THE LAST BASTION

GALLOW

THE LAST BASTION

NATHAN HAWKE

The right of Nathan Hawke to be identified as the author
of this work has been asserted by him in accordance with
the Copyright, Designs and Patents Act 1988.

First published in Great Britain in 2013
by Gollancz
An imprint of the Orion Publishing Group
Orion House, 5 Upper St Martin's Lane,
London WC2H 9EA
An Hachette UK Company

This edition published in Great Britain in 2013
by Gollancz

1 3 5 7 9 10 8 6 4 2

A CIP catalogue record for this book
is available from the British Library

ISBN 978 0 575 11512 5

Typeset by Deltatype Ltd, Birkenhead, Merseyside

Printed and bound by CPI Group (UK) Ltd,
Croydon CRO 4YY

The Orion Publishing Group's policy is to use papers that are
natural, renewable and recyclable products and made from wood
grown in sustainable forests. The logging and manufacturing
processes are expected to conform to the environmental
regulations of the country of origin.

www.orionbooks.co.uk

In the end it is our defiance that redeems us

WITCHES' REACH

WITCHES REACH

'So where's the Foxbeard then?'

Outside Witches' Reach, Sarvic stared at the pyre for a good long time after Valaric had finished his tale. Valaric shook his head. The Marroc from the fort didn't know either. They were exhausted, bleak-faced and grim even in their triumph. There were a dozen left and the first messages to reach the Crackmarsh had spoken of five or six times that number. Proud men, all of them, or they would be once it sunk in what they'd done. Names to be remembered.

'Varyxhun probably,' said a short needle-faced Marroc who stood in their midst, and it was only when she spoke that Sarvic realised she was a woman. 'He'll have gone to Varyxhun. And I'll be following him. The fortress is yours, Valaric the Wolf. Be sure you have a good look at the Aulian door in your cellar. Could be there aren't any forkbeards about know the secret of where it goes, but most likely there are. Still – could be a way out for a man clever enough to use it.'

Everything was black outside the circle of light from the pyre. Valaric stared at the flames a long time, Sarvic beside him. 'Strangest thing,' Valaric whispered, eyes fixed on the corpse of the iron devil still wreathed in fire. 'Couldn't have been that many forkbeards who saw him fall, but the ones who did, they just stopped. It was like they'd seen the sun go out and it went through them like fire through a hay barn.

I saw forkbeards truly afraid tonight, Sarvic, though I dare say they'll get over it.'

They talked some more then about how mightily upset the forkbeards waiting by the Aulian Bridge were going to be to find that Valaric had slipped around behind them. They'd know by morning and they were only a few miles down the Varyxhun Road. Valaric reckoned that gave the Crackmarsh men until maybe a couple of hours after sunrise. A busy night for most of them then.

When they were done with their own wounded and finishing off any forkbeards too hurt to get away, they collected their dead and dragged them to be buried in the snow of the deep woods below the ridge where the Lhosir wouldn't find them. After that they returned to the dead forkbeards, cutting the heads from the bodies. Valaric sent Angry Jonnic and a few others off to the Varyxhun Road with them, a trail of grisly little presents for the lot by the bridge to find when they came.

Sarvic had gone long before dawn but it was easy enough to imagine how that went. Brought a smile to his face every time, but by then he was slipping away to Varyxhun, up the valley with the needle-faced Marroc woman Achista and half a hundred others. Achista was off to rescue some Aulian wizard from the hangman, so she said, but Sarvic reckoned they might as well rescue a few Marroc while they were at it, and the two Jonnics figured that if they were going to be doing that, well then they might as well be 'rescuing' the whole of Varyxhun castle, and it was only afterwards that Sarvic realised this had been Valaric's plan all along – to keep the forkbeard army out at Witches' Reach while half his Crackmarsh men quietly crept off and did just that.

Gallow caught up with them that first day, set on the same thing as Achista. She asked him something about his family and his face went blank. The look Sarvic saw on him was a horror, like he really didn't give a shit about anything any

6

more. Like he just wanted to die with as many forkbeard corpses around him as he could possibly manage. It made him shiver, that look.

VARYXHUN

1

THE HANGED

There were riots in Varyxhun. Oribas couldn't see what was going on but he could hear the screams and he could smell the smoke. No one told him what had happened, but on the day they decided to hang him and hauled him up to the castle yard he could hear and smell the turmoil. He could see it written on the Lhosir around the castle, on their faces and in the way they held themselves. He looked up at the gallows. They were going to hang him but he wasn't going to be the only one. There were Marroc too. Pressed together with the other prisoners, he heard what had filled the streets of Varyxhun with revolt: the forkbeards were beaten. The iron devil was dead and Witches' Reach still held.

Witches' Reach still held.

He knew then that Achista was still alive and so he'd hang with a smile on his face.

There was an angry crowd somewhere outside the castle. Oribas could hear them shouting, calling out the names of the Marroc who were to die beside him. The snow was thick on the stones and the walls wherever it hadn't been trampled into ice. A heavy fall had come in the night but now the sky was clear, the sun cold and bright, the frozen air as sharp as broken glass. There were a few Lhosir in the castle yard, come up from Varyxhun to watch, but not many. The last time he'd been here Varyxhun had been thick with Lhosir fighting men, each sporting the forked braided beard from which they got their name. Today the castle felt empty. Maybe the cold was keeping them away or maybe they'd gone to Witches' Reach and now half of them were dead. The thought brought a flash of glee, quickly turning to shame. The death of a child, the death of a woman, the death of a man, he'd been taught there was never a place for joy in any of these things.

Then again... In the deserts of old Aulia people had robbed him, tricked him, lied to him, but no one had ever tried to kill him. Since he'd crossed the mountains with Gallow, it never seemed to stop.

An old Lhosir marched him up the steps onto the scaffold. At least the castle walls and the mountainside into which it was built kept them sheltered from the wind that scoured the valley; even so his hands were already numb in the cold. From the scaffold he could see a few Marroc among the Lhosir in the yard. Not many, but he could see the gates now too, the last of the six gates that rose in a single solid line up the mountain slope and barred the switchback road from Varyxhun to the castle. A line of mailed Lhosir soldiers with spears and shields stood across the entrance to the yard, barring the way to a crowd of hostile Marroc. Behind them lay the Dragon's Maw, a gaping hole in the mountainside barred so tight with thick rusting iron that even a child couldn't slip through. The dragon of Varyxhun lived in that cave, the castle's guardian, waiting to devour any army that breached the last gate. The dragon was only a story but the crowd was real enough. The air was taut with their anger.

He looked at the Marroc men beside him. He had no idea who they were or what they'd done but he'd heard their wails and their screams for mercy in the darkness over the last few days and it seemed to Oribas that they were mostly ordinary men from Varyxhun. He heard his own name called from the crowd now and then, or more often 'The Aulian'. He wasn't sure how the Marroc even knew who he was, never mind what he'd done, but they did. It was a terrible thing, shameful, not something to shout about, but the Marroc shouted anyway.

The Lhosir hangman positioned Oribas on the scaffold, hands tied behind his back, facing away from the crowd with the rope right in front of his eyes. *The iron devil is dead.* He had to wonder about that, had to wonder how anyone had managed to kill the ironskin and who else knew how a creature like that could be laid to rest; and then wonder who had made it and what for, and why the iron devils of the Lhosir seemed so akin to whatever had once been entombed beneath Witches' Reach; but he couldn't find any answers and there was a limit to how much wondering even Oribas could manage, staring at his own noose.

The hangman turned him round to face the crowd as the last of the Marroc were poked and prodded to the scaffold. The forkbeards inside the castle were mostly old or crippled; the ones who were fit to fight had gone with Cithjan to Witches' Reach. Now Cithjan was dead and half his army with him, but the other half was still out there, and while it was, the peace in Varyxhun remained fragile as a winter morning.

He hadn't taken everyone. The Lhosir who held back the Marroc at the gates weren't old or wounded. They were arrogant, these forkbeards, but not stupid.

A bull-like voice called out his name and began to proclaim his crimes. A few of them were true, the worst ones, although the Lhosir seemed to have added a few more for good measure. Oribas couldn't imagine why. Burning fifty men alive was enough, wasn't it? Certainly enough to hang a man but he'd have done it again in a flash if it was the only way to keep his Achista safe. At the edge of the crowd a Lhosir soldier with furs wrapped across his face against the cold was heading for the gatehouse dragging a Marroc woman in his wake, pulled along by a rope tied around her hands. A weight of sadness pinched Oribas's lips. Keep Achista safe? She was still in Witches' Reach and he was certain she wouldn't leave. Sooner or later the Lhosir would get in and then they'd kill her. The ironskin had promised them all clean deaths, but now the devil was gone. And Oribas was here and about to hang, and he'd promised her he wouldn't die first, and now there was nothing he could do. Nothing.

The reading of his crimes finished with the promise that Oribas would die here and now in front of these witnesses, and with a reminder that the Lhosir god – the Maker-Devourer – didn't give two hoots what a man did with his life or how terrible his deeds might have been as long as he was honest. Oribas didn't have too much of a problem with that. Here and now he envied the Lhosir for the simplicity of their belief. His own gods were more fickle.

Hands pulled Oribas towards the noose. They were surprisingly gentle. The Lhosir with the Marroc woman had dragged her to the gates and now he was arguing with the guards holding back the crowd. It was an odd thing to be watching when he was about to die, but it *was* strange. The Lhosir was mad. If the guards let him through, the Marroc outside would surely rip him to pieces!

There was something about the Lhosir though, something familiar. There was something about the Marroc woman too, but then the world went dark as the hangman slipped a hood over his head. Oribas yipped and shouted for it to come off, that he wanted to see – wouldn't any man want to see for every last second he lived? But the hood stayed. He felt the Lhosir step away to reach for the noose, and then a great roar went up from the Marroc outside the gate. A murmur rumbled around the scaffold and then sharp cries of 'To arms.' Hands grabbed him, not so gentle this time, holding him, pulling the rope over his head. Oribas let himself fall limp, slumping in the hangman's grasp before the noose could go round his neck. The Lhosir swore. For a moment he hauled Oribas right off his feet, then he grunted and let go, and Oribas fell hard to the wooden scaffold. He lay there, winded for a moment. The sounds around him now were of a battle.

A hand grabbed him by the foot and pulled him across the wood, then jerked. Something heavy – a body by the feel of it – fell across his back. Oribas pulled himself free and wriggled until he was on his knees, head so low that it almost touched his feet. He shook himself as hard as he could until the hood fell off and the first thing he saw was a dead Lhosir sprawled across the scaffold with two arrows sticking out of him. There was mayhem at the gates. The Lhosir with his Marroc woman was gone. The Marroc had surged forward and the ...

Gallow?

He stared. In the middle of the forkbeards at the gate, breaking their wall of shields from behind, was Gallow. And the Marroc crowd were pushing forward, and the ones at the front suddenly had swords and spears and shields, passed up from the men behind, and ...

The Lhosir with the Marroc woman – *that* had been Gallow. Oribas scanned the gates, looking for the woman and not finding her; then he saw a figure running up to the battlements where a single Lhosir stood watch. She'd thrown off her cloak and was carrying a bow. *Achista!* She was too far away for Oribas to make out her face but he knew her from the way she ran and how she nocked an arrow to her bow and drew back the string and hesitated a tiny moment before she shot. He knew her from the way she moved as surely as if she was standing right in front of him.

The Marroc on the scaffold had fled, taking their chances with the forkbeards below. Bodies lay around it, more Marroc than Lhosir. The forkbeards from the yard were mostly at the gates now. They might have been old or crippled but they were still Lhosir, and there wasn't a man among them who wasn't armed and ready to fight. But they weren't enough. From his perch Oribas watched their shield wall buckle and break and the Marroc force their way through. This was no mob – these were soldiers pouring into the yard, followed by the ordinary men and women of Varyxhun. People like the Marroc who'd been waiting to die with Oribas.

A Lhosir climbed the steps to the scaffold with a bloody sword in his hand. He snarled at Oribas and lifted it high. Oribas squealed and dropped to his haunches, ready to hurl himself into the snow below, but an arrow caught the man in the chest before he could move. The forkbeard sank to his knees, blood bubbling out of his mouth. Achista. Other Marroc were on the battlements now, some of them shooting at the forkbeards; still others hammered on doors with their axes, forcing their way into the gatehouse and the towers that overlooked the road below the castle. Oribas looked for Gallow again but the Foxbeard was lost in the seething melee. There must have been a hundred Marroc in the yard now and the Lhosir were falling fast. A last handful ran back to the inner gates, to the windows and halls and buttresses and towers and balconies built into the mountainside that passed for the castle's keep, but the Marroc were hard on their heels.

The yard quietened as most of the fighting moved inside to the old Aulian halls and galleries. Some Marroc rushed in, hungry for blood and plunder, others remained outside, surrounding the Lhosir who hadn't yet been killed, finishing them off and looting the corpses. Marroc soldiers moved through the castle towers, dragging out any Lhosir they found inside, dead or alive. It probably hadn't taken ten minutes from start to finish and the castle of Varyxhun had fallen. Varyxhun, which had once held at bay ten thousand forkbeards led by the Screambreaker himself, lost to a rabble of angry Marroc.

'Oribas!' Achista had her bow across her back and a knife in one hand. She ran straight at him and almost knocked him flat as she crushed him in her arms. Then she was behind him, cutting at the ropes around his wrists. 'Stupid Aulian! Do you understand what you did to me when I heard you were taken? Do you?'

He tried to laugh. 'It was quite deliberate. You should have seen the precision with which I threw my head against the edge of a Lhosir's shield. It was exquisite.' He tapped the lump on his head and the scar, still raw. 'I saw Gallow. Where's Addic? Did your brother escape too?'

'He did and he's here. Inside now, I expect.'

Oribas stretched his arms and rubbed his wrists. He looked at the noose behind him. 'It would have been worth it,' he said, almost in awe of his own words.

'What would?'

'To have died for you.'

Achista took a step away and slapped him. 'Don't ever say anything so stupid again!' And then before Oribas could think of what to say next, a gang of Marroc hauled a snarling Lhosir up onto the scaffold, all of them kicking and punching him. Down in the yard other Marroc turned to watch, shouting and cheering.

'Hang him! Hang him!'

More Marroc were trickling through the gates, the hungry-looking ones, the scared, the weak and the slow. The mob was after any Lhosir, alive or dead, and the Marroc soldiers who'd led the assault were letting it happen, turning away and heading inside the castle. The men on the scaffold hauled the Lhosir to his feet and slipped the noose around his neck. Oribas barged into them. 'What did he do?' They pushed him away. Even Achista had a hand on his arm, pulling him back. 'But what did he do?'

The Marroc who'd put the noose over the Lhosir's head shoved Oribas hard, knocking him down. 'He's a *forkbeard*!'

'But you can't ...'

The words died in his throat. Behind the scaffold someone pulled a rope. A trapdoor opened, the Lhosir dropped, the rope snapped taut around his neck, and that was that. Oribas thought he even heard the bones snap. The Marroc on the scaffold raised a fist and whooped and the crowd cheered. 'One less forkbeard! Got any more? Yes? Which one next?'

The soldiers on the walls watched and joined in with the cheers. Those Lhosir still alive were beaten down, a few simply murdered, others dragged toward the scaffold. Oribas pulled himself angrily to his feet. 'This isn't justice and this isn't right!' He made for the Marroc hangman again but this time Achista blocked him.

'This is war, Oribas.'

'No, this is murder.' Though was it any worse than fifty men burned alive under the ground? Hard to say, and maybe it was the guilt that drove him now. 'You're better than this!'

There was pain in her eyes, and Oribas realised with a sickening feeling that it wasn't guilt or shame, but sadness that he didn't understand why this killing had to be done. He faltered, and then another Marroc grabbed hold of him and was shoving him out of the way. 'They were going to kill you, darkskin.'

'For what I did, Marroc, not for what I am! It may seem small to you but on that difference the Aulian Empire was forged!'

'And now it's gone.' The rest of the Marroc ignored him.

'At least the forkbeards had a reason.' Although they hadn't had any real reason when they'd set out to kill him for the first time, when they'd carted him off to the Devil's Caves with a gang of ragged Marroc simply for knowing the name of Gallow Foxbeard. And, really, what was he doing here, defending the men who'd been about to kill him?

One by one the Lhosir were pulled and pushed and dragged and shoved to the scaffold. They were hauled up the steps, manhandled to their feet and nooses were shoved around their necks, and they were hanged. Five at a time because that was how many gallows the Lhosir had built, with the mob baying for the blood of every single one of them. Oribas turned away.

2

SARVIC

Before the fighting kicked off, Sarvic was with the mob, right at the front of it. Valaric was either on his way from Witches' Reach by now or else he was still there, taunting the forkbeard army that had meant to stop him and his Crackmarsh men from crossing the Aulian Bridge. Without Valaric, that left Sarvic and Fat Jonnic in charge. Jonnic was somewhere in the middle of the mob doing what he did best – shouting at people what to do. Sarvic was at the front, and that was just fine. He'd come a long way since he'd turned and run from the Vathen at Lostring Hill and been saved by a forkbeard. The same forkbeard he could see now, arguing with one of the soldiers at the gate.

The Marroc around him all wore thick heavy furs. This being the Varyxhun valley in winter, the forkbeards didn't think anything of it, but the nice thing about furs was what you could hide underneath. Mail, for example. An axe. A sword. Further back, other Marroc carried spears and helms and shields, things even a bear pelt couldn't hide. When Gallow appeared behind the forkbeards barring the gate, Sarvic quietly passed the word back. Fat Jonnic's shields crept forward through the mob.

Gallow shoved the forkbeard in charge of the gate into the spearmen facing the Marroc. One of the forkbeards in the wall of shields staggered and took a step forward. His spear dipped and that was all Sarvic needed. He lunged, grabbed the shaft just behind the point and pulled hard, pushing the tip down toward the road as he did. The forkbeard stumbled another step forward. The soldiers either side snapped back from the glances they'd been throwing behind them but by then it was too late. Sarvic had always been quick as an eel, and he was between their spears before they could run him through. He pressed up to the forkbeard who'd staggered out of the wall, getting in nice and close. He raised a long knife high where all the other Marroc could see, then he rammed it into the man's neck and pulled at him, yanking him out of the shield line while his blood spurted everywhere. Spears were fine weapons for keeping an angry crowd at bay but now the forkbeards had an armed man inside their points and it left them with an interesting choice: hold on to their spears and keep the mob back or drop them and take out an axe. So now was the time. Either the rest of the Marroc rushed the forkbeard line or Sarvic had about two breaths left in him before someone smashed his skull.

The Marroc surged forward. They didn't hesitate, and right there and then Sarvic knew they were going to win. Behind the forkbeards, Gallow had thrown back his hood and drawn out the red sword Solace and was shouting and roaring about who he was and what blade he carried and daring anyone to face him and all sorts of other nonsense. For a moment the forkbeards looked uncertain. It was enough. The crowd fell on them like a spring flood from a broken dam.

Sarvic barged on through, past the silence of the Dragon's Maw and into the yard. A few more forkbeards stood about, some of them still looking up at the scaffold, others frowning at the gate, the quickest-witted of them already starting to move. He let out a murderous roar. The more forkbeards he killed before they realised they were armed and should be doing something more useful than gawping, the easier it would be. He headed for the scaffold, intent on cutting down every forkbeard in his way. Up there was a man supposed to be an Aulian wizard, half the reason they were there, but at a quick glance Sarvic couldn't tell the prisoners apart. If he was honest, he wasn't all that bothered.

A forkbeard came at him swinging a hatchet. Sarvic raised the shield he didn't have, swore and threw himself sideways instead, rolling across the cobbled yard and crashing into the legs of another who bellowed a curse and lifted something big and heavy-looking. Sarvic knifed him in the foot and scrambled away from the scream that followed. He wasn't going to reach the scaffold after all, but back by the gates the wall of shields had stayed broken, and more Marroc soldiers were getting into the yard and throwing off their furs to show the mail they wore beneath. The men who'd been hiding deeper in the crowd rushed forward with shields and spears and more swords and axes. A good few carried bows. Sarvic snatched a shield off a Marroc he half-recognised from the Crackmarsh and shouted something he hoped sounded inspiring. Not that anyone needed much encouragement by the looks of things.

Beside him the needle-faced Marroc woman from Witches' Reach shot an arrow into a forkbeard stupid enough to make himself an easy target by standing up on the scaffold. Achista the Huntress, that's what the Marroc of Witches' Reach called her, and in reply she called them her Hundred Heroes, the dozen of them she had left. They deserved it after what they'd done. As far as Sarvic saw it, every one of them should be a lord or prince just as soon as the last forkbeard sailed back across the sea.

A hand on his hood yanked him back. He staggered and almost fell as an axe sliced the air past his eyes. 'Is it bedtime, Sarvic?' Angry Jonnic shoved him aside and drove the forkbeard back, battering him with his shield.

'Up yours!' Sarvic lunged low and fast with his knife, neatly hamstringing the man with the axe. He left Angry to finish him off and pushed on towards the castle keep.

The forkbeards were scattered now. One climbed onto the scaffold. A last prisoner was still up there, shaking off his hood. The prisoner's skin was dark and Sarvic had heard enough about the Aulian wizard to pause for a moment to see what would happen. But the forkbeard didn't turn to ice or explode or burst into flames, he just took an arrow for his pains. Apart from his dark skin the wizard looked oddly ordinary to Sarvic – scared out of his wits and close to shitting himself, much as anyone else ought to be.

The forkbeards from the gate were retreating to the steps of the Aulian Hall of Thrones. Marroc swarmed around them, swamping them. The stream of men passing into the yard turned to a flood. Sarvic snatched up an abandoned spear and stormed to where a few more forkbeards were making a stand on the steps. Cithjan the Bloody had once held his council here but he was dead now. The iron devil had burned him and spoken him out and then Gallow had killed the devil. Which was all a snarling shame: they could have done with hanging Bloody Cithjan high over the gates for every Marroc in Varyxhun to see, him and his ironskin too.

The forkbeards on the steps faltered and broke before Sarvic could get to them. He saw Gallow's massive frame thunder inside with a dozen Marroc in his wake and followed as fast as he could. He'd been starting to get the hang of killing forkbeards that night outside the Reach when they'd turned and fled, and he might have cut down one or two as they ran, but forkbeards never ran and it had taken him by surprise when they did. He'd watched for a moment before the savage inside had called for blood and by then they were away. Now his luck was out again. He forced his way into the Hall of Thrones. Marroc were on the floor, the kin-traitors who'd worked and lived in the castle and served the forkbeards, cringing and cowering and begging for mercy now as they were beaten half to death. Sarvic spat on them as he passed. The hangings would start as fast as they could. Every Marroc who'd made this place their home would swing and they'd deserve it too. Valaric might have something to say about that, but the Wolf wasn't here, and by the time he was it would be done and too late to argue.

Sarvic skidded to a stop. The forkbeards were mostly gone, but not all of them. Two stood in front of Bloody Cithjan's throne. Old men whose strength had long faded from their arms, but they were armed and armoured and already three Marroc lay dead in front of them, pricked by forkbeard steel. Sarvic grinned and started towards them. Strange lot, forkbeards. Wicked bastards, evil and vicious and mean in a fight, but they had their superstitions. Like back at Witches' Reach when the Crackmarsh men fell on their camp in the middle of the night and Gallow killed the iron devil. Some of the forkbeards had turned and melted away like any sensible man should, but the ones up inside the fortress hadn't. They'd retreated in silence behind their wall of shields. Even when Sarvic had run up close and taunted them and thrown spears and stones, they hadn't answered. Right in the middle of the battle and they'd left. Just lost all interest in it, as though the fall of the ironskin mattered more than fighting a rabble of angry Marroc, and Sarvic hadn't thought there was a forkbeard alive who'd give up a good fight for anything less than a severed limb. After the first few jeers, Sarvic and the other Marroc had mostly stood and watched them go, uneasy at their own victory.

Now two of them were ready to die to defend a dead man's chair. Sarvic was happy to oblige them, but another stood in his way. Huge in all his furs, even from behind there was only one person it could be: Gallow the Foxbeard, who'd faced down the iron devil of Varyxhun. Sarvic remembered clear as the sun: the Foxbeard standing beside the pyre and on it the ironskin, and then Mournful telling him how it was, how Gallow and the iron devil had fought as the

Crackmarsh men swept down the mountainside. How the iron devil's red blade Solace had shattered Gallow's sword and how the Foxbeard had killed him anyway, ramming the splintered remains of his blade through the devil's mask.

The rest of the Marroc scattered, looking for plunder or other forkbeards to kill or whatever drove them now. Sarvic looked the two old men up and down. Warriors once. Didn't take much of an eye to see that in the way they held themselves, in the way they gripped their spears.

'*Nioingr*,' hissed one of them. He was staring at the clean-shaven chin where Gallow's forked beard should have been.

Sarvic sidled up behind Gallow, too close for him to ignore but not so close he got in the way. 'Need a hand, forkbeard? You can leave them to me if you like. I'd take that as a favour.'

If Gallow heard, he didn't show it. His eyes didn't leave the men shielding the throne. When he spoke he sounded tired.

'*Nioingr*? The last man to call me that was Beyard Iron-skin. He ate those words.' He drew out the sword Solace and let them see the red steel of it. Sarvic stepped back, hissing at the cursed blade. 'Beyard carried this. We fought by the pyre of Tolvis Loudmouth and I sent him to the Maker-Devourer by his own sword. I placed his body on the pyre and I spoke him out and I have no doubt that the Screambreaker himself will welcome him. A better man than any of us.' He looked at the red sword. 'The Marroc named this blade the Comforter and call it cursed. The Vathen named it Solace, the Peacebringer. The Aulians called it the Edge of Sorrows.' He pointed the sword at the two forkbeards. 'You're Garran, named Fleetfoot once. I remember what they said of you, that you could run faster than the wind. You were with the Screambreaker at Selleuk's Bridge. I was there too and I saw you. You didn't run like the wind that day. You didn't run at all. The Marroc broke us yet your brothers had to tear you away. Lay down your spear, Garran Fleetfoot. Even the Lhosir can't always win. The Marroc have the day here. Cithjan is dead. Sixfingers' Fateguard is gone.' He shrugged. 'Our brothers of the sea who fought for the walls of Witches' Reach are scattered and broken. What sense is there in dying for all these things that went before you? Set down your spear, Fleetfoot. Walk the Aulian Way to Tarkhun and beyond. Sail your ship home and live your twilight years in peace among the family you left behind. You've long done enough to enter the Maker-Devourer's cauldron.'

Sarvic tried not to snort. *Walk the Aulian Way?* Let Gallow explain to the mob outside why they should let a couple of forkbeards go when they could just as easily hang them.

But it wouldn't come to that. The old forkbeard shook his head. '*Nioingr*,' he hissed. '*Nioingr. Nioingr.*' Three times, after which Sarvic knew there could be no going back. He breathed a quiet sigh of relief. No one would have to explain anything to anyone then. Just two more dead forkbeards. So much the better.

Gallow lifted his shield as the second forkbeard lunged and then jumped back as Fleetfoot stabbed at his feet. The red sword swung sharp and hard and sheared the shaft of Fleetfoot's spear. Sarvic started forward but Gallow was faster, lunging at both of the forkbeards, barging into the other Lhosir, shield against shield with enough force and weight to send the old man sprawling. Sarvic darted in quickly to put the point of his spear to the fallen forkbeard's throat. 'Very happy to kill you, old man. *Very* happy.'

The forkbeard didn't move. Gallow battered Fleetfoot back, driving him with blow after blow until he was pressed against a wall. 'Eat your words, old man! Eat them!'

Garran Fleetfoot glared. He dropped his broken spear, lifted an axe from his belt and lowered his shield. 'I know you, Gallow Foxbeard, and I'll unsay nothing. You took the sword you hold from the dead hands of the Screambreaker on the battlefield outside Andhun and you cut off the hand of our king with it, and instead of facing your fate you fled in fear. No, Foxbeard, I will eat nothing. *Nioingr.*'

Marroc were gathering around Sarvic now. Not the Crackmarsh men, who'd already pressed on deeper into the castle's labyrinth, but the Varyxhun mob that followed. They had an evil about them, a hunger for vengeance. Before Sarvic could see it coming, one seized the spear in his hand and jerked it down, too quick for him to stop. The spear sliced into the old forkbeard's throat. He gasped. When Sarvic snatched back his spear the Marroc let go but it made no difference. The forkbeard's blood sprayed into his face as he gurgled a curse and grabbed at Sarvic's leg, and then he was still.

The Marroc who'd done it laughed. 'Filthy goatbeard.'

Sarvic turned on him and then changed his mind and backed away. He'd barely taken a step when the rest of the mob fell on the dead forkbeard. Knives and clubs rose and fell as they beat and hacked him to pieces. Sarvic watched to see if he felt anything but he didn't. No pride, no shame, no joy, no regret. Nothing. The forkbeards were all going to die anyway, and when he looked at the angry men around him, come with cudgels and murder and hate to revenge themselves for everything that had been done to them, how was he any different?

Gallow had the other forkbeard pinned to the wall now. Garran Fleetfoot swung his axe. Gallow caught it on his shield and pushed and twisted it away. For a moment the old man was exposed, his shield useless and on the wrong side. The red sword lunged and drove into his ribs, cracking a fistful of them. The forkbeard gasped and staggered but his mail was good enough to keep the red steel out of his skin. Sarvic smiled to himself. He'd remember that. He'd have that mail.

27

The old man wheezed. He pointed at the mob ripping the other forkbeard to pieces. 'See what they are, *nioingr*? We're better than them!'

He dropped his shield, switched his axe to his other hand and lifted it high, wide open, as good as asking Gallow to finish him, and Gallow obliged him. The red sword flashed, blood sprayed across the Aulian walls and Sarvic watched the forkbeard fall. Gallow stood over him. 'You fought well, old man. Like Beyard. He never stepped aside from the path. It's the path itself that strayed. It's Medrin.'

The look on Gallow's face was like he'd killed his own brother; and then it changed to something dark and harsh – so dark that when he turned and strode away Sarvic forgot about the dead man's mail and followed. He'd seen that same look before, that morning after Witches' Reach.

3

ONCE A FORKBEARD

Gallow turned away from the Hall of Thrones and left the Marroc to their looting. Servants would be hauled out of their hiding places. If they were lucky they'd get away with being beaten bloody, but he'd been among a victorious army after enough battles to know what happened next. Nothing that a decent man would care to remember, and it would be like that here too. Worse.

He hesitated a moment then shook his head and moved on. Not his business. Let the Marroc sort out their vengeance without him. He'd come across the mountains to be with his family, that was all, and now he'd come here to this castle for his last real friend, the Aulian, and if Oribas was alive and safe then only one other thing mattered and it wasn't in Varyxhun. So he chose not to look at what was happening around him and pushed his way past the Marroc still surging into the hall. They were throwing down the braziers now and tearing the hangings off the walls, hangings that had been there long before any Lhosir had come to the valley. Their own treasures, if only they knew it.

Their business. Not yours. That's what Arda would say. Three years away and then a few days and nights trapped in a fortress and expecting to die, and then Valaric had come, and the forkbeards had gone away, and all of a sudden everything he sought was right there in front of him, begging to be taken, and he'd turned his back and left her there because ... because Beyard had sent Oribas to be hanged

29

and Oribas was his friend. Left her and lost everything, and he'd had to, because sooner or later Medrin would know he was back and the hunt would begin, and if he simply went home then one day he'd wake up to find Medrin standing over him with a thousand Lhosir and Medrin would kill them, all of them, slowly and with a great deal of lingering, because nothing would ever make up for the hand that Gallow had taken from him in Andhun. Medrin made the choice into no choice at all but Arda still wouldn't wait for him, not again, and he could hardly blame her for that. Better to blame fate.

He forced his way out into the yard. The mob was thinning, more and more Marroc crowding inside, pushing and shoving, climbing past each other, desperate for a share of the plunder. Around the scaffold he could see the bodies, Marroc and Lhosir both. Five Lhosir swung from the gallows. Small gangs of Marroc moved among the corpses, stripping them, shaking them. He saw the flash of a knife. Murdering them if they weren't quite dead then. The Crackmarsh men were up on the walls, but Valaric was back in Witches' Reach and the soldiers only stood and watched.

Not. His. Business.

Arda would be on her way home by now, back to the Crackmarsh to be with their children. *His* children. His sons and his daughter. He should have gone with her, wished he could, had always wanted to, but Sixfingers wouldn't let him. He turned away, sick of it all. 'Oribas? Oribas!'

The nearest gang of Marroc stopped what they were doing and stared at him. Their malevolence filled the air. There were four of them and their glances around the yard were already drawing in others. They dropped the Lhosir they were looting and closed in. Gallow took a step back. The Crackmarsh men had a hungry hate for forkbeards but they kept it to themselves around Gallow because Valaric had told them the story of the Foxbeard and what he'd done. The mob from the city beneath the castle, though, all they saw was another forkbeard even if he was shaven. They eyed him, and the longer they did, the more Marroc turned to look. Gallow had seen it before, a wolf pack setting itself to bring down a bear.

He'd seen how to stop it too. He stared right back at the four Marroc, picked out their leader, drew his sword and moved briskly forward. Marroc always turned and ran and this one would be no different. There'd be no need for blood; the threat would be—

A stone hit the side of his helm, hard even through the iron. He staggered sideways and suddenly a snarling Marroc was flying at him. He braced his shield and then there was another coming from the other side and another from behind and more of them all around. He raised the Edge of Sorrows but the first Marroc didn't flinch. The red sword sighed as it cut the air. Before Gallow could stop himself, he'd split the Marroc's face in two; and then the others came and the sword wanted more while he stared at what he'd done.

A second Marroc crashed into his side and tore at his shield. He battered the man away and tried to run but another tackled him from behind and staggered him; yet another grabbed his sword arm high around the shoulder and held on, trying to drag him down, and then another had his shield again, and however hard he forced his way onward, for every Marroc he shook off, another two came at him. He felt a knife stab at him, jabbing hard at his mail coat. Something hit his head, another stone or a stick, and then a hand had his leg and his foot, pulled hard, and he couldn't break free. He staggered, hopped, and finally fell with a half a dozen Marroc on his back.

'Hang him! Don't kill him down there; hang him for everyone to see! Hang the forkbeard!' He growled and snarled and twisted and writhed, trying to shake the

Marroc off, but there were too many. One got his helm and someone hit him on the head with a stone. Light crashed through the back of his head and the sound of everything changed as though he was underwater again. Drowning as he'd been off the cliffs of Andhun after fleeing the Vathen. Should have sunk beneath the waves there, but somehow the Screambreaker had come in a little boat, sailing away from his own death towards the Herenian Marches, given one more day of life to do whatever needed to be done; but in the moments before, as the water had swallowed Gallow, the sounds of the world had fallen away like this. He felt another sharp pain in his back and then the weight came away and he was being carried, dragged, and his eyes were still open but there was only light, horrible flaming lances of light.

The Marroc dropped him. He lay still, fingers clawing at a ground that was softer and warmer than the crushed-snow cobbles of the castle yard. Wood. The noises were slowly changing again. The Marroc mob, shouting and screaming. He opened his eyes. Everything was blurred. Bright blue sky above, a swirling sea of movement below.

Hang him! Hang him!

He blinked as the world swam back into focus. He was on the scaffold looking out over the heads of a few dozen angry Marroc. When he tried to get up, someone stamped him back down. He felt as weak as a baby. A great weight pressed on him, men sitting on his shoulders and his legs. They had his arms, were tying his wrists behind his back. Then hands reached under his shoulders and hauled him up. His sword was gone, his shield and helm too. He tried to shrug the hands away but the Marroc were too strong and too many. They pushed and shoved him and hauled a rope over his head, scraping it across his face, settling it around his neck. Panic washed away the dizziness, but too late. He snarled and raged and almost fell.

'Hang the forkbeard!'

The noose tightened and a vicious voice hissed in his ear, 'Ready to meet your uncaring god, forkbeard?' The voice grew into a shout. 'Shall we hang us another one?' The crowd howled with gleeful joy.

Something hit the scaffold by Gallow's feet. When he turned his head to look, an arrow was quivering in the wood. He couldn't turn enough to see his executioner, but he felt his shiver of hesitation. Then another arrow hit the scaffold, and this time the mob saw it too. A cluster of soldiers was coming down the steps to the Hall of Thrones and forcing its way through. He saw Achista with her bow and an arrow nocked, Achista and Oribas. They shouldered their way onto the scaffold. 'Jonnic! What are you doing?'

The executioner barged past Gallow. 'Killing a forkbeard.'

'Let him go!'

'Do I answer to you now? No, I answer to Mournful, and he's not here.'

'Are you dim? I said let him go!'

'Or you'll shoot me?' The hangman pushed forward. The soldiers around Achista pressed forward until they were all almost nose to nose. 'Kill a Marroc to save a forkbeard, would you? You know what we do to women who give themselves to forkbeards.'

Oribas punched him, and for a moment Gallow was so surprised that he forgot he was standing with a noose around his neck. The Marroc lurched back and drew a hand across his face and then laughed as Oribas clutched his fist. Achista shoved past them all and stood beside Gallow, looking out over the crowd. 'This is Gallow Foxbeard. The man who slew the iron devil of Varyxhun. The forkbeard who cut off Sixfingers' hand.'

'Still a forkbeard!' yelled a voice from the crowd.

'Hang him!'

'Look what he did!'

'He's a killer!'

The mob parted around the Marroc man Gallow had killed, eager to show his crime. He barely remembered doing it. An instinct, lashing out before he fell, that was all. Achista stared at the body, the fire stolen from her mouth. Then she looked at him. 'You did this?'

Gallow nodded. 'He came at me.'

'And you killed him.'

'I had little choice.'

'Angry Jonnic! Get your smelly hands off that noose!' Another Marroc soldier was pushing through the crowd. Another face Gallow knew from a long time ago. He squinted, trying to remember where it had been.

'Piss off, Sarvic. I don't answer to you either.'

'But you do answer to Valaric and Mournful'll string you up by your toes. I'll vouch for this one. Years ago he fought among the Marroc against the Vathen at Lostring Hill. I stood beside him in the shield wall. He's a forkbeard, yes, but we lost that day, and in the rout that came after the second Vathan charge he saved my life. Angry, I see you up there all hungry to kill another forkbeard and I have that hunger too. But a life for a life, I say. We both saw what happened here.'

'What I saw was a Marroc killed by a forkbeard. Seen too much of that these last years.'

Achista turned her back. 'This forkbeard is *nioingr* to his own kind. Do you understand what that means?'

'Means they won't care what we do to him.'

'Means you're doing their work for them.'

Jonnic snorted and shouted at the crowd. 'Anyone else? Anyone else want to spare this forkbeard, or can we get on with it? Just one of you and I'll let him live. Can't say fairer than that.'

An eager murmur rolled through the crowd, but then another Marroc pushed through them and climbed onto the scaffold. 'When the devil Sixfingers was prince of Andhun, three forkbeards threw me into the Isset and left me for dead. Then another one pulled me out, this one, and if he hadn't, I'd have drowned. I'll spit at him in the street now just as I did then. But I'm with Sarvic: a life for a life. Let this one go to never come back.'

Achista pushed past Jonnic. 'Now take him down.' There was steel in her voice. She snatched the rope and pulled it roughly off Gallow's head and no one moved to stop her. When she was done, Angry Jonnic punched Gallow in the kidneys hard enough to stagger him even through his mail and forced Gallow down to his knees. Achista squatted beside him. 'You're not welcome, Gallow Foxbeard. Varyxhun belongs to the Marroc now. Leave this valley and never come back. If you do, you'll be what Jonnic says: just another forkbeard to be welcomed with spears and arrows. Do you understand?' Her voice softened. 'Go home, Gallow. Go to Arda. She'll open her arms quick enough, for all her blunt words.'

Oribas pushed forward. 'Achista!'

She turned to him. 'You'd better choose whether you follow him or stay, Oribas. I know he's your friend and I know he came here because of you, but I can't change what has to be. If you have to go, I won't begrudge it.'

Gallow hauled himself wearily to his feet and shook his head. 'No, old friend. I've nothing to offer you and I don't want your company. I came home for my family, and if Beyard hadn't sent you here to be hanged then that's where I'd be; and I'd be there without you.'

He clapped Oribas on the shoulder and picked his way down the steps from the scaffold and through the hissing crowd. He walked to the Marroc he'd killed, picked up his helm and put it on slowly and deliberately. He found his shield and a spear and, last of all, the red sword. Then he turned to face the crowd, a Lhosir warrior dressed for battle.

The mob glared back, full of hate but with fear now too, and when he walked towards them again, they parted easily. He stopped by the scaffold. 'I wish you a long and happy life, Achista of the Marroc, and your brother too.' He glanced toward the Marroc who claimed they'd fought together at Lostring Hill. He remembered it, a distant thing: fleeing at full tilt down a grassy slope, a Marroc ahead of him, Vathan horse cutting at them as they ran, throwing the Marroc to the ground, catching a Vathan javelot on his shield. Angry Jonnic had called him Sarvic. Yes, that was him, but he'd changed, a frightened goat become another wolf. 'My greetings to Valaric when he comes. Tell him he'll be more than welcome to have his plough fixed or to buy some nails once Sixfingers is dead.' He almost laughed. Sarvic stood there looking confused, but Valaric would understand.

He looked at the other one, the Marroc he'd hauled out of the Isset three years back. He remembered doing it, but he hadn't ever seen the man's face until now, not properly. Then at his one last friend, the Aulian. He raised his spear in salute. 'Oribas. You were always a better man. Remember that. Remember what you told me.' He turned away from the Marroc and from Oribas and this new beginning they had before them, and rubbed his neck where the noose had touched his skin. His heart felt strangely empty. *Go home?* But he couldn't. Not until they'd be safe and forgotten, and that would never happen, not while Medrin was alive.

Inside the gates he stopped by the Dragon's Maw. The Marroc soldiers there looked uncertain, and when Gallow drew out the red sword they stepped back in alarm and drew their own. But Gallow reversed his grip and drove the sword into the hard-packed dirt between the cracked stones of the yard.

'Yours,' he whispered to the sky. 'For whoever is foolish enough to take it.'

*

Achista stood beside Oribas. They held hands as they watched Gallow go. 'What was it you told him?' she asked.

Oribas didn't answer for a very long time. When he turned to look at her, his face was pale and he looked as if he'd seen a ghost.

'What was it?'

'A long time ago.' He shook himself. Shivered as if trying to free himself of something. 'A long time ago I told him that every heart is wicked. That there are no good men in the world at all, just those who have the courage to look at their own deeds with honest eyes, and those who don't.'

A hundred fishing boats once sheltered in the sweep of Andhun Bay, protected by cliffs that swept the north-east winds from the Storm Coast up into the air and over the tops of their masts, but no more. The Marroc had taken to the sea when the Vathen came. Their ships had gone and the harbour had burned and the busiest port east of Kelfhun was gone in a single day. Few ships came now.

It was a sight then, when a white ship sailed across the mouth of the bay, driven by the freezing winds that blew down from the Ice Wraiths of the north. She didn't turn towards the harbour but men still stopped to look. Eyes followed her, wondering who might be coming; on both sides of the Isset they stared. In the eastern half of divided Andhun the ardshan of the Vathen paused at the window of his stolen castle and peered and then called for the Aulian tinker he'd taken to keeping around like a court fool. Across the waters of the Isset and the cliffs that kept the two halves of the city apart, the Lhosir looked with more knowing eyes, for she was a Lhosir ship and the white of her sails and her hull gave her away: she was a priest ship from the Temple of Fates on the edge of the frozen wastes, and that alone was reason to stare. White as though she carried the snow of the north through the waters with her, she passed Andhun Bay and sailed on a little way along the coast to the first cove where a party could put ashore. There she dropped her sail. Boats eased their way through the waves, and by the time they'd landed the first party and had returned to come back with the next, Lhosir riders from the city reached the cove. They came filled with questions from their lord of Andhun but their words died in their throats. The men on the stony beach were clad in iron. There were twelve of them.

The next boats brought men more familiar. Holy men, as far as the Lhosir had such things. Chanters of nonsense and rhyme who sent their words not to the Maker-Devourer but to the Fates themselves and to the frozen palace far to the north.

The boats went back a second time and headed for the shore once more. The holy men cried out for all to look away but the Lhosir were too curious and unafraid to do such a thing, and so their eyes burned as the last burden of the white ship came ashore. The ones who stared the longest remembered only white and light and a terrible brightness. The ones who looked away more quickly would say afterwards that what they had seen was another of the Fateguard, armoured in an iron skin but missing chest and back plates, and that what was there instead was the whiteness of ice and the brightness of the cold winter sun and patterns of both that wove with such a brilliance that for a while they thought they were blinded.

All understood at once what they saw: the Eyes of Time come down from the iron palace. A thing that had never happened in any remembered life.

The Fateguard commanded the Lhosir to get down from their horses and then took them, and the Lhosir – those who could still see anything at all – were left to watch the Eyes of Time and the iron-skinned men of fate as they vanished across the hills.

MIDDISLET

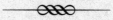

4

NADRIC'S SECRET

The wind roared and moaned and the rain beat on the roof of the forge and swirled inside, another winter storm come howling off the seas to the north. Arda stood, steadfastly ignoring it, drawing wire. The forge fire kept everything nearby comfortably warm and dry, even in the bitter tail of winter. Tathic and Pursic sat in the dirt nearby, keeping out of the rain, playing with the little wooden figures Nadric had carved for them while they'd been hiding in the Crackmarsh. Nadric wasn't much of a carver but they had at least the suggestion of legs and arms and a head, and that was enough. Pursic jumped his toy man onto Tathic's and the two boys started wrestling on the floor.

'I'm Valaric the Wolf! You're a forkbeard. Yaargh!'

Forkbeard. The word still made Arda stop. Made her look up too, eyes scanning the track to the big barn and the road beyond to Fedderhun, or else the other way, south to the Crackmarsh and then the long way round to Hrodicslet. A month ago she'd watched him leave Witches' Reach and head south for Varyxhun. An hour later she'd followed with a dozen Crackmarsh men, but they'd quickly turned from the Varyxhun Road and followed the secret trail through the Devil's Caves and Jodderslet. A mountain path had taken them to Hrodicslet and to the Crackmarsh, where the villagers of Middislet always hid in troubled times. To her children. To Nadric, who'd been father to the Marroc husband she'd had before the forkbeards had killed him. To

Jelira, the oldest, the one who wasn't *his* but remembered him better than the rest. To her sons Tathic and little Pursic. To Feya, their daughter. She'd vowed she'd never let herself think of him ever again and she broke that vow every single day. Gallow. Gallow, the clay-brained, sheep-witted, onion-eyed, flap-eared clod.

The boys roughhousing on the floor thumped into her feet and stopped and looked up. Pursic and even Tathic and certainly Feya barely remembered him. They'd come to know Tolvis as their father, and Arda quietly wondered if they understood that Tolvis Loudmouth was dead and gone for ever now. At least you could mourn for the dead. Speak them out like the forkbeards did or bury them and know where their bones lay and now and then go and talk to them. Couldn't do that with Gallow. He'd chosen something else. Found a thing that mattered to him more than her and his own children. Lhosir thought differently and there was nothing any woman could do about that, so she was better off with him gone, or so she told herself. She'd been miserly with the silver he'd sent back from Andhun and still had enough to make her worth a look from a Marroc man looking for a home, even if he'd have mouths to feed that weren't his and even if she was tainted by two forkbeards now. Although it was *her* silver and she wasn't sure she wanted another man anyway. If it wasn't for Nadric losing his strength, she might have kept things quietly as they were and done without, thank you very much.

She sighed and turned back to drawing her wire. Men would be knocking on the door for Jelira soon, not for her. She was Marroc through and through and close on her fourteenth year, which certainly made her old enough for the village boys to be interested.

Made her old enough to help in the forge too. She could cut wire into lengths for nails. Or wind it and cut it for links for all the mail that Nadric was quietly making. Valaric the

Mournful had done her a favour looking after her little ones and he hadn't forgotten who she was and where, and nor had his men still left in the Crackmarsh, and there were precious few forges where a man could make mail without the eyes of a forkbeard on his back.

She caught the thought. Snatched it out of the air and held it dangling, wriggling before her eyes, full of guilt. *Forkbeard.* She'd always called him that, right to his face, in good moods and bad. And he'd taken it. Never complained. And then she smiled and started to laugh, though the tears that came weren't of joy, because really what did it matter? She'd sent him away, and that had been the right thing, right for her and right for their children, though it hurt like a nail in the knuckle.

'Arda Smithswife?'

She almost dropped the draw plate. She spun round, hand reaching for the forging hammer that was never far away, but it was only Torvic, standing out in the wind and the lashing rain, leaning in around the corner of the workshop and flicking drips of water from his eyes. Torvic, who'd walked with her back to the Crackmarsh so she didn't get murdered by ghuldogs or the sentries Valaric had left behind.

'You're early,' she snapped. 'Wasn't expecting you for another two days.'

Torvic slid into the workshop. He cast an eye up and down the road. 'Sixfingers is on the move.'

She flinched. The name put her on edge every time. King Medrin and the doom looming over them all since he learned that Gallow was still alive.

'He's heading for Tarkhun.' Torvic snorted. 'The Vathen are getting restless again. When the weather breaks we'll be back to forkbeards and Vathen killing each other. And us Crackmarsh men, we'll be in the middle, happy as anything ...' He laughed and then caught himself and looked up sharply. 'No offence.'

Arda shrugged and shook her head. 'He's gone, Torvic. I don't know where and I try not to care. Say what you like.' She smiled. Forced it. Took some getting used to, being mistress of her own house again but knowing that Gallow was still alive after all.

A nasty grin spread across Torvic's face. 'Valaric let slip that he's got the Foxbeard in Varyxhun carrying the Comforter at his side. You ask me, Mournful can't wait to get Sixfingers across the Aulian Bridge so he can start picking and poking.'

'Is it true? Is Gallow with Valaric?'

Torvic's grin froze and then fell off his face piece by piece. He looked away. 'Best I know, your Gallow left the red sword in Varyxhun and headed out the valley. He hasn't been through the Crackmarsh. We'd know. Sixfingers holds Issetbridge and the forkbeards that were in Varyxhun have got Witches' Reach and no one crosses without their say-so. So I'd say he's still in the valley, but no one knows for sure.' The crooked grin grew back. 'Valaric's been putting it about that the Foxbeard had family in Hrodicslet and now they're in Varyxhun. Close enough to the truth, eh, but far enough to keep the forkbeards from coming across the Crackmarsh again.'

It was like the weight of a wet fur cloak coming off her, though she tried to sound as though she didn't care. 'As long as they're on the other side of the Isset, they're no bother to me.'

Torvic made a face. 'I'd keep my worries for the Vathen. Not often they come this far south but we see them now and then.' He hunched his shoulders and pushed out into the rain and came back again a moment later leading a bedraggled mule. 'Flour. Good for the rest of the winter.' He hauled a sheet of oiled leather off the animal's back and then threw down a couple of sacks and a pair of strong leather bags and emptied out a string of onions and a leg of cured ham. 'Keep your bellies full for a bit.' He went back to the mule. Arda picked up the onions and the ham and put them carefully to one side. She started to fill the leather bags with squares of mail. Making it up into a coat that sat well on a man was an armourer's job, but long hard hours went into drawing the wire, cutting the rings and riveting them together into lines and squares the size of a man's hand. Didn't take much skill, but it did take a forge and tools and a willingness for hard work. Nadric had the tools and the forge and everyone in Middislet knew how to work. Valaric paid in food and the winter had been a hard one. They were grateful, all of them.

She looked up when she was done. 'So. Are you all going to die up there when Sixfingers comes?' She spat out the forkbeard king's name. A ritual that was habit now.

'He could bring every forkbeard ever born, he still wouldn't get into Varyxhun castle. The Screambreaker had ten thousand men and even *he* couldn't do it. Anyway, you know the story. If the sixth gate ever falls, the Isset itself will wash the castle clean. Can't lose, can we?' He chuckled.

Arda snorted. 'The Screambreaker didn't bother trying, and his ten thousand were more like two by the time they got to Varyxhun. And they were knackered, worn to the end of their boots.' Little things she remembered. Gallow had never said much about the Screambreaker's war, all his years of killing good Marroc men. Hadn't been something either of them wanted to hear, but little things still came out now and then.

Torvic rummaged around in the mule's packs and threw a small leather bag at her, about the size of a hand. 'That's for Gallow,' he said when she caught it. 'If he comes by. From his Aulian friend.'

'What is it?' Arda opened the bag and sniffed. Some sort of pale crumbly grey stuff.

'Salt. In case.'

'Salt?' She laughed. 'Well *you* know how to keep a woman sweet!' Then she shivered and her smile died. Salt was for shadewalkers. And Fateguard too, as it had turned out, but the less said about *them* the better. One of the things you learned when you were stuck in a besieged fort with an Aulian wizard for company. Other things as well. Mostly things she didn't care to dwell on.

Torvic was looking at her like he had a bad taste in his mouth. 'Something else.' He stepped out and then came back in out of the rain with a second mule, even more bedraggled than the first. There were large pieces of metal tied across its back. He pulled one off, and it took a moment before Arda understood what it was. A mask and helm and crown made of iron, which could only mean it had once belonged to the iron devil of Varyxhun. The devil Gallow had said was once a friend, who'd taken her in a cage from her home. Some friend. She looked at the pieces of armour like they were a nest of snakes.

'Valaric said to give it to you. Maybe you can melt it down and make something. Or maybe if Gallow comes by there's some proper thing to do with it. Some forkb— some Lhosir thing.' He dragged the rest off the mule's back onto the floor. A whole set of iron plates. The iron skin of a Fateguard. She shuddered. The Aulian wizard had had things to say about the iron devils.

'Melt it down?' *If Gallow comes by*. Torvic had said that as if he was hoping for it but Arda wished he hadn't because a part of her was hoping for it too. A part hoping and another part praying that he didn't.

'Forge something with it.' Torvic shrugged. 'Whatever you want. Valaric wants it gone, that's all, and he doesn't want Sixfingers getting it back.' He nodded at the floor. 'It's good iron that. Worth a bit.'

He wasn't wrong either, and maybe it would feel good to turn those pieces of cursed metal into something of value.

The other villagers would help. They'd be glad to. A little victory, but still, the very sight of it made her skin crawl. Valaric wanted it gone? She could understand that. 'You want me to hammer this out into wire and make it into mail for your men. Will they take kindly to wearing the skin of the iron devil of Varyxhun?'

Torvic shook his head. 'Not when you put it like that, no.' He shrugged. 'Do what you like with it. No one wants it back, not in any shape. Just get rid of it. Bury it if you want.'

Across the yard, the back door of the house opened. Nadric stood at the threshold. He stared at Torvic, scowled at the rain and then hunched his shoulders and hurried across to the forge. 'This your friend from the Crackmarsh?' He looked Torvic up and down. 'Rotten day to be living in a swamp when you could be under a roof with a nice warm fire.' He flashed a look at Arda. 'Getting ready to stick some forkbeards?'

'This is Torvic.' Arda stepped away from Nadric, distancing herself. They'd never quite got past what he'd done three years ago on the night that Gallow had left and never came back. Gallow's choice, but a part of her would always blame Nadric for doing something so stupid.

Nadric beckoned Torvic closer. 'Come over here then, Torvic of the Crackmarsh. I have something for you.' He pushed his way past Arda to the back of the workshop, to the corner full of dust and cobwebs where he kept the bits and pieces he couldn't bring himself to throw away. The scrap corner. Arda had never paid it much attention except to note that in the three years Gallow had been away all it had done was grow. Gallow had kept his armour there once, his sword and shield and helm. There was still a single Vathan javelot.

Nadric pulled away an armful of old tools and broken wood and then some sacking. Underneath was a wooden chest bound with iron and three thick leather straps. Torvic

49

crowded closer as Nadric started to undo them and even Arda couldn't help peering over his shoulder. She'd had no idea the chest was even there. 'Pull it out where we can all see it, then!'

'Pull it out, she says.' Nadric chuckled. He finished with the straps and threw open the lid. Arda stared.

'Diaran preserve us.'

'Holy Modris, old man. Where did you get them?'

Nadric cackled. '*Get* them, young man? I *made* them. Me and that other forkbeard, the one who's dead now.' Tolvis. Arda winced. 'Been making them for the last three years. Still got *some* strength in these arms.'

Inside the chest were arrowheads. Thousands of them. Arda and Torvic and Nadric stood together, staring at the pile. Torvic couldn't keep his mouth closed and Nadric couldn't stop chuckling.

'How long?' asked Arda. 'How long were you making them?'

'Ever since Gallow left.'

'No.' Arda shook her head. 'You didn't make all of these. I'd have known.'

Nadric laughed. 'I made a lot of them. It started after the Vathen—'

He stopped abruptly. They'd both said everything they had to say about that night long ago, loud and furious, and they both thought they were right. Gallow had brought a wounded forkbeard back after Lostring Hill. The Widowmaker. When the Vathen came looking, Gallow had killed them and he and the Widowmaker had gone and never come back, and it had been Nadric's fault and Arda had never forgiven him.

'It wasn't so bad. Not like what the forkbeards did across the Isset.' Torvic coughed and Nadric turned to him, shuffling away from the anger in Arda's face. 'They killed the animals we couldn't take with us, you see. That was how it

50

started, because they left all their arrows behind and that was money that was, if there was anyone who'd buy them, only no one wanted to be making the trip to Fedderhun to see if the Vathen would trade them for food, not when they were Vathan arrows in the first place.' Nadric shook his head. 'Was a hard winter after that summer with so many animals dead. We were back from Varyxhun by then.' He peered sharply at Torvic. 'Was Arda who kept the village alive, not that she'll tell you. Her and that silver the forkbeard brought with him. They had food in Varyxhun and the Wolf was in the Crackmarsh.' He nodded at Torvic and the mule outside and then the sacks of flour and the onions on the floor. 'Was how that all started. Arda here and that other forkbeard. We did what we could. No one in the village had money or anything to give that winter. They had them arrows, though, and so they gave them to me.'

'And you never said a word?' Arda snapped. 'Money, that is!'

Nadric waved her away. 'Ach, you've enough to keep this house fed for a good long while.' He leered at Torvic. 'She hoards that silver like a squirrel hoards his winter nuts.'

'And for much the same reason!'

'Anyway.' Nadric shrugged her aside. 'People owed us and there was plenty of old pieces of metal about after all the fighting that summer. Broken bits of this and that. People took to keeping whatever they could find, and that winter it came to me. I thought a fair time about what I might do with it.' He kicked the box. 'There you have it. Broad heads mostly, the older ones, but later I took to making them like the Vathen do. Narrow points. Up close they'll put a hole in a forkbeard, those ones, even if he's wearing mail.'

Torvic bent down and tried to pick up the box. He heaved and huffed and his face went red.

Nadric laughed. 'Careful, friend. You'll do yourself an injury trying to lift that. Needs a wagon, that does. There's a few pieces of Vathan mail at the bottom too and some other bits and pieces. I been hoarding it for you, for when the need was right.'

'Can't take a wagon into the Crackmarsh.' Torvic winced. 'And I've only got two mules here and no spare bags.' He gave Nadric a long look. 'I'll come back, old man. I'll bring more mules and take them off your hands. What do you want for them?'

Nadric shook his head. 'Nothing. Was forkbeard silver that bought the metal when it comes down to it. Give it back to them, nice and hard. That'll do nicely.'

Arda stepped between them. 'I'll take six sacks of flour and two legs of pork, Torvic.'

'No, you won't.' Nadric glared. Wasn't like him to stand up for something but he had a fierce look on him now. 'Forkbeards killed Merethin. Your husband, woman, your first one, and my son in case you've forgotten. Forkbeards can have this lot back for nothing.'

Arda's face tightened but she kept her peace. Torvic looked from one to the other and then nodded to Nadric and backed away. 'Take me a few days. When I see Mournful I'll see what he says.'

5

HRODICSLET

The drunken forkbeard was going to be a problem. Mirrahj watched him, keeping a careful distance. He was sitting in the mud in the middle of Hrodicslet, not doing much except singing to himself, and that was fine until any of her riders got anywhere close, when he stumbled to his feet and lurched and started shouting and swinging his axe. No one wanted to go anywhere near him and Mirrahj Bashar could see why.

'Let me shoot him,' grumbled Josper. 'Put an arrow or two in his legs, that should shut him up.' Josper was sulking. The rains might have broken the day before but the Marroc town was soaking wet. The streets were rivers of mud and the houses were all built on stilts, as if mud was only the beginning. Josper liked to burn things, but around here he couldn't even find tinder to start a flame.

'No.' Mirrahj waved him off. 'Circle the place again. Find some Marroc and chase them into the marsh. See which way they go.' Josper rode away laughing. He'd enjoy himself with that until it got dark and the ghuldogs came out. He'd be back sharp enough then though, tail between his legs.

Which left her with the forkbeard. Other times she'd have let Josper have his way, but this one interested her. A forkbeard on the wrong side of the river. Just the one, not some raiding party, which begged the question: how did he get here? And that in turn begged the answer she was secretly looking for: a southern passage around the Crackmarsh and across the Isset. Because there had to be one, there simply *had* to, and if the forkbeard knew it then she wanted it out of him.

Mirrahj got off her horse. She checked the buckles on the little round shield strapped to her left arm and headed towards him. Shrajal and two of his riders came out of a house dragging a pair of screaming Marroc children. 'Don't get too close!' He was laughing at her. 'That one bites.' He made a show of stringing up his captives but he was watching her all the time. Waiting for her to fail, just like Josper was waiting too.

The forkbeard stopped singing and started staring as Mirrahj came close. He tried to get up, fell over and then finally found his feet. Mirrahj drew the short curved sword at her side and stabbed it into the mud. Her helm followed. She shook her hair, letting the braids fall around her neck. Sometimes men didn't know what to do when they realised she was a woman. The forkbeard stumbled a step towards her, half drew the axe from his belt and then put it back. 'Men all too scared, are they? That's you horse buggerers. No pride.'

She smiled. He was a big one, even for a forkbeard, but it made no difference. The rest of the ride could have him once she'd got what she wanted. She turned to Shrajal. 'You hear that, Shrajal? Forkbeard says you're scared of him.'

'Forkbeard can come here and say that if he wants. I'm not going anywhere.'

They both laughed. Mirrahj turned back. 'They're not scared of you. They're waiting for me to tell them what to do with you. What are you doing here? There aren't any forkbeards on this side of the Isset.'

He seemed to forget she was there. He tipped back his head and howled. 'Medrin? Medrin! Waiting for you. Here I am! Come and get me!' His eyes dropped suddenly back to Mirrahj again. 'I'm the one who took his hand.'

'You took King Sixfingers' hand? I don't believe you.'

'Believe what you like, Vathan.'

'You were in Andhun when we stole it from you, then?' She took a slow step closer. 'I was there too.' Another step. 'How did you get across the Crackmarsh, forkbeard? Did you walk or did you ride? How did you get past the ghul-dogs and the Marroc who live in there?'

The forkbeard sat down with a heavy *splat* in the mud. 'I didn't. I came through the caves and down the mountains like everyone else.' He rocked back and put a finger to his lips and a lazy smile moved over his face. 'But don't tell the other forkbeards.'

So he does know! A surge of anticipation sparked through her. Behind the forkbeard another handful of men spilled into the mud from the big hall at the heart of the town. They were whooping and cheering. A moment later a curl of smoke followed them out through the door. Mirrahj laughed. Someone had finally got a fire going and Josper had missed it. She took another step closer. 'Tell me about these caves and this path down the mountains.' When he didn't answer, she stifled a flash of irritation. 'You were in Andhun, were you? Does that make you a soldier?'

'Always a soldier.' The forkbeard laughed. 'Too much of one.' He started to rise, slipped in the mud and fell flat on his back and then finally stood up again. 'You look mighty fine for a Vathan.'

'And you're ugly even for a forkbeard. If you're a soldier, how many came with you? Where are they?' There were flames under the eaves of the burning hall now. A haze of smoke and steam hung over its thatched roof. More of her riders were coming, looking to light a brand and see if they could fire a few of the other houses too. They were watching her.

The forkbeard rubbed his misshapen nose. 'Soldier? I'm not anything. Nothing. *Nioingr*. That's what they call me.

55

You can say it three times if you like. Then I have to kill you.'

Nioingr. A traitor and an outcast. In that case, maybe he'd tell her what she wanted freely. 'What's your name, outcast?'

'Gallow Foxbeard.' He grinned at her as though that was supposed to mean something.

'You're a long way from home, Gallow Foxbeard.'

'Home?' The forkbeard howled with bitter laughter. Mirrahj took another step closer. 'Careful, Vathan. I've killed plenty of your kind.'

'I'm unarmed, forkbeard.'

'Lhosir don't make war on women and children.' He spat. 'Didn't used to, anyway.'

'You're a strange one.' And not much use drunk. She'd have him alive and let him sober up in a cage and then she'd set about finding out whether he knew a way across the Isset or not. Or maybe Josper would find one for her after all, or one of the Marroc prisoners would know of one and the forkbeard wouldn't matter any more. Either way her ride would take some pleasure from a forkbeard's screams. Another scratch of vengeance for what they'd done outside Andhun.

She walked towards him with purpose now. He cocked his head and his face screwed up, trying to make sense of it. He waved his axe at her. 'Piss off, Vathan.'

'I don't think I will.' She stopped right in front of him, so close he could have swung at her, but he didn't. 'Well, forkbeard, whatever you think, you're going to fight a woman today. Look.' She threw aside her shield. 'I've made it easy for you. Fists. No steel.'

'Girl, I'm twice your size.'

But he was steaming drunk too. Mirrahj stood in front of him.

'Leave me alone. Go away.'

'Make me.'

Down the street behind him there were about a dozen of her men watching them now. Even the ones who'd lit brands were waiting. 'My men are watching us, forkbeard. I'm their bashar.' Which made it a matter of pride and face. He had to understand *that*, didn't he?

He closed his eyes. For a long time he stood like that, head tipped back to the clouds, and Mirrahj reckoned she could have just walked up behind him, wrapped an arm around his neck and choked him and he wouldn't even have noticed. But she waited. Eventually he looked at her again and groaned because she hadn't vanished like she was supposed to. He sighed and threw down his axe and his shield. 'Maker-Devourer, girl. Come on then. I'm going to pull those leathers down and spank your arse.'

She crept closer, one shuffle at a time until he lunged and she ducked and darted behind him, and it was even easier than she'd hoped. She jumped onto his back and wrapped her legs around his waist and one arm around his neck, gripped it with the other and squeezed as tight as she could. He staggered, turning round and round as though he didn't quite understand that she wasn't simply behind him. Damned forkbeard was built like a bull, with a neck so strong that she had a moment of doubt. Shrajal was watching her though, and the others who weren't out chasing Marroc. She'd staked her right to be their bashar on taking this forkbeard down, and that made it a bit late for doubts.

'I had a daughter like you,' slurred the forkbeard. 'Like a bloody limpet. Could never shake her off.' He didn't do any of the obvious things, like run backwards and smash her into the wall of a hut or throw himself down on his back and try to drown her in the mud. If he did, she wasn't sure she could hold on. Wasn't sure her ribs wouldn't snap, if it came to it, but then it had always been a gamble. He was stinking drunk and it made him stupid.

One hand tried to get a grip on her arm. The other pawed over his shoulder, trying to grab her face. 'I had brothers,' she said. 'Lots of brothers.' She grunted at the effort. The muscles in her arms were burning at the pressure she was putting on the forkbeard's neck, and he was still talking? She squeezed harder. 'Lots of brothers. All bigger than I was.'

'No brothers, me.' The forkbeard was losing his strength. 'Made my own. All brothers. Before …' He stumbled and sank to his knees.

'Well I had lots.' Mirrahj forced herself to keep her arms tight. 'I had a man as well, and he was big like you, and I always beat him even so.'

'I had a wife.' The forkbeard's arms dropped to his sides. 'So where is he, your man?' Another few seconds and he finally went limp and toppled over into the mud.

'He died,' she said quietly. 'Fighting forkbeards like you.' She stayed on his back, squeezing until she'd counted to twenty in her head. Then, only then, she let go and stepped back. Her furs were covered in mud. It was oozing through the forkbeard's fingers. He was face down and so heavy that she almost couldn't roll him over onto his back to stop him from drowning. She did, though, and then put an ear to his chest. He was still breathing.

'Shrajal! Bind him and get him out of here.' She made a sharp gesture to the riders who'd stopped to watch. They turned and set about what they'd come to do: looting everything they could carry and burning whatever would burn in this godforsaken swamp. Mirrahj climbed back onto her horse and rode among them, watching, shouting encouragement here and there. Her arms were still burning.

They dragged the last few Marroc out of their homes. There wasn't much worth taking and only a little food this far towards the backside of winter. The sky was darkening, more rain on its way. As it started they rounded up the Marroc animals they'd taken. They'd slaughter themselves a feast before they moved on, sleep in the houses they didn't burn, warmed by the fires of the ones they had, and tomorrow they'd leave. Deeper into the mountains or further around the fringes of the Crackmarsh, one or the other, looking for the south passage across the Isset. They wouldn't stray far though, not for another day or two. Josper deserved his chance with the Marroc.

'Bashar!' It was almost dark when Shrajal caught up with her again. As he reined in his horse he was brandishing something that looked like a sword but wasn't. A scabbard.

'Shrajal.' Mirrahj let her face settle into an amused disdain. Shrajal was young and eager – a little too eager.

He thrust the scabbard at her. 'Look! Look!'

She looked, and at first there was nothing to see. A scabbard for a Vathan sword. An ornate one, and she wondered for a moment if he meant it as a courting gift, which made him more stupid than she'd thought. But the scabbard was too long for a Vathan blade, and then the designs in the metal around the top of the sheath caught her eye, and she knew she was wrong and Shrajal was sharper than he looked. 'Where did you get this?'

He answered with a grin. 'The forkbeard.' He probably hadn't ever even seen it before but he still knew what it was. Mirrahj, who *had* seen it, had no doubt at all. He was holding the scabbard they'd lost at Andhun. The Peacebringer's scabbard, and if the forkbeard carried that then maybe he knew the fate of the red sword itself and Shrajal had every right to look pleased with himself because nothing mattered to the Vathen more than the Sword of the Weeping God.

Mirrahj nudged her horse a step closer so her mount was almost touching his and leaned over. 'Spread the word and then go after Josper and bring him back. After we're done here we head straight back for the ardshan in Andhun.'

She smiled. 'Have some fun with Josper. Tell him what you found.'

6

ARROWS AND SALT

It was more than a week before Torvic returned, and when he did he came with three other grim-faced Crackmarsh men. Arda waved them into the house and they tied up their mules and came inside, pleased to be out of the gales blowing from the Storm Coast. While the other Marroc exchanged greetings with Nadric – because he was the man of the house – Torvic went back outside and Arda went with him. He had two enormous hams. 'No flour,' he said. 'But I've got this.' He passed her a bag of cured fish strips, tough and oily and salty and delicious. 'Valaric thanks you for your kindness. We'll take the arrowheads. After that ...' Torvic scratched his beard.

Arda hoisted one of the hams over her shoulder and turned to go, keen to be out of the wind, but Torvic put a hand to her arm and caught her. He leaned in close. 'There's a band of Vathen about. They sacked Hrodicslet. About a week ago. They burned what would burn and took a few slaves and chased off everyone else. Seems like they're look-ing for a way across the Crackmarsh. Could be they'll come here before long.' They were face to face now, close, Torvic looking at her intently. She felt her pulse quicken. Stupid really, but she hadn't had anyone stand so close to her since Witches' Reach and it made her think of Gallow in all the good ways she was trying to forget. She took a step back, giving herself a little space.

Torvic raised his voice over the wind. 'We followed them

most of the way here. They were pushing a hundred. They turned north but that doesn't mean they won't be back.'

Back in the house the stale air was a relief. Jelira was staring at a soldier who couldn't have been much older than she was, and he was staring back, and they were both smiling and looking away and then looking back and smiling again, and Arda wasn't having any of *that*, not with a man from the Crackmarsh who'd vanish at the drop of a hat and probably be dead before the year was out. She slid the ham off her shoulder and thrust it at Jelira. 'You can take this out to the workshop and hang it round the back where the birds and the rats won't get at it.'

The young soldier began to get to his feet. Arda glared at him until he squatted down again.

'The Vathen must have passed only a few miles from here.' Torvic shook his head. 'Heading for Fedderhun, and in a hurry.' He was looking at Nadric now, a steady gaze full of some meaning that filled Arda with unease. 'Haven't seen the Vathen come so far south in a while. They're looking for something. Only a matter of time before they come back.'

Arda fixed Torvic with a hard stare. He was leading to something, if only he'd spit it out. Only he was gazing at Nadric, as though she didn't count, and she wasn't having *that* either. 'Well, if they do then we'll be sure to be nice to them.'

Torvic reached into the bag he'd given Arda and helped himself to a fish strip. He cocked his head. 'Valaric could make good use of anyone who knows their way around a forge. In Varyxhun.'

'How interesting.' Moving the forge then, that's what he wanted, and when she looked at the three men he'd brought with him, she wondered if that was why they'd come. 'Any travelling smiths come through, I'll be sure to mention it.' She glared at Torvic, trying to make sure he understood she wasn't moving anywhere for anyone, not now, and he'd said his piece and now could he please have the sense to let it go?

'We'll be here a few days,' he said. 'Going to head north and have a look around between here and Fedderhun. Keep an eye in case there's more Vathen on the move. You mind if we leave the mules here with you?'

'You do that.' Arda's voice had a finality to it. 'You're welcome to stay under my roof as long as you're here. Mules too.'

Torvic smiled. He had an easy smile, not forced. 'That's kind of you, Arda Smithswife. When we're back, we'll talk a bit more about what we've seen.' And the forge, she supposed. He'd talk about the forge and moving it and her and all of them up into the mountains again where Gallow had sent them three years back. She'd be buggered if she was going to let that happen a second time.

She nodded. 'You do that, Torvic. I'll be made of ears.'

Torvic took his Crackmarsh men and left the next morning, nice and early. The Vathen had had a beardless forkbeard among the slaves they'd taken but he hadn't seen any need to mention that. Might have been Gallow, might not. Either way he reckoned Arda didn't want to know and so he kept his peace and made sure the others did too. They all knew who Gallow was. They'd all followed the Wolf to Witches' Reach and seen what happened there.

He sent two of his men north-west, scouting the fringes of the marsh in case the Vathen were doing the same. He kept the young one, Reddic, close, with his eyes for Arda's daughter, and trudged up the north road towards Fedderhun until they picked up the trail of the Vathen from Hrodicslet. The Vathen were travelling too fast to catch on foot but Torvic followed them anyway until he was sure he knew where they were heading: north and west to the coast road and Andhun. Then he turned north and for another day they followed the winding waters of the Fedder. The winds off the Storm Coast fell away and the air grew still. A bitter cold drifted out from the Ice Mountain Sea and settled over the land.

By the time they slunk into Fedderhun, the ground was freezing at night and it was snowing again. They spoke to the Marroc there and kept their ears open but all they got was a name: Mirrahj Bashar, who'd taken her ride south to look for a passage around the far side of the Crackmarsh and had never come back. By the sound of things, no one had expected her to. Full of ghuldogs and Marroc bandits, the Crackmarsh. Torvic often wondered whether there might be some way to get the forkbeards and the Vathen into the Crackmarsh at the same time, have them kill each other in the swamps and water meadows and then let the ghuldogs finish them off while the Marroc just watched it all happen. Fat chance, but it was a nice dream.

The Vathen around Fedderhun helped themselves to whatever took their fancy and largely left the Marroc fishermen of the town alone. They didn't seem to be doing anything much except kicking their heels and as far as Torvic could tell most of them didn't want to be there at all. They wanted to be in their home pastures for the winter, curled up in their tents, not here in this godsforsaken outpost. They were here because someone had told them to be and so they were making the best of it until whoever that someone was allowed them home. Or so it seemed to Torvic.

They learned as much as they could, which seemed like it wasn't much at all, and left after a couple of days, and they were hardly out of the town when the snow started again. It fell steadily all through the day, thick and heavy, covering the land with white and then, as the light faded, the clouds cleared away to the south and Torvic was looking up at a deep blue sky. They'd need more than a fire and some warm furs out in the open tonight, but it wasn't much of a worry.

Nice thing about moving through this part of the world: the farms were scattered and easily missed but they were there if you looked for them, and the Marroc who lived here were happy to share their fires and their shelter and even a little food to hear a few travellers' tales. And there weren't any forkbeards, but there *were* old friends here and there.

Torvic stopped at a house with a pair of small barns nestled beside it in a hollow, almost snow-bound already, and banged on the door. When a scar-faced Marroc opened it, Torvic grinned, and the scarred Marroc hugged him and dragged him inside.

'Stannic. Long time.'

'Torvic!' Stannic let him go and looked Reddic up and down. 'This lad yours?'

Torvic shook his head, chuckled to himself – no daughters here for Reddic to make eyes at, thank Diaran! – and sent Reddic back outside to settle the mules and strip their saddles; and by the time he came back Stannic's wife had fetched some cheese and milk and a few turnips, and Stannic had opened a jug of mead and his three young boys were peering from behind the curtain to the night room with eyes hungry for stories and the evening was looking very comfortable indeed.

'He ever tell you about Lostring Hill?' asked Stannic as soon as Reddic sat down, and then he told the story anyway, even though Reddic had heard it a dozen times by now, about how he and Torvic and Sarvic and the two Jonnics and a few others had fought the Vathen with Valaric the Wolf, and how they'd run away with a forkbeard who'd turned out to be Gallow Foxbeard. Reddic listened as though he'd never heard it before, which made Torvic smile even more. By the time he was done, the food was gone, the fire was dying and the eyes gazing out from the night room had long since closed.

'The Vathen came as far south as the Crackmarsh after,'

said Stannic as they settled down for the night. 'Valaric ever tell you that story, Torvic?'

Torvic nodded, because yes, he knew all about it, and so did anyone who'd lived through Andhun and the months afterwards, but then he saw Reddic shake his head. Reddic was too young to have been at Lostring Hill or at Andhun after. The first forkbeards had probably come from across the sea before Reddic was even born. To him they were simply the way of the world. Hadn't stopped him running away to the Crackmarsh though.

Stannic belched. 'Lad, you've heard of the Widowmaker, curse his soul, the Nightmare of the North? That was who the forkbeards sent to hold the Vathen outside Fedderhun. Well he lost, didn't he, and it was Valaric who found him after the battle, out of his senses, and he let the Widowmaker go. Let Gallow take him away.' He jerked his head down the track towards Middislet and the Crackmarsh. 'That's why half of Middislet looks like it was only put up yesterday. Vathen tore a good piece of it down.' He poked the fire with a stick and watched the sparks rise with the smoke.

Reddic leaned sideways and let out a long fart. 'Did they find him?'

'The Widowmaker? He died fighting them outside Andhun the day before the city fell.'

'I knew *that*.'

'Well, how'd you think he got to be at Andhun a month later if the horse shaggers had found him Middislet?' Stannic laughed and shook his head.

'Could have escaped.'

'No. He got away.' Stannic stared into the flames, remembering, and Torvic stared too, remembering much the same, fleeing through the woods with Valaric and the Foxbeard and then the two Vathan horses and the rest and the aftermath of the battle, and then the days after, riding for Andhun. He looked suddenly up at Stannic.

'You ever face him? The Nightmare of the North?'

'Go against him?' Stannic shook his head and laughed. 'Never wanted to go and fight when I was younger. Scared, I suppose. I was about the age of your lad here when the Widowmaker came and I didn't have the balls to run away and be a Crackmarsh man even if there'd been such a thing. Forkbeards didn't come by these parts for years, and when they did they weren't as bad as everyone said they'd be, not back then. That was after Tane died and Varyxhun fell. Just wanted to go home, I think. Most of them did, too.'

Reddic looked awed. Torvic grinned. Lostring Hill wasn't something he talked about that much because everyone who hadn't been there made out that the Marroc who'd survived the battle were heroes, whereas Torvic knew perfectly well that most of them had been shitting themselves as much as everyone else and just kept their heads a little better and got lucky. He snorted. 'You remember the Foxbeard said he saw horses? And then he and Valaric went on their own to look, and Valaric came back and it was just him? How we all thought he'd done for the forkbeard?' He chuckled again and looked at Reddic. 'The Wolf only told us the truth later, and even then only because there were some Vathen who just wouldn't stop following us until Valaric skinned a few of them to find out why. That's when it came out. Ask Sarvic if you like – he was there too. Don't ask Valaric though. Valaric doesn't talk about it. He and the Foxbeard got a history ...'

He froze. A noise. Outside. The look on Reddic's face said he'd heard it too. Then it came again. A heavy broken shuffle, as though someone was dragging a load through the snow in long slow pulls with a good rest between each one. Reddic jumped up, startled, eyes darting from one door to the other and one hand already on his axe. 'Forkbeards?'

Torvic shook his head. 'Not out here.'

Stannic waved at them both to sit down. 'Wolf maybe.

If it is then it's got something. Leave it be. Dead of night in that cold?'

He snorted but now Torvic got up too. 'Didn't sound like an animal to me.' He crept to the door and opened it. Cold air froze his face but at least the winds weren't the gales they'd been a week ago. The moon was full and high, its light bright on the snow except where long deep shadows spilled from the wood pile and the low barns. A soldier in mail and a helm stood not more than a dozen yards in front of him. Hard to make out much in the moonlight but he had a naked sword hanging loose and long from his hand and he was too big to be a Vathan. Torvic snatched his shield from beside the door and whipped out his axe. 'Reddic! Stannic!' The soldier was a forkbeard. Had to be, although only Modris knew what a forkbeard was doing all the way out here. He couldn't see the forkbeard's eyes but he felt them staring at him, and when the forkbeard moved, he lurched a stride closer, dragging one leg as though crippled. Crippled was good. Torvic tried to tell himself that one crippled forkbeard was more a gift than something to fear but he couldn't quite make himself believe it. One forkbeard out here all on his own? One?

Then again, the Vathen had taken a forkbeard from Hrodicslet. It made him pause a moment. He took a step closer and peered. 'Foxbeard?'

The forkbeard took another step and this time it wasn't so slow. His sword came up fast and lunged and Torvic barely got his shield in the way. The sword was odd. It wasn't a forkbeard sword. Too long, Torvic thought as he brought his axe down hard on the man's helm, not hard enough to split the iron but hard enough that the forkbeard would see stars long enough for a killing blow. But the forkbeard grabbed at his shield as though he hadn't felt anything, and Torvic stepped back, and that was when the moon caught the forkbeard's face and he saw it wasn't a man at all. The sight froze him stiff, and in that moment the shadewalker drove its long Aulian sword through Torvic's guts and then caught him as he crumpled. While one hand still held the sword, the other grabbed Torvic by the throat and pulled him close. The shadewalker stiffened; and as it squeezed Torvic's life out of him, its crippled leg twisted and straightened and its eyes gazed hard at the door.

And that was how Reddic found him, Torvic gasping and gurgling while his blood ran out of him over his belly and down his legs and dripped off his dangling feet to pool blackly in the snow, and the shadewalker on the other side of him, crushing his throat. For an instant Reddic was paralysed, and in that second the only sound was the snap of bones as the shadewalker finally crushed Torvic's throat. Reddic struggled for breath and backed away. The shadewalker dropped Torvic and looked at him. It stepped forward, almost into the doorway, and that was when Reddic remembered there were five more people in the house behind him and three of them were children.

'Shadewalker!' He slammed the door in its face and hurled himself against it. 'Shadewalker! Stannic! By Modris! Get up! Run!' He was screaming now, willing the others to get out of their beds and into their furs as fast as they possibly could. There wasn't anything to do when a shadewalker came except run, every Marroc knew that. Even the forkbeards didn't try to fight them because they couldn't be killed, and they couldn't be killed because they were already dead. They wandered aimlessly, served no purpose. No one knew what they were or why, save that they came across the mountains from Aulia now and then,

The door rattled. The shadewalker slammed into it hard enough to knock Reddic back a step. The Marroc were piling out of the night room, the children already wailing in fear. Stannic pulled on his boots and wrapped another fur around himself and picked up a hay fork. He threw open the other door and roared at everyone to get out. Against Reddic's shoulder the door rattled again. The shadewalker pushed it open another inch.

'I'll hold it here as long as I can.' Reddic wasn't sure why he'd said that except that he was the one holding the door closed and no one was helping him and so he was pretty much stuck with it and never mind how much he wanted to piss himself and sink to the floor. Stannic was still throwing cloaks and furs and blankets to his wife and his children. Reddic's feet slipped back. A gap opened wide enough for a finger to slip through and then for two and then three, and that was when he turned and let go, and Stannic was out the other door a step ahead, still carrying armfuls of furs. Stannic ran, glancing over his shoulder now and then, while Reddic shot past them all, legs pumping as hard as they'd go, flailing and floundering in the snow. After a minute he stopped to catch his breath. When Stannic's wife caught him, gasping with her children pecking at her heels, Stannic snapped at them all to wait. He stood and stared back at the farm and at the tracks they'd left behind them in the snow. The shadewalker was following, out in the open now, walking fast and steady, clear as anything.

Stannic stared at it as he handed out the furs, then met Reddic's eye. 'Not the first time I've had to run from a shadewalker and probably won't be the last. They're not so quick and they don't run but they don't give up easy neither, and they don't feel the cold. Follow us until sunrise, this one, most likely, and pick off whoever drops. So we go steady, quick as we can but slow enough we don't have to stop much, and we keep warm, and we don't leave anyone behind. I'll take the front, you take the back. Keep your eyes on it, lad, and if the cold bites too hard, you shout for help and I'll come.' He slapped Reddic on the shoulder. 'You did good, lad. Held it back long enough so we got what we need.

Modris walks with us and we'll all live to see the sun again.'
The shadewalker was getting closer. Stannic set off. 'Shout
to me, lad, if it gets too close.'

Sometimes Reddic forgot he wasn't many years from
being boy. Others he felt it sharp as an Aulian knife.

7

MIRRAHJ

'Forkbeard king's on the move.' Gallow woke up slumped over the back of a horse. The ground was right in front of him, swaying from side to side, lurching up and down with the animal's gait. He flinched. His hands were tied behind his back, his ankles bound together and the whole of him lashed tight to the saddle beneath. His head throbbed. Bits and pieces of Vathan conversation drifted over him. 'Where?' 'Somewhere down south.' He tried to remember what had happened the night before. Trouble. Fighting. He'd been drunk. Marroc running and screaming and men on horses ... Vathen. And then the Vathan woman, and then ... And then he didn't remember.

A dozen Marroc trailed along behind the horsemen, hands bound, pulled by ropes tied to Vathan saddles. If anyone fell then the Vathen wouldn't stop. Gallow closed his eyes again. No point letting them know he was awake because then they'd only drag him like the others. He let himself drift, trying to doze away the throbbing between his eyes.

The sun was still high when the Vathen finally stopped and made a small camp. They threw together a fire and sat around it roasting haunches of meat while they left their animals to graze. The horses looked thin and hungry and the Vathen tucked into their feast like starving men. Some of them taunted the Marroc with strips of fat, dangling them and then whipping them away again, but they stopped when the woman from Hrodicslet came past and barked at them. Gallow's eyes followed her. The other Vathen deferred to her. She was their bashar then. And now he dimly remembered. Hadn't she told him that before ... before whatever had happened?

She saw him watching her, and while the other Vathen stamped out the fire and rounded up their horses, she cut the ropes that held him and tipped him onto the ground and poked him with her toe.

'Come on, forkbeard, move. Else I'll think you're dead. You might think I'll leave you and you'll slip your ropes and escape, but there are some things I want from these Marroc, and I'm thinking that if I let them bleed a forkbeard it might loosen their tongues a little.'

Gallow rolled onto his back and looked up at her. 'Lhosir make poor slaves. What do you want from me, Vathan?'

'Right now for you to get to your feet.' She tied a rope to the horse's saddle. As Gallow struggled to rise she hauled him up and then strung the rope around his waist. When that was done she cut the ropes around his feet. She didn't touch the ones around his wrists.

'It's easier to walk with your hands at the front.'

She flashed him an unkind smile. 'So it is. You want to know what I want from you?' She walked a little way to her own horse and led it back and tapped at the scabbard tied across its saddle. *His* scabbard. 'I want to know where to find the sword that goes with this.'

Gallow shrugged, but she was laughing before he could even open his mouth. 'Of course, forkbeard, of course you don't know, haven't the first idea, can't even imagine what I'm talking about. Save your breath for the walk since I won't believe a word you say right now. When you're ready you can tell me how you came to have the scabbard, at least. Or do you propose to tell me that some Marroc hung it on you for a joke when you were drunk last night?'

Gallow twisted his neck from side to side, trying to ease out the knots in his muscles. He felt the joints and the bones crack. 'I'll tell you exactly, Vathan, for I see no secret to it. My name is Gallow. Some once called me Truesword. Most call me Foxbeard now. I fought beside the Screambreaker at Andhun. I was there when he defeated your giant and took the red sword and I was beside him when he fell. That's how I came to be carrying both that scabbard and the sword you're looking for. Is that what you wanted to hear?'

The Vathan cocked her head. 'Go on.'

Gallow closed his eyes. 'Let your Marroc slaves go.'

The woman howled with laughter. 'A forkbeard asking mercy for Marroc slaves? There's a thing. I'm sure *they* won't beg for *you*.'

'No.' Gallow bowed his head.

'Well, if ever you find a Marroc prepared to take your place, I'll let you go, forkbeard. But for now there are other things I want from these Marroc and so you'll have to tell me more about what happened to Solace as we walk. Do you think you can manage that?'

'You told me to save my breath.'

She smirked. 'Are you the forkbeard who threw Solace off the cliffs of Andhun into the sea?'

'Yes.'

'And you jumped right after it?'

'Yes.'

The woman looked at him askance. Behind her the rest of the Vathen were getting ready to leave. 'I've stood at the top of that cliff, forkbeard, so I'm quite sure I don't believe you. But suppose for a moment that I did: how are you still alive?'

Gallow wasn't sure he had much of an answer to that. When he didn't speak, the Vathan woman laughed and her eyes called him a liar. She turned away and vaulted onto her horse. She didn't free his wrists so he could walk more easily but as the Vathen rode off, she circled back to take the reins of his horse and led him to the front where everyone could see and had him trot along behind her. She didn't once look back at him.

The Vathen rode at a hard pace for walking. Gallow didn't see what happened to the Marroc at the back of the ride, but when they stopped again in the evening on a ridge looking down over a steep valley, most were still there. No one came to untie him so Gallow sat down and stretched his legs while the Vathen set out their camp and lit their fires. He looked down at the valley. He knew this place. At the bottom was the road that ran from Hrodicslet and round the hills to Fedderhun. On its way it passed Middislet only a few miles from Nadric's forge. *From home and from Arda.* As he gazed he walked deep among those memories, so deep he didn't notice the Vathan woman until she squatted beside him, drinking water from a deerskin bottle. 'I imagine you could keep up that pace for days.' She drank deeply.

'I imagine I could.' Gallow closed his eyes. The sun was setting and the air would get cold quickly even this far from the mountains.

'Yes. A forkbeard like you should manage well enough. I'm guessing three more days to Fedderhun and then we'll pick the pace up. Another five or six to Andhun.'

'I'd like some water, please. Walking makes me thirsty.'

'Polite too?' She laughed. 'But where's your beard, fork-beard? I feel stupid calling you that when you haven't got one.'

'I cut it off.'

'Why?'

'Talking makes me thirsty too.'

'Sit up then.' When Gallow managed to get himself sitting, the woman moved closer and tipped the bottle against his mouth. She was careful and he managed to drink more than she spilled.

75

'This is your ride. The others answer to you. You're the bashar here?'

'So I am. Where's the sword, forkbeard?'

'I left it behind.'

'Where?'

'A place I passed through.'

'Why?'

'Because it's cursed.'

She snorted. 'I hear the Marroc say so. I thought you forkbeards knew better.'

Gallow turned and smiled at her, though there was no friendliness there. 'I carried the red sword for long enough to know that the Marroc are right. If I had it, I'd give it to you.'

She laughed. 'I doubt that very much, forkbeard.'

'That doesn't make it any less true.'

'You're not going to tell me where it is. But you know. I can see that. That or it's all been lies right from the start and you just found the scabbard empty washed up on the shore somewhere. I think if I try to beat it out of you, I might kill you before you talk, and the ardshan would have my hide for that. So you can keep your secrets, forkbeard. I'll take you to Andhun and the ardshan can try. I'll be curious to see if it can be done.'

'It's a long way to Andhun, Vathan. A lot could happen.'

'It could.' She stood up and took the bottle away. 'Hungry yet?'

'I'll live.'

'I bet.' She chuckled. 'I've killed forkbeards. Two. Three years ago in Andhun. I hated your people once but not so much now. Don't think for a moment that'll help you if I have to hunt you down. I'm the bashar of this ride, as you say. Challenge me and I'll open your throat and damn whatever it is you might know.' She turned and started off, then stopped and looked back. 'One thing puzzles me, forkbeard.

76

What were you doing in that Marroc town, just you and none of the rest of your kind?'

'Looking for a place to get drunk.'

'In a town full of Marroc?' She hooted with glee. 'You forkbeards are mad. I'm surprised they didn't slit your throat.'

'But they didn't.'

She went away then, back to the fires to be among her men, but later, when it was dark and the Vathen were settling to sleep for the night, she returned with a ragged half-eaten leg of fire-burned meat, cold again now, with the fat congealed among the flecks of charred flesh and skin. She poked Gallow with her foot until he stirred, and when he sat up she dropped the meat on his lap. He wriggled until he had it wedged between his knees. Doubled over he could reach it with his teeth. He tore at it carefully, wary of dislodging it. The woman watched him. 'You're a strange one, forkbeard. The Marroc all scream and cry and wail to be let go. They beg and wave their hands. The forkbeards I've met before were all full of curses and threats. They never gave an inch and they all came to bad ends. But you? You just sit here as though none of this really matters.' She snorted and laughed at the same time, an odd squeaking sound.

Gallow glanced up between mouthfuls. 'Your ropes are strong and your knots are good, Vathan. I told you already that Lhosir make poor slaves and I'll be no different, but why waste my strength fighting what cannot be fought?'

The Vathan shook her head as she got up. 'You intrigue me, forkbeard, but that was a dull answer. Do better.'

He slept as best he could in the lashing winds blowing off the Storm Coast to the north. In the morning the Vathan woman poked him in his shivering ribs until he was on his feet and they were away again. She ignored him for the rest of that day and for most of the next one too, until his throat was swollen with thirst and his legs ached and his

77

belly knotted with hunger, but on the third night, as the Vathen camped amid a wind that howled like a fury and whipped the trees and the grass and staggered men whenever they took a careless step, she came back to him again. She held water and meat still warm and dripping from the fire in front of him, and shouted over the gale, 'Amuse me, forkbeard. Never mind the sword, if that somehow troubles your honour. Tell me the story of how a drunken forkbeard found himself in a Marroc town so far from his fellows and then simply didn't care when a Vathan bashar took him for her slave.'

Another day without water would be the end of him. He wasn't sure if the Vathan woman would let that happen but the smell of hot fat drove him wild. And in the end what did it matter? He laughed. 'Strange that you should ask that tonight.' The land around them had been familiar for hours. He remembered riding across it with the Screambreaker after Lostring Hill. Middislet was less than a dozen miles away, somewhere to the south and the west – Middislet and Nadric's forge and Arda and home – but he didn't dare breathe a word of any of that. So he told her instead how the ghost of the Screambreaker had been waiting for him after he'd thrown himself into the sea from the cliffs of Andhun, of the choices he'd been given there and of the choice he'd made. Of how storms and slavers had taken him ever further from his home. A year as a slave, an arena fighter, then a wanderer and a corsair, and finally on a ship again, looking for the way home and yet another storm that sank him and washed him up on a beach in a distant land to the very far south. And always he had the sword. He told her how he'd clung to it, gone back for it, always kept it somehow with him in each escape, the red sword and his old shield of Medrin's Crimson Legion. He watched her eyes as he told her and saw the hunger there, and so each night he told her more.

The Vathen reached Fedderhun and then the sea and the coast road to Andhun. The gales blew themselves out and in their place a stillness settled in the air. A cold was coming, a bitter cold drifting down from the Ice Wraiths in the distant north. The Vathen stopped in Marroc villages, each one quietly getting on with its life until a hundred Vathan riders threw them out of their homes and hearths for a night and ate their food and moved on. In a Marroc house around a Marroc fire Gallow told the Vathan woman of Oribas – how the Aulian had found him washed up on the beach with the last of his crew and nursed them all back to life – and of the Rakshasa, the great monster they'd hunted together while Gallow always looked for roads north that would take him home. As snow fell outside, he spoke of how he found the pass through the mountains, the Aulian Way to the Varyxhun valley, and at the same time the secret that would kill the Rakshasa, how he'd gone back to the desert and to Oribas to finish their hunt and how he'd lost the red sword in that battle, the one and only lie in everything he said. She looked at him hard when he told her that and asked many questions, and he knew she didn't know whether to believe him but here and now he didn't care. In a way he was speaking himself out, since the Vathen in Andhun would surely kill him once they knew who he was. They'd ask him about the sword over and over, and either he'd break as they tortured him or he wouldn't but the end would be the same.

She came back, that was what mattered, and when the cold came as he knew it would and the snow lay thick and men shivered and died under their blankets at night, she made sure they kept him warm. He got her name out of her. Mirrahj Bashar. He couldn't think of much reason to lie about the rest and so he told her how it was: how a forkbeard had come across the mountains after three years of looking for the way home and found himself caught between the Marroc and his own people. How other forkbeards had been looking for the sword too and how they wouldn't let him be. How he'd found himself fighting his own brothers of the sea, killed the man who'd been his best friend in the world and found his family at last only to leave them again. How his wife had sent him away. How the Marroc had thrown him out and how he'd long ago burned all bridges with his own kin.

'So you see, Vathan, there's no peace for me and never has been, except for this. I'm done. Kill King Sixfingers and then perhaps I can go home. I'd like to see my sons grow into men, even if they want nothing to do with me. But if that's not to be then best I stay away. Far away. It's no hurt what you're doing, taking me from where I was.'

Mirrahj Bashar listened quietly to it all, and when he was done she didn't laugh or spit, only shook her head. 'I'm sorry, forkbeard, but I don't think that's your future. We'll see the walls of Andhun tomorrow.' She touched his face, a finger on his cheek. Gallow had lost count of the days they'd been on the move since Hrodicslet but it had been more than a week. Like it or not, he was growing a beard.

As she'd said, the middle of the next day brought them to Andhun. Gallow looked up at the gatehouse as they rode beneath it, thinking of the times he'd been this way before. With the Screambreaker more than a decade ago. With Tolvis Loudmouth on the day he'd decided not to go home just yet after all. Walking the other way with Valaric the morning after he'd burned Jyrdas on the beach, with a hundred Marroc howling for his blood. They crossed the square where he and Valaric had stood, side by side, alone against Medrin and his men. He'd never thought to see Andhun again.

Instead of the castle, the Vathen swarmed into the horse market. If they'd been Lhosir they would have kicked a few Marroc for the fun of it, and the Marroc would have shouted back and maybe thrown stones and fistfuls of dung, and then before you knew it there would have been blood and dead men all over the place. The Lhosir liked a fight, and once they started they weren't that keen on stopping. But the Vathen simply told the Marroc to go and then waited, and the Marroc went and no one killed anyone.

'Last chance, forkbeard.' Mirrahj came and sat beside him after she'd eaten with her ride. She offered him a piece of gristly meat and a skin of water. 'I'll give you to the ardshan tomorrow. If you're who you say you are, he'll remember your face and kill you slowly. I've been kind to you, forkbeard, kinder than others might have been. Tell me where the sword is. The ardshan will get it out of you in the end anyway.'

'In the desert of Aulia, far beyond the southern mountains.' Gallow smiled and drank the water. Mirrahj snatched the meat away from him.

'You're lying to me, Gallow Foxbeard of the Lhosir.'

'It's the only answer I have for you, Mirrahj Bashar of the Vathen.'

'If I let you go?'

'But you won't.'

'I might promise to kill you quickly and without pain.'

'I wouldn't believe you.'

'What if I told you that I meant to find the sword for myself and overthrow the ardshan and proclaim myself Daughter of the Weeping God and rule over all my people?'

'Then you're no different from any other.' He almost smiled. 'A dull answer. You can do better.'

Mirrahj Bashar laughed and threw the meat to him anyway. 'Enjoy it. It's the last you'll see.' She made as if to leave and then stopped and looked at him intently. 'You know what I think? I think you're telling me the truth when you say you left it behind. I think you're telling me the truth when you say it's cursed and when you say you want nothing more to do with it. All that happened to you, you choose

81

to blame on Solace. Foolish, but then you *are* a forkbeard. There's a change in your face when you talk about things that matter, and so I believe you, all of what you say except the where.' She shuffled closer. 'You *did* leave it behind, but not in Aulia. That's the lie. So where is it, forkbeard? It's somewhere closer, isn't it?'

Gallow shook his head and looked away. Saying nothing, that was the best defence when the questions started. The whole truth or else say nothing at all.

'If you'd left it somewhere that was beyond grasping, you'd have told me, safe and sure that it didn't matter. So it's not in Aulia, but if you didn't lose it in Aulia then you brought it back.'

Gallow caught her smiling at the corners of her eyes. He shrugged.

'Nothing to say, forkbeard? You left the sword up in the mountains, didn't you? There's a road from Andhun that heads south on the other side of the Isset. Goes all the way up there. The Marroc call it the Aulian Way. Not too hard to guess where it goes.'

'It's on the other side of the river,' murmured Gallow. 'There's no place to cross. You know that.'

'Oh, but there is. Go far enough and there must be. Tell me, forkbeard. Tell me and take me to it and I'll let you live. I'll let you go. I know what it's like to want to go home.'

Gallow shook his head. Mirrahj got up and patted him on the shoulder. Later she came back and brought him the remains of a roasted goat's leg, one with some decent meat still on it, and Gallow knew it was a goodbye of sorts. Made him wonder if Medrin's Lhosir would have treated Mirrahj Bashar as kindly if they'd taken her. Probably not, all things considered. He ate his fill, rolled onto his side and let his thoughts drift. If they killed him, so be it. Tomorrow was another day.

8

KING SIXFINGERS

In the darkness of the new moon the Legion of the Crimson Shield slipped into the waters of the Isset in a hundred tiny boats and pushed away from the banks. Each had a muffled paddle, but for the most part there was no need for them for the river was already beginning to swell with the first meltwater from the mountains. In each boat a handful of soldiers hid under fur cloaks, eyes at the front to watch their way, tugging on strings to one man at the back trailing a paddle in the water to steer them. There were no words, no whispers. They floated in silence.

On the far side of the river Thanni Ironfoot and two dozen men had crossed the Isset at dusk, hours before the little boats left. Now they ran, trotting along the bank in ones and twos, watching for Vathen. It was a dangerous sport. There might not be any Vathan sentries on the river at all so far north of Tarkhun and the massing Lhosir army. Or there might be any number. If that was the case then Ironfoot and his hunters had to find them and kill them quickly and without alarm, and all the while they had to stay ahead of the little boats, and that meant they had to run through the night. Which was just as well, because the night was as cold as an ice witch's kiss.

Three miles short of Andhun they found their first watchers. Three Vathen, clustered up close to a fire. The cold was a blessing, Ironfoot reckoned. Man stood around for long away from a fire on a night like this, he froze and died. So the Vathen were beside their fire, two snoring like old drunks while the third sat on a log, head drooping and jerking back up again. Ironfoot got close enough to hear the Vathan's breathing. The Vathan's head jerked up one last time. Ironfoot came from behind and covered the space between them in three long strides, clamped a hand over the man's face and opened his throat with a long-edged knife. He held the Vathan good and tight well after the blood stopped spraying out towards the river. He'd done it quietly enough, but by then the other Vathen had stopped snoring. They'd stopped breathing too. The Lhosir cleaned their knives and ran on.

A mile out of Andhun they slowed. The banks of the river grew steeper as the Isset closed in on the sea, as though the land itself had risen to try and keep the water back and the river had simply cut deeper and deeper. A steep ridge rose in front of them and Ironfoot smelled smoke. He crept closer and saw a Vathan down by the bank, awake and alert. He threw a stone. The Vathan looked the other way and Ironfoot ran silently up behind him and split the back of his neck with an axe. Then he waved the men running behind him to a halt, made a circling motion and pointed to the ridge. He took a moment to catch his breath and then led them away from the river at a fast jog, following the bottom of the slope until they'd covered a good half a mile; then they climbed it, quiet as thieves. The men with the best legs went on over and down the other side to keep on to Andhun; the rest followed him, creeping back along the top of the ridge. He had no idea how far behind the little boats were by now, but no real distance.

Close to the river again he could finally see what he was dealing with – fifty or sixty men, so surely at least one other sentry watching the river and probably two. He waited for his Lhosir to get ready. They looked at one another and closed their eyes and muttered words to the Maker-Devourer, then went forward on their hands and knees, silent as owls. Close up he could hear the Vathen talking, the handful who were awake – away on the side of the camp looking down over the Isset. Half his men spread out behind him and got on with the business of slitting sleeping throats. He led the rest himself, just four, creeping silently through the night like shadows, closer and closer to where the Vathen sentries—

A shout broke the silence behind him. What or why made no difference and he didn't look back, just rose and rushed forward. The Vathen turned. They saw him coming, but only so the surprise was still written on their faces when he ran his spear into the belly of the first and buried his axe in the face of the next. The other two sentries cried out before they died but it made no difference now. The Vathen were waking up faster than his Lhosir could kill them. Then again, his Lhosir were in mail and furs and had their spears already in their hands. Made for an interesting fight for a while. Short, maybe a hundred heartbeats before it was done, but tense as a drawn knife.

When they were finished, Ironfoot looked out over the river where the Vathan sentries had sat. He could see the first shapes in the water, silently drifting with the current towards Andhun. Hard to see what they were without a moon, but then he didn't need to see to know they were the boats.

When the first shouts woke him, Moonjal Bashar jerked upright to see the dark shape of a man standing over him. The man had a spear raised ready to run him through. In that moment Moonjal couldn't have said whether the man was a Lhosir or a Vathan or a Marroc but the sight was enough. He threw himself sideways, rolled as far and fast as he could and tipped himself off the side of the ridge. He tumbled and bounced down the slope and landed in a thicket beside the river, too winded to do more than lie still.

'Where are you, bandy-legs?' When he looked back he could make out the shape of a man coming cautiously down the slope after him. The words gave him away: a forkbeard. Moonjal stayed exactly where he was, still as a mouse. The Lhosir wouldn't see him unless Moonjal moved or the forkbeard trod on him. The man had a shield as well as his spear and he probably had a sword or an axe on his belt. Moonjal had all of these things too, only they were lying on the top of the rise next to the furs where he'd been sleeping.

He was shivering already. *That* was what was going to give him away. Or the mist of his breath. Cursed cold!

The forkbeard wasn't stupid. He was coming at a steady pace, not rushing, keeping his shield low to guard his legs, poking his spear into each clump of grass. He was heading the right way too. 'Come on, horse boy. Come and play.'

Moonjal's fingers touched the haft of the knife strapped to his calf. It was a nice knife, an old piece of Lhosir steel sheathed in Aulian gold and looted from Andhun. Strapping it to his calf had been to make sure no one stole it but he'd not say no to luck, however it came. He bent forward now, fingers closing around it, as slowly and gently as he could, trying to stay invisible.

A twig snapped beneath him as the knife came free. The forkbeard's head whipped round, looking right at him. The man growled under his breath. 'That you, horse boy?' He was coming straight at Moonjal now, crouched low, shield covering almost all of him, spear jabbing. Moonjal froze. If he moved a muscle, the forkbeard would see him now, or hear him. If he tried to get up and make a dash for it, the forkbeard would run him through with his spear. If he tried scrambling deeper into the thicket ... He had no idea how thick the undergrowth was. He might get away or he might not, but the forkbeard would still be after him and he'd still be on his hands and knees.

The Lhosir eased in closer. Moonjal stayed absolutely still, hoping the forkbeard didn't tread on him. A snapped twig. *Could* have been an animal. The forkbeard stopped with his feet so close they were practically touching Moonjal's arm. The Vathan heard him breathing, slow and harsh, the long deep breaths of a stalking hunter. He was whispering to the air, 'Where are you, Vathan?'

The bushes rustled and shifted above Moonjal as the forkbeard lunged with his spear. Moonjal held his breath. The spearman took another cautious step. His foot came down on Moonjal's leg and slid sideways. Moonjal jerked – couldn't help it – and for a moment the forkbeard lost his balance. He grunted in surprise. Moonjal rammed the knife into the forkbeard's thigh, nice and high under the skirts of his mail, and hacked hard. The forkbeard staggered back, tripped and fell. For a moment as he toppled over they were face to face in the blackness, but then the forkbeard was down and Moonjal was hauling himself to his feet and never mind the thorns that shredded his hands. He started to run but then realised the forkbeard wasn't moving. When Moonjal went back to look, the forkbeard was dead. The grass around him was sticky and wet with blood.

Shouts rang out from the top of the ridge. He crouched beside the body for a moment and looked up. The slaughter was still going on but no one else was coming down. Good enough. He stayed with the forkbeard long enough to help himself to the man's shield, helm and spear, but by the time he'd armed himself, the sounds of fighting were dying down. He could hear voices, forkbeard voices, which meant his ride was destroyed or fled and the forkbeards had won, and that was when he realised he had no idea how many of them were here, just a short march from the walls of Andhun, in the middle of the night and on the wrong side of the river.

He dragged the dead forkbeard into the thicket and started to strip him. He was mostly done when the first of the boats began to drift by. At first he couldn't imagine what the large misshapen lumps were, then he saw one of them move, saw a forkbeard head poke out from under the furs at the front, and understood. But by then it was too late.

King Medrin Sixfingers, king of the Lhosir and the Marroc and bearer of the Crimson Shield of Modris the Protector, peered at the walls of Andhun rising ahead on either side of the river. The Vathen had spent three years making sure he couldn't simply build a fleet of boats and cross the Isset into the eastern half of the city and now only a fool would try an assault from the river. There were walls along the eastern bank and lookout towers and simply nowhere for boats to land short of the harbour. There were a dozen sentries, all carefully protected from arrows and archers in walled-in posts that could only be reached through long stone passages from as far away as the city gates, and each lookout had a bell and a small fire to light, both of which could raise the alarm. Three full rides of Vathan warriors had their barracks along the river defences, armed with thousands of javelots. The ardshan's Aulian tinker had shown the Vathen how to make little stone throwers and ballistae to fire their javelots harder. They had a good collection of Marroc fish oil too, for throwing into the river and setting the water alight. More to help their eyes than to burn Lhosir maybe, but to the Vathen watching the river either was as good as the other.

For three years Andhun had been split in two like this, and for three years Medrin had waited, but no more. He gave the word, and the little boat that carried him turned towards the shore still a full half-mile from the city walls. Behind him a hundred other boats did the same.

Only a fool would try an assault from the river.

At the edge of Andhun harbour, among the rocks and the breaking waves at the foot of the cliffs, a handful of men encased in iron rose out of the water and clawed their way to the shore. No one saw them come. There were caves at the bottom of the cliff and some of them led up into the castle. A few of the iron-skinned men clambered into them, but most crept and scraped along the foot of the cliffs. The passages under the castle were no secret any more. They'd be guarded and the ironskins had other duties tonight. They walked around the cliff paths, fourteen of them clinging to the shadows. Now and then they stopped, pausing as idle eyes awake in the middle of the night swept across them. They were no ordinary men, these warriors. They were the Fateguard, servants to the Eyes of Time, all Lhosir once but something else now, thieves and murderers and rapists and traitors, the worst *nioingr*, outcasts handed over in chains to the white ship that sailed now and then to the land of the Ice Wraiths. Now they had come back.

The Eyes of Time had not made them to be subtle tools but they had instincts beyond those of ordinary men. They slipped through the edges of the lower city, away from the castle, away from all the places where the Vathen might keep watch, sidling through the darkest narrowest alleys where the Marroc lived. Once they saw a Marroc thief coming the other way. The thief saw them too. He squealed and ran to cower in the darkest place he could find. They let him go – he'd not warn any Vathen, after all. They climbed steep and narrow alleys, closer and closer to Andhun's gates, past the door to the Grey Man inn and along the very same alley where Valaric and Gallow had once held half an army of Lhosir at bay long enough for the Marroc to flee to their ships and boats – or so the story was told among both the Marroc and the Lhosir in their very different ways.

There wasn't much to be done about the gatehouse itself. There were Vathan guards outside the doors, standing close to their braziers and rubbing their hands, and then there were the doors themselves, thick iron things held shut and barred from the inside. The Fateguard entered the square. They walked quickly now, keeping to the shadows for as long as there were shadows to be had, then brazenly out in the open.

'Stop! Who goes there?'

The Vathen were quick to pick up their spears and shout the first alarms. When one turned and ran, a Fateguard threw his spear and brought him down. The guards screamed and threw themselves forward. The Fateguard barely slowed their pace. They shattered spears and bodies and bones without a thought and then the Vathen were dead or fled and broken.

One of the Fateguard stood before each iron door and placed a palm against it. Fingers of brown rust spread across the iron like cracks in glass – across the door and across the skin of the Fateguard alike. The fingers spread in fast fits and starts, fattening as they went until both the doors and the skin of the Fateguard were crazed with brown cracks.

Alarms sounded up and down the city, then finally a bell from the castle itself. More Vathen came but they were too few and too late. The Fateguard ringed the gatehouse doors, their iron skins turning aside the Vathan spearheads, their swords striking with the deadly speed of snakes. A dozen Vathen died, their blood spreading in dark puddles across the stones. The last few backed away, fearful yet entranced. The iron doors were flaking and so too were the two Fateguard whose magic was eating them. Both were pitted and cracked. Dead leaves of corroded metal peeled away and snapped and fluttered to the ground. With a crack one of the rusting Fateguard snapped at the waist and toppled sideways. His hand remained pressed to the door, welded in place by the rust. The rest of his armour broke into pieces as it hit the cobbles. The armour was hollow now, nothing but dust left of the man who'd once been inside.

The other Fateguard kicked at the doors. Ruined iron

buckled and twisted and then the hinges snapped and the bolts shattered. The gates fell, the iron turning to powder, doors and rusting Fateguard both. Inside the gatehouse the Vathan soldiers hurled their javelots and fired their crossbows. Bolts struck iron and did nothing. A well swung axe severed an iron hand at the wrist but the Fateguard barely seemed to notice. The axeman had enough time to see there wasn't any blood, to feel the horror rise inside him before a sword slammed into his belly, doubling him over, and then came again, point first down on the back of his neck and out through his mouth. He spewed his own blood over his feet as he died, and there on the floor right in front of him was the severed hand, still in its iron skin and not a drop of blood at all. Nothing but old dead meat.

Andhun's gates were already opening as the last of the Vathen died. Back outside the gatehouse, shadows began to move – Lhosir, running out of the darkness, their king leading the way. They poured through the gates and swept as fast as they could through the upper city, straight for the castle. The Fateguard retraced their steps toward the sea, down to the foot of the cliffs and along the shore.

This time they turned for the caves.

9

THUNDER AND LIGHT

A crash woke Gallow in the night. His eyes flicked open but the rest of him stayed perfectly still. The sky was dark, just starting to grey where the sun would rise in another hour, as shouts spread through the horse market: 'Arms! To arms! Forkbeards!'

A Vathan ran past him, throwing mail over his head. The riders who'd been his guard were scrambling to their feet, snatching up their javelots, casting their eyes around wildly in the dark, searching for the enemy. Gallow rolled into the far corner of the yard and curled up in the moonshadows, trying to make himself small. Trying to be unseen.

'Get up! Get up!' He recognised the voice. One of the men who wanted to be bashar in place of Mirrahj. Josper, was it? Something like that. 'Forkbeards inside the walls! Arm yourselves! To your horses!' Three Vathen ran past heading the other way, then more and more spilled out into the yard, and now Mirrahj was screaming at them to stay together, and right in the middle of the chaos a dozen Lhosir burst in through the market gates and launched themselves at the Vathen, who almost broke even though they had three times the numbers. He saw Mirrahj and Josper both hurl themselves at the Lhosir, stalling their charge as the men around them wavered; and then at last the Vathen rallied and the Lhosir pulled seamlessly back behind their wall of shields and spears and withdrew to leave a dozen Vathen dead in the yard. Josper screamed at the Vathen to charge after them and Mirrahj screamed at them to hold and for a moment the two of them stood nose to nose ready to fight, but by then the Lhosir were gone. Josper swore something and spat. The Vathen dragged their horses into the yard and threw themselves into their saddles, some of them barely dressed but all of them furious. They hurtled away in dribs and drabs, Mirrahj's last cries echoing back: 'The castle! The castle!'

Forgotten, hobbled and with his hands tied behind his back, Gallow was alone. A quiet settled over the yard. In the distance he heard shouting and screams. He waited a moment in case the Lhosir came back or any last Vathen came rushing through, but none did. The sounds of fighting were fading.

Among the fallen lay one dead Lhosir. Gallow rolled across the yard towards him. Vathan javelots – light things for throwing from the back of a horse – were useless for what he needed, but a Lhosir spear was heavy with a good sharp edge that sliced and slashed as well as stabbed. He fumbled with his fingers, sliding the haft behind him, easing the bladed head against the ropes around his wrists and then rocking back and forth, slicing them thread by thread. The spear kept slipping and he kept having to find it again and line it up right, but one by one he felt the strands of rope snap, more and more pieces of it tickling his fingers. He felt the rope give, a bigger jolt this time, and then the spear slipped again and the rope unravelled and fell apart and his hands were suddenly free. A few seconds more and he'd untied the other ropes. He scrambled over to the fallen Lhosir and took the soldier's belt and his boots and all his weapons bar one. The last was a knife. He wrapped the dead Lhosir's fingers around it. 'I don't know this man, Maker-Devourer, but I saw him fall. His death was brave and worthy of your cauldron.'

He picked up the Lhosir's shield and saw its design,

painted like the Crimson Shield of Modris the Protector. The last time Gallow had been in Andhun, the Legion of the Crimson Shield had been Prince Medrin's personal soldiers. He stared at it and at the dead Lhosir on the worn stones. Did that mean that Sixfingers was here? Until now he'd had every intention of running, caught between Vathan and Lhosir armies, none of whom were friends. But if Sixfingers himself was here ...

A terrible purpose swept into him. He hurried through the horse market. His sword hand itched. *Medrin.* If Medrin was here they could end it between them. One of them would die, and either way Arda and his sons would be safe. A snarl curled his lip – best if it was Medrin who was the dead one. He crouched in the black shadows of a doorway. No one would hunt him if Medrin was dead. The two of them could finish it; and even if the war wasn't done and the fighting wasn't over, he could leave all this far behind and go back to who he was, throw away his sword and hammer his spear into something more useful. Arda would have him again if he could promise her that was how it would be. Forget the red sword. Leave it with the Marroc in Varyxhun or lead the Vathan woman to it. He didn't know, didn't care. But Medrin had to die first. Right here and now nothing else mattered.

He picked up his Lhosir spear and walked out of the horse market, turned the first corner and was almost ridden down by a dozen Vathen.

'Forkbeard!' One of them threw a javelot. Gallow lifted his shield to knock it aside and then dived into an alley too narrow for the horses to follow. Jeers came after him. 'Coward! *Nioingr*! Sheep lover!'

'Leave him!'

The voice that rose over the others was Mirrahj. Gallow ran back to the end of the alley. 'Mirrahj Bashar!' The horsemen were disappearing back into the market, half-lost in the shadows cast by the houses pressed tight around them; but as he stood and watched she came back. She kept her distance on the back of her horse, spear levelled at his face, while Gallow kept his back to the alley and his feet ready to run.

'My pet forkbeard! Fortune smiles on you.'

'I mean to look for King Sixfingers so that one of us might kill the other. These are his men here. Where might I find him?'

'The forkbeards are at the castle. I'm sorry to tell you that they're already inside, so you might find it hard.' She lifted her spear. 'I'm glad the ardshan won't be ripping you apart, forkbeard. I'll look for you on the battlefield so I might do it myself.'

'I mean to kill him, Mirrahj Bashar.' Gallow saluted and backed away. 'You were a fine enemy. Better than many a friend.'

He turned, letting the night swallow him, and ran uphill, always uphill towards the castle. The alleys of Andhun, all too narrow for a man on a horse, made it easy. Now and then he darted across open streets, and sometimes there were riders and sometimes they saw him and shouted and threw their javelots but they were always too slow and they never gave chase. Some of the streets were empty, others he had to wait while dozens of Vathen cantered past, but they never looked down or to the side, always up and towards the castle. In one small square he had to creep around fifty riders. He could hear the Lhosir by then, their battle shouts splitting the night, barked cries of men with weapons ready, and he heard the beating of swords and spears on shields and the bellows of men readying themselves to fight and then the clash of arms, the animal howls, the screams of horses and of the dying. Yet as he drew close to the castle square, the sounds of fighting dropped away. For a few minutes the city fell quiet, and in that stillness Gallow reached its heart.

In the grey gloom of almost dawn, dead Vathen littered the cobbles. A hundred Lhosir barricaded the castle gates, shields pressed tight together, spears arrayed over the tops. They had their own dead too, dragged back through the ranks by now, but Gallow could see them through the thin line of spears, the Lhosir who were too wounded to fight dragging the dying back into the castle yard, talking among themselves to see who knew each man to speak them out. Scores of Vathan horsemen rode back and forth in front of the shield wall, just out of reach, taunting with words and javelots. The Lhosir held their ground, howling insults of their own and throwing the Vathan javelots right back at them. Fists clenched, spears shook, horses snorted and men bellowed, each side firing itself up for the next crash of iron.

At the edge of the square Gallow watched them all, and then he stepped out from the shadows and strode between them. Spears and eyes swivelled to greet him as he ignored the Vathen, stopped a pace short of the Lhosir wall and lifted his spear over his head and let out a roar: 'Medrin! Medrin Sixfingers! King *Nioingr*! Gallow Truesword waits for you!'

The Lhosir looked at one another and cocked their heads and shook them. One of them started to laugh and soon they all were. 'You just stay there calling for him.'

Someone threw a stick. A stone pinged off his shield. Then the ground under his feet was trembling – he could feel it tickling his soles – and the Lhosir weren't looking at him any more, they were looking across the square to the wide road down to the harbour.

'Medrin!'

The rumble of hooves grew louder still, and with a great roar another hundred Vathan riders thundered into the square and hurled themselves towards the Lhosir line, veered away from the spears at the last second and hurled their javelots. Stranded between them, left to choose whether to run or to be trampled, Gallow ran, and as he did he cast a glance back. The reluctant sun was creeping over the horizon now and the tops of the castle towers lit up, suddenly bright. In the square the Lhosir bellowed and roared their taunts, the Vathen howled and hooted back, javelots flew into shields, spears reached out to stab at man and horse alike. Animals and soldiers screamed and the air reeked of blood. Back in the shadows Gallow looked wildly for another way through, a weakness in the Lhosir wall. Then he saw the rising dawn light the balcony over the castle gates. Men stood there, and Gallow stared at them until the sun touched the square and struck his eyes, dazzling him, pulling him out of its shadows.

'Forkbeard!' A Vathan horseman pointed a spear at him. In a flash, a group of riders had turned towards him. He was still dazed by the light and the figure on the balcony. He turned to run and a javelot hit him between the shoulders hard enough to hurl him forward and sprawl him across the cobbles. The horsemen came up behind him. He could barely move. For a first helpless moment he couldn't tell whether his mail had held and turned the point or whether the javelot had driven right through him and he was about to choke on his own blood. He'd been kicked by horses a few times and that had hurt far less less.

Spears prodded at him. And then they stopped. 'Where is it, forkbeard?'

He laughed. When his mouth didn't fill up with blood, he hauled himself to his hands and knees and Maker-Devourer damn the pain that came with that. 'You followed me here to ask me that?'

He could hardly move his sword arm at all. He pushed himself up and rose shakily to his feet. There were half a dozen Vathen around him, all with their spear tips an inch from his mail. Mirrahj looked down at him. It was a cold look. 'Where is it? Tell me and walk away.'

His back was agony but he still looked up past the Vathen, back to the castle and the men standing on the balcony over the square. He squinted until he was sure, but he'd known it right from the start. Medrin. Medrin had taken the castle. The Lhosir had won Andhun. Which meant there was nothing to stop them from marching on Varyxhun.

The Vathen followed his eyes, even Mirrahj. 'The ardshan,' she whispered.

'It's in Varyxhun,' said Gallow quietly. 'I left it in Varyxhun. Did you hear me?' He looked from one Vathan to the next to the next. 'Your sword Solace. It's in Varyxhun.'

Mirrahj leaned down and hissed, 'And where is this Varyxhun, forkbeard? Tell me!' It hadn't even crossed his mind that she wouldn't know.

'I'll do better.' He offered the hand that still worked. 'Keep your word, Mirrahj Bashar, and I'll show you.'

She smiled and laughed again, though it was a bitter sort of laugh. Once he was on the back of her horse, she turned and rode for Andhun's gates.

10

SHADEWALKER

Come the morning, Reddic was still alive, barely. He was still scared too and there was no barely about *that*. None of them knew how long the shadewalker followed them. Certainly for a while after they left the farmhouse. Stannic had been happy enough to pace it for a while. 'To see how fast this one goes,' he said. Reddic had stayed at the back as he'd been told. Once he got over his terror he caught up with Stannic and his family. He could see by then that the shadewalker wasn't about to catch them and kill them and eat them and rip out their souls and turn them into more shadewalkers or whatever it was they did. So he went to the front with Stannic because he was supposed to be a soldier of Valaric's Crackmarsh men, hard as nails and ready to fight forkbeards, and so that's where he ought to be. Stannic hadn't been best pleased but he'd stopped moaning once he decided the shadewalker had given up on them. This was the third he'd met this winter and the fourth in his life, and yes, the first one had made him shit his pants too, thanks for asking. But they weren't too terrible once you knew they couldn't run, and any man with his wits and both his legs could escape. They'd follow a scent through the whole night sometimes, so a man had to pace himself, but they always stopped at sunrise and disappeared into the dark. Or the three he'd met so far had all done that. When Reddic asked whether this one might be different, both of them wished he hadn't.

Come morning they were exhausted, blue with cold and half frozen, but Stannic had had the cunning to lead them in a great circle and so they weren't that far from the farmhouse where they'd started. They all stopped for a bit and agreed that Stannic would stay where he was and keep watch for the shadewalker in case it was still following them, and that Reddic would go on to the farmhouse with everyone else because, well, because they were all blue with cold and half frozen but also because they were scared the shadewalker might have gone back to the farm, all of them except for Stannic, who said he knew better. So Reddic went with the others and felt stupid because he didn't know the land and could only follow while they scrambled through trees and crossed streams and floundered in drifts of snow, and then it turned out that the shadewalker *had* gone back to the farmhouse after all, some time in the middle of the night, and eaten Torvic's face. Or just possibly it had dragged Torvic from where it had killed him and left him hung up in a field and then gone away, and it was some wild animal that had come and eaten his face afterwards. Didn't seem likely, but after he'd found Torvic and finished with puking everywhere, Reddic thought he liked that idea somewhat better.

'What are they?' he asked when Stannic finally came back, but he only shrugged.

'Cursed men,' he said. He followed the tracks the shadewalker had left around the farm. It had come back and taken Torvic and done what it had done and then walked around the farmhouse three times before heading away again. 'South,' said Stannic, squinting in the bright morning light. 'Middislet way, I'd say. Walking pretty straight.' He chuckled and punched Reddic in the arm. 'Brave man could follow its trail in this snow. Find where it's hiding from the sun and put an end to it if he knew how.' Reddic shuddered and Stannic laughed. 'Braver man than me, that'd be.'

'There was a man in Varyxhun who did that,' Reddic said. 'An Aulian.'

They cut Torvic down. Wasn't much they could do for him now. Couldn't even bury him, not in this cold with the ground all frozen and covered by snow, so they took him out into the woods. Reddic said some words, though he didn't know much about Torvic or who he was or why he'd thrown in his lot with Valaric and the Crackmarsh. He took Torvic's mail and spear and his shield because Valaric would skin him for leaving good stuff like that out in the middle of nowhere. Not much else to do. Stannic seemed to know him better, so Reddic left the two of them alone with the winter trees and went back to the farm and tried to get some warmth into his skin again. When Stannic came back he gave Reddic some food and some kind words, and later that morning Reddic took his leave and headed south. Seemed like someone ought to warn the folk of Middislet there was a shadewalker coming. Didn't follow its trail though, not for long.

He spent the next night under the roof where he and Torvic had stayed on their way north with a surly old farmer Torvic had known, like he had seemed to know everyone between Fedderhun and the Crackmarsh. They barred and barricaded the door and took it in turns to keep watch. None of them got much sleep but the shadewalker never came, and by the end of the next day he was in Middislet again. He went to the forge first, thinking they could spread the word and thinking too that it might be as well to load up the mules Torvic had left there, ready to leave in the night if that was the way it went, but when he got there and banged on the door, it wasn't Arda or Nadric who answered but Jelira. Reddic stared at her, not sure what to say, and Jelira stared back and then turned bright red and looked away.

'Where's the smith?' he asked when he found his tongue again.

'In the big barn.' Jelira flashed him a glance. 'Mam's there too. With everyone.'

'Right.' So he ought to be there as well, to tell them about the shadewalker, but his feet weren't moving.

'You staying or heading off?' asked Jelira.

'Staying.'

She nodded. 'I'll make sure there's some more furs airing then. Cold as the Weeping God's tears these last few nights. Hard work for some keeping warm enough to sleep.'

She was smiling and Reddic wondered whether he was missing something, and then realised that yes, he was. He blushed furiously.

'Your friends here too?' Reddic shook his head, and she must have seen the death in his face because her smile vanished. 'You best go up to the barn if you've got news.'

When he reached it, most of the village was gathered inside. As he listened, Reddic realised they were already talking about the shadewalker, except they were talking about at least two – two seen last night, one the night before. He said his piece and told them how one had killed Torvic and eaten his face. Half of them left before he'd even finished, off back to their farms to hammer their doors closed or to take what they could and get away, although where they would go in the middle of nowhere with the nights cold enough to freeze a man's beard Reddic had no idea.

When they were done talking, Arda grabbed him and pinched his ear and marched him back to the forge. 'Don't know what you were thinking telling them about Torvic like that.'

'But that's what it did!'

'Doesn't mean people need to be hearing it. You saw them. They're afraid enough.'

'Aren't you?' She didn't look it and didn't sound it either, but when they got back to the forge she had him bring Torvic's mules into the house and keep their saddles on them, loose so they wouldn't trouble them but still on their backs, and while Reddic loaded them up with Nadric's arrowheads, Arda piled furs beside them. When they were done with that she put the children to sleep in the night room and then sat with him and Nadric. They both fell asleep, snoring curled up on the floor, but when Reddic closed his eyes he kept seeing the ruin of Torvic's face, which was no good for sleeping, and that was why he was awake when the scraping noises started in the yard between the house and the forge. He sat there listening, chills like ice running through his blood, and it struck him hard then that there wasn't any man in the house except old Nadric, who hardly counted, and that meant it was down to him to go and see what it was, and he was scared like he hadn't been since that first night in the Crackmarsh when the ghuldogs were all set to eat him. He prodded Arda awake. Might have been a rat after all, or a dog or a mule broken loose or a sheep wandered into the village. Could have been any of those things but he woke her anyway in case it wasn't.

'Heard something,' he hissed.

'Might be a pig. Roddic's keep getting loose lately.' But she sat up, sleep falling off her like he'd thrown snow in her face. He tried to believe it was a pig. Nothing had come knocking on the door after all, not like Stannic's place.

'Well, go and look then,' Arda said. Reddic looked at his mail and wondered if he should put it on, but then Stannic hadn't had any mail and it hadn't troubled him. He picked up his shield and opened the door a crack.

There were three of them crouched in a circle in the middle of Nadric's yard, scratching at the dirt as though they were searching for something. Like one of them had dropped a coin. They didn't look up. Reddic eased the door closed again, quietest thing he'd ever done. Then he nearly crapped himself. 'There's three of them.'

'Three what? Pigs?' She was poking Nadric.

'Three shadewalkers!'

There was something sharp on her tongue waiting to come out but it died before it was given sound. The colour drained from her face. 'Sure that's what they are, boy?' And he was, and she knew it too.

Boy? Damn but he was fed up with people calling him that. He drew himself up, trying to find some courage from somewhere. 'Yes, quite sure, old mother, may Modris protect us.' He liked the way her eyebrow shot up when he called her *old mother*. Took his mind off the death waiting outside.

'Go and see whether the way's clear outside the other door.' She scurried through the curtain to the night room and started shaking the children, whispering urgently in their ears. Reddic went to the front door and put his hand on it and then stopped. Something made his skin crawl. Instead of opening it he bent to peer around the cracks at the side. Couldn't see much but …

It was right there. Standing in front of the door, waiting for him, still and silent as a statue. The one from Stannic's farm. He whimpered and pointed. 'Right. By. The door.'

In the night outside a scream broke the silence. It came again and again, a shrill cry of terror. After a bit another voice joined it, lower and deeper, shouting out the alarm. Arda was shushing the children, putting them into their furs, all urgent movement, leaving herself until last. She snatched up a bag of something from the corner of the house where she kept her pans and pressed it into Reddic's hands. 'Never mind swords and axes, the best weapon we've got against their sort's in there. They come smashing in, throw it in their faces and run. Don't you worry about us. Nothing wrong with our legs.'

He looked at the pouch. Opened it and sniffed.

'Salt,' she said. 'The Aulian wizard from Witches' Reach sent it to Gallow. For the shadewalkers. Suppose he knew they'd be coming. Don't know how, but that's wizards for you.'

Reddic flinched. Salt? What use was a bag of salt? He scurried to the back door and peered through the cracks. The shadewalkers were still there, crouched together. Three in one place, four if you counted the one standing by the front door – he'd never heard of such a thing. The three in the yard looked like they were looking for something. He'd never heard of that either.

As he watched, one of them stopped scratching and cocked its head. It began crawling on all fours from the middle of the yard towards the forge, scraping away the snow and sniffing at the dirt beneath as it went. 'What are they doing?'

'As long as they keep doing it outside.' There was a nervous edge to Arda's voice, and the only thing that stopped Reddic from falling to bits was the way Jelira kept looking at him. She looked terrified and so he kept his face straight. Couldn't show how scared he was in front of women and children and an old man.

The crawling shadewalker vanished into the forge. The other two followed. Reddic hissed at Arda, 'They're out of the yard. We can run now.'

Arda was already stuffing her feet into a pair of fur-lined boots. She hurried Nadric to the door, dragging the two oldest children after her. Reddic didn't even know their names, only that the boys had been fathered by Gallow the forkbeard. You could see it in the older one. He had forkbeard eyes, ice-blue and cold as a winter night. Arda took the smallest in her arms and pushed the younger girl at Reddic. 'You'll have to carry her. She can hardly walk all night.'

Nadric stood by the door. Arda opened it and ran, hauling the mules out after her. She was carrying a pan, brandishing it as though it was an axe. Reddic pushed the two older children outside. From the shadows of the forge the shadewalkers re-emerged. Each carried a piece of the iron armour Torvic had brought from the Crackmarsh. They moved quickly, not quite running but walking fast. Arda was still struggling with the mules. Reddic ran out between them. 'Go! Quick!' He lifted his shield and waved his sword, and for some reason the shadewalkers stopped short. Arda got the mules going and hauled them away from the yard. Reddic stayed close, moving as fast as he could, while the shadewalkers simply watched them go. Around the corner another one was striding towards them, the one from the door. Arda started to run, but this shadewalker ignored them too and turned for the yard and the forge instead. When Reddic looked back into the village he could see there were others. A dozen maybe. He followed Arda and the mules out into the fields.

The shadewalkers were converging on the forge, all of them. When she saw this Arda stopped to catch her breath. 'What have you brought here?' she asked in horror. 'What have you done?'

A scream from the village spurred them on again. 'Nothing. I didn't bring anything.' But Torvic had brought the cursed armour of the ironskin, and that was what the shadewalkers were after. Last he saw of them they were all gathered around it, sniffing at it, pawing at it.

And then they were gone, lost in the darkness.

11

THE RIVER

Mirrahj kicked her horse and cantered through the chaos of Andhun to the gates and another heaving mass of horsemen milling in helpless anger. The gates were open but no one seemed to know what to do, whether the city was won or lost, how many forkbeards had come, whether to flee or to rally and fight. As they fought through the press of riders, a voice pierced the confusion. 'Mirrahj Bashar!' Mirrahj pushed towards a score of Vathen pressed tightly together. They were her ride, part of it. 'The forkbeards have destroyed the gates! They can't be closed.'

'We leave.' She had to shout over the cries of the other Vathen.

'No!' Josper's voice. Gallow had come to know it and now the Vathan was pointing a javelot at him. 'And what's that forkbeard doing here? You should kill him.'

Mirrahj raised her own javelot and levelled it back at him. 'We leave because I say we leave, Josper, and the forkbeard comes because I say he comes.'

Josper folded his arms and shook his head. 'You're no bashar, Mirrahj. We need to fight these forkbeards. We need to kill them.' He glared at Gallow. 'Starting with that one.'

'Then lead them, Josper. If you can.' Mirrahj looked past him. 'You all know me. I say we leave. I have good reason but I will not say what it is.'

Mirrahj's horse stumbled sideways as another barged into it. The shouting rose to almost deafening and then a river of horses surged into the square from deeper in the city, pushing and shoving their way to the gates and riding out into the fields beyond. Josper looked at them and sneered. 'Hakkha Bashar. You say we should turn our tails and flee like he does?' He turned to the other riders. 'I say we stand and fight! Look at our numbers! The battle is barely begun and this ... this *un-woman* would have us turn and run!'

Mirrahj spat. She didn't say a word, only turned her horse and joined the push for the gates. The walls and the towers either side were empty, held by no one. Gallow looked back. He saw Josper rise in his saddle and raise his javelot to hurl it – whether at Mirrahj or at him he couldn't tell – but the spear stayed in his hand and Gallow and Mirrahj were through the gates. The press of horses burst into the open space beyond. The other Vathen veered east, but Mirrahj turned south towards the river. She galloped away, full of eagerness to be gone from Andhun and everything it held, but her horse had barely found its stride before ahead of them, lit by the dawn light, Gallow spied a handful of figures walking towards the city.

Mirrahj hissed, 'Forkbeards,' and Gallow thought she'd turn and ride away since there were six or seven of them and only one of her, but instead she lowered her javelot and kicked her horse faster, heading straight for them. The Lhosir scattered as she came, jumping out of her path. Half of them were limping. 'Die!' she screamed at them as she turned her horse for another pass. 'What are you waiting for?'

Gallow pressed into her. 'No, Mirrahj of the Vathen. These are still my people.'

She reined in sharply, twisted and wrapped one arm around his back then heaved and tipped him sideways so he fell off. It was done with such fast grace that Gallow was on the ground before he knew it. 'Then get off my horse, forkbeard.'

The Lhosir had gathered again, protecting their wounded with a tight line of shields and spears. They watched but didn't come any closer. Gallow walked slowly towards them. The one in the middle had a face he knew. 'Thanni Ironfoot.'

Ironfoot laughed out loud. 'Well, well. And what should I call you, Gallow? I remember your name was Truesword once, but I've heard other names since. I heard you married a sheep. Doesn't look like a sheep to me.'

'Call me what you like, Ironfoot. Seems the Crimson Legion has taken Andhun castle. Don't know that they're going to hold it. There's a lot of angry Vathen inside those walls. Best you go and help where you can if that's what you're minded to do. Are my eyes still good, Ironfoot? Did I see Medrin in Andhun as the sun rose?'

Ironfoot laughed again. 'And why would I answer a man who rides with a Vathan?'

'Tell Medrin something for me, Ironfoot. Tell him, in case he doesn't already know, that Gallow Truesword came looking for him to finish what he started. Tell him I'll be waiting for him in Varyxhun if he has the stomach for it. Tell him the Comforter waits there too, if he has the strength to lift it in those crooked fingers of his.'

'If he's there, Gallow-who-rides-with-my-enemies.'

'He's there, Ironfoot, and you know it. But I'll not make you lie for him.'

Thanni Ironfoot dipped his spear in salute. 'The Scream-breaker loved you, Gallow. I wonder what he'd make of what you've become. Maybe it's as well he's gone.'

'I wonder what he'd make of us all, Ironfoot. What he'd make of a king who deals with the ironskins, who makes war on women and children. What he'd make of those who follow such a king. I wonder that all the time. I'd not head for the gates, if I were you. Not yet. More Vathen there than even you can bite.'

He turned his back on the Lhosir. Mirrahj was still where she'd dumped him off her horse and so he walked back to her. She didn't stop him from climbing behind her again, though it was hard with his shoulder so swollen and stiff from the blow he'd taken beneath the castle. Ironfoot and his Lhosir watched but they didn't move.

'What did you just do, forkbeard?'

'Told Medrin where to find the things he most desires. Called him to where I can kill him. And then I can go home.'

Mirrahj didn't reply. After a long pause she turned her horse and rode away leaving the Lhosir behind. She stopped again on the top of a ridge overlooking the river. Long shadows of morning sun streaked the ground now but there was no missing the bodies or the streaks of bright red blood in the whiteness of the snow. Mirrahj dismounted and poked at the dead with her foot. Caught by surprise, half of them murdered in their sleep, throats slashed, the others cut down before they could lift their shields or don a helm. Gallow counted a score of Vathen and there were clearly more. A couple of forkbeards too.

'They did this.' Mirrahj was looking down from the ridge towards Ironfoot and his Lhosir, limping on towards the city. In the morning light there was nowhere to hide. 'This was Moonjal Bashar's ride. The ardshan's son.' She sat heavily among the corpses and closed her eyes and then stood up again and walked among the dead, turning them over one by one and looking at their faces. Gallow left her to it; by the time she was done the sun had risen a hand higher and he'd lost sight of Ironfoot's men, still heading for the gates. Chances were they'd be dead soon.

'He's not here.' Mirrahj Bashar leaned on her javelot and held her head in her hand.

'Why didn't you stay and fight?' Gallow asked. 'Your riders were ready for it. Best I could see, Andhun could still go either way.'

'Because I'm sick of it, forkbeard, that's why.' She rounded on him. 'Did you count the size of my ride when we entered Andhun? There were eighty of us. I knew them all. More than just their names. I know the names of the children they left behind when they followed the Weeping Giant across the plains. I know the names of their wives who'll never see them again and of the brothers they once rode with who are nothing but bones now. We don't belong here, forkbeard. This isn't our land and none of us wants to be here, but we have no choice any more. We brought the Sword of the Weeping God here and then we lost it and now we can't go back. We just can't. Were you lying in Andhun or was that the truth at last?'

'The truth.' A pall of smoke was rising over the city now.

'Then take me to it and I'll take it back where it belongs and every Vathan for five hundred miles will follow me. We just want to go home, forkbeard.'

The words touched him deep enough to make his eyes swim. 'Three years I carried that burden.'

'Three years.' Mirrahj nodded. 'And more for those who followed the Weeping Giant and his dreams in the early days before he had all the clans drawn to his banner. The start wasn't so bad. Riding and riding and riding across lands almost bereft of anything but grass and wind. We smashed a small Marroc army at Fedderhun and we felt the calling in our blood. And then Andhun. Bloody Andhun, and yet we took everything this side of the river in the end, but what it cost us ... What you forkbeards did to us.' She shook her head and wiped her eyes. 'I was just a rider then. I had a man, a bashar himself, though I dare say I wouldn't have kept him long. But he was strong and wild, and you took him from me, you and yours, like you took the sword. After that nothing was right.'

Gallow watched her. He might have offered her the comfort of an arm but she was his enemy and he was hers, even

111

if the pain they shared was deeper than any race or creed. He forced himself to look away. 'Many died at Andhun. Why did you come back looking for me?'

'Because without you I'd never find the sword.'

'But I'm a forkbeard.'

'But you know where the red sword rests.'

'And now I've told you, shall I be on my way?'

Mirrahj laughed. 'I took you, forkbeard, and you didn't care. There was no fear in you, no anger. All I ever saw was relief. And it took me a while, but by the time we reached Andhun I understood – I understood why it sang to my heart. Whatever it was you were fighting, it was over, and you were glad, because in the end there was no victory to be had, not really, and you've known that for a long long time. And I saw that in you and I saw that in myself, and the moment I did I was no longer fit to be the bashar of my ride. That's why I let Josper have his way. Are you done now, forkbeard, or shall I show you my other scars? I have plenty.'

He couldn't answer that. She was right. He'd never have seen it for himself, only ever felt the relief that nothing he did would matter any more, and yet this Vathan woman, a stranger to him, had put it into words. That was why he'd gone after Medrin instead of fleeing. To die. To make it all end. The knowledge made him shiver.

'Take me to it and I'll take my people home.'

Gallow shook his head. 'It's just a sword.'

'The Sword of the Weeping God, forkbeard! Older than the world.'

'I carried it for three years, Mirrahj Bashar. It's a sword with a strange colour to its steel and a very hard sharp edge, and that's all.' He sighed. *Home.* They all wanted the same, really. The Marroc of Varyxhun busy hanging forkbeards. The Vathen. Even the Lhosir, most of them. He'd seen it in Thanni Ironfoot's face clear as day, just as he'd seen it in the eyes of all the Screambreaker's men a dozen years ago before they'd finally sailed back across the sea. Home. Peace. To built their houses and farm their land and raise their sons and daughters. For a moment Gallow wasn't sure who was left who wanted anything else. Medrin? The red sword itself perhaps? Hard to see why they were all still fighting.

Mirrahj threw down her javelot with a snort and vaulted into her saddle. She rode away along the ridge, out of sight, and was away for so long that Gallow wondered if she was coming back. When she did she was leading another Vathan horse. 'Can you ride, forkbeard?'

Gallow nodded.

'I mean actually ride, not just sit there tight as a drum and hope you don't fall off like most of you forkbeards do.'

'I learned across the sea.'

'Then she is yours.' She handed him the reins. 'Treat her well. Which way to the sword?'

They made their way through the snow along the bank of the Isset. Gallow's thoughts wandered as they rode. He'd been lost when the Marroc threw him out of Varyxhun, but not any more. Medrin would come after him, and Medrin would come after the sword, sure as the sun rose each morning, and there'd be no peace until he was dead, and killing him wasn't going to be easy, even if it was what had to be done.

'I'll take you to the sword,' he told her when they stopped by the river to drink and rest. 'But I can't give it to you. You'll have to fight to make it yours and then you'll have to fight a deal harder to keep it. And then later you'll wish you hadn't.'

He turned away from the river when they mounted again, heading to the south and east toward the distant Crack-marsh. He'd come this way once before.

12

THE CRACKMARSH CAVES

The Crackmarsh had been full of Marroc when the winter began. Most had left with Valaric. He'd taken every about man he could spare; but when he wasn't called Valaric the Mournful, he was Valaric the Wolf – so the old Marroc knew him – and he'd always known that one day the forkbeards might drive him back and so he'd prepared for that. A few men stayed behind then, left to watch the hideouts, keep the tame ghuldog packs in line and to watch what the forkbeards were up to nearby. The old men, the injured, the crippled, the ones who couldn't fight and a few that Reddic thought Valaric had left behind just to spite them.

The two old men left to keep watch over the Crackmarsh caves near Middislet might as well have been a pair of blind goats for all the good they did. Arda led the mules along the hill path and through the woods at the frozen edge of the water meadows and right inside the caves before either of them even knew she was there, and when Reddic woke them up from their snores, they were obviously both drunk as lords. He left them to it. They had half a night of darkness before them and the air was as cold as death's fingers.

'We'll be needing a fire.' Arda was bad from the cold. She'd been the last to dress and she hadn't put on enough. Her hands were blue and her head kept sagging. The children weren't much better, their sobs of exhaustion long since fallen silent. Only fear kept her going. Truth be told

Reddic wasn't much better either, what with the nights he'd had after Stannic's farm, but he was the man among them now and so he made his shaking fingers rummage through the bags lying open beside the snoring watchmen. He found tinder and then their stash of dry cut wood and painstakingly blew on the embers of their old fire until he had a flame again and lovingly carried it to a new spot. Nadric was already asleep by the time he got it burning and Arda was fussing with the children, settling them around him, wrapping them all in the furs off her own back to keep them warm. 'Any more blankets here?' she asked after Reddic had been staring at the fire for a few minutes, rubbing the feeling back into his fingers, and he could have kicked himself for not thinking of that before. He ran off to look but came back empty-handed.

'Sorry.'

She'd found some straw from somewhere and piled it as close as she dared to the fire. Now she was sitting cross-legged on it, hands stretched out to the flames, shivering. Reddic took off his cloak and laid it over her and then took off his mail and sat beside the fire on the other side, watching her shudder and curl up tight and rub her hands and blow on her fingers. He'd spent the winter in the Crackmarsh, a good few nights in places with no fire at all. He'd seen men shiver like this and fall asleep and not wake up again, the life stolen out of them by the winter. Fire or no fire, without his furs he was already cold. Nadric had all four of the children wrapped around him, bundled up so tight that Reddic couldn't have said how many were in there. Arda had given them too much – or rather she hadn't left enough for herself.

He got up and came round the fire and lay down beside her, wrapping his fur tightly around both of them, pressing up against her, giving her his warmth. She was cold, just a thick woollen shift and a thin linen dress underneath the fur cloak she wore, and beneath it her skin was like ice. He wriggled closer and wrapped an arm around her. She never moved or said a word. Within minutes they were both asleep.

His dreams were strange that night in the cave. He was paralysed and there were shadewalkers everywhere. He was in the cave and they were shambling around him, talking. Then he was back in Middislet. He watched them tear open doors and drag women and children out into the snow and the air was full of screams. He never saw what they did, but he knew anyway because he kept seeing Torvic with his face bitten off, walking about the place. Then they were coming for him too, and he could run, only these shadewalkers could run too. They chased him for what felt like for ever until he reached the edge of a cliff and had to stop because there was nowhere left to go, and they were all around him and they closed in and dragged him down and tore off his helm. He was about to die but suddenly he was somewhere else, somewhere warm. Now he wasn't seeing a horde of hungry shadewalkers but Valissi, the girl he used to see in Tarkhun washing clothes by the river, only now she was leaning over him and she was naked and she had one hand pressed between his legs.

He woke with a start. There'd been enough nights when Reddic had been huddled up like this with others of Valaric's men trying to keep warm, and there was no accounting for dreams. There were no women in the Crackmarsh. He'd seen men disappear together now and then, and they all knew what happened, said nothing and looked the other way.

His hand was pressed into Arda's breast with her own hand clasping it. He could feel the nipple, hard as stone, and when he shifted his legs, trying to find a more comfortable way to lie, she followed him, her buttocks pressing into his crotch. He had no idea whether she was awake or asleep.

He twitched. Couldn't help himself. He tried closing his

eyes, tried to think of other things, even made himself think of the shadewalkers and Torvic with his face ripped off, but it wouldn't go away. He kept seeing Arda's face and Jelira's too, seeing for the first time how alike they were. Without even realising he was doing it, his hand slid off her breast and slipped downward. Arda's hand stayed with him. As his fingers slipped between her legs she let out a little whimper and twisted slightly towards him. Her legs opened and his hand went on under the fur, feeling along her thigh until he found her skin and then reaching underneath the wool and linen and round to the inside of her leg and sliding back again; and then he shifted himself and pulled up his own shirt and pushed down his trousers and pressed his hands between her legs, pushing them apart from behind. She shifted now and then. Little movements but all to make it easier for him. He slid inside her and thrust hard. His hand ran up her skin, reaching for her breasts. He grunted with each push but Arda didn't make a sound, only perhaps breathed a little harder, and then came and was still. She shifted once or twice more as he twitched inside her, then a moment later he was asleep.

The morning woke him, late winter sunlight bright through the stunted trees at the mouth of the cave. He was still wrapped in his own fur but Arda was already up. She sat across the re-kindled fire, boiling a pot of water and chewing on a strip of black bread, and there was a bewilderment of people around him who hadn't been here the night before. He stared at them, wondering who they were and how they were here and why he didn't remember them. Most were still huddled under their furs but a few were shuffling about or squatting by the fire. When he grunted, Arda shot him a sharp look.

'If those two in that other cave are supposed to be your lookouts, I'd have a word with them if I were you. Still snoring fit to bring down mountains, they are. I dare say there's forkbeards standing right across the Crackmarsh with their ears tipped to the wind wondering what they're hearing. We had a look around, found where they kept their breakfast and helped ourselves. Hungry?'

'We?' Reddic was still staring at the other Marroc. It was as if they'd appeared by magic in the middle of the night while he'd slept.

'Did you think everyone else in Middislet was just going to stay there?' She snorted. 'These caves were ours to hide in long before your Valaric came along.'

Reddic nodded. He wrapped his fur around him and came closer to the fire. 'What if the shadewalkers come here too?' He leaned in, peering into Arda's pot, but before he could see what was cooking she smacked him across the knuckles with the stick she'd been using to poke the fire.

'Then we go somewhere else. Mother not teach you manners, boy?'

He stared at her. That was exactly the thing his mother had done before the forkbeards had killed her. 'She died last summer. And yes, old mother, she taught me some.'

Arda poked another stick into the pot and stirred it. 'Well I'm sorry to hear she's gone. Been a lot of people dying these last few years and not many of them for much of a good reason, if you ask me. Still no excuse for having no manners. Even little Pursic knows better and this is barely his fifth winter.'

'I'm sorry.' Reddic sat and looked at her and opened his mouth and closed it again. Fidgeted and opened his mouth a second time. 'About—'

'Manners, boy,' she said again. 'Manners.' Her voice softened very slightly. 'You did nothing wrong, if that's what you were wondering. And you did good with those shadewalkers.'

Reddic shook his head. 'No, I didn't. I practically shat myself, I was that scared.'

'No different from the rest of us then. Reckon my Gallow would have said the same too. Kept your head, that's what matters. Better than some would do.'

'You didn't look like you were scared at all.'

Nadric and the children were stirring now – the light or the smell of Arda's pot perhaps – and more of the villagers from Middislet were coming to sit around the fire, muttering to each other, whispering their stories. Arda picked up her pot and came and settled beside Reddic. 'I was scared right enough, lad. I've had one husband lost to the forkbeards and another lost to the sea only to show up again three years later. I've carried five children and lost one when it could barely lift its head. Jelira and Tathic I've seen sicken and nearly die and then fight their way to the living again. I had one forkbeard in my bed for eight years and another for nearly two. I had the Widowmaker himself in my house and stitched closed a hole in his head – though not until after I'd had a good long think about dashing his brains out, mind. Shadewalkers? I've met men who've hunted them. I was in Witches' Reach when the forkbeards were about to storm it. The Wolf hadn't crossed the bridge out of his swamp and we were all going to die, and badly too. I had the iron devil of Varyxhun in my yard once and his fingers around my throat. So I've seen a lot that's made me scared and would give me the shits again if it cared to, but I know how to deal with it. Put another few years on you and you will too.' She glanced behind Reddic to where Jelira and Feya and Tathic and Pursic were sitting in a row, all quietly watching her. 'Them.' She nodded, and for the first time Reddic had seen, a smile settled over her face, a real warm smile full of love. 'They're what keep me going. There's nothing in this world or any other that scares me like the thought of losing my little ones.'

'I'm not little any more,' grumbled the older boy. 'Pursic's little. I'm not.'

'You're all still little to me,' Arda snorted. 'Who wants to eat?'

She lifted the pot and passed it round, tipping some sort of runny white sludge onto old wooden plates she must have liberated from the same place she'd found the food. The children eyed it hungrily and Nadric already had his fingers in it when Arda raised a hand. 'Wait!' She took out the pouch she'd thrown at Reddic back in the house, the magic Aulian salt. He watched in amazement as she sprinkled a few flakes onto each plate. 'Just a little, mind.' She crouched in front of her children. 'Remember how I told you I met a wizard from Aulia last time we all had to run away, when the iron devil came?'

'Before da killed him and made you safe again,' said Jelira loudly.

'Which da?' the smaller of the two boys turned to look at the bigger one.

'Both of them, actually,' said Arda without even a blink. 'They did it together. And that was when I met a wizard from Aulia. He gave me this magic powder to keep us all safe. Just a pinch of it and those shadewalkers won't hurt us.'

'Is the wizard here?' Pursic's eyes were as wide as saucers.

Arda shook her head. 'He had to go somewhere else.'

'He was sent away to be hanged for helping our real da,' said Jelira. 'And then our real da went away to save him.'

'That's right.' Arda looked uneasy now. She put a hand to her mouth and heaved a long deep breath.

Tathic sniffed at the porridge and tasted it. His face lit up. 'Does that mean we can go home now?'

'I don't want to go home,' said Jelira. 'I want to find Gallow.' She turned to Reddic. 'He's still in the mountains near Varyxhun. He went to help Valaric the Wolf fight the forkbeards and send them away.'

'If he didn't get himself killed already,' whispered Arda.

Reddic leaned forward. He smiled at Jelira, taking her attention for a moment. 'Not many call him Valaric the Wolf these days. Mostly the Crackmarsh men call him Mournful. Wolf was his name in the war against the forkbeards.'

'So why do you call him Mournful?'

'Because he lost his family in the war, and even though that was more than a dozen years ago now, he still mourns for them.'

Jelira's eyes grew wide. She took a step closer. 'Did the forkbeards kill them?'

'No.' He almost told them how it had been cold and starvation and how a shadewalker had walked through their village one late autumn day and cursed them all, but then he looked at them, cold and hungry and with their village filled with shadewalkers, and thought better of it. Instead he dipped his fingers into Arda's porridge. He looked down at the children and made a happy face. 'Mmm! Good! I might have all of this!'

It might have been an accident that Arda kicked him right after he said that, but he could have sworn he saw just the tiniest flicker of a *thank you* on the corner of her mouth. They talked for a bit after that about what they should do, all of them together. Go back to Middislet maybe, since shadewalkers were wandering things who never stayed in one place for more than a night. In the end they agreed that Reddic and a couple of the men from the village would go and have a look and see whether it was safe. They didn't wait for Valaric's two guards to wake up, and Reddic spent half the walk imagining Arda giving them a good shaking and shouting-at until they were awake enough to realise their caves had been overrun by fifty-odd men and women and children and they hadn't even noticed.

It was an easy enough walk to Middislet and back and the air was a lot warmer that morning. Dull grey clouds filled the skies and a wind was blowing in from the north and the west, freshening with each hour they walked. They reached Middislet with the sun at its zenith and found the village half empty but not dead. The shadewalkers were gone. When Reddic looked, there were a few villagers already back in their homes, those who'd hidden in their cellars or walked or fled a different way and come back in the morning, as Stannic had done. He talked to them until he had a dozen different stories saying which way the shadewalkers had gone or how many they'd been – five, fifty, a hundred, and every possible way except north. Reddic settled for there being maybe a dozen and they'd headed roughly south. It amazed him that no one had been killed. It was the forkbeard Gallow, he heard one of them say, who'd told them about shadewalkers and what to do when they came. He'd played games with the children, the ones whose parents would let a forkbeard monster anywhere near them, and he'd pretend to be the shadewalker and they had to see how close they could get without him touching them.

Reddic even tracked the shadewalkers a little way, before a fine drizzle made him think better of it. On the way back to the Crackmarsh the rain fell steadily heavier, blurring the snow and then washing it away, but the last tracks he'd seen had the shadewalkers going south, close past the caves, and maybe it would be better to get back to Middislet tonight after all. He hurried and ran the last few miles, leaving the others to follow, but when he got back to the caves, Arda came running out. She grabbed him by the cloak and shook him, and this time there was no hiding her fear.

'Jelira's gone.'

And all he could think of was that it was cold and it was raining and it would be dark soon and then it wouldn't just be the shadewalkers that came out. Here in the marsh it would be the ghuldogs too.

13

CROSSING THE WATER

'I came this way before,' Gallow told her after he'd settled the argument about how to get to the Crackmarsh by simply riding off, and after she'd finished shouting at him and threatening to kill him when she'd had no choice but to follow. 'After Lostring Hill I went back home, close to the edge of the Crackmarsh. This is how I came to Andhun from there.'

They stopped beside a frozen pond. Mirrahj reversed her spear and smashed the ice around the edge so their horses could drink. Gallow drew a map in the snow with a stick. 'The Crackmarsh is here, the Ironwood here. We go around the top of the Ironwood and then cross the marsh to the Aulian Way. The road leads to the Varyxhun valley.'

Mirrahj pinched her lips. 'Crossing the Crackmarsh? So there *is* a way.'

'Probably about a dozen.' Gallow yawned.

'And you know them! Tell me!'

Gallow shook his head. 'You'll see soon enough. Until then it gives you another reason not to kill me in my sleep.'

'And why should I do that?' Mirrahj spat a laugh at the snow. 'We've both turned our backs on our people now.' When he took her hand she flinched and snapped it away, got up and went back to the horses. He understood her bitterness. 'Well, I have no secret to hold over you, fork-beard, yet I'll sleep easily enough. I don't think you're the throat-cutting sort.'

'No.'

They passed two nights together, huddled up in the best shelter they could find with the horses standing over them among a thick stand of trees on the first night, with a fire Mirrahj managed to light from the last handful of tinder she carried. The air was still bitter with a killing cold and snow still lay on the ground, but at least the winds hadn't come back to flay the skin from their hands and faces and strip the last of their warmth away. On the second night they found a crumbling shepherd's shelter. When morning came, Gallow's horse was dead. After that, a wind picked up. Heavy grey clouds scudded in from the north and the west and it began to rain, dreary, relentless and grey; but Gallow *had* been this way once before, and although years had passed since the Vathen had driven the Marroc from this part of the land, none had come back. When he finally found the farmhouse where he and the Screambreaker had fought a handful of Vathen together, it was still there, still with a roof and its torched barn, empty and abandoned for all those years. Mirrahj nodded and looked impressed. 'And I'd thought you were bringing us this way just to see whether a Vathan was tougher than a forkbeard or the other way around.'

There were benches. Blankets. Everything the way he remembered it. There were dead Vathen too, three of them out the back by the remnants of the burned-out barn, one out the front, the one the Screambreaker himself had killed, and one still in the house, all skeletons long since picked clean by whatever animals had found them. Gallow dragged the one in the farmhouse outside in bits and pieces, a reminder of the war that neither of them wanted to remember. Mirrahj coaxed her horse into the shelter of the house and tended to it while Gallow searched through the larder. Everything was long gone, eaten or dissolved into mould, but outside in the ruined barn he found a crate with a sack of grain in it that was dry and only tasted slightly bad. He took it back to the hearth and filled an old pot with rainwater that had collected among the ruins. There was even firewood in the house, cut and ready underneath thick cobwebs, sheltered from the rain. Farm tools too, and when he searched he found a handful of precious flints. By the time they'd scraped enough shavings of wood to make tinder and lit a fire, the sky was dark as pitch. Neither of them said a word. They listened to the hammering of the rain and the wild tearing of the wind and stared at the fire, warming themselves, always watching to make sure the flames kept alive. As the house shed its icy chill they stripped off their soaking furs. The grain, after Gallow had boiled it soft, tasted of mould, but after three days without warmth or food it was like seeing the sun again after weeks of storms. They ate in silence, and for the first time since they'd left Andhun, Gallow eased himself out of his mail and let the warmth of the flames bathe his skin. 'We'll be in the hills tomorrow. There's not much shelter. Then we cross the Crackmarsh, dawn to dusk. The ghuldogs won't trouble us as long as we're out by sunset. The water meadows will be growing now. Might have a skin of ice at sunrise if the rain stops but don't let it fool you – you'll go right through as soon as you put any weight on it.'

Mirrahj shrugged. 'We have warmth and shelter. We should wait a day here. Rest until the weather breaks.'

Gallow drew out a knife and sharpened it on a whetstone. When the edge was good enough, he tugged at the stubby beard he'd grown in the days since Hrodicslet and lifted the knife to it.

'You should leave that,' said Mirrahj.

He stopped and looked at her. 'To what end?'

'What are you, Gallow? Are you Marroc or are you Lhosir? Which is it?'

'Can't I be both?'

'No. You may live among both and worship the gods of both but you cannot *be* both. What were you born?'

'You know very well I was born a brother of the sea.'

'And in your heart which are you?'

'Both and neither.' Gallow lowered the knife and poked angrily at the fire.

'You left your family to fight Sixfingers. Is that what a Lhosir would do?'

'Yes.'

'Is it what a Marroc would do?'

Gallow hesitated, which was answer enough in itself. 'Some of them,' he said.

Mirrahj looked at him hard. 'You're a Lhosir, Gallow Foxbeard, not a Marroc. However much you want to be, deep inside you have a forkbeard soul. That's how you were made and it's a thing you can't change. Be what you are, forkbeard.' She bared her teeth at him and then nodded across the fire. 'In my saddlebags you'll find a piece of waxed paper wrapped around some cheese. It's more than a year old and it comes from my homeland. It has a flavour strong enough to kill children and it's the most delicious taste in the world. Get it and I'll share it with you.'

Gallow found what she wanted and unwrapped it. The stink climbed up his nose and stabbed him right behind the eyes. 'Maker-Devourer!' He almost dropped it, then tossed it to Mirrahj. She cut off a piece and tossed it back.

'Vathan horse cheese, aged to perfection.'

He sniffed and promptly sneezed. 'That stinks, and of strong stale piss.'

Mirrahj waved the knife at him. 'You found us this house, forkbeard, so I'll forgive you a lot, but not that. You eat or you fight now.' Her mouth was angry but her eyes were smiling. Gallow took a deep breath and bit a piece. For a moment he let it sit inside his mouth, trying hard not to taste anything at all. Then he felt it wriggle, made a face and spat it across the room. 'It moved!'

Mirrahj collapsed with laughter. 'Your face! O forkbeard, your face!' He glared as she cut a piece for herself and chewed it. 'I'm not trying to trick you, forkbeard. This is what we eat, but I've yet to find anyone other than a Vathan who has a taste for it.'

She turned the cheese and pinched at something and then delicately withdrew a slender reddish wriggling thing. A worm. Gallow screwed up his face. 'You can keep your cheese, Vathan.'

'Forkbeard, this is how we welcome one another when clans meet. I invite you into my shelter. We share milk and I promise to protect you as long as you remain in my house; and by accepting my food you promise to protect me too, and my family. We might be enemies the moment you cross the threshold, there might be blood as bitter as wormwood between us, but when you come into my home and drink my milk, you vow to be my brother until you leave. You forkbeards welcome your guests by breaking bread and sharing ale with them but we don't have bread and ale.' She cut another piece of cheese and picked out the worms. 'Here. It's not exactly milk either, but it was once.'

Gallow forced himself to swallow as quickly as he could and washed it down with a long gulp of water, trying not to be sick. His stomach rumbled. Mirrahj got up and walked into the shadows in the far corner of the house. She stripped off her mail and her woollen shift and wrapped herself in a blanket. She hung the rest of her clothes neatly around the fire. 'You should do the same. It'll be nice not to be sodden for a while.'

Gallow was already stripped to his woollen shirt. 'Aye, before I sleep I will.'

'It's customary, as a stranger who's shared my milk, that we should tell each other of our deeds.'

'You already know mine. I've told you everything that matters.'

Mirrahj shuffled closer and sat next to him beside the fire. 'But not the Vathan way.' She touched his face and ran a finger along the length of his nose, over the dent near the bridge and along the old white scar that ran beneath his eye. 'Some wounds tell their own stories, others speak in hints and whispers. Where did this one come from?'

'A Marroc.' Having her so close was unsettling. He felt on edge, tense, and was suddenly very aware that she was naked under her blanket.

'A Marroc? Just *a Marroc*?'

'It was my first proper fight under the Screambreaker. Not far from Kelfhun. The Marroc then weren't as they are now. They still knew how to be fierce. It was a hard battle.'

'A whisker closer and you wouldn't have seen the end of it.'

For a moment Gallow laughed, remembering the day. 'I knew he'd hit me. I felt it. I didn't feel the pain but I felt the blow and suddenly I couldn't see. I thought he'd taken my eye out.'

'He very nearly did.'

'I hit him and hit him and hit him until I knocked his shield down, but I didn't kill him. The man behind me did that. Quick fast lunge through the throat the instant that shield dropped. The man who held that spear was Thanni Ironfoot's cousin. He died a year later. Ironfoot spoke him out. I was there to make sure he remembered that thrust.'

She traced another line along his cheek, fresher and redder though still years old. 'This one?'

'A Vathan. Lostring Hill. I don't remember his face or anything about him. I didn't kill him either.'

Her finger moved across the side of his throat. 'This one?'

He froze. He forgot that one, now and then, and then he'd find himself running a finger over it. 'From a Marroc, but a different kind of battle.' That was the night he'd found Arda. She'd been on the road from Fedderhun to Middislet with little Jelira on her back and a basket on her head. And it was late and there was no one else about and he was lost and trying to find his way to Varyxhun and the Aulian Way and so he'd walked towards her, a forkbeard, and she'd stopped and put down the basket and little Jelira and come to him swinging her hips because she had a child to protect and everyone knew what forkbeards did to Marroc women. And he'd stopped to stare at her, wondering what she wanted and why, and when she'd come close he started to ask her the way to Varyxhun and she'd flung her arms around him and then slid behind him, and the next thing he knew she had a knife at his throat and was making a fine effort to cut it. It had been a close thing but he'd thrown her off, bleeding from the gash in his skin, and he might have killed her or done what she'd thought he wanted in the first place, but he'd seen five years of that with the Screambreaker. So he'd taken the knife and then helped her to her feet and carried her basket for her while she carried her little girl, and he'd asked her about Varyxhun and found that he'd gone completely the wrong way out of Andhun and would have to cross the Crackmarsh. And she'd brought him into her home and they'd broken bread together, and he might easily have gone away the next morning but it turned out that there was a forge in need of a smith, and he was a smith in need of a purpose, and so he'd stayed a few days to help with a few things, and somehow one thing had led to another and he'd never left.

He touched the scar again. She'd marked him on the day they'd met so that everyone else would know he was hers. He'd said that, years later, and she'd laughed and called him a clod, but the twinkle in her eyes had given her away.

And now she was gone and here was the Vathan woman

Mirrahj sitting beside him and suddenly Gallow found he wanted her very much. He turned.

'Deep, that one?' She didn't stop him as he unwrapped her blanket and pushed it away.

'Deep.'

14

GHULDOGS

Reddic rolled his eyes and stamped his feet. He was sodden to his boots from walking in the rain and he wanted the dry and the warmth of the caves and their fires. 'When?'

'Hours ago!' Arda's face was red and puffy and her fingers kept curling like claws. 'I tried to make those other two look for her but they're worse than mules. So I went myself but she's gone into the Crackmarsh and I don't have the first idea which way. And I couldn't leave the others. Nadric and Harvic and a few of the men went out looking but none of them know where to even start.' She put a hand on his chest. 'You do. You live here. Find her, Reddic. Please.'

The men who'd come with him to Middislet were moving among the villagers, telling them what they'd found. Men and women were already gathering up their furs, their children, whatever they'd brought with them when they fled. They wanted to be home before dark, behind doors and shutters they could bar before the shadewalkers came out from their hiding places. When Reddic talked to the two old Crackmarsh men Valaric had left to watch the caves, they only shrugged. 'No point looking now,' muttered one of them. 'She's long gone. Ghuldogs might get her tonight or they might not, but you won't.' And they were probably right, but Arda wasn't going to understand the cold logic to waiting. What she'd understand was that, between the rain and the wind and the ghuldogs and the night, there wasn't much chance they'd find her if they left their search to the morning. So he pressed the old men and they told him Jelira had asked the way to Varyxhun and the two daft buggers had as good as told her how to cross the Crackmarsh to Hrodicslet and that there was a trail up into the mountains from there. And after that she'd gone. Gone looking for Gallow.

Reddic went back to the mouth of the caves, looked at the sky and reckoned he had three hours before dark. And the rain didn't look like it had plans to stop any time soon. He sighed and dressed himself as warm as he could, taking a few more furs from the two old men – not that they much liked letting them go, but Arda was about ready to kill them – and left. Him and Arda, while Nadric stayed to look after Tathic and Pursic and Feya and Jelira if she came back. Arda promised to flay the two old men alive if they didn't help too. She hung on to Reddic's arm. 'Promise me! Promise me we'll find her!' And she wouldn't stop, and so he promised and then wished he hadn't. Valaric was always loud about that sort of thing. A man gave his word to something, he'd best see it through.

They set off together in the rain, wrapped up in as many furs as they could wear, partly to keep warm and partly to keep ghuldog teeth at bay. The old men had been certain about the trail to Hrodicslet, at least, so Reddic followed the path as they'd described it. They ran, keeping up a steady pace, but after an hour Arda had to stop.

'I can't keep going like this. I'm sorry.'

'Then you shouldn't have come.' Which sounded harsh but he was right. He probably ought to have run off again there and then and left her with not much choice but to follow or get left behind alone in the swamp in the dark or else go back to where she ought to have stayed in the first place. He couldn't though, and if she'd said he had to go more more slowly then he'd have done that too.

But she bowed her head and turned back alone, hiding her face so he wouldn't see the tears. Better this way, Reddic reckoned. Better she wasn't there if the ghuldogs came, because then there wasn't much to do except run or fight, and Reddic had been chased by ghuldogs before and had learned how to run a lot faster after that. Better too that she wasn't there if he reached Jelira after the ghuldogs did. He shuddered at that, and with the light slowly failing he ran on alone into the Crackmarsh. To a man who didn't know the place, the water meadows and the swamps were a maze, tricky at best and often deadly. You came here and you didn't know their ways, you vanished, and Reddic could have filled a day with the stories he'd heard of men who'd disappeared. But he was a Crackmarsh man now. He'd lived among them for months and he'd learned their fickleness. He slowed to a walk when the sun set and true darkness came, but he didn't stop. A few stars were enough light. Give it another few hours for the air to freeze and there'd be a scum of ice over the water meadows, if the rain ever stopped. The ghuldogs didn't like that. It cracked and snapped under their feet. You heard them coming, if you knew what to listen for.

He stopped and swore. Somewhere he'd taken a wrong turn and now the path was getting muddier and turning him east instead of south. Hummocks rose out of the marsh ahead, little mounds covered in tufts of thick grass that rustled in the breeze. He stared, reaching out with his ears for the distant howls of ghuldogs a-prowl, but all he got was the wind. He knew where he'd gone wrong. Ten minutes back where the path was dry it came to an old tree stump, dead a hundred years. There was a fork. He'd gone right. He should have gone left. He turned around and then stopped again. He knew he should have gone left because he'd walked the track from the Middislet caves to Hrodicslet before. But Jelira hadn't. If she didn't know the way, maybe she'd made the same mistake too. In the dark he'd walked straight past it. Too busy thinking about how he wanted to be back in the caves. Jelira would have come past in daylight, though. She'd have seen it, wouldn't she?

What if she didn't?

He didn't know. He ought to go back now and he knew it. Come out with others in the morning and all go separate ways, but he couldn't. He could see Arda's face, how she'd look if he came back alone. How his own mother had looked the day his sister hadn't come back. And he could see Jelira too, eyes filled with hope and promise – what if she *had* come this way without realising she'd gone wrong? She'd follow the path as best she could, wouldn't she?

He walked on. After another half an hour the path was gone, no trace of it left. The hummocks that rose out of the water were bigger now. The first stands of stunted trees weren't far ahead, where the hummocks grew into hillocks and the water meadows grew deeper and swallowed a man who wasn't careful with his feet. Where would he go, lost and alone and with the light failing? Back, surely, but if Jelira had gone back why hadn't he found her? What then? What had he done when it had been him? He'd gone for the trees, that's what. For the shelter they seemed to offer, even though they didn't.

He heard a howl far away, and then another. The ghuldogs, talking to each other. Too far to worry about but that didn't stop his heart racing. Stupid. Trees meant shadows and the ghuldogs liked shadows, and yet the trees called out nevertheless, offering him the haven of their branches, and he almost started running, and never mind that he knew perfectly well that any ghuldogs nearby would be waiting there. And that they could climb.

A distant scream ripped the night over the steady hiss of rain. Not a ghuldog scream this time but a girl scream. *Now* he ran. In the dark with the rain it was hard to know which way or how far but it had come from somewhere ahead. Almost at once another ghuldog howl went up, closer this time, the howl of scent found and of calling the pack. Reddic's heart pounded. He glimpsed movement to his left, something bounding through the water. Not towards him but alongside, slowly converging. He almost turned to chase it off but he didn't have the nerve. Made him wonder though – how was he going to face down a whole pack of them if that's what it was? – but he kept running anyway. The ghuldog pulled ahead of him. Reddic let it lead. Thing clearly knew where it was going.

'Jelira!' He felt suddenly stupid now. And guilty. Guilty for leaving her. 'They can climb the trees!' People who didn't know better thought ghuldogs were just big dogs but they weren't. They had dog-like heads but their limbs were the arms and legs of a man and they had no tails. Man was chased by wolves, man climbed a tree. Everyone knew that, and so men chased by ghuldogs climbed trees too, and then watched in horror as the ghuldogs climbed after them. Not that they were much good at it, but usually it was enough that they could. Truth was, there was wasn't much you could do about ghuldogs except turn and fight them. They weren't keen on fire but there wasn't much chance of that out here, not tonight.

The rain answered his thoughts, falling more heavily. Over the hiss of it he heard Jelira scream again. A scream for help. They hadn't got her, not yet, not quite.

The ghuldog he'd been following reached the edge of the trees and vanished into the shadows. There couldn't have been more than a dozen trunks but there could have been a dozen ghuldogs too for all Reddic knew. He saw one of the trees shake as the first started to climb.

'Help! O Modris! Help me!'

The ghuldogs would have seen him by now. And yes, as he looked hard into the shadows he saw at least four still on the ground, as well as the one easing its way up the tree. Those on the ground turned to look at him, one by one. It was Jelira's scent that had drawn them and so it was her they were after, but it wouldn't take much for them to change their minds. Reddic drew his shield up in front of him and lowered his spear. Against a Vathan or a forkbeard, a man crouched, hiding himself as best he could behind his shield. Against a ghuldog a man stood tall and broad and made himself as big as he could. 'You look big enough, they all just run away.' Although the man who'd told him that was Drogic, who was about as big as a horse. Even bears thought twice when they saw Drogic coming.

If you were lucky the first ghuldog came straight at your throat and all you had to do was lift your spear a little and watch it skewer itself. Trouble with ghuldogs was they learned. As Reddic came closer, two of them split away from the tree and circled him, one coming from each side. They stopped, letting him know that he wasn't welcome, that he should leave, that the prey in the tree was theirs and not for sharing. Changed things, that did. A ghuldog in close turned a spear into a useless lump of wood and then it was time for a stabbing knife. Or his hatchet would do. He lifted the spear high, took careful aim at the ghuldog climbing the tree, threw it as hard as he could and ran straight forward. The spear caught the ghuldog in the chest and it crashed out of the branches. Reddic roared at the top of his lungs. The two still by the tree shied away, startled. He turned sharply back. The other two had chased after him as soon as he'd run and the closer one was already leaping. He ducked behind his shield, gripped it with both hands and slammed it into the ghuldog as it came at his face. It bounced off and landed and rolled snarling back to its feet. The other one skittered round behind him and for a moment he couldn't see it. He slipped the hatchet off his belt and jumped at the first. Keep moving, that was the thing. Keep moving, because when you fought a ghuldog pack there was always *always* one of them creeping up behind you.

Modris smiled on him for a moment. The first ghuldog scampered warily back out of reach but the creature from the tree, dead with his spear stuck through it, was right in front of him. He slipped his hatchet into the hand holding the shield and snapped the spear out of the ground. The ghuldog in front of him growled and bared its teeth. Reddic held the spear high up the shaft, disguising its reach, then stabbed out with it, almost throwing the spear and then catching it again by its end. The ghuldog jumped away but the blade still raked its flank and left a long bloody cut. It whimpered and fled.

Always one from behind. He spun around. The creature was already in the air, so close he had no chance to put his shield between them. He raised his arm to protect his face, dropping the spear as he did. The ghuldog's fangs closed around his elbow and bit down hard. Reddic screamed. He had no mail there, only furs, and yes they were good and thick, but the ghuldog's bite was like nothing he'd ever known. Like the blow of a forkbeard's axe, maybe, only it didn't stop. He howled and snarled and shook his arm but it didn't let go. He changed his grip, let go of his shield and brought his hatchet down on the ghuldog's skull and cracked it in two. The bite loosened but Reddic was past caring and he brought the axe down over and over until the ghuldog fell off his arm. His elbow felt as though the bones had been crushed to powder. In the dark he couldn't see if there was blood. Blood was bad. Blood meant the ghuldog had broken his skin. He wasn't sure what happened then, only that the Crackmarsh men whispered that if the wound from a ghuldog's bite went bad – and they always did – then a quick clean death was for the best.

There were still two ghuldogs close by. One howled, no more than a dozen yards away, summoning more of the pack. He couldn't find either his spear or his shield and his sword arm was too hurt to be much use. He looked up.

'Jelira, where are you?' He heard a voice. His foot trod on something hard and he almost stumbled. His spear! 'Can you see me?'

'Yes.'

'Take this then.' When he looked up he could see her as she moved. She was good and high, well out of reach of the ghuldogs if they jumped. He waved the spear at her. 'You know how to use this?' He looked about for the other ghuldogs and then jumped at the tree, hauling himself up fast with his one good hand and scrabbling feet, driven by a surge of fear. 'You stab it at their faces. Brace well and use both hands and pull quickly back so they don't grab hold of it. Strike hard and fast and don't be afraid to hurt them.'

He was gasping for breath. Maybe a braver man would have got her down from the tree and walked them home in the night and seen the ghuldogs off, but Reddic wasn't that man and, besides, his sword arm flared in agony whenever he moved it. Now he was up in this tree, he was staying.

He sat in the crook of a branch with his axe in his lap, and when more ghuldogs came he slashed and kicked at their clambering muzzles and Jelira stabbed with his spear until they'd bloodied three and the rest gave up. It was hardly what anyone would call heroic, but when the sun rose they were both still alive, and that was what mattered.

15

SCARS

Gallow and Mirrahj lost themselves in each other's skin. The night passed and then another day. They fingered each other's scars and stroked each other's hair and touched one another's faces. Gallow's lovemaking was angry and insatiable; Mirrahj was hungry and fierce. In between, lying naked around the fire, Gallow licked the salt off her skin and she drew his eye to the longest scar of all, a slice low across her belly. She'd had a child once then, and they'd cut her to get it out. An Aulian birth.

'I had a son and I had a husband. I lost my son not long after he was born but I lost my husband on the day they cut me and he came out. They said I'd never carry another child, and what use is a woman who can no longer make sons? He left me to go and serve with the Weeping Giant, and I followed because I could fight as well as any man I knew, and we went with the ardshan to the disaster of Andhun and there he vanished. I suppose some forkbeard killed him but maybe he ran away. By then I could beat him at everything by which a man measures himself. I learned to wrestle among the warriors of his ride. I learned ways to beat men who were bigger and stronger than me. It was to humiliate him after what he did in leaving me behind. He tried to throw me away and I wasn't going to have that. I don't know why the ardshan raised me to become a bashar after Andhun but I was a good one. You've been wondering that since the day we met – how is it that a woman leads men into battle?'

'But I watched and I learned the answer.'

'As no man's wife I could never have another Vathan. If I gave myself to a man then I would have belonged to them. So I didn't, because I wanted my ride, and men laughed at me and eyed me askance but they did what I said. Several tried to take what they couldn't freely have. A rightful challenge of my strength, they said, and so it was equally rightful when I killed them with their own knives. Josper was the first one I let live. I beat him to within an inch of his life in front of the rest of the ride. When I was done with him he could barely move for days, but I was careful not to break him. It was a lesson to the others. Mostly it stopped after that.' She pulled Gallow closer and clutched his head. 'You'll take me to the sword, forkbeard. You will. And then I'll take my people home.'

'I'll take you to where I left it.'

'Why is it that a bashar who is a man can take as many women as will have him and be admired and envied by his ride, yet I could not take even one man to be mine? Where's the justice in that?'

'A woman's place is raising children.'

'And a man's place is in the fields, flapping his arms to scare away the crows.' Mirrahj bit his ear. 'I carried one child, Gallow of the forkbeards. I know that pain. I've had an arrow through my arm and I can tell you that hurt a good deal less. Remember that when you go back to your Marroc wife.' He tensed and she laughed. 'Oh you will, forkbeard, and she'll have you too. You'd be stupid not to and so would she. Stay alive, do what you need to do, go back to her and never leave her again.'

They knew each other a little better by the time they left the farmhouse. A day and two nights out of the wind and the rain lifted their spirits, as did warm food, even if it tasted of mould. Even their horse seemed to feel better. The storms had lessened to a breeze and drizzle now, and they made good time to the edge of the hills and through them to the fringes of the Crackmarsh. For a while Gallow turned south until the Ironwood closed in and forced them to choose between the trees and the water meadows. Mirrahj eyed the wood with uneasy suspicion. 'I never heard of a ride who ventured far into any forest. I forget, is it a giant spider the size of a horse or an enormous snake that lives in this one?'

She spoke with scorn, as if laughing at such foolish superstitions, but her words carried a nervous edge. Gallow raised an eyebrow. 'I'd heard it was shadows and trees that came alive. The shadows start to move and frighten their prey and herd them towards groves of Weirtrees in the forest's heart. The groves close around you and the roots and branches wrap you up and the trees themselves devour you. Then too I've heard there's a race of people who live there, as old as the world itself. Small like children and dark like an Aulian. They were here before any Marroc.' As Mirrahj's eyes darted nervously about, Gallow laughed. 'The Marroc have their stories, but that's all they are. One day I'll tell you some Lhosir ones about the mountains of the Ice Wraiths.'

They sheltered on the fringe of the forest for a night and lit a fire and slept warm and dry under the branches, and perhaps Mirrahj slept with one eye open but no trees or shadows came alive and no fey-folk tried to eat them, and the next day they rose early and moved with the dawn as Gallow guided them into the water meadows of the Crackmarsh. He walked ahead and Mirrahj rode behind, but before the sun reached its peak she stopped him and pointed back the way they'd come, and when he followed her finger with his eyes, he saw riders, six of them, some half a mile away. He squinted, trying to work out who they were.

'Forkbeards,' said Mirrahj with a touch of wonder. 'They've crossed the river.'

Gallow climbed up behind her. 'They did that back in Andhun. Let's get away from them.'

'They've been behind us a while and they're following us. But I'll try if you like.' Mirrahj set off at a canter. Gallow wondered how she could be so sure they were Lhosir but then a horn blew and he knew she was right. Gallow looked back now and then. The riders chasing them were gaining, slowly but surely.

'Cover.' Gallow pointed out an island of trees rising out of the marsh a mile ahead of them. Mirrahj rode for it, but as they came close she suddenly veered away; a moment later their horse stumbled and fell and threw them both into the water. The horse thrashed and then found its feet and bolted and Gallow saw an arrow sticking out of its rump. He caught a flash of movement in the trees and a second arrow hit him in the shoulder, biting through his mail far enough to draw blood. He roared as he yanked it out of his arm. The Lhosir were still after them, gaining quickly now. Another arrow zipped from the trees. Gallow lifted his shield to cover himself as best he could and Mirrahj ran close behind him as they raced for the land. Another arrow hit his shield and then another, and then they were out of the water and into the trees and Mirrahj had her sword drawn with her own shield in front of her. She pulled one of the arrows from Gallow's shield and waved it in his face. The tip was nothing more than a narrow metal spike, no barbs or blades. 'This isn't a Marroc arrow; this is a Vathan war arrow. From close up it'll go right through mail, deep enough to kill.' She bared her teeth. 'We make them for hunting forkbeards.'

'Why are there Vathen in the Crackmarsh?'

'I don't know!'

They pressed close together, covering each other with their shields, crouching low and moving fast, deeper into the trees. The Lhosir on their horses weren't far behind but now they too were being peppered with arrows. Then the swish of a branch made Gallow freeze. He spun round in time to lift his shield and catch an axe flying at his head with an angry Marroc on the end of it. He stepped back, ready to lash out with his spear.

'Gallow! There are more!' Mirrahj had her back against his in a flash, always lightly touching him so he'd know where she was, so he could feel her movement.

'How many?' He caught another blow and jabbed his spear, trying to keep the Marroc away. 'I don't want to kill you, you idiot! You must be one of Valaric's Crackmarsh men. Leave us be and let us pass.' He felt Mirrahj push hard against him as she caught a blow with her shield. 'I fought with the Wolf at Lostring Hill and at Andhun against Six-fingers. I fought with him at Witches' Reach when the iron devil had it under siege. I was in Varyxhun when the castle fell. I'm not your enemy!'

The Marroc paused. One of the men facing Mirrahj shouted over their heads, 'Don't listen! He's just another filthy forkbeard.'

'Do these names mean nothing to you? Sarvic? Achista the Huntress? Addic? Oribas of Aulia? We fought together, all of us.'

Another shout came from deeper in the trees and now the Marroc facing Gallow backed away. 'You want to fight for Valaric, forkbeard? Now's your chance.' He circled them and then was away, bounding through the trees with his friends. The Lhosir riders had come. There were five of them now and Gallow wondered whether the sixth was dead but then caught sight of him cantering through the water meadows back the way they'd come. The horn sounded again. Mirrahj started as if to run but Gallow shook his head. He pushed her down, crept behind a tree and put a finger to his lips.

'Fan out and find the Foxbeard. Never mind the sheep.' The Lhosir began to move into the trees, slow and cautious. With luck the first pair would die quickly and then it

143

would be three on two and he'd finally find out whether this Vathan woman could fight as well as she said.

Find the Foxbeard. So they knew who they were chasing. Had they followed him all the way from Andhun? He pressed himself against the bark, letting the trunk of the tree shield him from the Lhosir. They'd do what they always did, fan out until they were a dozen paces apart and walk in a line, scaring up everything in their path. In the dead of night you could still hide when a search line like that came past, but not in the middle of the day.

Only one way to find out how far they'd come. Cripple one instead of kill him and then ask.

He could hear them getting closer, each careful pace. The *swish* of a caught branch as a man tried to duck beneath it. The crack of a dead twig, the squelch of a boot in the soft earth, the *clink* of a careless shield on mail. He waited until a Lhosir was about to step past the tree where he hid, then struck low and fast and hard, spinning out from where he crouched and slashing with his axe. Legs and feet, they were the weakness he'd learned in his years in the battle lines. His axe hit the Lhosir below the knee, snapping his shin and slicing it in two. The Lhosir screamed and dropped like he'd been hit by a stone, but Gallow was already up and moving, racing at the next; and even as he did he heard a second scream from behind. Mirrahj, and it was a scream of bloody fury.

He had two Lhosir in front of him. He charged at the nearest but the man was quick and had his shield round fast. They smashed into each other and staggered apart, and then the other Lhosir was at the first one's side and Gallow was facing two, shields overlapped, closing on him with the length of their spears against his axe.

'Forkbeard!' He didn't dare look back but he heard the rush of footsteps. 'On your knees, forkbeard!' He dropped to a crouch and then fell forward as a weight crunched into his back and sprang over his head, and there was Mirrahj, in the air between him and the other Lhosir, and for a moment they were too surprised to raise their shields. She rammed her spear into one of them, straight into his face. 'Behind you, forkbeard!'

He picked himself up. The second Lhosir jabbed at Mirrahj as she levered herself away from the first. Gallow saw the metal blade of his spear flash past her knee but by then there was another warrior almost on him. He stayed low, flicked his axe in an arc and let it go to fly at the Lhosir's legs and then sprang at him. The man jumped, letting the axe spin past him, and lunged. Gallow caught the thrust on his shield and turned it, and then he was inside the man's guard with a sword in his hand and a moment later he had it jammed through the Lhosir's throat. He let his eyes linger on the face for a moment in case it was someone he knew, but no: a young face, barely old enough to have a proper beard.

When he turned back again, the fourth Lhosir was running. Gallow let him go. Mirrahj was limping but she still held her shield and her spear high. When he looked for the last of them, he found the body close to where she'd been hiding, a great bloody pool over his chest. She'd stayed exactly where she was and waited, and then rammed her spear up under his chin, straight into his skull. Another face he didn't know.

'Medrin sends children to kill us.' He spat and went back to the Lhosir whose leg he'd shattered. That one would talk. One thing was answered already, though: the Vathan woman could fight.

16

SOUTHWARD

Up in their tree neither of them got much rest. They were cold and sodden and miserable and sorry for themselves when the sun rose but at least they weren't dead. Reddic almost had to force his legs to move again when the light finally drove the ghuldogs away. They weren't happy about it but slunk off, often looking back, sniffing the earth around the trees as though remembering who he was. Reddic watched long after they were gone before he finally jumped down. He landed hard and fell, and the jolt sent such a shock of pain through his arm that he cried out and for a moment couldn't move. His elbow was so swollen he couldn't bend it at all without feeling like he was being stabbed by hot needles. Jelira was little better. She could hardly keep her eyes open, and when she let herself slide out of the branches, she fell more than jumped. He tried to catch her and they sprawled among the mud and the hard roots of the trees, knocking his arm again. He lay there curled up, cradling his elbow for a while. When the pain finally died down enough for him to think again, he eased himself out of his furs and looked. Half his arm from shoulder to wrist was bruised. His elbow was purple and swollen to almost twice its proper size. Even touching it burned. There wasn't any blood though. As far as he could see, the ghuldog's teeth hadn't punctured his skin.

He made himself a sling, then slowly and painstakingly pulled on his furs again and turned to Jelira. 'Can you walk?'

She nodded and so they set slowly off back the way they had come. Jelira leaned on his spear more and more but they were almost halfway back to the caves before she stumbled and fell and couldn't get up again and Reddic had to carry her the rest of the way. It was hard enough getting her over his shoulder with his damaged arm, but it was either carry her, leave her or stay out with her for another night with the ghuldogs. Besides, she was lighter than he'd thought, and carrying her did a strange thing to his heart, as though her very presence gave him strength.

'Why did you leave?' he asked as he carried her, and she murmured this and that and none of it made much sense, but it wasn't like they had much else to talk about and he got it out of her in the end. Yes, she'd gone looking for the forkbeard she'd called her father and yes, she'd been stupid, and yes, she was almost more afraid of the scolding she'd get when they got back to the caves than she'd been of the ghuldogs.

They stopped a lot. He made her drink water and fed her what food he had. Later she managed to walk again for a while, but never for long, and by the time they reached the caves it was almost dark. He staggered across a line of grey sand that someone had laid inside the cave mouth and fell to his knees and dropped her. The other villagers from Middislet were gone, but Arda and Nadric and the children were still there, and the two old Crackmarsh men. They fussed over Jelira and barely noticed Reddic was even there, and it was Arda who finally brought him a bowl of warm water and a pot of beans and barley boiled soft and flavoured with slices of onion and a pinch of Aulian salt. It was the best food he'd had for a long time.

'You found her. I owe you a debt, boy.'

He laughed. What he should have been thinking about was that he'd saved Jelira's life, how scared he'd been, whether his elbow would ever heal or that there were ghuldogs not far away and more than one pack of them too – not to forget the shadewalkers either – but what he was actually thinking was that it wasn't right that she still called him *boy* now that they'd lain together.

Arda backed away with a snort. 'Funny, is it?'

Reddic shook his head. But it was.

'I'll give you something else to laugh about then. There were shadewalkers here in the night. Two of them. Came right into the cave.'

The smile dropped off his face like an apple off a tree. 'Where did you run?'

'Didn't.' She went back to the line of grey sand and started poking at where he'd scuffed it, and he suddenly knew that it wasn't sand but salt.

'Did it work? Your wizard's salt?'

Arda nodded. 'Won't say we weren't all shaking scared it wouldn't. They walked right up to it and looked right at us. Stayed there staring for half the night but they never crossed it. Then they just went.'

'It does have magic then.'

'It's salt, Reddic. Just salt. I put a bit in that stew you're eating. Nice. Used most of it up on the entrance though.' She finished with the line across the cave floor. 'Them two useless old men went out after you did, after I poked and kicked and hid all their spirit and made it plain they'd get no peace from me until they did something useful. Came back screaming their heads off. Shadewalkers. Dozens of them, they said. All heading straight south.'

She looked pleased with herself. Reddic sat straighter. 'They're going away from Middislet then. You can go home.'

'Maybe, but not tonight. We'd best take it in turns to keep awake in case they come back. Make sure they don't get past.'

Arda stamped away, deeper into the caves and back to Jelira, and when Reddic hauled himself to his feet and went looking for her, she barely seemed to notice him and he couldn't think of what to say. He found himself following her from place to place like a lost sheep. As the darkness drew in she turned on him and told him he should get some sleep. 'Long day tomorrow.'

There were no shadewalkers that night after all and Reddic slept until late in the morning, the first good night of sleep he'd had since Stannic's farm. He woke and found Jelira sitting beside him, watching, and as soon as he moved she pushed a bowl towards him. 'Marsh deer stew,' she said. 'Morric made it.' One of the old men, and Reddic wondered whether he'd told her what a 'marsh deer' actually was. Probably not. There were no deer in the Crackmarsh. Hardly any animals with any good eating on them at all. What there was was plenty of ghuldogs.

He tasted it. Nodded. 'Good.'

Jelira smiled at him. 'Thank you for coming after me.'

There was a part of him that wanted to tell her how stupid it was to run off like that. But even as he was thinking it, he was looking at her and he couldn't. She wasn't that much younger than him. A couple of years, that was all. As he watched her, she watched him back and he felt himself blush and looked away. 'I suppose everyone's already had a right good time telling you how you shouldn't have gone off like that.'

The smile wavered. 'But I want to find him. I know he's not my father, but he was my da.'

'It was only a few ghuldogs.' Which was probably the stupidest thing he'd ever said and Valaric, if he'd heard it, would have hit him. He shuffled across the stone floor of the cave and sat next to her, wanting to be closer. 'It was a brave thing you did.' And Valaric would have slapped him for saying that as well. A *stupid* thing, and idiotic and outright selfish perhaps. But brave?

Jelira shook her head. 'It was stupid.'

149

And yet here he was, taking her hand and holding it in his and squeezing. 'Well, maybe a bit of both, but no harm done in the end. We're all still alive.'

She touched his arm. 'How is it?'

'Not so bad.' By which he meant it still throbbed and ached and was more swollen than before and he certainly didn't dare move it, not unless he wanted to double up in agony. But not too bad if he simply let it be.

She hugged him and held on to him a while. 'Thank you.'

'Jelira! Girl!' Jelira jumped like she'd bitten by a snake. Arda was staring at them from the mouth of the cave. 'Finish your eating and bring your walking legs. You too, boy.'

Reddic bristled as Jelira hurried away and left him to finish his stew – and it *was* good, and if you were a Crackmarsh man and you knew what was in it, you soon learned not to let it trouble you when your belly was rumbling. When he finished they were waiting for him outside. Arda looked him over. No smile or anything. 'Well then,' she said. 'Lead the way.'

'Lead the way where?'

'Varyxhun. That's where you're taking these mules, isn't it?'

He nodded.

'Right then. You'll be getting some company.'

He wondered why but he didn't ask. Maybe it was the shadewalkers. When he looked at the two old men they shrugged and looked away as if to say they thought she was mad, that he was mad too and they'd be having nothing to do with it. He ought to be saying something, he knew that, something about how it was a bad idea to cross the Crackmarsh with an old man, a woman and four children, but there was Arda staring at him, waiting for him to get on and do something, and he found he couldn't move or talk.

'Or are we waiting for night again and the ghuldogs and the shadewalkers? I know there's both about but I know there's places that are safe too.' Her eyes narrowed. 'Must be, and I reckon you know them, even if these old dodderers say there's no such thing.'

There were places. Little shelters that the Crackmarsh men had built. He looked about. Glanced at Jelira. Didn't know why.

'Well?'

'What happens after? What happens in Varyxhun?'

'After?' Arda's eyes bored into him. 'Valaric will pay well for those arrowheads I'm bringing him, that's what happens in Varyxhun.'

He couldn't read her face. Couldn't read it at all.

The crippled Lhosir had a shield with the mark of the Crimson Legion on it – Medrin's men. He was pale and he'd lost a lot of blood but he was alive. Gallow picked him up off the ground and slammed him against a tree. 'Where's Medrin?'

'You're the Foxbeard?'

'Some call me that. Heard of me, have you?'

The Lhosir's eyes flickered and he glanced at Mirrahj and spat. 'The *nioingr* who lies with the sheep.'

'You have my name. What's yours?'

'Forris Silverborn. For now.'

Gallow smiled. The Lhosir was young like the rest and hadn't yet done anything worthy enough to earn a name of his own. Silverborn meant he had riches in his family, that was all. Plunder from the Marroc, most likely. 'Were you even born when the Screambreaker first crossed the sea, Forris Silverborn?'

'*Nioingr. Nioingr. Nioingr.*'

Said three times, which meant they had to fight, and Silverborn could barely hop, which made it nothing more than a rude demand to die. Gallow slapped him. 'You don't end that easily, Silverborn. And is that truly what you want?

To bleed out in the middle of this swamp where no one will ever find you except maybe a Marroc who'll laugh and piss on your corpse? No one to speak you out?'

'I know what I've done, Foxbeard. I don't need a reminder.'

'Do you now? And what *have* you done, Forris Silverborn?' He let that hang between them. 'Where's Medrin? Still in Andhun? I bet he isn't. On his way to Varyxhun yet?' Silverborn shook his head but there was a look about him as though he'd seen the king not so long ago, as if Gallow was close to the mark. And then there was the shield. Gallow hit him. 'The Maker-Devourer has no place for lies, Silverborn.'

'He's looking for you, Foxbeard. If you want to find him, all you have to do is stand in one place for long enough.' Silverborn stopped and looked up, suddenly staring into the trees behind Gallow. Gallow craned his head around. Away among the shadows stood two Marroc with bows drawn back and arrows ready.

'Turn round and face me!' snapped the closer of the Marroc. 'Hands where I can see them, and keep still or I'll poke your liver with my iron.'

Gallow glanced at his shield, leaning against a tree. These were the Marroc who'd shot him once and made him bleed through his mail, the Marroc with the Vathan arrows, and they were closer now, much closer. Beside him Mirrahj gripped her spear. She was limping from the slash on her knee. Gallow gave a little shake of his head. The first Marroc took a few cautious steps closer and slowly lowered his bow. 'You were the forkbeard at Witches' Reach. You're the one who killed the iron devil.' He waved to the other and sniggered. 'Gallow Addlewits, that's what Valaric called you.' He looked at Mirrahj. 'Why is there a Vathan in the Crackmarsh?'

'We're after Sixfingers.'

The Marroc shook his head. 'No Vathan in the

Crackmarsh.' He lifted his bow again and Mirrahj moved like a pouncing cat. She threw herself sideways and rolled behind her shield just as the Marroc's arrow struck it, quivering in the wood. She crouched behind it with her javelot poised, hidden except for her helm, ready to spring. Gallow jumped between them. 'No!'

The Marroc both had their bows drawn back. 'No Vathan in the Crackmarsh. Valaric says.'

'He's just another forkbeard,' snarled the other archer. 'Shoot him and I'll do the woman.'

'Shut your hole, Remic! No one shoots anyone.' The first Marroc narrowed his eyes.

The second laughed, and as he did, Mirrahj sprang. The first let out a startled cry but all there was to see of Mirrahj was her shield. His arrow struck wood and then she landed on him, knocking him flat. Gallow leaped forward as the second loosed his shaft. Mirrahj's head jerked sideways and she stumbled a moment, then she had the tip of her javelot pressed to the throat of the archer on the ground. Gallow crouched behind his shield as the second Marroc trained yet another arrow on him. 'Forkbeard! I don't care what anyone says you did, you're all the same!'

'Move and your friend's blood feeds this swamp,' hissed Mirrahj.

Gallow kept his eyes on the Marroc with the bow. 'Remic, is it? Weren't you with Valaric at Witches' Reach? We mean to cross the Crackmarsh, nothing more.'

'No.'

There was a moment before he let the arrow go. Gallow saw it in his eyes, the slightest narrowing in the set of his face as a resolve and a belief settled there. Even as his fingers slipped off the bowstring, Gallow ducked and raised his shield. The arrow thudded into its rim exactly where his eyes had been a second ago. The Marroc on the ground let out a piercing cry of anguish, cut off as soon as it started into a lingering dying gurgle. The archer reached for another arrow. Gallow turned his head, caught in indecision, looking at Mirrahj, but the Marroc on the ground was already bleeding out from where her javelot had ripped his throat.

She had her arm drawn back to throw it.

'No!' He was far to slow, and if she had heard him, she didn't listen. Her javelot hit the archer in the chest, punching straight through him and hurling him back. By the time Gallow reached him he was already dead. He whirled and glared at Mirrahj. 'Why?'

She put a foot on the dead man's chest and pulled on the javelot with both hands, tearing it out of him, then flicked a glance to the arrows in Gallow's shield and her own. 'Why? You have to ask me that, forkbeard?'

'They were Marroc!'

'And Marroc have your permission to fire arrows at you as the mood takes them? Very generous of you, but they certainly don't have mine. Let's find the horses these forkbeards were riding and go.'

Gallow shook his head. 'We've spilled Marroc blood in the Crackmarsh now. There'll be others. They'll hunt us.'

Mirrahj snorted. 'No, they won't! Some forkbeards came upon some Marroc and most of them died. Five forkbeards, two Marroc. They'll be heroes if they're ever found at all, and who's left to say exactly how it played out?'

She turned away and vanished back among the trees. Gallow left Remic and knelt for a moment beside the other Marroc. 'I don't know you, but you followed Valaric to Witches' Reach and I know how many Marroc died there and how they fought.' He turned to look around at the trees. 'A brave man, Maker-Devourer. He belongs in your cauldron.'

He went to the Lhosir with the shattered leg to see if he wanted to die with a sword in his hand but when he got there, he found that Mirrahj had beaten him to it, and when he looked for her, she was already out among the water meadows, cooing and clucking at the horses the Lhosir had left behind.

It wasn't long before they rode off, each on their own Lhosir mare. They left the bodies as they lay. No point burying a man in the Crackmarsh, even if you wanted to. The Ghuldogs just dug them up again.

VARYXHUN

17

THE WITCH OF THE NORTH

Achista and Oribas lay hidden in snow halfway up the mountainside. Half a mile away around the mountain at the edge of the treeline waited a dozen Marroc soldiers. They were the last remnants of the Hundred Heroes, the Marroc who'd crept into Witches' Reach and taken it from the forkbeards and started the fire that now burned across the valley. They'd been more like seventy, even at the start, and now most of them were dead, and Oribas knew all that because he'd been with them from the start, because he'd opened the Aulian seal beneath the Reach that had let them into the forkbeard tower above. But a hundred sounded better and no one felt like arguing.

He'd stood in this very same place that day. Witches' Reach perched on a small stumpy peak overlooking the Aulian Bridge across a saddle in the mountain. The Reach was full of forkbeards again now, which was why Achista was here with her heroes, watching them, sending runners and riders every day back to Valaric in Varyxhun across the secret mountain paths with word of their movements. The forkbeards had taken much of the lower valley back. They owned the bridge and the road as far as the Devil's Caves, or at least Valaric allowed them to think they did. Oribas wasn't sure anyone owned the road or the land between Varyxhun and the Reach any more. Neither army made much move to venture out from its walls. The Lhosir rode out in packs of fifty or sixty now and then, but never further than a single day's ride. They raped, pillaged, murdered, looted, took whatever farmhouse they fancied as shelter for the night and then rode back the next day before the Marroc could muster. After a few weeks of this every house and barn within a day of the Reach was a burned-out shell and the forkbeards didn't have any shelter any more. At the same time Marroc archers roamed the mountains from tiny caves and hideaways, shooting at any forkbeard they saw. No, it was winter that owned the road, and if Oribas had been in Varyxhun then he might have told Valaric to do something about that before the spring thaw came. Or Valaric might have quietly led his army into the Devil's Caves and out of the mountains and across the Crackmarsh and maybe bloodied the garrison at Issetbridge instead. Might, but Valaric was set on making his stand, on the Vathen crossing the Isset again to take war to the forkbeards once more, and so Oribas was here with Achista because she needed a scribe and because Oribas was very glad indeed to be beside her. Love was a strange beast.

'There. Again.' He pointed.

The forkbeards of the Reach were little more than dark specks on the snow, but now and then Oribas caught a flash of light from among them. He might have put it down to lanterns in the dark, but he saw the flashes in the daylight too, and at night they were too bright. They came and went like tiny stars exposed and then quickly covered. In the last week Medrin Sixfingers had come to the Reach. They knew that from all the flags and the fuss the forkbeards had made – the forkbeards had stopped riding out to burn Marroc farms too – but something else had come, days before, and Oribas had no idea who or what, only that he'd felt a deep and abiding unease ever since.

'We need to get closer.'

Oribas shook his head. Achista's idea of getting closer was to slip away when he was asleep and creep down the slope as close to the walls as she could get without the forkbeards seeing her. She was good at that while he was almost useless, but every time she did it he always woke up almost as soon as she was gone and then spent the rest of the night pacing the woods and chewing his nails until she came back.

Later, as the sun sank, they went back to the camp in the woods and Achista told Oribas what to write for Valaric. When that was done she dragged him to their tent before it was even dark and they made love to the quiet amusement and occasional hoots of the Marroc outside. Another sign Oribas understood. Amusing him, occupying his thoughts and leaving him dozy and happy as twilight fell and she quietly dressed and slipped away. He watched her through lidded eyes, pretending he was asleep. Watched her look back at him with a lingering glance full of love and with a sadness he understood perfectly. He didn't try to stop her, but when he was sure she was away from the camp, he rose and quietly followed.

The Marroc nightwatchman was ready as soon as Oribas crept out of his tent. 'She's gone,' he said.

'I know.'

'See if you can keep quiet tonight, Aulian. People need their rest.'

'I'll be off in the trees. I won't keep anyone from their pillow.'

The Marroc shook his head and snorted. 'Pillow? Keep close, Aulian. There might be wolves or forkbeards out there.'

'I won't be far. But I will be quiet.' He spoke lightly. It was only half a lie after all.

He walked away and then wandered aimlessly in the trees as Achista had shown him to make his trail a hard one to follow, then climbed back past the place where they'd spent the afternoon wrapped around each other while they watched the Reach. He carried on around and down the further slopes until he was in among the massive trees where he'd once seen twenty Lhosir massacred and where, a month later and not all that long ago, a hundred Marroc dead had been carefully hidden where the Lhosir would never find them. There had been flowers on that first day. Deep blue midwinter flowers, the first colours of the year, or the last depending on how you measured such things. He'd slipped out and brought back three and given them to Achista on the day he'd asked her to be his wife. Silly sentimentality perhaps, with death as close as it had been, but he'd never regretted it, not once. It was one thing he'd done since he'd crossed the mountains that made him proud however he looked at it. One thing among many that did not.

He walked quickly through the immense Varyxhun pines, guided by the starlight. Out to the north over the plains and the hills that led to the sea the sky was filled with grey cloud, but here in the mountains it was as clear as Aulian glass. The stars twinkled and sparkled and the half-moon glowed bright. They reminded him of home. Of the desert. Those night skies had been cold and clear too. Sometimes he wondered if he'd ever go home but mostly he thought not. He couldn't think of a single reason why he should.

He passed through the trees until he was around the back of the Reach and began to climb again, cautiously now because the cave that led into the mountain and to the shaft beneath the Reach likely wasn't a secret any more. He crept as close as he dared without crossing open snow and then lay in the cover of a boulder for a good hour, watching and waiting, feeling the bitter cold of the night slowly dig under his furs and into his skin and deeper. No one moved. No guard on the cave then, and so he ran across the open snow to the crack in the side of the mountain and slipped in. There were no lamps here and the starlight quickly vanished as he walked deeper. He carried a lantern but didn't light it, not yet, knowing how far it would gleam and shine off the wet walls of the cave. In the dark he felt his way along as quietly as he could. It took longer and seemed further than he remembered but finally he felt the air change. Space opened ahead of him. He dropped to his hands and knees and crawled the last few yards until he reached the shaft and touched the surface of the water there. A thin crust of ice broke beneath his fingers. No one had tipped more barrels of fish oil down here then. He smiled bitterly at the thought. His finest hour, as far the Marroc were concerned, and the most terrible thing he'd ever done.

The walkway around the shaft was too narrow for crawling. He took the bag off his shoulder and left it in the tunnel, and then his boots as well, and inched around on his feet, pressing his back against the wall and feeling his way with his toes. Far above him another tunnel led to an Aulian seal that the Marroc had smashed open. For all he knew there might be a Lhosir on watch up there now, picking his fingernails, half-crazy with boredom. It made more sense than standing a man out in the open by the mouth of the cave. If nothing else, the inside was warmer.

Rungs set into the wall led up. Oribas climbed them slowly and with care. Here and there he found the loose ones and the ones that were missing. The Marroc hadn't needed to make the climb any more treacherous than it already was – age had done that well enough – but they'd given it a good go nonetheless. At the top he half expected to peek over the edge and find himself staring at the boots of a forkbeard but there was no one there, and no light coming from the half-smashed door into the tomb. He almost relaxed. Almost, but not quite. Something still set his teeth on edge. Maybe it was the thought of entering an Aulian crypt in the pitch dark, even if he knew perfectly well that whatever it had once entombed was long gone, turned to dust or vanished away centuries ago.

Yet still …

He hadn't understood, from the moment he'd left the Marroc camp and even before, quite why he was doing this. If there was a way into the Reach to be scouted then he was the last person to be doing it, and yet he'd come and he'd come alone and only a part of it was because of Achista. There was a sense of something. A sense of something here and he'd had it for weeks, long before the Lhosir king had come. The sliver of bone that he carried with him in a silver rune-etched tube quivered the way it had once quivered whenever the Rakshasa was nearby. The coin he carried that bore no face now bore the face of death. Something had changed, something that wasn't about Lhosir and spears and swords and arrows but had to do with darker things, and so here he was. Alone.

He eased himself over the rim and onto his hands and feet. Everything was silent and still, yet he was suddenly certain that the tomb was no longer empty. He pulled himself up and took two steps forward, then walked to the wall and took out a handful of his precious salt and spread it in a line across the passage. Most of the things he wished he had with him right now were back at the bottom of the shaft but salt was the one thing he never left behind. A part of him felt stupid for being so nervous. He'd been through the tomb a dozen times, after all. He'd found what had been imprisoned there and it was long gone, a couple of pieces of old iron armour all that was left.

Iron. Iron like the ironskins of the Lhosir Fateguard. The same design and style. He finished his line of salt and stepped over it and immediately there was a presence. It had felt him make his wall and now a noise came from the other side of the broken seal, the grinding of metal on metal. He crept to the door, feeling his way, half of him wishing he'd brought a lamp, the other half glad he hadn't. He held a fistful of salt in each hand. It was right there. He was sure of it. Right on the other side of the broken seal, silently waiting for him to step through. His heart was pounding so loudly that the Lhosir in the tower above must be wondering what was going on in their cellar.

On the threshold he paused and threw a handful of salt ahead of him. A soundless dazzling light bloomed inside the tomb. The air shook as though the mountain had fallen and a silent shock trembled the air, throwing him away from the seal and back the way he'd come. As he scrabbled to his feet, a figure came through the shattered door covered in a skin of iron armour save for a black cloth wrapped around its torso. It wore a mask and a crown and from under the mask glowed pale blue eyes like glacier ice. It stepped through and lifted its hands to its head. Iron armour. Like the Fateguard but missing a breastplate, and Oribas suddenly knew it was missing a back plate too because those were the pieces that had been left in the tomb. The pieces it had once been forced to leave behind.

His salt lay scattered across the floor of the tomb, each grain glowing white like a tiny star.

The abomination lifted the crown and mask off its head and the ice-blue light of its eyes burned brighter. 'An Aulian.' Its words were in the old tongue, the perfect high speech of the priests and the magi of the empire at its height a hundred years ago. 'Come, Aulian!'

Not a Fateguard. Worse. Far worse. Oribas took two quick steps toward the monster and threw his other handful of salt in its face, then turned and screwed up his eyes. The blast of light came again. He saw it red through his eyelids and then another shock of air caught him and threw him back. He stumbled, almost scuffed the line of salt he'd laid across the passage and landed heavily on the other side. The creature opened its arms wide and strode towards him and Oribas couldn't stop himself from stepping back until he was on the brink of the shaft. It reached the line of salt and stopped and hissed. Oribas had to pinch himself. *It worked!*

Mere salt was actually holding it. He made himself look at it now. Take it in, good and long though his eyes squealed and squirmed to look away. The armour of a Fateguard, without question, but the face behind the mask was of a man much longer dead. A shadewalker, perhaps.

A wisp of wind started around the creature's feet. A crumb of salt flew up into the air and swirled around it, touched its metal leg and flared into light. The creature looked at Oribas and smiled.

18

GHOSTS

There was a part of him that wanted to turn and leap into the darkness to get away. There was water at the bottom of the shaft, it wheedled, and it would break his fall, wouldn't it? And it didn't matter that he hadn't the first idea how to swim, because if he took a deep breath he'd float once he threw off the furs, and then surely he could haul himself out into the tunnel, even if he'd once seen a Marroc man almost drown trying the same with three men to help him. He thought these things as he swung over the edge of the shaft and started climbing down the rungs as fast as he dared. But no, the water wouldn't cushion his fall, not from this height, and chances were good he'd hit the wall on the way down and maybe the walkway at the bottom, and even if he didn't, he'd break his bones and his clothes would drag him down, and he'd drown before he could shed them. If he was even still conscious.

Up above, the dim light of the *thing* – he had no idea what it was, some creature half dead and half like the Fateguard and the shadewalkers – lit up the shaft enough for him to see how far the water was below, black and glistening like a hungry mouth. He saw the air swirl around the entrance to the tomb. *It*, whatever it was, was making a wind to blow away his salt, and he could be thankful now that he hadn't done such a good job of keeping it dry out with the Marroc in all that snow – it was sticky and crumbly and not the nice fine powder he might have wanted it to be. He tried not to look up, only down, one foot after the next, hand over hand as fast as he could, and when he slipped on a loose rung, he simply let himself fall to the next and clung to it for dear life.

A whistling began. It filled the shaft and a low moan rose behind it. And then it stopped and everything was silent, and Oribas did look up now because he still wasn't quite at the bottom of the shaft and the silence meant the wind had stopped and *that* meant ...

It was looking down at him. Its pale blue eyes gleamed and there was a white wind swirling around it. It seemed to smile. 'Aulian ...' whispered the white wind, and it whirled into the shaft overhead and dived towards him. Now he forgot about how hard the water might be. He threw off his cloak and let go of the rungs, all other thoughts and fears wiped away by the ghost-thing hurtling towards him. He fell straight as an arrow, arms stretched up, cringing inside. He didn't even know how deep the water was, and then it hit him like a mountain, shaking his bones. It tore at his arms, almost pulling them from his shoulders, and snapped at his neck like a hangman's noose. It gouged the air out of him.

The cold might have been what saved him, a deep killing ice-cold that forced itself into his nose and his mouth and the back of his throat and stabbed him awake as he felt the impact suck him away. It crushed into his ears, a deep hard pain, and all he could hear was a terrible roaring. The light was gone. He kicked, half expecting to find the bones in his knees and hips and spine shattered into fragments but to his amazement they seemed whole, and whatever pain they had waiting for him, the shock of the cold and the fear had killed it for now. He burst to the surface, floundered, grabbed at something that turned out to be his fur cloak floating beside him and began to sink again. He clawed at it, pulling himself some way or other. Caught a glimpse of the passage out of the mountain's heart as he looked wildly around, and of the walkway, and then of the ghost-thing above still arrowing down at him. Instinct made him duck under the surface, but as he began to sink again he knew his instinct was wrong. He needed salt for a ghost, not ice-water. That was for other things. Desert things.

The ghost plunged in beside him and for a moment they were face to face under the water, the empty sockets of its eyes boring into him. It seemed to speak, though it had no mouth. *I've never had an Aulian. Your skin is already on its way.* Oribas kicked away, frantic to escape. He surfaced again and the ghost floated beside him, mocking him, but he reached out of the water and clawed at the stone floor of the passage and hauled himself up into the tunnel, inch by freezing inch, dripping, already shivering, driven by terror. The ghost opened its mouth impossibly wide and swallowed him. He felt it run through him, a bone-shiver deeper than the shakes born of cold, a weight on his soul and on his consciousness, dragging him into a place far deeper and darker than the water of the shaft. His eyes began to close, so heavy that nothing would keep them open.

His bag! Right there beside him! His fingers reached it. Touched it as his eyes closed. Fumbled at the buckle as his mind began to drift. Reached inside and found what they were looking for. Salt. And then the weight was suddenly gone and he opened his eyes and the ghost was hovering above him, swirling and spitting. His fingers clenched tight, Oribas drew out another handful of salt and threw it and the ghost dissolved in a shower of light and sparks and was gone. From high up the shaft came a cry of fury. Oribas didn't wait to see what followed. He stuffed his feet into his boots and snatched up his bag and another fistful of salt in case he needed it and stumbled away, forgetting in his fear how icy cold he was, how bitter the night air would be outside the cave to a man already soaked in freezing water. Forgot until he felt the first gasps of wind like knives into his skin.

In sight of the cave mouth he stopped. A monster was behind him, a cold seeping death ahead. Despair almost took him then but that wasn't who he was, not who he'd been taught to be. He opened his bag and let his numb fingers feel at the pots and the parcels and the waxed paper wrappings and the glass vials, questing for something that would turn back the cold.

Saltpetre. He could set fire to himself. *That* would keep the cold back. He snorted bitterly and closed the bag and sat there for a moment in the dark, lost. Then uttered a tirade of Marroc curses that he'd been learning in the company of so many soldiers.

A spark of light flashed by the mouth of the cave. The spark of a man striking a flint. He started to laugh. That would do nicely, wouldn't it? If there *had* been a Lhosir guarding the cave mouth after all and somehow they'd missed each other, and now maybe he wouldn't die of the cold after all but something even worse. They'd wanted to hang him for what he'd done in this very tower, and sometimes in the dark at night, as he saw the flames again, he thought that a mere hanging would be a kindness. Then again he'd seen a Marroc made into a blood raven and that had been far less kind. On the whole, hanging sounded better then freezing, but freezing sounded better than having his ribs snapped off his spine and two metal spikes driven through his chest.

The spark flashed again. He could always go back and drown himself in the water. Not that drowning sounded all that pleasant either.

'Oribas?'

He froze. *'Achista?'*

'Oribas! What in the name of Modris are you doing?'

'Shivering.' He picked up his bag and ran. In the starlight he could see her standing inside the entrance. He threw himself at her, burrowing under her furs for her warmth.

'Modris and Diaran! You're freezing! And sodden! What were you doing here? What were you thinking?'

'I was thinking that something hasn't been right here for quite some time, even before the Lhosir king came. And now I know I was right.'

'How?'

He shivered, squirming closer. 'Ah, you're so warm!'

'And you're freezing. What do you mean something not right?'

'There's a monster here.'

He felt the growl in Achista before he heard it. 'I know. And we'll find a way to cut off his head as well as his hand!'

'No, not the Lhosir king. Something worse. The creature my ancestors imprisoned here has returned. And I know why, and the iron-skinned men are its children.'

She stepped away, or would have if he hadn't been clinging to her like a leech. 'Tell me later. You're freezing. We need to get you shelter.'

'We need to get back to the camp.' To a fire, except the Marroc hiding up the mountain didn't ever dare to light one.

'No.' Achista started to drag him down the mountain. 'It's too far. You'll freeze.'

He ran after her, tumbling and slipping through the snow back to the trees. He was shaking uncontrollably, steadily freezing to death, but at the edge of the wood Achista stopped. Something was ahead of them, ploughing through the snow, and Oribas would have said it was a man from the steady sounds of its shuffling except what was any man doing out in the forest at the dead of night?

Achista reached for her bow. She pointed. In the starlight he saw something move. A shape shambling through the trees. They stood there, both of them frozen to the spot as the shadow moved through the wood and passed them by, and when it was gone Achista stared after it and Oribas had no idea what it was that they'd seen. Tall enough to be a man. A bear, perhaps? 'I can't feel my face,' he whispered. At least his boots were dry and warm. Otherwise he'd probably have lost his feet by now. Good chance he'd lose a finger or two.

Achista shook herself free of her wonder. She pulled him into the trees until she found a deep drift and made him dig a hole for them both. She took his wet furs off him and laid them out and then took off her own and squirmed into the burrow, and Oribas squirmed in after, pulling her furs too. They huddled there together, as close as could be, the two of them wrapped in a cocoon for the night, shivering.

And in the morning they rose, stiff and half frozen but alive, and saw three sets of footsteps ploughing through the trees towards Witches' Reach. When they got back to the rest of Achista's Marroc, the watchmen in the night said they'd seen shadewalkers and the iron devils of the Lhosir Fateguard too; and over the days that followed more of them came, and forkbeards crossed the Aulian Bridge until the Reach was full and their camp sprawled around it, and it was barely another week before Oribas wrote his last message from Achista the Huntress to Valaric the Wolf in Varyxhun: *The forkbeards are coming.*

19

THE DEVIL'S CAVES

The paths through the Crackmarsh were slow and winding. A month or two earlier and they might have simply walked straight over the frozen boggy ground. Another month, when the waters were at their highest, they might have poled their way on a flat-bottomed raft. But in these months of early spring while the waters were rising but still far from their peak, there were only so many ways to go. Reddic led the mules and the children took it in turns to ride them. Arda followed, then Jelira and Nadric. They stayed in the hideaways that riddled the water meadows and the swamps and Reddic took them to what was left of Hrodicslet; and when they were through it Arda led him along a trail that ran south and east into the hills among tiny clusters of farms tucked away in the valleys. The Vathen had never come this far, nor any forkbeards, but it was a path Reddic knew well. They all did, all the Crackmarsh men who'd marched with Valaric to Witches' Reach.

They crossed the ravine where Valaric's men had built a new bridge of ropes. On the other side lay the Devil's Caves which ran right through the mountain to the Varyxhun valley. Marroc soldiers waited inside, Crackmarsh men, and when they saw Reddic and Arda their faces broke into smiles of welcome, though the smiles faded quickly when Reddic told them of the shadewalkers he'd seen. In the warmth of the caves, in the cathedral-like chamber of spires and columns near the passage out to the valley, Valaric's soldiers of the Crackmarsh told him in return of everything that had passed, of Sixfingers himself at Witches' Reach only a half-day's hard march away, of the forkbeard army that was massing, bigger and bigger, and more iron devils too.

'You staying here?' Arda asked him that night as they settled down around stones warmed beside the fires lit outside the caves.

Reddic shrugged. It would be nice to be among friends and to stay in one place for a while. To have other men around him so that he wasn't the one to whom everything fell when difficult things needed to be done.

Arda cocked her head. 'Well, you can do as it pleases you. No need for you to follow if you don't want to. First thing in the morning we're off to Varyxhun.' In the dim flickering light of the few torches kept going under the ground Reddic saw a pair of eyes watching them from where Nadric and the children had lain down to sleep. Jelira. Arda saw them too. 'We all are,' she added sharply.

'You should go back to your forge. To your home. You'd be safer. There's a war coming here and people run away from wars.'

Arda stared as though she hadn't heard.

'He's not here, you know.'

She looked at him hard now, as if she was waiting for more, but Reddic had nothing left to say. They both knew who he meant. 'I know.' She looked away at last. 'I asked too.'

'He killed a Marroc.' Jelira was still watching them.

'I heard. We didn't come here for Gallow anyway. Middislet isn't safe any more.'

Reddic had to laugh. Did she really believe her own words? 'And Varyxhun is? Sixfingers is going to march an army on it any day now. He'll sweep every Marroc in the valley out of his path. They'll all go running to the castle and he'll sit outside and wait until we all starve, because after Varyxhun there's nowhere left to run.'

'Still, it's where I'm going. So you staying here, are you?' She looked him over, and now he was the one who had to look away, though he stole a glance at Jelira as he did.

'I don't know.'

Arda smiled. 'You should. You've done good for us. If you were my son, I'd be proud. At least here you've got a way out when the forkbeards come. Might not be much back the way we came but you'll have a chance.' She reached out a hand and touched his cheek, stroked his face. 'You're young, boy, and you have a good heart. Live.' She touched his sword arm, still in its sling. The pain wasn't quite as bad now, but only as long as he didn't move it.

He put his other hand over hers but Arda pulled away and shook her head. 'Live,' she said again, and rose and backed away and lay down with her family, with her children and the old man Nadric, and Reddic watched as they huddled together and slowly fell asleep, one by one. He felt a great longing wash through him. He'd had a family of his own once, not all that long ago, and he'd thought of the Crackmarsh men as his new one; and they were too, but it only went so far.

He turned away. Forced himself to look somewhere else. Despite everything they'd been through he didn't feel tired, not tonight. *Stay or go?* Varyxhun was a dead end. Sixfingers would have the Isset running red with Marroc blood. He wouldn't leave anyone alive, not a man, woman or child. He'd wipe the valley clean and behind him there'd be nothing but a legion of blood ravens to be picked to bones by the crows. There weren't many here who'd stay to fight that future, not those men who still had a way out through the caves.

Live?

He looked at Arda and her sleeping children. They'd need someone to look after them. Ought to go with them then. Except the more he thought of Arda, the more he thought that maybe they didn't need anyone at all, thanks very much. And besides, with his arm as it was, a fat lot of use he'd be when an army of forkbeards came sweeping up the valley.

Another hand touched his shoulder. 'Hey.' He turned quickly, thinking it was Arda again, but in the flickering light of the candles the face was much younger. Jelira. 'So you're not coming with us?'

Reddic tried to smile. 'I don't know. I sort of think I should actually, but what use am I?' He shrugged. 'And I don't know the way.'

'We stayed there for a while when I was younger. After … Gallow went away to fight and didn't come back.' A smile spread across her face. 'It was so big! So many houses and so many people.'

'He's not there, you know.'

Her face hardened. 'That's what ma says but he'll come. He will. He came back before.'

And left again. That's what Arda had said and her face had said a whole lot more – anger and despair and wanting and resentment, and even Reddic had thought better than to pry.

Jelira bit her lip and touched his injured arm, her fingers light as a falling feather. 'You fought off those ghuldogs. That's what use you are.' Reddic lifted a hand and then didn't know what to do with it. Before he dropped it again, Jelira took it and pressed his palm to her heart. He could feel it beating under her shift. 'I want you to stay. But not like the other forkbeard did.' Her eyes were huge in the candlelight. She put her other hand to Reddic's chest.

'Then I will.' He shuffled closer. His hand stayed pressed to her heart, his eyes snaking past her to where Arda and Nadric and the children lay. Jelira stepped closer. She tipped back her head until the tips of their noses touched together.

'If the forkbeards win, I don't want to die alone.'

'Nor do I.' He reached his injured arm around her and pulled her closer still.

'Forkbeards!' A sudden shout split the rumble of snores and echoed through the cave. Reddic and Jelira jumped apart, looking about in panic as the shout came again: 'Forkbeards! Forkbeards are coming!' It ran through the caves like fire and suddenly Marroc everywhere were scrambling for their shields and their spears, jamming their helms on their heads while the few who had mail struggled into their shirts or hauberks. Reddic stood frozen. He stared at Jelira and she stared back, and then an old Marroc grabbed him by the arm and Jelira nodded and turned away.

'Live!' she cried after him.

'This way, boy.' The old Marroc ran up a slope at the side of the cavern and into the passage that led outside to a tiny valley beside a stream. A dozen Marroc soldiers were already there, clustered together with their shields held up and their spears wavering towards the night. Out in the snow Reddic saw figures moving in the moonlight. He couldn't tell how many there were. As he watched, more Marroc came in ones and twos, running and out of breath.

'Marroc!' A forkbeard voice pierced the chill. 'Traitors and rebels! This is your king. I'd ask you to throw down your arms but we both know that you won't. Good enough. I don't want you to. I don't know how many of you are in there, but I haven't brought many men. Most of them simply couldn't be bothered with you. So I'm going to sit here and watch. Come and get me if you have the heart. If you have women and children with you, you may send them out. They'll not be harmed. They may go back to their homes.'

In the semi-darkness figures formed into a line, a dozen of them, maybe a few more, but still less than half the number of Marroc now at the mouth of the caves. They came on slowly.

'Those aren't forkbeards.' The old soldier who'd dragged him out frowned and let go of his arm. Reddic peered. 'No spears. No shields.'

The moonlight caught them for a moment. The old Marroc gasped and Reddic felt himself wilt inside. The men coming towards him were clad in iron from head to toe like the devil that had led the last assault on Witches' Reach. His mouth felt dry. He took a step back and the other Marroc around him did the same. He could taste the fear in the air. They began to back into the cave and it was all he could do not to turn and run. Iron devils. Men who couldn't be killed. Already dead, some said, but they said it in fright-filled whispers. Then shouts rang out from the passage behind him too, and screams, and a moment later a half-dressed Marroc bolted out of the tunnel. 'Shadewalkers!' Maybe he didn't see the iron devils or maybe he didn't care. He ran straight at them. 'Modris preserve us!'

The iron devils broke into a run, slow at first but building speed. The fleeing Marroc swerved from their path but one ironskin veered from the rest and cut him to the ground. The others charged in silence, each with an axe in one hand and a sword in the other, straight at the mouth of the cave. Faster and faster they came, while the Marroc soldiers wavered, wilted and then broke and turned and ran back into the tunnel before a single blow was struck, and Reddic ran with them, clutching his arm to his chest, and they were screaming in terror, only now there were Marroc fleeing the other way too, getting in their way. Someone barged Reddic from behind. He stumbled and tripped and fell as the iron devils crashed into the fleeing Marroc and began to cut them down. A man fell beside him, the back of his head split open by an axe. Another Marroc came the other way, bellowing with rage and fear, battering the iron devils back for a moment before they cut him to pieces. Reddic pulled himself free. Between the pressing walls of the tunnel some-one trod on his leg, then his head. He managed to stagger to his feet but he could hardly see a thing and all he could hear were shrieks of terror, and there were men all around him, thrashing to get past each other but with nowhere to go. He dropped his shield and pushed forward in the dark. Men kicked and cursed him, and he shouted at them to turn back because there was nothing waiting for them but the iron devils and at least a man could outpace a shadewalker, but no one heard. He pushed his way out of the passage at last to where the tunnel opened into the cathedral of stone and jumped down off the ledge, wincing as his ankle hit the cave floor below and as he jarred his damaged arm. Inside the caves he could hardly see a thing. The only light came from those few candles that hadn't been tipped over and trodden out, yet sounds echoed everywhere, the rattle of iron on stone, the hiss of the shadewalkers, the scratch of steel, the shrill screams of men trapped with nowhere to go. 'Arda! Jelira!' A candle lit up a cluster of spires near where they'd been resting and he stumbled towards it. A lurching shape loomed at him out of the darkness. He yelped and jumped away but it was only a Marroc soldier with his arm almost hacked off at the shoulder, staggering in blind agony. 'Arda!'

'Reddic!' He heard Jelira but he couldn't see her. Another shape moved across the darkness in front of him. A shade-walker this time. He didn't see it, didn't see the swing of the sword until the very last moment, too late to do much except twist and lean back. The point of the shadewalker's sword scraped down the front of his mail hard enough to spark, hard enough for his chest to feel as though he'd been ripped open. He tripped over a ridge in the stone floor and landed hard on his shoulder. His damaged arm exploded with pain and he screamed. The shadewalker came after him. He scrabbled back to his feet and stumbled away. Anywhere.

'Reddic!' A deeper voice. Arda this time. He almost walked into a stone column, and then an arm grabbed him and pulled him and suddenly he was in among a small huddle of Marroc pressed tight against a cluster of the stone spires. Arda. He recognised her smell. And Nadric and Jelira and the children. 'Stay still and be quiet, you daft bugger!'

'Stay still?' His arm was agony.

'Yes!'

'We have to leave! We have to run!'

Arda gripped his shoulder so hard it hurt. 'Run where, boy? Now be *still*.'

Jelira's hand took his. Squeezed tight and didn't let go.

20

THE WIZARD OF AULIA

Oribas ducked under the shadewalker's sword and threw a handful of salt at its face. It let out an unearthly scream and reeled back. He shoved a flaming torch at it, burning it some more. Salt and fire and ice, all those things together had once stilled a shadewalker long enough for a stab of cold iron through the heart to finish it. 'Addic!' He looked desperately for the other Marroc but all he could see was the flicker of torches in among the trees. A handful. Everyone else had fled.

A heavy stone fizzed past his head and hit the shadewalker in the face and suddenly the air was filled with the stench of fish, and Oribas understood it hadn't been a stone at all but a pot of oil. He rammed his torch at the reeling shadewalker again, held it there until the oil started to burn and then stumbled back as flames engulfed the monster's face and chest.

'Iron! Cold iron!' Oribas took another handful of salt from his bag for when the flames started to fade. 'Addic!'

'Oribas!' Footsteps crunched the snow behind him but it wasn't Addic. Achista had a shield in one hand and a sword in the other – not that she had much idea of what to do with a sword any more than he did but she held it anyway. 'Everyone else has run. You need to come.'

Oribas shook his head. 'We can put this one to rest.' The flames were dying now. The shadewalker had stopped struggling and stood swaying from side to side. It stank of burned flesh and scorched fish, and when Oribas threw his second handful of salt into its face, it collapsed like a puppet with its strings cut. Oribas jumped on it at once, pulling at the mail coat it wore. 'Help me with this!'

Achista recoiled and shook her head. He understood. There was something about the touch of cold dead flesh on the skin. Oribas had cut up a dozen bodies in his youth, long ago when he'd been learning his arts, and yet it still made his skin crawl, the clammy touch of the dead. The shadewalkers felt the same only they weren't quite dead, which made it worse. He pulled the mail up around the shadewalker's hips and then rolled it over onto its back and pulled further. The dark was a blessing. The last time he'd done this had been in daylight. What he'd seen he still carried with him, clear as yesterday.

He had to push hard to get at the creature's ribs. He couldn't get the mail any further without taking the whole coat off. 'Can you finish it?' The last time he'd done this the shadewalker's mail hadn't been so long. Easier to pull back.

Achista shook her head. She backed away. 'No. I can't. Not one of *them*.'

'A knife. Please. Iron.' Oribas reached out a hand. Achista pressed a haft into his palm. He levered back the mail and tried to get the knife as straight as he could over the space between the ribs where the shadewalker's heart ought to be. He almost had it and then paused. 'You have the courage to stand this close – why not one step closer still? I need both my hands to hold back the mail and that leaves me with none for the knife.' A half-truth, but there was a better reason: here was Achista the Huntress, the woman who'd led the Hundred Heroes into Witches' Reach and held it for a month while forkbeard bodies piled up around its walls and she shouldn't be afraid of a thing like this. 'You once stood and faced a forkbeard army with a sword you could barely use, my love. This is a dead man. Nothing more.'

'A dead man that lives.'

'I have stilled him.'

She took a step closer. 'I remember the forkbeards. You started throwing lumps of snow at them.' She laughed, high and nervous, and Oribas chuckled too, even with a dead man under his fingers.

'I could not think of anything else.' He knelt down by the body again and put the knife in place as best he could. 'Help me.'

She knelt beside him, shaking badly, face screwed up in fear though she'd stood and faced death from the forkbeards more times than he could count and he'd never once seen her afraid. Sad, perhaps, and often angry, but never afraid like this. 'It isn't right. It's a thing spurned by the gods themselves. Touched by the Weeping God's tears.'

'In this land it is a monster, Achista, nothing more. And I have slain many monsters.' The gods of the Marroc weren't the same as the old gods of Aulia and the shadewalkers came from across the mountains, not from here. He took her hand and put it over his own on the hilt of her knife, took her other hand and put it there too and then pulled at the shadewalker's mail. 'Close your eyes if you wish. It will go in easily. I'll count to thr—'

But she pushed down before he even finished and the iron blade slid as easily as he'd said between the creature's ribs. Oribas let go of its mail, grabbed Achista and pulled her away. 'Open your eyes. Look! Look!' The shadewalker was disintegrating at their feet, all the years of death and decay that had been held at bay let loose at once. Achista gagged and doubled over and threw up. The stink from the corpse was terrible. Oribas took up her knife when it was done and handed it back. 'How many were there?' he asked, but Achista only shrugged.

Later, after the shadewalkers had gone, the Marroc slowly came together again, calling out to each other. Dozens of the creatures had passed through the wood. Not as many as a hundred but perhaps half that number, and they'd walked with a purpose, and it was only chance that had taken them close to the Marroc camp and the Marroc had come out to kill them, thinking that they were forkbeards.

It was only much later that Oribas realised where the shadewalkers were all going with such purpose. To the Devil's Caves, but by then it was too late to do anything but bury the dead.

Reddic cringed. A shadewalker was standing right in front of him. Not that he could see it because the caves were now black as pitch, the last of the candles burned out or crushed under iron boots. The shouts and screams and the clash of arms had long since died away, fallen to a dwindle of distant wails as the last men in the caves were winkled out of their hiding places. The shadewalkers were searching and they had eyes that pierced the utter dark and saw some light that ordinary men did not. And now the shadewalker was there, in front of him, and if Reddic reached out with his sword, he was certain he could have touched it. When it stood still it was silent, no hoarse rasping breaths to give it away, but he'd heard its feet scraping on the stone as it came closer and closer. Heard it come up to the line of salt that Arda had lain across the stone floor around where they hid.

For a long time it didn't move. Then he heard a clink of mail and more scraping as it turned away. He started to breathe again. It was the fourth to have found them. They showed no sign of leaving. He went back to rocking slowly back and forth, holding his arm, biting back the tears.

Oribas and Achista and her Hundred Heroes were most of the way to the caves when the Lhosir caught them, galloping up the road in the dead of night, guided by the moon. The sounds gave their coming away before anyone saw them, but they came fast. The Marroc threw themselves off the road among the grass and stones at the edge of the Isset and lay flat, praying to Modris that the forkbeards wouldn't see, but Modris wasn't listening. The Lhosir stopped a little way up the road and dismounted and came back. A score of them, thereabouts, not that many more than the Marroc themselves and so the Marroc got to their feet and dusted themselves down and readied themselves for a fight. Yet only one of the Lhosir carried a shield and wore the dark bulk of forkbeard furs. The rest of them ... In the moonlight they gleamed. They wore metal. They were the Lhosir Fateguard, iron devils to the Marroc, but Oribas knew them better still. Shadewalkers that hadn't yet lost their minds. Children of the thing he'd seen in the crypt under Witches' Reach. He reached for his salt as the ironskins moved closer, steady and cautious while the forkbeard stayed in their midst with his shield held in front of him. 'Well, well. I was after your friends in the Devils' Caves tonight, but I'll thank the Maker-Devourer for giving you to me too. Throw down your swords, Marroc. Give yourselves to me and I'll show mercy.'

Beside Oribas, Achista tensed. She hissed. 'Sixfingers! It's Sixfingers himself!' She whipped an arrow out of her quiver and drew back her bow. 'Sixfingers!' she cried. 'The one with the shield! Kill him and the forkbeards are beaten right here!' The arrow flew straight and true at the forkbeard's face and Oribas didn't see how any man could move so quickly, yet the Lhosir king did. His shield jerked up and caught the arrow squarely in its centre. The other Marroc jumped up and howled and ran at him but the iron devils stepped into their path with a casual disdain. Spears and swords struck sparks off their armour but nothing more, and then their own swords and axes fell, hooking shields aside, striking hard into mail, searching out hands and arms and necks and faces and all those places where men who weren't clad in iron showed their skin. Oribas sprinkled salt in a wide circle. Achista let another arrow fly. It caught one of the iron devils in the face, went straight through the bars of the mask he wore over his eyes and struck deep into whatever skin and bone lay beneath. It barely flinched. Oribas scattered more salt.

The Marroc turned and ran now and the iron devils chased them, all but a few who stayed by their king. Achista loosed another arrow at Sixfingers and again his shield caught it. She turned to Oribas, held out a hand to pull him away and then froze. Addic was staggering, hobbling from a terrible slash across his calf and there was a Fateguard right behind him already raising an axe. Achista let Oribas go, screamed and hurled herself at it, smashing the ironskin sideways so hard that the two of them crashed to the ground.

'Addic!' Oribas darted out of his circle, took Addic by the hand and pulled him inside.

And then stopped and stared, aghast. The Fateguard had Achista. The Lhosir king held up a hand, stopping one as he lifted a sword to kill her. 'Lhosir don't make war on women and children. Hold her still!'

Two of the ironskins held her arms and her shoulders. Sixfingers stood in front of her. 'How many Marroc women fight with their men? I've seen a few and I've heard of another one. They call her the Huntress. Is that who you are? I should wring your neck.' Ten figures now stood around Achista, nine clad in iron and armed with swords and axes, the tenth a king, and Oribas carried no sword or spear or shield, but he ran at the iron devils howling like a dervish. In each clenched fist he carried salt which he threw in their faces, and for a moment Achista was free and the Lhosir king was right in front of him.

'And her Aulian wizard. I should have known. I'm not like them, Aulian.' He drew back his sword. Achista barged Oribas out of the way. She whipped out a knife and lunged, but Sixfingers only laughed at her and slammed her with his shield, knocking her down again. Oribas threw one last handful of salt into the air and bolted back to Addic, dragging Achista with him. She tried to haul Addic to his feet so they might all run together but Addic couldn't move.

She set her jaw and turned to face the iron devils and their king.

'A fine gesture.' Addic shook his head. 'And now what? The river, Aulian. If you can make the river you might escape. Run, both of you! Run!'

Oribas stared at the iron-skinned men of the Fateguard. 'Did you see any bows on their horses?' Addic looked at Oribas as though he'd gone mad but Oribas started to laugh. He stood beside Achista and put a hand on her shoulder and faced the Lhosir king and his Fateguard. 'I won't run from you. None of us will.' He leaned closer to Achista and hissed in her ear, 'Stay close. He cannot touch us. Trust me.'

Sixfingers moved nearer, his iron devils around him, his shield held in front of him again. 'Salt, is it? It hurts my Fateguard like a hornet's sting but nothing more. And hornets who sting are crushed.' He closed his fist.

'Come closer if you dare, Lhosir king. I travelled with Gallow the Foxbeard for a year. I know how you lost your fingers of flesh and bone, and now it seems you have new ones. Did the creature you keep in the crypt beneath Witches' Reach give them to you? By all means bring them into my circle.'

'Is it true, Aulian, that you burned fifty of my soldiers in the shaft beneath Witches' Reach?'

Oribas looked down for a moment. The shame of that still ate at him. 'I did.'

'How did it feel, Aulian, to send so many to such a terrible death?'

'I hear you hung as many blood ravens along the streets of Andhun in your time, King Sixfingers.'

'Far more than fifty, Aulian. Have you even seen a blood raven?'

'More. I have stood and watched it done.'

Sixfingers came to the circle of salt. 'A blood raven is there to be seen by the gods. Those men who died in your fire will wander the Marches for ever. No one will send them to the Maker-Devourer, nor speak out their names.' His eyes flicked to Achista. 'Her Marroc did the same, beheading every corpse so no one could say which was which.' He shook his head. 'War is war, Aulian. A man who fights well and stands up for his word will be rewarded in what comes after, Marroc or Lhosir or Vathan. Yet you deny men their just reward for honest courage?'

Achista drew back another arrow. Sixfingers stared at her and laughed. 'You know what shield I carry, Marroc? The Crimson Shield of Modris the Protector, stolen from your King Tane years ago by the mighty Screambreaker, taken from him by the Fateguard, stolen and lost at sea and found again. Loose your arrow, Marroc, and see what happens.'

Achista let fly at his face but the shield seemed to move even before her fingers slipped from the bowstring. The arrow hit the wood of it, close to the rim this time. She readied another.

'I want them alive.' Sixfingers was still laughing at them from behind his shield.

And Oribas laughed right back, because as the ironskins reached his circle of salt they stopped as though they'd walked into a wall. 'My people caught that creature you keep in your crypt hundreds of years ago. They defeated it and brought it here. Your iron-skinned men are nothing more than shadewalkers who don't yet know they're dead. My salt does more than sting, King Sixfingers. They cannot pass.'

Sixfingers drew his sword. He pushed through his Fateguard and stepped into the circle. 'But I can, Aulian.'

Oribas nodded. He opened his hand and held out a flat

palm piled with salt. 'Yes. You can. If that is what you wish. You alone may pass.'

Addic hopped forward on his one good leg, swinging his sword at the king's head. The Crimson Shield flew up and caught the blow, but at the same moment Achista let fly again. The arrow hit Sixfingers in the ribs and stuck in his furs. He had good enough mail to turn the point but it still made him scream.

'Come, king forkbeard,' offered Oribas. 'Enter my circle.'

For a while, lit up by the moon and the stars, Medrin Ironhand, King Sixfingers of the Lhosir, clutched his side and stared in disbelief. Oribas watched. Crimson Shield or no Crimson Shield, Medrin wasn't about to fight alone against three, even if one was wounded, another was a woman and the last was armed only with salt and words.

Medrin smiled, mocking his own hubris perhaps, for with even just one other man beside him, everything would have been different. 'I salute you, Aulian. I see I shall lose more men than I would like when I take Varyxhun. My soldiers will know not to kill you. But then the Vathan ardshan of Andhun had an Aulian and they all knew I wanted him too, and that still didn't save him.'

He bowed and turned, beckoned his ironskins, and Oribas and Achista and Addic watched them walk to their horses and ride away. When the last echoes of their hooves had long since died, Oribas breathed a huge sigh.

'You work magic.' Addic shook his head. 'I said so from that first day. You're a wizard.'

Oribas laughed. 'I'm a scholar. I know things, that is all. And we can all be thankful that the king of the forkbeards isn't as clever as he thinks.' He touched the circle of salt with his foot. Medrin could have broken it – kicked the salt aside and made a path for his Fateguard to step through – and he hadn't thought of it, or else he had but had been afraid, and that was the only difference between the three of them being alive and the three of them being dead.

'Now what?'

'Shadewalkers. Iron devils.' Addic shook his head. 'Where does it end?'

'Varyxhun.' Achista offered him her shoulder. 'Valaric.'

It was a while before the other Marroc returned, slinking through the darkness to reveal themselves. Their talk was muted. Another handful of men killed and no forkbeards slain. It had turned that way of late, ever since Sixfingers had come. There were only nine of them left. Some said that the forkbeards could never win as long as even one of the Hundred Heroes was alive but none of the Marroc there that night much liked the notion.

They took it in turns to carry Addic. Achista led them to a ridge overlooking the road and then over it and down and into a sharp valley on the other side and then along another ridge until Oribas hadn't the first idea where they were any more; and then suddenly, as the dawn broke, he found himself overlooking a sharp ravine and realised they were above the Devil's Caves; and they kept very still and very quiet as they watched the Lhosir king and his ironskins file down the road, finished with massacring the Marroc hiding in the caves, and turn back towards Witches' Reach. In the quiet of the early morning Oribas made Addic lie on his belly and stitched his gashed calf closed, bandaged it as best he could and told Addic that if he ever wanted to run again then he'd best rest in a nice comfortable bed with plenty of food and water. They both laughed at that until Achista snapped them out of their joking.

'Look.'

Down around the mouth of the caves a single figure was moving.

*

The shadewalkers stayed for hours. For a whole day, or that's how it felt to Reddic, but at last they left and didn't come back and everything fell silent and dark. And of course it fell to him to be the one who crossed the line of salt and crept away in the pitch black, feeling his way on his one good hand and his knees until he reached a wall and then along it until he saw the light from outside. Dead men littered the cave. He couldn't see their faces but he felt them, felt his hand press on someone's cold dead fingers or his leg slide in something sticky and wet that he didn't want to think about yet couldn't not. The passage out was the worst. More than half the Marroc of the Devil's Caves – fifty men or thereabouts – had died caught between the shadewalkers and the iron devils. A little sunlight reached in but being able to see the bodies he had to step on to get outside didn't make it any better.

There was no sign of the shadewalkers outside, or of the iron devils except the footprints they'd left in the snow. He realised that he had no idea, in the end, whether the shade-walkers had gone back the way they'd come or followed Sixfingers. He took a good long look around and then went back to the cave and started pulling out the bodies. Took a while with one arm, but clambering over dead still wet with blood was no thing for children. When he was done, he went back along the passage and called out, guiding Arda and Nadric and Jelira and the children with his voice. He let them pass and sat there alone in the dark a little while, contemplating all that he'd seen, and then went looking for Torvic's mules, still with Nadric's arrowheads bagged over their backs. When he led them back out to join the others, he heard a shout, harsh and hostile, and he was still blinking the sun out of his eyes when he realised an archer was crouched over the top of the cave mouth. Just the one, but her arrow was pointed at his heart. 'And you! Name yourself!'

He sank to his knees, too tired to be afraid. 'Reddic of the Crackmarsh men.'

'Who's with you?'

Arda threw down the axe she'd been holding. 'Arda of Middislet, and for the love of Modris put your bow down, girl. I know your voice, Achista of Witches' Reach. We had a few days together if you remember it, and if you're so keen on having someone to shoot then you should have come here a little earlier in the night. Plenty of choice then.'

The archer lowered her bow and scrambled down and Reddic started to laugh. He stared as tears streamed down his face. *This* was Achista the Huntress? He'd expected someone ... well, *bigger*. But she smiled at Arda as she came close, though her face was full of worry and sadness.

'Smithswife! What brings you to the Devil's Caves?'

'Middislet isn't safe, that's what. Seems like there's no-where safe, from what I see. Beginning to wish I'd taken my chances where I was.'

Achista spat. 'Sixfingers is in the valley. He'll be marching on Varyxhun in days.'

'We have two thousand arrowheads for Valaric,' said Reddic, gathering himself together. He slapped the mules they'd brought all the way from the Crackmarsh. It hadn't been easy finding them, nor leading them out of the cave.

'Then Valaric will thank you. We'll have need of them soon enough.' The Huntress waved up the slopes and a few minutes later there were a half a dozen more Marroc around them and a dark-skinned man that she called Oribas, and Reddic knew that this was the great and terrible Aulian Wizard, though Arda glared at him as though he was a snake.

'So you got him back, then.'

Achista turned to Arda. 'Barely. They were about to hang him. He was on the scaffold when we took Varyxhun castle. Addic rescued him off the gallows.' She swung back to her men. 'Sixfingers turned back for Witches' Rea—'

'Oi.' Arda glared. 'Where's my husband?'

Achista ignored her. 'Hasavic, you know the paths best. Can we get mules to Varyx—'

Arda stepped around, planted herself in front of Achista and poked her in the chest. 'I asked you a question, woman.'

Everyone stopped. Hands went to swords and axes but then fell away. What were they going to do – draw steel on an unarmed Marroc woman in front of her children? Achista frowned. 'Gallow left Varyxhun, Smithswife. He killed a man. Angry Jonnic wanted to hang him. And others. People who didn't know him. We sent him away. Probably for the best, what with him being a forkbeard. So he didn't come back to you?'

All the anger fell out of Arda. Her shoulders slumped. 'No,' she said. 'He didn't.'

21

THE AULIAN BRIDGE

The Aulian Way ran from Tarkhun almost due east to Issetbridge, through the fringes and spurs of the Shadowwood and then the Crackmarsh, roughly following the Isset with a typical Aulian straightness of purpose. Issetbridge itself lay at the foot of a mountain a few miles short of the bridge from which it took its name, the great Aulian Bridge that crossed the Isset and led to Varyxhun. From the town the road wound up the slope like a coiled rope spilled down the mountainside.

The town and the Aulian Way were both thick with Lhosir who had marched from Tarkhun. Gallow and Mirrahj followed the edge of the Crackmarsh, slipping between the bands of soldiers that swept the water meadows. They travelled at night and in the day they hid close to the cascade of the Isset falls, the impassable cataracts that divided the river in two. They skirted Issetbridge the next night, picking their way along trails and paths that wound up into the mountains, and rejoined the Aulian Way on the other side. Now and then they rode past bands of Lhosir heading towards the bridge in their dozens and hundreds, but no one challenged them. Gallow carried a shield of the Crimson Legion, stolen from the Lhosir in the Crackmarsh, and his beard was long enough now to split into two stubby little forks. He was one of them, one of Medrin's Men with a Vathan prisoner, and all the old soldiers who'd once fought for the Screambreaker and might have known his face were dead or far away. Medrin didn't want them.

They reached the bridge not long after dawn. Gallow and Mirrahj stared at it open-mouthed. A single arch of grey stone reached across the river from the base of the gorge cliffs on one side to the base of the cliffs on the other. Its peak rose a hundred feet above the water rushing beneath it, and was level with the sides of the gorge and the two halves of the Aulian Way. Whole trunks of Varyxhun pine, split down the middle and laid side by side, reached from each edge of the gorge to the centre, the midpoint held up by that one stone arch. In the Screambreaker's day that was all there had been, but now someone had built a crude wooden watchtower over the middle of the bridge.

Gallow pointed. 'Guards.'

'I saw the bridge in Andhun the day the Marroc burned it down,' murmured Mirrahj. 'But that was nothing like this. Who built it?'

'Aulians.' No one could match the Aulian masons. It left him wondering whether Oribas had the knowledge to build such a thing if he had the craftsmen to work the wood and stone. Gallow reined in his horse. The bridge was visible from the road for miles and so the road was visible from the bridge. Judging by the smoke of their morning fires there were soldiers at each end and some in the watchtower. He was about to ask her if she'd be his prisoner for one more time as they crossed the bridge, hoping that no Lhosir would question his shield and his face, but he saw the look in her eyes and knew the answer before he spoke. A part of him was glad. They'd enter the valley together as they meant to leave it, one way or the other, with shields held high and spears levelled at the hearts of their enemies. He laughed. 'You would have made a good Lhosir, Mirrahj Bashar.'

She turned her horse in a circle, shook her head at him and set off at a canter along the road, calling over her shoulder, 'And you might even have passed as a Vathan, Gallow Smallbeard, though your riding is poor. Mind, since you're a forkbeard, it's a constant surprise that you don't fall off.'

Gallow galloped after her. The Vathen made better riders it was true, but the Lhosir knew perfectly well how to deal with soldiers on horseback. A hedgehog of spears and shields and some archers, and once the riders were all rolling around on the ground wondering what had happened to their horses and why they were stuck full of arrows, then you fell on them with axes. Men who wouldn't face you toe to toe deserved no better.

The Lhosir at the bridge saw Mirrahj and Gallow but did nothing until Mirrahj spurred her horse to a gallop and lowered her spear. Two of Medrin's men hastily raised their shields and ran out into the road, saw they were alone and hastily ran out of the way again. As he reached the bridge, Gallow kicked his horse faster and rode alongside Mirrahj, putting his shield between her and the Lhosir behind them. Mirrahj's eyes were already on the archers in the watchtower, her own shield raised to ward off their arrows. Medrin's Lhosir threw their spears. One flew over them; the other hit Gallow's shield, stuck for a moment and then fell out a few paces later. His eyes shifted and he brought his shield around in front of him. 'The horses!' he shouted. 'They'll shoot for the horses.'

'And that's why we Vathen hate you forkbeards so much!' Mirrahj leaned suddenly forward until she was almost lying flat on her horse's back, her shoulders across its neck and her head almost resting between its ears. She raised her shield over them both. One of the archers on the watchtower released a shaft but his arrow flew long. The second was aimed at Gallow, who sat up straighter and drew his axe from his belt.

'Do you know who I am?' he roared. 'Gallow Foxbeard,

come to take your king's head because his hand wasn't enough!' He threw the axe. The archer hesitated and then let fly too, but the moment cost him his life. Gallow lowered his head and the arrow glanced off his helm while his axe took the archer square in the chest. The Lhosir fell back onto the platform, tumbled over the edge and fell to the hungry river below.

Mirrahj slowed to let Gallow pass. Now she was lying right back in her saddle with her head over her horse's arse and her shield covering both her and her horse from the one archer that was left. Gallow galloped past her. 'Crazy Vathan!'

The Lhosir soldiers at the far end of the bridge had seen it all. They blocked the road now, seven of them in a wall of shields, spears bristling. Gallow slowed. He looked for a way past but there wasn't one, not wide enough for two horses, not without one of them taking a spear in the flank, and so he stopped a dozen feet short of their spear points and dismounted. Mirrahj drew to a stop behind him. His shoulders itched from knowing there was an archer still in the tower, but only a *nioingr* would shoot a man in the back.

One of the Lhosir facing him stepped forward, bold with a strong clear voice. 'Name yourself, enemy.' He was young, too young to have fought with the Screambreaker unless it had been against the Vathen. Gallow grinned at him and twirled his spear.

'Gallow Foxbeard. And you?'

'Bedris One-Eye. I've heard your name, *nioingr*. We know who you are.'

Gallow twirled his spear again. 'Call me that two more times, Bedris One-Eye, and you'll be obliged to stand against me to prove your mettle.' He peered. 'Seems to me you have two good eyes, boy, so how did you earn that name?'

'I'll stand against any *nioingr*, Foxbeard. I call you *nioingr*.

And again, *nioingr*. That good enough for you?' Bedris stepped out from his men and faced Gallow.

Gallow laughed at him. 'Your name, Bedris One-Eye. You didn't earn it for yourself, so you've taken it from someone. I knew a Jyrdas One-Eye once. Fierce he was. I wouldn't have wanted to cross my sword with his when he was in his prime, that's for sure.' He lifted his spear slowly as he spoke, sinking down behind his shield so there wasn't anything to be seen of him except his feet and his face.

Bedris hissed, 'Jyrdas One-Eye sired me.' He'd settled into a fighting crouch now too. The other soldiers eased back, their eyes following the fight.

'Old One-Eye sired a great many bastards, I'd say.' Gallow crept sideways. 'He was a fine brother of the sea. One of the best. Be proud to have his blood in your veins.'

'I'll have yours on the—' Gallow's spear flew straight at his face, so fast and hard that Bedris didn't see it coming. He screamed and staggered back. Gallow caught the spear by its butt and pulled it back. Bedris collapsed onto the roadway, hands clutching at his head, blood running between his fingers. Gallow turned to face the other Lhosir but Mirrahj was already moving. One-Eye's warriors had lowered their guard to watch the fight and her horse jumped straight into the middle of them. She stabbed down and a Lhosir screamed and she stabbed again. Then she was past them and on the road the other side and two more Lhosir were on the ground. Blood dripped from the tip of her javelot. Gallow eyed the men left guarding the bridge. Four of them and they would still fight. He aimed his spear at them but when they drew no closer he lowered it and pinned Bedris to the road, his spear point at the Lhosir's neck. 'Do you know how Jyrdas died? It started when he was hacked in the back with an axe. He killed the man who did it. Then he took a Marroc arrow in the side but he still killed three more and he was standing when the rest of them fled. He would have faced the Screambreaker himself had there been a need, without a doubt or a moment of second thought. He called your king *nioingr* and died with Medrin's dagger through his one good eye. I built his pyre and I spoke him out and then I found Medrin and I took his hand. Now I've taken your eye, Bedris One-Eye, and so you've earned your name. I'll not kill you today but I might just come for you again.' He turned to the others. 'Stand and fight us if you want. Only two of us and four of you, though you might remember you were seven a moment ago. And you might wonder if a Lhosir might serve his king better by living, by telling him that Gallow Foxbeard has crossed the bridge and waits for him in Varyxhun. Or not. Either way, as you wish it, brothers of the sea.'

He started to move, creeping towards them, covering himself all the time with his shield and with his spear aimed at their faces. If they were going to fight then they'd split and come at him from all sides, and then he'd have to run and it would all depend on Mirrahj, still on her horse, and how she could fight four men when they were packed so close around him. But the Lhosir only turned their shields to face him as Gallow circled past and stood beside Mirrahj and clucked for his horse. Nor did they move as he climbed into the saddle; and when he turned and took the Aulian Way to Varyxhun, the Lhosir by the bridge were still standing there, watching him go.

22

VALARIC THE WOLF

Trouble always came in threes. The first trouble was the trouble Valaric had expected: Sixfingers had left Tarkhun and come to the valley with his army of forkbeards. Well, that was the way it was supposed to be and the Wolf had known this day would come ever since his Crackmarsh men had slipped away from the Reach and helped themselves to Varyxhun instead. That had been a slap in Sixfingers' face and a taunt too: *The Widowmaker never took this castle. Can you?* Valaric had been preparing for the siege since the day he'd arrived. If was honest with himself, he was itching for it.

He sighed. There was always someone in the shrine to Modris up at the top of the castle – Sarvic or Angry Jonnic or one of the others quietly praying for the Vathen and the forkbeards to fight to a bloody stalemate. Valaric hadn't bothered. He'd been at war with the forkbeards for more years than he had fingers and that was never how it went. The Lhosir were charmed. Luck never sent a plague to make their armies vanish into smoke or made the rivers flood and wash them away. The best luck he'd ever had was a bit of mud that made a forkbeard shield wall back up a hill a bit more slowly for fear of slipping, and what the mud had given, the rain that made it had taken away with what it had done to the Marroc archers. It hadn't surprised him when he'd heard that Sixfingers was in Witches' Reach, that he'd turned his back on the Vathen and chosen to crack

Varyxhun first. No surprise that his iron devils had come with him either. Could have done without the shadewalkers. Even the whisper of them put the shits up his men. The Aulian would deal with them though. His men needed to see that.

He stared at himself in the mirror – another Aulian treasure left behind when they'd abandoned the valley to the Marroc warlords who'd claimed the castle until the first kings of Sithhun had tamed them. It was gold and a finer silver than you ever saw in Andhun. Every time he looked at it, he felt a warmth inside him, a reminder of who he was and why he was here, for not long ago a Lhosir had sat where Valaric sat now. Braiding his forked beard, no doubt.

The Aulians had left other things too. Like a great big cave right behind the sixth and last gate to the castle with great big bars across its mouth and, if you believed the stories, a great big dragon inside which would drown anyone who broke those gates down if you could somehow find a way to wake it up.

He sighed. Stories like that kept his men happy but stories didn't kill forkbeards. The Aulians had left behind a library too – the biggest on this side of the mountains. Not that Valaric cared, but Oribas spent half his time there and the other half wandering the castle, looking and poking, although what he was looking and poking *for* only the gods knew. So far all he'd managed to do was find some underground pools and get soaking wet. Books. Books wouldn't save them from Sixfingers any more than stories. Was it too much to hope that Oribas would find some other treasure, something he could actually use?

An angry fist banged on the door. Valaric glanced out the window at the sun and yes, it was about time. His second trouble was more straightforward on account of being locked up in the castle prison, but doing that had made his third. He took a deep breath. Stared at himself in the mirror and sighed again and then turned to face the door. At least it had a latch on the inside so she couldn't just barge in. 'No!' he shouted. 'And still no, and I'll have some more no for you later. Now go away!'

'It's not right, Valaric, and you know it.'

'He killed a Marroc, Arda Smithswife.'

He waited to see if there'd be more today but after a pause he heard her walk away. Maybe she was giving up. And then he looked at himself in the mirror again and laughed. *Arda Smithswife? Give up?*

Five minutes later he was breaking his fast with the Marroc who'd lead the defence of the castle: Achista and Addic of Witches' Reach, who spoke for the Marroc of the valley; Sarvic and the two Jonnics, who'd come with him from the Crackmarsh; and the Aulian, whom everyone said was a wizard, dragged away from his books. They'd all fought the forkbeards before but he always got the same feeling whenever he sat with them: they were too young. They were brave and they'd fight and they'd stand on the walls of Varyxhun until someone cut their legs from under them, but they barely even remembered the days when the Screambreaker had rampaged. Except for Sarvic and Angry Jonnic, who'd been with him at Lostring Hill, none of them even knew what a real battle looked like.

'Sixfingers is moving up the valley now,' said Achista. Her men were watching them come. 'He'll be in Varyxhun tomorrow with five hundred men.' She didn't say anything about the iron devils but all the Marroc except for Valaric made the sign of Modris anyway. Valaric didn't bother because Modris wasn't going to help them, not this time. He closed his eyes. No point banging the table.

'As many men as we can spare. Get them down into the city and sweep it one last time. Food, arrows, weapons, oils, anything that burns.' He glanced at Oribas. 'Salt. If there's anyone still left they can keep whatever they can carry but nothing else. Forkbeards will just take it anyway. Make sure they understand – the gates close when Sixfingers comes and they don't open again for anyone. Anyone.' Felt like he was plundering his own people. He knew he was right – whatever he left he was leaving for Sixfingers – but that didn't make it any easier to do. 'Might be shadewalkers in the city tonight.' He glanced at Oribas while the others all quietly made the sign of Modris again. 'Salt. Do you have enough?'

'Enough to fight them, yes. Enough to bar them from the whole city?' Oribas shook his head. 'It cannot be done.'

Valaric's foot twitched. Oribas had laid lines of crumbly brownish powder across every entrance to the inner castle but people kept forgetting. Kept treading in them and scuffing them and Valaric was no better than anyone else. He wouldn't even have considered it if Achista and Addic hadn't told him how Oribas had faced down Sixfingers and all his ironskins armed with nothing else.

'There are more than a thousand forkbeards in the valley now.' Achista passed her hands over the table where a map lay spread out, another relic of the forkbeard Cithjan. Valaric had found it helpfully marked with all the places where forkbeards had been killed on the roads, and so the first thing he'd done was send his Crackmarsh men out looking for the Marroc who'd done it to see if they wanted to do it some more. Forkbeards had a thousand men in the valley? Fine. He had about half that, but most of them were proper fighting men with decent arms and he had an impregnable castle too and enough food for months. Sixfingers would have to do better.

'There's more crossing the Aulian Bridge all the time.' Sarvic had been the one to come up with the idea of putting watchers on the other side of the river. The western side of the valley was wild and rugged and hardly anyone lived there. The forkbeards had never bothered much with it except for Boyrhun. Sarvic's men lit torches each morning before dawn to say how many forkbeards had crossed the bridge the day before.

Addic's fists were getting tighter every minute. 'You can't just—'

His sister put her hand over his. *You can't just abandon the town.* That's what stuck in Addic's throat. Truth be told, it stuck in Valaric's as well, but if they tried to fight out in the open then the forkbeards would smash them to pieces and they all knew it. The road from the city to the castle, on the other hand, was a series of switchbacks with a gatehouse in the middle of each all stacked one on top of the next and walls overlooking every inch. 'Jonnic, lead the sweep of the town. Achista, go with him.' Maybe the sight of their Huntress would give the Marroc of the valley who hadn't already run some heart; he'd not say no to a few more fighting men. 'Addic, the salt. Sarvic, sort him out some men.' Addic might never walk properly again and he certainly couldn't fight, not yet, but he understood the Aulian wizard's protections and railed about them more than the wizard himself. 'Sarvic, go to the fourth gate and work your way up one more time. Make sure everyone understands when to close the gates and yes, yes, I know they'll be bored to tears hearing it by now but they can hear it again. I'll be at the lower gates doing the same. Oribas, you can come with me.' They'd both be standing watch with the men at the first gate tonight but he didn't need to say that just yet.

He left the others to it and walked through the castle, taking his time, stopping to talk to the men whose names he knew. There was a chance, after all, that he wouldn't see them again, and so wherever there was any problem he stayed until it had been resolved and it was past noon before he even got out of the sixth gate and onto the road. There he looked down.

The sixth gate was different. The first five barred the

middle of each switchback and made a neat line up the mountainside, with ladders running up from the top of each gatehouse to the next. When the forkbeards started up the road and began their assault on the first gate, the men behind the second would be standing fifty feet over their heads, shooting arrows and dropping rocks and whatever else they could find. When the first gate fell, the men behind the second would fall back to the third and do the same again. As Oribas had shown him, the Aulians had designed their fortress so that each gatehouse could be left and allowed to fall, one after the next, while the attacking army would be bombarded all the way to the top, and even the men who manned the roof of each gatehouse could escape after it was overrun by climbing the ladders so their feet would never touch the road. The sixth gate was separate, built right at the end of the castle road, a notch of wall jutting out from the battlements with a small space behind it and then the Dragon's Maw, while the castle yard opened up to one side. The forkbeards, if they reached the sixth gate at all, would be exhausted, battered, bloodied, the road behind them littered with their dead, and not a single Marroc would have had to raise his shield to defend himself. And yet when Valaric looked at the piles of stones and firewood, at the pots of fish oil carefully lined up along the roadside, it left him with a hole in the pit of his stomach. Their defence was based on an assumption that none of them spoke but all quietly made. One by one the gates *would* fall; one by one the forkbeards would take them, and in the end the forkbeards would win because the forkbeards always did, and all Valaric was doing was making it as bloody as possible. The feeling stuck with him right down to the first gate, looking down the castle road to Varyxhun. A grubby muddy market town when you put it beside Andhun and Sithhun and Kelfhun, not even a big one; but to the valley folk Varyxhun was a city and it was hard to imagine anything greater. Now a steady stream of carts was heading up the Aulian Way to the higher valleys. He watched them, suddenly not having much else to do, while Oribas wandered the gatehouse for what must have been the tenth time. When he came back he still hadn't found whatever he was looking for.

'My people liked to dig,' he said. 'I thought there would be tunnels. We were always good with stone.' He brightened. 'Sometimes when my people built a defence like this, there would be a stone with a chain. A dozen strong men pulling on the chain would bring the stone down and without it the building would fall in on itself and block the road. A last defence, you see.'

'Not much fun for the men pulling the chain.'

'In those days they were usually slaves. Sometimes even the officers didn't know. Famously so, in the battle of Iri—'

Valaric cut him off. 'Will the Vathen be any better?'

Oribas stared, mouth still open at what Valaric had just said. He shrugged. 'I don't know the Vathen. The only one I've ever seen is the one you have in your cells.' He paused, and Valaric already knew what the Aulian was thinking before he spoke it. 'Gallow would fight for you. You should let them both—'

'Don't you start on me too, Aulian!' Oribas was right though, and Arda was right. They were all right. Gallow would stand and fight Sixfingers to his last breath, and maybe the Vathan woman would too. And he could use every sword he could get, especially ones that had seen their share of fighting. But to have this castle defended by the very enemies he was trying to kill? He struggled with that. 'I suppose you don't know whether there's any truth to what the Vathan says about the sword either.'

'I've looked through the histories my people left in your library, but …' Oribas only shrugged. 'There's a secret to this castle.' He nodded up the slope to the tarn lake above it and then tapped the sacks of salt by their feet. 'A secret to its stories, to why my people came here and what they brought and why they built this castle where they did.' Salt. The castle cellars had been full of it, a thousand sacks, a hundreds years old. Valaric saw no reason not to drop it on the forkbeards when they came. Sack of salt was as good as a rock, after all.

'When you find out, you let me know,' he said, after they'd both been quiet for a bit.

'I will.'

Together they settled down to wait. To see what the night would bring.

23

SHIEFTANE

Spring came late to the mountain valleys, but it came at last. The sun shone bright and the air was warm and scented with pollen. Under his mail Reddic was sweating. On the top of the first gate beside him Valaric the Wolf and Sarvic and the three Jonnics and a dozen other men were probably sweating too. He hoped so, because that would mean it was the sun and the heat and not fear. On the road beneath the gate, within easy range of an arrow, stood a single forkbeard. He carried a shield and a spear with a white streamer tied to its top and he was just standing there. Further down the road, outside Varyxhun and away from the castle walls, another thousand forkbeards lined the valley, a single solid mass of shields blocking it from the Isset to the mountainside. The forkbeard on the road had Reddic's attention though, all of it, because the forkbeard on the road was Medrin Sixfingers and the shield he carried was the Crimson Shield of Modris.

Nearly three weeks since the ghuldog had bitten him and his arm still hurt. Nowhere as bad as it been on the way to the Devil's Caves but still sore. He hid it as best he could.

'I could shoot him,' muttered Sarvic. 'It wouldn't be any bother.'

Valaric growled, 'He comes to parley.'

'Fine. I'll take that up with Modris when I see him.' But he didn't lift his bow and they all watched in silence a while longer, sweat dripping off them. Reddic wiped his eyes. He didn't understand why they were all just standing and look-ing at each other and no one was talking. Down on the road Sixfingers looked bored and was leaning on his spear.

'Oh, get on with it.' Fat Jonnic nudged Valaric. 'He might not have sweated enough but I have.'

Reddic winced, but instead of throwing Fat Jonnic off the top of the gate Valaric sighed and closed his eyes and lifted the spear that had been sitting beside him all this time with its dirty white shirt knotted beneath the blade. He took one step closer to the edge and looked down at King Sixfingers. Took a long drink of water and then spat on the road below. 'Well then, Sixfingers?'

Medrin squinted up at them. 'I've heard your voice be-fore.'

'You have. In Andhun I stood against you on the beach and behind the city gates, and I stand against you now. Pox-scarred prince of filth! Twelve-fingered son of the Mother of Monsters. I'm Valaric of Witterslet. Valaric of the Marroc. Valaric the Wolf and I carry the red Sword of the Weeping God. Do you care to face me this time, Sixfingers, or are you the coward that even your own men know you to be?'

Sixfingers lifted his spear, stretched his arms and yawned. 'Three years in your swamp, Valaric of the Crackmarsh, and not a single new rebuke? Truly, the turgid waters have seeped into your head. Or perhaps the ghuldogs have taken a bite out of you? As for your challenge?' He shook his head. 'I'll fight you, Valaric of the Marroc, Valaric of Witterslet, you and I alone, but I'll fight you at the top of this road not the bottom, between sundered gates ringed by the burned corpses of those who follow your foolishness. It won't satisfy me just to kill you now; I mean to make an end of you that all Marroc will see.' His voice rose as though he addressed the mountain itself. 'For a year and a day this will be a castle of ghosts. Not one who hides behind these walls will I spare. Not one. Men will hang and women too. Children will burn.

Gibbets will rise and blood ravens will fly. The curse of the red sword lies on you all, Marroc of Varyxhun.'

Sarvic strummed his bow and then put an arrow to it. 'I've had enough of this.' But Valaric knocked the arrow aside.

Sixfingers looked up to the gatehouse again and cocked his head. 'Marroc who serve their king with good hearts tell me that tomorrow is your festival of Shiefa. They tell me you celebrate with ale and mead and dancing and singing and beckon the blushing bride of summer to shed her last clothes of winter. I'm told it's a time for bonfires and bedding maidens and that even the dead rise to watch. Make your festival a grand one, Valaric of Witterslet, wherever that is. I'll give you three days of kindness before I return with iron and fire.'

He turned and walked back down the road to Varyxhun. The army of waiting forkbeards lifted their shields and spears and roared and beat them one against the other in a slow steady rhythm. Sarvic drew out another arrow, and this time Valaric rounded on him and pushed him so hard he lost his balance. Sarvic threw out an arm to catch himself and almost barged Reddic off the battlement. 'Sixfingers, Valaric! Sixfingers the demon prince of Andhun! Have you forgotten?'

Valaric grabbed two great fistfuls of Sarvic's mail and pulled him close. 'Have I forgotten?' For a moment his face twisted into such a fury that even Angry Jonnic paled and took a step back. Valaric set Sarvic down. 'No, Sarvic, I haven't. But that doesn't make it right to shoot a man in the back when he comes to parley. Not even if that man's the devil.'

'Took a finger of courage, coming up here like that all on his own.' Fat Jonnic sniffed and scratched his chin.

'And don't you go and start admiring him, don't you dare. *You* didn't see Andhun.'

Reddic and Angry Jonnic stayed on the gate with a

handful of the Marroc from Varyxhun while Valaric and the rest of the Crackmarsh men climbed back to the castle. They slept the night on the battlements, eight of them out in the open wrapped up in their winter furs – the warm spring days didn't change how cold the nights could be. They spent the next morning there too, and by the time Valaric sent his Crackmarsh men to relieve them, Angry Jonnic was ready to go and fight the forkbeards on his own. They climbed the ladders from gatehouse to gatehouse, all the way to the castle walls where Sarvic and a few others stood watch, looking down at Varyxhun and the forkbeard camp and the glittering rush of the Isset winding off to the north. Sarvic nodded as Reddic came past. 'You wait and see. Sixfingers says he'll come the dawn after next. But he won't; he'll come tonight when he thinks we're all in our cups, raising them to Shiefa. Faithless forkbeard.'

Reddic thought he might go and look for Jelira, but even before he'd come down off the walls and crossed the castle yard, Valaric was waving at Angry Jonnic and so Reddic went too, and Valaric had the Aulian with him and a barrel full of arrows. He clapped Reddic on the shoulder. 'Those iron heads you brought? Fletchers from Varyxhun have finished making them into arrows. There's three thousand, give or take. That's ...' He frowned.

The Aulian smiled. 'Make them into bundles, ten arrows in each. One bundle to every man with a bow. What's left to stay in the armoury.'

'Ten arrows in a bundle?' Jonnic picked up ten arrows and then looked at the barrel. 'That's all? That's—'

'Not enough arrows,' finished Valaric curtly. 'So they'd better count.'

'Going to take us all day is what I was *going* to say!'

Valaric shrugged and pointed to two more barrels tucked in the shadows against a wall. 'Needs to be done though, so best you get on with it.'

Jonnic took a deep breath but Reddic got in first and put a hand on Jonnic's arm. 'Go and find the children who came with the smith from Middislet. They can do it. I'll stay with them and make sure it's done right.'

Valaric smirked as Jonnic stamped off. 'Arda won't let you anywhere near her. You know that, don't you?'

He was about to say he hadn't any idea what Valaric was talking about but by then the Wolf and the Aulian had turned away. The Wolf was laughing. And he was wrong too, because when Jonnic came back he came with Nadric and Jelira and the three children and there was no sign of Arda at all, and for a while Tathic and Feya helped with counting the arrows into tens and tying twine around them, until they got bored and wandered off to where Nadric and Pursic were playing. Jelira and Reddic finished the rest on their own. They talked, hardly noticing the time, Reddic about the family he'd had once and his new family in the Crackmarsh, Jelira about the days she remembered back before the Vathen, before the forkbeards came again, the days when Gallow had been her father. They talked about happy things, times and places and people that made them smile and forgot for a while about the harshness that over-shadowed them. By the time they were done with the arrows, the sun was setting and Angry Jonnic was coming across the yard. He clutched a jug of something, held it close like it was a lover, and for once he looked more merry than angry.

'Looks like Sarvic and Valaric are wrong and the fork-beards aren't coming tonight after all.'

Reddic reckoned that was the mead talking, given the night had barely begun, but kept the thought to himself. Jonnic beckoned Reddic forward, but when Jelira came too he shook his head and put an arm around Reddic's shoulder and walked him away, whispering loudly and stinking of drink. 'Got something for you.' He struggled for a bit while he tried to hold on to Reddic and the mead jug and get something off his belt all at once. Eventually he pressed a key into Reddic's hand. 'Valaric says to let him go. I don't like it, mind, but Mournful don't ever listen to me any more.'

'Let who go?'

'The Foxbeard.' He snorted and shrugged. 'Valaric says for you to do it. So go on then. Do it.' He staggered off.

Jelira looked at him, face filled with worry. Reddic smiled and showed her the key. 'Valaric says to let the Foxbeard g—' He shook his head at his own stupidity. 'I mean Gallow. Your d—'

And then he couldn't have said how she covered the ground between them except that one moment they were a good ten feet apart and the next she was wrapped around him, head pressed against his chest, arms squeezing him as though she was wringing water out of a blanket. She led him by the hand to the sixth gate, skipping past the Dragon's Maw and down the winding stairs to the dungeons beneath, past the cell where the strange-looking Vathan woman hissed at them and on to another. There was a guard on watch, sitting beside Gallow's cell, pressed up against the iron bars. Gallow was on the inside, pressed up against them too, and it seemed odd to Reddic that Valaric would waste a man to guard the forkbeard and stranger still that any guard would sit so close; and then he realised this wasn't a guard at all, this was Arda, and this was where she'd been when Angry Jonnic had gone looking and for the rest of the day too.

She stood up as she heard Reddic and Jelira and scowled. 'Whatever you two want on Shieftane, I doubt very much I'm going to like it.'

Jelira threw herself at Arda and hugged her the way she'd hugged Reddic. Reddic just slipped the key into the cell door, opened it and stood back. And then took another step away as the Foxbeard unfolded himself from where he'd been crouched beside the bars and eased to his feet.

In the cramped space he looked huge, a head taller than Reddic and twice as wide, with arms to wrestle bears and fists strong enough to stun a boar. But then Jelira let go of Arda and ran into the cell and threw herself at him, and that and the bemused pain and joy on the Foxbeard's face took away his menace.

'Valaric the Wolf says you're free to fight beside us,' said Reddic, which wasn't quite what Jonnic had said but it would do. But they'd already forgotten him. He watched the three of them wrapped up together tight in each other's arms, and a pang of longing built up inside him and he had to turn away. He went up to the yard and stared at the moon for a bit and then found Angry Jonnic and stole his jug of mead. In the Hall of Thrones half the Crackmarsh men and most of the Marroc from Varyxhun were singing and dancing. Up on the walls Sarvic and a few others kept watch, those who wouldn't trust a forkbeard's word, not ever. Reddic let them all be. For now he wanted to be alone.

When the moon reached its zenith, Jelira came and found him and asked him if he'd seen Nadric and the little ones. He pointed her to the hall and she went away again, but after she'd found them she came back and nestled beside him, and later Reddic took her hand and led her up to the castle walls and they sat on the battlements together and got drunk on Angry Jonnic's mead. Noises wafted up from the valley below but Jelira and Reddic were both lost, drunk on mead and each other, staring out over the Isset, which was lit up like silver by the moon.

The sun rose on the morning after Shieftane and then rose on the next and Reddic stood atop the first gate once more. Low grey cloud hung over the valley. The forkbeards were massing. The abandoned houses and taverns and stables and barns of Varyxhun had become their camp, and on the morning after the festival, as the Marroc nursed their sore heads, the forkbeards had erected an avenue of wooden poles along the castle road. Reddic didn't understood what they were at first, and then when he did, he wished he hadn't. Gibbets. While he'd been sitting and dreaming in the moonlight with Jelira, the forkbeards had rounded up the Marroc of Varyxhun who were too stubborn or too stupid to leave. Now they lined the road, dangling.

A column of forkbeards was winding its way out of Varyxhun. He watched a while longer until he was sure and then he ran to the wall. 'They're coming! The forkbeards are coming!' And when he peered closer he saw what it was that had kept them in the city these last few days. It wasn't some simple gesture of kindness that had made Sixfingers leave them alone until the festival of Shiefa was past. They'd been building, and now four siege towers eased their way onto the road.

There wasn't much to do now but watch and wait and pray to Modris.

24

THE FIRST GATE

Standing beside Valaric on the second of the six tiers of walls that rose up to the castle of Varyxhun, Gallow watched them come. The Lhosir marched up the road in the cool morning air singing an old song of the sea that Gallow knew well, a mournful lament for drowned men. A hundred feet short of the first gate they stopped. A few dozen pushed a ram towards the gate but they stopped short too. Gallow waited for the surge forward and for the fury of the battle to begin but it didn't happen. The Lhosir stood below him, out of reach of the gatehouse but right below the feet of the men lining the second tier, shields locked together over their heads, looking up in anticipation. For a long minute an eerie quiet fell over the road. Then Valaric raised his hand and held it high for three long heartbeats and let it fall, and as he did, a storm of stones and arrows flew into the shields from right above them.

The Marroc yelled and howled and hooted. The Lhosir held firm and took their punishment. Arrows stuck out of their shields. Men screamed and howled curses as stones hit them. Here and there Gallow saw a Lhosir fall, crippled or dead, but there were few. The air had a touch of sweat to it now, forkbeard sweat, men already sweltering under their mail and helms though the road to the castle lay in the shade of the mountain. No burning skin yet though. Valaric was saving his fire for when he needed it. The Lhosir simply stood there. They didn't even try to raise any ladders.

Gallow caught Valaric's arm and shook his head. Arrows into a wall of shields was a waste, even if they did hit a Lhosir now and then. 'They're drawing you in, Valaric. They're making you spend your arrows while their shields are strongest. Wait for them to make their move.' He looked at the stones around him. The Marroc had already thrown most of what they'd brought and the battle had barely started. Three hundred archers with some dozen arrows each and the same again waiting in the castle thanks to Arda and Nadric. Enough to kill almost every Lhosir who'd ever crossed the sea, but only if they were used with care.

Valaric's eyes blazed, itching for the fight. 'Every arrow, you beef-witted clods! Every arrow has to count! Every arrow and every stone! Hold! Hold!'

The first of the siege towers was getting close. The Marroc bowmen fell silent, and now it was the turn of the Lhosir to hoot and taunt and howl, peering from behind their shields and sticking out their tongues. There was a rhythm to their shouting, as if they were at the oars of their ships. The towers weren't for the gates, Gallow saw that now. Medrin meant to scale the walls directly from one tier of the castle road to the next, bypassing both the first gatehouse and the second. And Valaric, who had seen this too, meant to stop him. Marroc scurried to and fro, readying every stone and missile they could find. Valaric raised his hand again as the first tower came higher, as its top came close to the level of his feet. Every Marroc eye turned to follow him. The Lhosir watched too, hunched behind their shields. They understood what would come when that hand fell.

'Now!' Valaric's hand dropped, and the Marroc along the walls cried out to Modris, to old King Tane, to Diaran, even to the Weeping God. Stones and rocks and boulders rained on the Lhosir once more, and now lighted pots of fish oil burst among their shields. The Lhosir wavered and Gallow felt a pang of sorrow for them, for deep down these were his people. Nothing wrong with most of them, just men on the wrong side of a wall as stones smashed down shields and broke bones and snapped sinews. Arrows flew. Men wrapped in flames tumbled over the edge to the Aulian Way and the Isset below. Others slipped and fell, rolled on their backs; burning shields were hurled away. Medrin's Lhosir had no answer, no arrows of their own, no javelins, no stone throwers. Yet the towers came on.

'More! More!'

The Lhosir were packing themselves tight, pushing their shields closer. A jagged piece of stone as big as a man's torso went over the edge and smashed into a dozen of them clustered together. Half were crushed where they stood, the others sent sprawling. Gallow saw one man stagger to his feet with two arrows in his chest and vanish back under the wall of shields. How deep they were through his mail was anyone's guess. Smoke rose up the walls now, acrid, thick with the stench of burning men, of fish and hair and skin. Over the shouting he heard Valaric whoop as the Lhosir died.

Gallow closed his eyes. Medrin. Medrin had made this slaughter. Medrin and no one else and so Medrin would pay to make it right.

The first tower began to slide slowly back. For a moment Gallow's heart was in his mouth, begging and praying and willing for it to slip and roll and topple and fall and crush the others. The Lhosir were yelling to hold it steady. Yet now, when it mattered most, the stones and the arrows gradually wilted. The boulders became pebbles. The road fell quiet again as though both sides were holding their breath, waiting to see, all except Valaric who was screaming at his men for more. But when Gallow looked, he saw why Valaric's Marroc didn't respond. There was no more. They'd thrown everything they had.

The Lhosir shouts found a rhythm again. The tower

stopped then ground back up the road once more until it slid to a halt in front of Gallow, right in front of him because he'd been watching it and was waiting for it. A ladder on wheels, that's all it was, draped with heavy furs to protect the men climbing inside. At the very top the forkbeards had built a ramp like a drawbridge to cover the gap between the tower and the wall. Gallow readied his spear and waited for it to fall.

Now the tower was actually here, Valaric wished he'd saved some of the oil or the boulders. There was a runner on the way to the third gate calling for both but they wouldn't come in time. This wasn't how it was supposed to go. The forkbeards were supposed to die battering their way through the gates. Now his men were in the wrong place. He needed his soldiers here, all of them, and he sent a second runner for reinforcements, but it was all too late to make a difference. Cursed Sixfingers had out-thought him, that was the truth of it, not that any man around him would ever say so.

A dozen archers stood ready for the ramp to come down. Valaric stood in the middle of a semicircle of twenty men with spears and shields, the best of his Crackmarsh men with Gallow in the middle beside him. In his hand he held Solace, the Comforter, the red sword of the Vathen. In Andhun he'd told Gallow that the sword was cursed and he'd believed it too, but now he had no choice. 'When that ramp comes down, sod the arrows.' The forkbeards would be ready for that. They'd have their shields up, but maybe that meant for a moment they wouldn't see what was coming. 'When it comes down, we charge them. We hit them like bulls and we take their tower and throw it down on their heads!'

The forkbeards below fell quiet. Valaric and his men gripped their spears, waiting for the ramp to fall.

'Are you ready for us, Valaric of Witterslet, Valaric of the

Marroc, Valaric of the Swamp? Are you ready to die now?' Sixfingers was somewhere below and not far from the foot of the tower but Valaric couldn't see where.

Beside him, Gallow let out such a howl of hate that Valaric winced. 'Medrin!'

There was a long pause and then Sixfingers seemed to be closer. 'Is that you, Foxbeard?'

'My sword hungers for you!'

'They say you killed Beyard outside Witches' Reach. I hear he had the better of you and let you win.'

Valaric threw Gallow a glance then nudged him. 'Answer! You have to answer!'

'I'll not be as accommodating, Foxbeard.' Sixfingers was taunting them now. 'I'll be with you as soon as I can. While you wait, perhaps you might discuss with your Marroc friend which one of you I should kill first.'

Valaric shoved Gallow again. Idiot. 'Bring your worst, king of dogs,' he bellowed. 'My wolves hunger for you!'

'Then enjoy your feast!' There was a venomous glee to Sixfingers' voice but Valaric didn't have time to wonder about that because the tower shuddered and the ramp crashed down, and he was already moving and so were his Crackmarsh men because if there was one thing that got you killed in a battle more surely than a spear or an axe then it was doubt.

But the men waiting for them when the ramp came down were no forkbeards. They wore closed helms and ragged mail. They carried long Aulian swords and small round shields and their skin, where it showed, was chalky white. Shadewalkers. Sixfingers, somehow, had sent shadewalkers, and for a moment Valaric felt every part of him turn numb. The Marroc beside him thrust a spear through one porcelain throat. The shadewalker staggered but it didn't bleed and it didn't fall. Valaric heard a wail of fear and a cry of despair. He felt the air turn cold and sour and his men falter.

Gallow smashed a shadewalker with his shield. Another lost its hand, cut off at the wrist. It dropped its shield and grabbed a Marroc by the throat and throttled him while the Marroc stabbed it over and over, but Valaric had his own dead man to deal with, slamming its sword into him, battering him back with a strength that wasn't human. 'Stand!' he bellowed. 'Stand and hold them! Get the Aulian!' Salt, that was the trick wasn't it? But none of them had thought the forkbeards would send shadewalkers to do their fighting – who would have thought they could? And, besides, shadewalkers only came out at night, didn't they? How had Sixfingers done this?

His men were already breaking and running around him, the shadewalkers stumbling after them and then stopping, staggering in the daylight. Valaric screamed a roar of rage and frustration and hewed at the dead thing in front of him. He slammed two blows into its shield, and then it blocked a third with its long sword but the iron blade snapped. Solace carved a line across the shadewalker's face. The creature howled, its skin fell in on itself, and before Valaric's eyes it crumbled into dust and bones and a dizzying stench of death. Valaric reeled and swung at the shadewalker strangling one of his Marroc and half severed its head. It too crumbled before him.

'See! They die!' But he was too late. His men had left him, even Gallow. Fled, and now there were shadewalkers all around and he could feel the tower shake as the forkbeards climbed through its guts, and then suddenly there was one looking right at him with his shield over his shoulder as he climbed. Forkbeards he understood, and this one couldn't do a thing about it when Valaric lunged. The point of the red sword split the forkbeard's mail as though it was cloth and bit straight through to his heart. The forkbeard's eyes rolled back in surprise. He fell limp and dropped among the others behind him. Valaric bared his teeth and grinned:

this, *this* was what he wanted! He was standing at the top of the ladder and the forkbeards had to get past him. He'd kill them all, every single one of them. Alone if he had to.

'Valaric!'

And he *wasn't* alone. On the road behind him the shade-walkers staggered and lurched. Not a single Marroc had stayed, but two men stood firm nevertheless. The Aulian wizard with his satchels of salt and Gallow, battering the shadewalkers away from him.

From atop the first gate Reddic saw the Marroc surge into the forkbeard tower and then fall back and scatter and break, screaming as though they'd walked into the gaping maw of the Maker-Devourer himself. They ran like they had the devil at their backs and Reddic could see at once that the creatures who stepped onto the road were no forkbeards. They stood in a daze as though they'd never seen the sun. He gasped. 'Shadewalkers!'

'Look sharp!' Angry Jonnic didn't want to know. On the road beneath them the forkbeards were coming, a hundred or more with the ram they'd left short of the gates. A second tower was coming up the road and the next two weren't far behind. Reddic squinted at where the forkbeards had driven his Crackmarsh brothers away. The walls of the second tier overlooking the ram were already all but abandoned: where there should have been a hundred men with arrows and stones, now there were none. At the start of the day he'd been scared but there'd been a part of him that had thought they might win. Not any more.

'Ladders!'

The stone quivered under Reddic's feet as the ram hit the gates. He looked for something to throw but Jonnic caught his arm and shook his head. 'Wait.' He pulled Reddic away from the edge and pushed him down behind a merlon then shouted at the others to abandon the gate and go up to the next and pull the ladder up behind them. When Reddic made to get up to join them, Jonnic pushed him down again. 'I said wait!' He grinned and his eyes were wild and mad. 'The six of us up here won't stop them breaking through. Let them think they've got an easy ride of it. Let them think we've all run away like the rest. Keep nice and quiet and still. Then we can rain rocks and oil on them when they're not expecting it. Hurt them where it counts.'

'And then?'

Jonnic patted Reddic on the shoulder. They both knew what *and then* looked like. Reddic closed his eyes and shook his head. 'Scared?' Jonnic chuckled. 'There's no shame in that.'

But Reddic found he wasn't really, not any more. He'd gone long past scared and it was something else. 'There's a girl up in the castle. We spent Shieftane watching the moon together. I wanted to tell her something but I never did.' He shrugged and whispered a prayer to Modris the Protector. Beside him Jonnic did the same.

Valaric killed the next forkbeard to show his head at the top of the ladder. Oribas was scattering lines of salt on the road and Gallow was smashing the shadewalkers away, keeping the Aulian free to do his work. One by one he penned them in, and it seemed to Valaric that these shadewalkers were slow and clumsy and not so frightening after all. Yet there were no other Marroc here now. Just him and Oribas and Gallow against Sixfingers and all his army.

'Come on up, Sixfingers!' he bellowed. 'We're both here. The Foxbeard says I get to have at you first!'

'The sun, Valaric,' Oribas shouted. 'The sun steals their strength. But I have no fire to burn them, nor iron to kill them.'

'Your sword, Valaric!' Gallow had one of them wrestled to the ground and was smashing it over and over but it still thrashed and its mail turned his blade. 'The red sword. End them! I'll keep Medrin's curs whimpering in their holes for you!'

Valaric ran out from the tower and across the ramp. He smashed the red sword into the head of the one wrestling with Gallow and then watched as the Foxbeard ran to take his place. The red sword hacked down another shadewalker. Now that he was outside he could see the forkbeards were bringing their ram up to the first gate and the Marroc on top were already scaling the rope ladder to the roof of the second, fleeing without putting up a fight. Valaric raised his fists at them all, screaming at the top of his lungs, 'Cowards! You sheep! You're everything they say of us! If this is the best we are then we deserve everything they do! Mewling hedge-born clay-hearts, all of you!' Tears were running down his face. The Crackmarsh men he'd had with him, those surly old soldiers he'd quietly thought as good as any forkbeard, they were all gone, cowering along the zigzag road, past the next gate where they had stone and wood and iron to keep the shadewalkers at bay. Probably none of them could even hear him. No one except the Aulian wizard, who shouldn't even be here, and Gallow, a forkbeard. It made him want to fall on his own sword.

The second tower was close. Soon it would reach the road and fall open and there'd be no stopping them. He let out a furious howl, grabbed one of the shadewalkers from behind, picked it up and and threw it over the wall onto the throng of forkbeards below. He turned back. 'I have iron enough for these, Aulian!' He swung the red sword and listened to the air moan as the steel split the wind. A shadewalker fell with its head torn from its shoulders, the next with its face split in two, a third with the point driven through the back of its skull. They tried to defend themselves, but against the red sword, out in the sun and doused by Oribas's salt, they were as feeble as children.

Peacebringer. The red sword wanted them. One by one the shadewalkers crumbled to dust.

25

THE RAM

A movement from inside the tower caught Valaric's eye, another forkbeard shield creeping up. Gallow was there. He brought his axe down and the forkbeard beneath bellowed an oath. Valaric laughed. The last two shadewalkers were helpless quivering things, paralysed by Oribas's salt, and they didn't even try to stop him as he took their heads. He looked up the road to the third gate, praying to Modris that his Crackmarsh men had found their spines again, but no.

The second forkbeard tower reached the road and stopped, and even Valaric knew better than to stand alone against the dozen angry forkbeards who'd come howling out of it. He grabbed Oribas, turned and ran, shouting at Gallow as he did and didn't look back until he reached the elbow where the road turned from the siege towers and second gate behind him and doubled back on itself up towards the third. Past the elbow there were Marroc on the walls over his head again, more men with stones and arrows and fire. Forkbeards were coming out of both of the siege towers now, scores of them, and Gallow still stood alone to face them. Valaric could have murdered him for that. A forkbeard facing dozens of his own kin when a hundred Marroc had been too afraid? And for a heartbeat Valaric thought about running back to Gallow's side, facing them together, the two of them against the whole of Medrin's army just like it had been in Andhun. Utter madness, but when he held the red sword he felt immortal.

The forkbeards were advancing slowly behind a wall of shields, taking their time, content to walk the Foxbeard slowly back. As Valaric watched, an arrow from up on the fourth tier took one of them in the legs. Gallow threw back his head and roared out his challenge once more: 'Here I am, Medrin! Waiting for you!' The first gate was being smashed in without a single Marroc holding his ground to defend it. The second gate had the forkbeards from their towers behind it already. They'd just walk up to it and open it.

Valaric walked through the third gate with the red sword over his shoulder. He growled and looked at the faces around him, the men who'd broken and run at the first drawn sword. But as he prepared to bellow out his furious contempt, Oribas touched his arm. The Aulian took his hand and raised it high, the red sword still firm in Valaric's gasp. 'Men of the Varyxhun valley! For years you've feared those creatures. Shadewalkers that many of you thought could not be killed. Today one man alone with this sword has destroyed them.' He dropped Valaric's arm and lifted one of his satchels of salt. 'I have fought them too. You saw me. I didn't kill any and I had no sword, but I didn't run because I did not need a blade.' He sprinkled a line of salt across the road. 'Salt! Nothing more, yet it is like a wall of stone to them. They cannot pass. Throw it on their skin and it burns them like fire. Salt!' He threw the satchel down and pulled Valaric up the road, muttering under his breath, 'You'll have to give salt to every man now. I have no idea how many shadewalkers are in this valley but it's many more than you put to rest today. Tell them it works on the ironskins too. Men must know how to fight whatever enemy stands before them. You cannot blame them if they run when they do not.'

Valaric looked back through the open gate at Gallow, still alone, still facing the forkbeards. He didn't understand why the forkbeards didn't simply charge and overwhelm Gallow with their numbers. He stopped at the edge of the road and looked down. The ram was still at the first gate but the forkbeards must have smashed through already because he could see them clearing rubble on the other side and trading insults with the Marroc atop the second. Now and then an arrow flew down. One good charge and he still might sweep the forkbeards off the road and smash their towers. One good charge, but that was what the gates were for. So that he didn't have to. So that he didn't have to lose so many men, not yet.

Stuck in his throat though. He yelled down the road at Gallow, 'Foxbeard! Save it for the sixth gate, not the second.' He sighed and shook his head because walking away wasn't what forkbeards did when they could stand and fight instead, however stupid it might be. Yet after a moment Gallow backed away and the forkbeards didn't follow. Valaric took a deep breath and let it out between his teeth. The second gate wouldn't hold long, not with forkbeards on both sides. 'Two gates lost in a single day.'

Oribas touched his arm. 'They still have to open it. Then they have to clear the road and bring up their ram and you can drop rocks and arrows on them all the way. Your men have seen that shadewalkers can die now and the forkbeards cannot easily bring those towers any further; and if they do then I have an idea or two about how we might stop them.' His eyes were gleaming. 'Imagine many stones hitting the men behind that ramp as it opens. Hitting them very fast and hard.'

Valaric felt suddenly light-headed. 'What I want, Aulian, is to imagine the dragon coming out of that cave behind the sixth gate and eating them all. That would do nicely.'

Gallow was walking through the third gate while the Marroc there all looked away, pretending he didn't exist, closing the gate behind him. The Aulian was nodding to himself, lost in his own plans. 'I'll go back up to the castle now. You've got enough carpenters there and rope and wood. I could have one made by sunset. And the dragon of your stories will drown them, not eat them.'

Valaric unexpectedly sat down, because it was suddenly that or fall over. He felt dizzy and had no idea what the Aulian was talking about. He looked at his feet in front of him. One of his boots was light and one of them was dark. Which was odd because they'd both been light at the start of the day.

It was blood. 'Oh …'

Oribas was staring at him. The Aulian knelt down and pushed at the mail surcoat that Valaric wore down to his knees. He poked at something and a sharp pain shot right up Valaric's spine. 'One of the shadewalkers.'

'I don't even feel it.' Did he want to look? That was a lot of blood, but he'd run all the way up the road so it couldn't be too bad, could it? But Oribas wasn't even looking at him. The Aulian was waving his hands at the nearest Marroc and yelling for a mule, and at Gallow, and calling for his satchel, and all with an urgent panic in his eyes. Valaric sat humming to himself. Some old tune his mother had used to sing when he was a boy, one he'd forgotten for years.

Reddic listened to the forkbeards yell at each other and then tuned his ears for the scrape of wood on stone that would be a ladder but it never came. After another hour, when there still hadn't been any forkbeards climbing over the battlements, he needed a piss. Jonnic snarled at him. There were forkbeards all over the road below clearing stones so they could move their ram. They hardly weren't going to notice if some Marroc stood up on the gates and relieved himself over them.

Reddic turned his head. There were more forkbeards further up the road. The second gatehouse was surrounded. But more to the point, the forkbeards on the second tier could see him if they cared to look down. He couldn't even sit up. Didn't dare move at all. After another hour he just let it out. It was an odd feeling, lying down and pissing in his pants. Couldn't say he could remember ever doing that before. And there they stayed, the two of them alone, lying still as statues because that's what Jonnic said, while the forkbeards pushed their ram and then their army on up the road.

Oribas had barely got two Marroc to bring a mule when Valaric tipped over sideways, white as a sheet. Gallow caught him and eased him to the ground but the bleeding was worse than the Aulian had thought and so there wouldn't be any taking him up to the castle to patch him together. He'd do it here. They needed him. Without Valaric, the Crackmarsh men would simply break.

Oribas waved back the Marroc with the mule and beckoned Gallow closer instead. 'Hold him.' He eased Valaric onto his back. Blood still ran freely out of his leg, though it should have clotted by now. 'Pull back his mail.' He rummaged in his satchel wondering why the wound wasn't closing. If the shadewalker had hit an artery Valaric would have died back on the road so it wasn't that, but it just kept bleeding. There were desert animals that used the same trick on their prey. Bit them and then left them to bleed until they were too weak to run. He'd never understood how they did that. Spirits. Bad spirits, his masters had said, which was another way of saying that they didn't know either.

'I never thought I'd come back,' said Gallow out of nowhere. 'It was right that I did. I've made myself whole again.'

Gallow had Valaric's mail pulled back. 'Now get his trousers down.' Needle and thread and Firaxian powders to make the bleeding stop. Marroc clustered to see what he was doing. They stared at him and so Oribas stared back. 'Do you want to be the ones fighting the shadewalkers? No?

Then give me space to work! Fetch some wine. Good strong dark wine. The best you can find.' It might help Valaric or it might not but it would certainly help an Aulian scholar who'd never been so close to a battle in all his life until Gallow had brought him over the mountains. He set to work with Gallow crouched beside him with his weight on Valaric's shoulders.

'I made an oath on Shiefa's night. It was three years to the day since I left Middislet with the Screambreaker. I made an oath in blood, Oribas, a promise to fight no wars once this one is done. And after that I dreamed of how it would be if Medrin Sixfingers simply ceased, if he changed his mind and went home, if there was more to our horizon than bloody war and starving siege and a slow and unwelcome death. Can you do that, Oribas, wizard of Aulia? Can you make Medrin simply disappear?'

'No.' Oribas snapped. His stitching was ragged and there was blood all over his hands and yes, he was staunching it at last, but far more slowly than he should have. He shouted at the Marroc, 'Water! Bring water!'

Gallow stood up. 'I'll see we're ready for Medrin when he comes. We've lost two gates already. Yes, I'll be seeing to what needs seeing to, whether these Marroc like it or not.'

Oribas muttered and kept to his sewing, and of course Valaric woke up when he was only half done and almost jumped straight into the air even though he was lying down, and Oribas had to persuade him back and never mind how much it hurt. At least the wine helped with that, when it came.

The forkbeards were moving on now, swinging their ram around the elbow in the road. Past the second gate they were already clearing the stones the Marroc had left there to bar the way. A few Marroc still held the top of the second gatehouse, shooting the odd arrow to keep the forkbeards on their toes. It was never going to amount to much, holding the roofs of the gates, but Angry Jonnic still just shook his head when Reddic said they should go and climb on up to the second tier before the forkbeards cut them off.

'Sooner or later Sixfingers is going to come up that road. He's going to think he's safe, right until we put a pair of arrows into him.' Jonnic grinned and drew a finger across his throat. The ram rounded the corner.

Valaric just about managed to wait for Oribas to finish before he jumped up again. 'Gently on it!' The Aulian snapped at him. 'There must have been something on the shade-walker's blade. A wound shouldn't bleed like that. You should rest.'

But Valaric laughed and waved him away. 'Rest? You still have eyes and ears to see and hear that army, right? Rest? Don't you worry Aulian, there was nothing on the blade that cut me. I bleed. It's just the way it is.' Stupid thing for a man who'd made his life fighting, but then that wasn't how he'd ever thought he'd spend his time. A farmer like his father, like his brothers, like his uncles, like everyone he knew, and that's how it had been until the forkbeards had come and set to their rampaging. After that, knowing every wound would bleed had made sure he'd learned how to fight, how to take the other man down first, fast and hard.

He made himself forget the pain. Sixfingers was down there somewhere. He took a long look at the forkbeards and their ram and then moved among his men. He knew every one of them. Knew their names and who they were and what had dragged them from their homes and into the Crackmarsh to fight the forkbeards. Some had lost their families or their wives or their sons or their daughters. Others had stood up for themselves. A few had killed. And of course they had men come to the Crackmarsh to get away from Marroc justice too, but the marsh always heard the truth of what a man was running from in the end and when it did, they made their own justice.

He moved among the men who hated the forkbeards most of all. The ones who'd lost everything. The ones who'd come here ready to die, wanting it even. Men like him. He knew who they were, for they were the ones who looked at Gallow with stony dead eyes. Whose lips stayed tightly shut while their knuckles clenched white as he passed them. They stood together and watched the forkbeards below, threw taunts at them while the Lhosir laughed back from behind their shields and shouted insults of their own. One of the forkbeards threw a spear. Valaric plucked it out of the air and threw it back and it hit a shield hard enough to sprawl the forkbeard beneath across the road. The man wrenched it free and shook his fist. The others around him laughed.

The ram moved up towards the second gate. Marroc archers still held the roof, sneering at the forkbeards on the road and loosing an arrow now and then. A few men dead but it didn't amount to much, not unless you were the one with the arrow sticking out of you. Valaric waited until the ram was right up to the gate, until the forkbeards were getting ready to swing it, then he smiled and nodded. This time his stones were in the right place.

The first fell squarely on the nose of the ram, shattering its frame and smashing the front wheels. It slithered off the wood and into a half-dozen forkbeards and dropped them over the edge to the tier below. Valaric didn't see them land but he heard the screams as they went. The next two stones landed short. Men were crushed flat and the ram smashed sideways, throwing another few forkbeards over the edge as it slewed. The last stone was perfect. It bounced off the cliff and landed on the front of the ram again, and this time the back end jerked into the air, scattering forkbeards, twisted and then rolled as it landed and slipped over the edge. In a great rumble of stone and cracking wood and howling men, the ram tumbled off the road and smashed itself to pieces behind the first gate below, crushing a few forkbeards more as it did. Valaric picked up a bow and let fly a couple of arrows while the forkbeards were still reeling. After that he told his men to hold their fire and watched to see what the enemy would do. He looked at the siege towers, still where the forkbeards had left them. They'd be back with those, he thought, and that made him start looking for Oribas. Maybe the Aulian could think of a way to bounce a stone straight on top of them from right up in the castle. Save them the bother of all that walking back and forth.

He winced. The wound *was* going to be a bother. He could tell that now.

26

THE THIRD GATE

They felt the gate shake as each stone hit the road above then shudder as the ram crashed beneath them. Jonnic was grinning like a snake. Reddic could hear the Marroc up above shouting and forkbeards shouting back, but from where he lay he couldn't see much of what was going on. Later Jonnic moved across the gatehouse roof until he was overlooking the road up from Varyxhun. By then the fighting had moved on. A while later still, he cackled. 'You know what I see? I see a banner coming up the road.'

The forkbeards from the siege towers opened the second gate from behind and then held their ground wherever they found shelter from the Marroc above them, yelling taunts and insults up the mountain. Gallow stood on the fourth tier now, looking down. The men around him threw rocks when they thought they saw something they could hit, but for the most part the battle had gone quiet. In places the two armies were only a few dozen paces apart, but as the sun came round the mountain, even the insults stopped. The Lhosir crouched behind their shields and the Marroc archers taught them the hard way where was safe and where was not. Gallow understood exactly what Medrin was doing. He could have drawn his men back to the first gate until they were ready but he was trying to make the Marroc waste what missiles they had before the charge came.

Down below, the forkbeards lifted something up to the

road behind the second gate. 'Another ram,' said Oribas.

Gallow frowned. 'They'll not split one of these gates with something that size.' He squinted, trying to make out what it was for. There were a score of forkbeards pushing it, maybe half a dozen on the ram itself, the rest with huge shields to keep the Marroc arrows at bay. Then as it climbed the road, a figure stepped out from the huddled mass of shields behind, an ironskin, and as the Fateguard rounded the corner of the road and passed the men with their ram, it suddenly broke into a run and raced for the third gate. A storm of stones and arrows flew at it until Valaric screamed at his men to stop. They were all wasted on an ironskin and besides one Fateguard could hardly take a castle gate. It wasn't even carrying an axe.

The Fateguard ran to the gates and slid to its knees. It spread its arms wide and pressed its hands against the wood and iron and didn't move.

'Salt!' shouted Oribas. 'Rain salt on him!' Gallow was puzzled. Just another way to make the Marroc waste their arrows? Around him the Marroc pointed and laughed. Then fracture lines of rust spread out over the Fateguard's iron skin like water freezing on glass. The lines of rust spread across the iron of the gate too, to its bars and bolts and hinges. Oribas was still shouting, hurling salt over the edge of the road, the Marroc still laughing and taunting the forkbeards. The ironskin stayed where it was, perfectly still, until it finally fell under a barrage of stones from above and broke into pieces as though its iron armour was all but empty. And then the forkbeards charged.

Sarvic had a little line of stones each the size of a man's head lined up on the top of the third gatehouse. He stood poised behind one, waiting for the ram. The forkbeards hadn't even bothered to build a roof over it and they were going to suffer for that. He had a torch and his buckets and pots of fish oil too, ready to set alight and drench the forkbeards and burn them back down the mountain. He felt a strange elation. The forkbeards were doomed. They had their shields against the rain of stones and arrows, but here and there he saw men fall, arrows finding their way through the gaps, and Valaric still had his stone slabs to smash the ram off the mountainside.

The first blow of the ram hit the gates under his feet. The Marroc threw their stones and their burning oil. Sarvic watched the pots burst on the shields below and rivers of fire flow over their sides and pool on the road. Men screamed and the smell of fish and burning hair rose around them. The smell of victory. And then he heard the cry behind the gate, and when he ran to look the Marroc there had already turned and were fleeing up the road, waving their arms and screaming, 'The gates! The gates!' And the gates hadn't simply been split; they'd been smashed right down, their hinges shattered. They lay on the road now, twisted and askew on the rubble the Marroc had piled behind them and forkbeards were already scrambling through. They left bodies, plenty of them, and their ram. A score and a half of dead maybe, but Sarvic's heart pounded and filled with dread as he saw how many were still alive.

Valaric watched the third set of gates shatter. The iron devil had done this. He glanced at Oribas, who looked aghast. More forkbeards were coming already, their shields raised high, hiding something in their midst. When Valaric looked hard, he saw what it was: two more of the iron devils. They ran past the abandoned ram as stones and arrows showered them. A rock the size of a man's head hit one of the forkbeard shields, flattening the warrior who carried it, breaking a dozen bones and knocking the man beside him down into a pool of burning oil. The flames embraced him. As he screamed and rolled, three arrows hit him and he lay still.

Another forkbeard fell and then another, and then they were climbing through the rubble behind the gate and Sarvic was screaming at his men to stop them. Another head-sized rock hit one of the iron devils, knocking it down and crushing its shoulder and arm but it hauled itself back to its feet and carried on. Stones and arrows pinged off its armour. The men on the gate were throwing everything they had at this one handful of forkbeards, and Valaric wanted to scream at them to stop because they'd have nothing left when the rest of the army passed beneath them.

The forkbeards and their iron devils were through, onto the open road past the third gate, to the elbow where it turned back on itself and rose towards the fourth. Sarvic was already shouting up to Valaric for it to be closed. Fat lot of good that would do if the iron devils got to it, Valaric thought – might as well leave it open and fight them on the road. Around him his Crackmarsh men were milling about, not sure whether to stay and throw stones at the forkbeards below or to form up behind their shields and face the ones coming up the road or whether to simply flee back to the fifth gate now. For a moment Valaric didn't know what to do either, and then Gallow came and stood beside him like an unwelcome ghost. 'The red sword, Valaric. The Edge of Sorrows will put an end to your iron devils.'

Valaric pushed him away. He knew he couldn't fight that many, not when he was limping with a bleeding hole in his leg.

'I'll do it.' Gallow held out his hand. 'Give it to me.'

'And if you do and then Sixfingers' forkbeards take you down and take that sword, what then?' He barged past Gallow. 'Oribas? Aulian!' The Aulian was arguing with Sarvic, the two of them bawling up and down the mountain at each other. A shout went up from the forkbeards below and they started to move again, surging for the third gate. 'The ram!' Valaric bellowed. 'Smash that ram down there off the road for a start.' He looked up towards the fifth gate but the Marroc behind it couldn't hear, not from so far away. He'd just have to trust them to drop rocks on the forkbeards as they came. Not too much of a worry. Fat Jonnic was up there. He'd be good for that.

Oribas was yelling at him: 'Salt! Salt will stop the Fate-guard. But it takes only one Lhosir to scrape it away.'

Cursed leg was hurting like buggery. Everywhere around him people were shouting, wondering what to do. 'Go to the fifth gate, Aulian. Put your salt there, everything you've got.' More and more forkbeards were coming up the road, hundreds and hundreds of them. Arrows flew, whether Valaric wanted them to or not, and stones too, and Sixfingers had to be in among them somewhere, didn't he? Yet Valaric was damned if he could see where. The Marroc of Varyxhun were starting to edge away, turning in dribs and drabs to run back to the fifth gate. His own Crackmarsh men were on the edge too.

He felt a door close inside him, and then another and another until only one option remained. He nodded quietly to himself, pleased with where it led him. 'Sarvic!' Oribas was halfway up a rope ladder to the top of the fourth gate, a sack of salt over his back. 'Sarvic! Sarvic! Come up from up down there and go up to the fifth gate! Close them and then put every piece of stone you can find behind them. Tell Fat Jonnic to smash any ram off the road the moment it turns the elbow. Then get as many arrows as you can find and bring them here.'

The fourth gates stood closed. The forkbeards were almost on them, one iron devil in their midst. Arrows and stones rained uselessly on their shields. Valaric closed his eyes and took one long deep breath and then another. Enough. And when he opened them again, his voice was changed. Calmer now, more certain. Sooner or later it had been coming anyway. He raised the red sword over his head and stood atop the rubble behind the fourth gate. 'Marroc of Varyxhun! Shields and spears!' Maybe some of them had heard the orders he'd given to Sarvic, maybe not. 'Marroc of Varyxhun! Sword and axe!' If they had maybe they'd know the fifth gate was about to be sealed and that they were on the wrong side of it, that there was no going back. 'Marroc of Varyxhun!' Now he had their attention, he jumped from the rubble. With the tip of his sword he drew a line in the dirt across the road. 'When that gate falls, this is where we stand. Sixfingers comes no further!' He stood in the middle of the line and turned to face the gate, crouched behind his shield, the red sword ready to spike the first forkbeard who dared come close. Two hundred Marroc fighting men in stolen mail and helms with forkbeard swords and shields and spears all of their own. Ten abreast they'd bar the road. The iron devils would break these gates as they broke the last, and when they fell, the forkbeards would come though, and these men would either turn them back or else they'd die.

The first man to stand beside him was Gallow.

Angry Jonnic moved suddenly. He looked at Reddic and nodded. 'Get your bow ready and some arrows. Nice sharp ones. Easy now. Don't let anyone see us. That banner's coming closer.'

Reddic risked a peek between the merlons. There were a dozen or so forkbeards on horseback and everyone on the road was getting out of their way. 'Sixfingers?'

'How many banners do you see in this army?'

'Just the one.'

'Well then, who else?'

It still took him a moment to get his head round it. The forkbeard king himself, and he and Angry Jonnic were going to kill him. He found himself a good sharp arrow as Jonnic had said. One of the ones they'd made from Nadric's arrowheads, the narrow Vathan ones for poking through mail.

The Fateguard was almost at the gates. Oribas watched it. Its head was tipped back as though it was looking right at him.

'Well, wizard?' Sarvic was up from the third gate, twitching like a mouse who'd seen a hawk and then suddenly lost track of it.

'Salt and fire and iron.' Salt and fire and iron killed shade-walkers. He was fairly sure they'd work on the ironskins as well. *Fairly* sure. 'Can you shoot well enough to put an arrow though that mask?'

Sarvic laughed. 'I can shoot as well as any man, but that? That's luck.'

'Make sure one of your archers is lucky then.' Oribas closed his eyes briefly and ducked back behind the battlements, letting the Fateguard come a few steps closer before he rose with a pouch of salt in his hand and emptied it straight down onto the Fateguard's upturned face. His old masters had never taught him to lift a sword but everyone learned to throw: salt, water, holy oil, a dozen potions and powders. The salt burst over the Fateguard and it froze and then staggered as if blind. Oribas picked up the sack he'd carried over his back and hacked it open with his knife. He hefted it over the battlements, shaking more salt over the Fateguard and where it stood. The Marroc around him lit pots of fish oil and poured them over the wall. A choking stinking smoke of burning flesh and fish wafted up amid the screams of pain and the howls of rage.

'Arrows!' Sarvic fired first, his arrow pinging off the Fateguard's mask. The next arrow missed completely and the next bounced off its armour. Amid the cries of burning men, more Lhosir pressed up the road. The ram was coming.

Another arrow struck sparks from the Fateguard's mask. The ironskin turned its head away. Oribas swore, but then an arrow came up from the roof of the third gate below. It struck the Fateguard in the face, straight through its mask. For a moment Oribas was transfixed, and then the iron devil toppled back, wreathed in salt and flames, and Oribas screamed with glee. It *could* be done! He ran to the edge of the gate and looked down to see who'd fired the arrow but a spear struck the stone beside him and he cowered instead. Another hit the Marroc next to him in the throat.

The forkbeards charging up the road. He'd almost forgotten them.

Achista watched the Fateguard fall. She drew out another arrow and nocked it to her bow and waited for another one of them to make a mistake. Sooner or later they always did.

Reddic risked another look over the edge. The riders were trotting up the road and there weren't as many as he'd thought. Seven. Six iron devils, four at the front and two at the back, and one man in the middle carrying a bright shield that could only be the Crimson Shield of Modris the Protector, the holy shield of the Marroc which had stood in King Tane's throne room until the forkbeards had pillaged it.

Sixfingers.

'You ready?' Angry Jonnic clenched his teeth and spat. 'Pity Sarvic's not here, but he's not. Quick and steady and take your time to aim. Chances are we won't get a second shot. And he'll have mail on, and good mail at that. If you can, shoot him in the face.'

Reddic glanced at the rope ladder up to the second gate. The forkbeards had the whole second tier now, and the third tier too by the look of things, but the ladder was still there and no one had come down from above or up from below to make sure there were no Marroc left on the roof of the gatehouse. Their mistake.

'Now!' Jonnic rolled into a crouch and then stood straight with his bow drawn back in one smooth motion, all far too perfect for Reddic, who tried to get to his feet and draw back his bow at the same time but stumbled and almost fell over. He saw Sixfingers on the back of his horse look up. He saw Jonnic shoot his arrow straight at the forkbeard king's face, just like he'd said, and he saw the Crimson Shield jerk up with an impossible speed to catch the arrow and turn it away. He didn't see his own arrow because as he let it fly he slipped sideways and he had to drop his bow to catch himself as he fell. He landed on his sore arm and howled.

Arrows and stones and fire poured into the press of Lhosir around the fourth gate. A part of Oribas recoiled in horror and another part clenched in fierce glee. The gates hadn't fallen and the Marroc at last had the Lhosir helpless. Overhead, behind the fifth gate, they were tipping down every piece of stone they could find, oblivious to Valaric's orders. Oribas watched a chunk as big as a man crush a handful of Lhosir warriors and sweep three more off the road. He tried to spot the second Fateguard in the melee but it was impossible with all the forkbeards lifting their shields overheard to keep the arrows and stones at bay. Now and then when he thought he caught a glimpse he threw salt, but it was lost in the chaos. The forkbeards were being crushed and burned with no way to fight back. It made his stomach churn and yet he'd seen what they did to the Marroc who defied them. He'd been there and watched as they'd sliced open a man's back and snapped his ribs off his spine and drawn out his lungs, and these Lhosir would do the same to all of them if they won. To his Achista and to her brother Addic, to him and to Gallow. To Gallow's children and to every single Marroc they found, man, woman or child.

A Marroc beside him lurched and fell with an arrow in him. Oribas peeked long enough to see a few dozen archers back at the elbow of the road. Marroc archers bought with silver that the forkbeards had stolen from their fathers, that's what Valaric would say. He ducked, but most of their arrows were going up to the fifth tier. A few more arced overhead.

'The gates!' Oribas barely heard the shout. 'The gates! It's happening.' He ripped open another sack of salt and pulled it to the edge of the battlements, heedless of the arrows now. All he could see were shields packed together. He threw the salt anyway in case some of it found its way somewhere useful, but even as he did, the forkbeards suddenly moved apart and Oribas saw broken and empty pieces of iron armour lying on the road. Now the ram rushed forward. It took a dozen blows this time. Small consolation; but before Oribas could get to the ladder and scamper up to the fifth tier, Sarvic was pulling him face down into the stone as the arrows began to fall again.

Gallow saw the iron of the fourth gate brown with rust and flake and peel and split. He saw the dust rise off it with each blow of the ram and the first hinge snap. The stones piled behind the gates held the ram a while longer; and the gates, when at last they cracked and fell, toppled awkwardly, and the Lhosir had to clamber through them, over them and around them, picking their way through the rubble. Not that it made much difference. It was tempting, when the gates gave way and the enemy came screaming through, to give in to the fury, to let out his own scream and charge right back at them. Yell to shake their very bones and eat their souls, as the Screambreaker had done on the day he'd shattered King Tane's Marroc outside Sithhun. He felt the urge, hot and fierce, and beside him Valaric felt it too, but the forkbeards had to climb over the rubble and there were Marroc archers who still had arrows to shoot them as they did, and it was better to hold the line, to keep their shield wall waiting for the Lhosir when they finally reached clear ground. They growled at each other then, he and Valaric, snarled at one another to hold fast come what may. The first forkbeards came screaming with their spears raised high and Gallow lifted his shield to meet them and turn their sharp iron aside as he stabbed back with his own, while beside him Valaric savaged them with the red steel of Solace. They were mad, these Lhosir, swept away by fury. They'd survived the press of the gates, the fire and stones and arrows. They were burned and battered and now they charged without any thought for themselves. They hurled their spears at the very last with such force that the men who took them in their shields reeled and staggered, and then they smashed into the ranks of the Marroc with their axes raised high and brought them down, splitting skulls, hooking away shields, stabbing with knives, and for a moment Gallow felt the Marroc line waver under the ferocity of that first rush; but then beside him Valaric's red sword lashed out left and right with a fury that even the forkbeards couldn't stand and Gallow felt the Marroc harden again. They would hold. They could. They believed, and for once Marroc would face Lhosir and win, toe to toe, shield to shield.

He lost his spear, torn out of his hand when he drove it into a Lhosir's foot. He hacked and slashed with his axe, battering at each man who stood in front of him, and it was strange fighting in a line of Marroc because the soldiers behind him didn't do what they should, and when his axe hooked a shield, no killing thrust came at once from behind.

A spear sliced him open along the back of his arm. He barely felt it. An axe hit his shoulder, turned by his mail and he might not even have noticed. He couldn't hear over the noise, and it was a long while before he realised that most of the screaming was his own.

*

Angry Jonnic dragged Reddic to his feet. 'You crazy Marroc!' He was yelping with joy. 'Did you see what you did?'

Reddic stumbled up. Down on the road only a few dozen yards away the iron devils had stopped. They were staring up at him and in their midst a man lay sprawled across the road, hauling himself sideways by one arm, screaming in pain. Reddic blinked. *That's King Sixfingers?*

'I did that?'

'I think you shot him in the foot.' Jonnic loosed another arrow at the forkbeard king but he twisted and lifted the Crimson Shield in the way even as he screamed bloody murder at the pain. 'His horse threw him too. Now let's finish it!' But the iron devils had already jumped down to shield Sixfingers with their own bodies, and other forkbeards on the road were pointing and shouting. Some were already running at the gate with a ladder. Jonnic let another arrow fly, swore, let off one at the forkbeards with the ladder instead and then threw his bow over his shoulder. 'No use us staying here now.' He pushed Reddic ahead, who climbed as fast as he could with Jonnic right on his heels. When he got to the top of the second gate and looked back, the forkbeards had raised their ladder and there were iron devils climbing after them.

Reddic lunged for the ladder up to the third gate. They were rope ladders, lowered from above and just as easily pulled up again. He shouted out in case any Marroc were still holding the roof up there. 'Iron devils! Help!'

There were. Hands reached over the edge to haul him up and out of the way. He heard a woman call for the Aulian wizard to come down from the tier above. He twisted, looked back down and reached for Jonnic right behind him. Their hands touched and then the first iron devil threw an axe from its belt. Angry Jonnic arched and spasmed. His hand slipped out of Reddic's and he crashed back to the gatehouse below and lay still.

'No!' Reddic screamed. He almost climbed back down, even though he knew in his heart that Angry Jonnic was already dead, but other hands pulled him away.

'No,' said another voice, and then the wizard was there, breathless and wild-eyed. He pressed something into Reddic's hand. A pot of oil. 'Wait for it to climb. When I throw my salt, you throw this in its face. You understand?' The wizard sounded angry and suddenly Reddic was angry too. Red-hot furious angry. He nodded as the sounds of iron scraping on stone came closer. The ladder ropes shook. An iron-gloved hand reached over the battlement and there it was, the face of the devil. Its mask and crown. Reddic had never seen one so close. He wasn't sure any of them had. He saw it for a moment, long enough to remember for ever, and then the wizard threw a cloud of brown salt into the iron devil's face. It hissed and froze and Reddic smashed the pot over its crown. The wizard jabbed a burning brand into its face and it burst into flames.

'Move! Back to the fourth gate now!' An arrow tore the air and buried itself in the iron devil's face, straight through the slats of its mask. It tipped back, toppled and crashed into the tower below, knocking another ironskin off the ladder as it went. Reddic stared over the side. They'd landed on Jonnic, both of them. The one with the arrow through its face was still burning. It didn't move.

'Get the ladder up.' The archer reached past him. A woman, and with a start he recognised Achista. Then the Aulian wizard was pushing him.

'Up! Up! Plenty more of those to kill if you have the stomach for it. Plenty more.'

As he climbed, he heard the wizard and the Huntress behind him, arguing about who should go last.

Valaric didn't understand how the forkbeards were doing it but they were slowly turning the tide and winning. Never mind that they had to run through the gatehouse with men firing arrows down on them. Never mind that they had to clamber through the stones strewn across the road to break their shield wall and stop their rams, never mind the ribbons of burning oil and the stones that still fell among them, slowly they were winning, and the Marroc around him were falling one by one – falling dead or falling back. The red sword danced in his hand, happy and filled with purpose, yet no matter how many forkbeards he killed there were always more.

A spear stabbed at his leg, reaching under his shield. The red sword split it in two and lashed at the forkbeard who held it, but Valaric felt the pain as the wound Oribas had stitched together ripped open again. And he could hear the sword humming, he really could, but the noise was in his head, not in the world outside, and it was getting louder and louder, drowning out everything else, and then for a moment it stopped and suddenly there were no forkbeards left in front of him any more because they were backing away, turning and running, and the Marroc had won after all, for once they'd really won.

Valaric's eyes rolled back. He pitched forward and smacked face first into the hard stone road.

27

THE RED SWORD

Back on the top of the fourth gate now, Oribas watched the Lhosir leave. Others might have routed and fled but the Lhosir didn't. They moved quickly enough when the Marroc were shooting and throwing rocks at them but this was no broken rabble, no matter what the cheering Marroc thought. They'd had enough, that was all. They'd taken the first two gates and smashed in the third and the fourth, and all in one day. Against a castle that was supposed to be invincible, they might well feel pleased with themselves.

'Oribas!' Gallow was crouched over a body, beckoning. Oribas rolled his eyes. There was going to be a lot of this. He could probably resign himself to spending every day of the rest of his short life stitching Marroc back together just so he could watch them go and get killed again, but then what else? Was he going to sit and do nothing and watch them die? No.

He climbed down to the road and turned his head from the bodies as he walked. Lhosir mostly, this close to the gates. The air and the stones stank of burned flesh and that wretched fish oil and the road was slick with blood and a greasy ash. He wondered if someone ought to organise a counter-attack but none of the Marroc seemed to have the heart. If anything they looked more battered than the Lhosir they'd driven back.

Gallow's waving grew frantic. Oribas trotted to him and saw that it was Valaric. He'd ripped himself open again and lost a whole lot more blood and this time he wasn't going to drink a few cups of water and get up again. Oribas swore and set to work, and when he was done Valaric was still alive and even had a chance to stay that way as long as someone could convince him to just lie down for a few days. He found some Marroc to carry the Wolf to his bed and had Gallow swear in blood to see Valaric up to the castle and to sit on him if that was what it took to make him lie still. Then he took the red sword and put it in Gallow's hand. The Foxbeard, when he took it, held it as though it was a snake.

Oribas waved Gallow away after that and forgot him almost at once. There were a dozen other Marroc who needed him, a few lives to save that would otherwise have bled out and a few he couldn't help at all except to make them more comfortable. There would be many more, he knew, as the fighting moved up the tiers and the Marroc couldn't simply drop things on the forkbeards any more. By the time he was done, the sun was setting, a blazing fiery glory sinking behind the mountains across the river. Achista came and sat beside him and gave him some water. He drank it without any thought and passed it among the injured, and it was only when she took his hand and pulled him away that he realised she'd come for more.

'Valaric has sent for you.'

'Is that stupid man up and walking again?' Oribas ground his teeth. 'He has only so much blood inside him, and when it comes out I can't simply put it back. I've told him myself but perhaps my accent confuses him. Please explain to him that the next time he tears himself open he might die whether I am there or not. Even if I am, I'm not sure I'll be minded to stop it.'

'You can tell him yourself.' Achista dragged him to his feet. He followed with a numb reluctance, exhausted, and they walked up the road between knots of Marroc soldiers who clearly felt the same. As they passed through the sixth gate he looked up at it and at the Dragon's Maw beyond, barred to keep its mythical dragon at bay. Oribas didn't believe in dragons. Valaric had said that the castle was unassailable and Gallow had said much the same, yet they'd lost four gates in a day.

'I'm missing something.' He shook his head. 'My people came and settled this forsaken place with its bitter winter cold. They built this castle and their bridge over the river and the forts that look over it. They built a road halfway to the sea. They traded with the Marroc but they didn't stay and after fifty years they left. And the story they left was of a flood that rose to the very gates of their castle and swept everything before it.'

He turned to look Achista in the eye and stopped. He'd thought she meant to drag him back to the hall where Valaric held his war council but the look on her was quite different, a look he'd come to know. And she did drag him to Valaric's hall in time, but only after she'd taken him somewhere more private first, and when they finally walked in, long after nightfall, and Valaric snarled at him and demanded to know where he'd been for so long, Oribas only smiled. He felt calmer now.

'The tomb under Witches' Reach,' he said. 'The Aulians came here to bury something. All this way, and now King Medrin has brought it back. I've seen it.' He stopped to look at Valaric. The old Marroc looked white as a shadewalker himself, droopy-eyed, holding himself up by clutching on to the table. 'And you need to rest, Valaric the Wolf.'

Valaric smashed a fist into the table. 'And how long can I rest before the forkbeards are smashing in my doors? At this rate they'll be here by tomorrow! How do we stop them, Aulian? Your people made this place – how do we stop them?'

'Shadewalkers and Fateguard, Valaric the Wolf. We must

put an end to their monsters. You still have walls enough to deal with the rest.'

Gallow sat in the castle yard, his back against the wall among the Marroc soldiers, exhausted and rocking back and forth, picking at the dead skin on his fingers and yet quietly smiling. Arda sat beside him and held his hand while the little ones played tag in between the Marroc. Jelira was somewhere else with the young soldier Reddic. A little storm crossed Arda's face whenever she spoke of him, and Gallow didn't know whether it was because Jelira was still so young or because the Marroc boy was a soldier, or perhaps because that's simply how mothers were. Reddic seemed brave enough and Gallow felt churlish standing in the way of any happiness at a time like this and so he let it go and sat quietly with his Arda. They didn't say much, even if they hadn't seen each other for most of the last three years. Somehow talking seemed a waste of the little time they had left.

He slipped slowly out of his reverie to see Oribas and Achista coming across the yard with Valaric hobbling and limping beside them. Arda squeezed his hand, a little warning – a reminder of what he'd promised, perhaps, but she needn't have worried. She looked up as Valaric reached them. 'You look terrible, Mournful.'

'Shut it, woman, or I'll throw you at the forkbeards. Might do a sight better than throwing rocks at them. Rocks just come at you the once.' He looked half-dead. 'And no, Foxbeard, before you ask: I don't want a plough fixed or an axe sharpened.' He tossed a belt and a scabbard and the red sword onto the ground at Gallow's feet. 'You were supposed to take this away from me.'

'I did.'

Oribas glared at him. 'You know very well I meant you to carry it, not simply leave it lying on the floor.'

'I don't want it.'

Valaric lowered himself painfully to his knees and sat down beside Gallow, breathing hard. 'Well who else? I'm done, as you can see. Your wizard says I'll fall down and die if I try to fight any more. So I can't use it so I'm not giving you a choice.'

Oribas hissed between his teeth. 'You should not even be walking. Lying still! Perhaps, Gallow, you can tell him that. Gods know I've tried enough times to make him understand!'

'Oh please stop, you clucking old hen!' Valaric leaned into Gallow. 'Four gates fell today, Truesword. That leaves two. With their shadewalkers and those iron devils, two gates won't last us long.' He glanced again at Oribas. 'The wizard says someone has to take this sword to Witches' Reach and kill the creature Sixfingers keeps there.'

Arda still held his hand. He felt it tighten again but she didn't speak. Valaric's fingers closed on Gallow's shoulder, digging deep. 'Sixfingers is killing us. Go to Witches' Reach. Take your cursed sword. The wizard has a way out of the castle. He hasn't seen fit to share it so for all I know he means to fly, but he says it can be done. There's a Marroc as can take you through the mountains past the forkbeards. Paths your sort don't know. You can be there in a couple of days, maybe three. We'll hold as long as we can but, for the love of Modris, be quick! The wizard says you're a killer of monsters, Foxbeard, so kill whatever it is Sixfingers has under Witches' Reach and do it soon. I can't spare you any men, but if you happen upon Sixfingers while you're out and about, you're very welcome to him.'

'Killing Medrin won't make any difference, not now.'

Valaric pushed hard on Gallow's shoulder, levering himself up again. 'Have some time with your wife before you go, Foxbeard. I'll never hear the end of it anyway but you might as well.'

253

He limped away, leaning on Oribas, arguing with him about arrows and some such. After they were gone Arda let go of Gallow's hand and turned his face to look at her. 'Promise me,' she said with eyes as wide as mountains. 'Promise me that when this is done you'll give away that sword and you'll come back and we'll live in old Nadric's house and make wire and nails. Promise me that and I'll be glad I came all this way to find you again. Promise me, if that wizard's got a way out, you'll take us all away when you've done this thing, and never mind anything else. Promise me that too.'

Gallow cupped her face in his hands and kissed her. 'I already did.' Somehow it was easy this time. 'When Medrin's dead they won't be looking for us any more.'

'And you'll leave Valaric to his war and come back home and sod the Vathen too?'

'I made you an oath, Arda. A forkbeard blood oath. I mean to keep it.'

'Good.' A hint of a smile twitched the corner of her mouth. 'And you'll fix the roof in the barn?'

'Leaking again?'

She wrinkled her face and nodded. 'You never did it before you left and Nadric was next to useless, and even your old friend Loudmouth couldn't make it right. Stayed good for a bit but now it needs fixing again.'

'First thing I'll do.'

'Promise? Most important promise of all?'

He laughed and smiled and took her in his arms. 'I promise.'

For a moment she let him. Then she pulled away and glared. 'Actually no, I do have an even bigger and more important promise for you. Promise you stay alive. Promise me you send these forkbeards and their shadewalkers and their iron devils all to the Isset and into the sea. Promise me you win, Gallow Truesword.' Her eyes were aflame.

'You know I can't promise those things.' He reached for her again and again she kept her distance.

'You can try.'

'That I can, Arda, that I can. I can promise that much'

She let out a snort and then a shrug and then let him hold her. 'Well, then I suppose that'll have to do.' She took his hand and started to lead him away. 'Come on. Your children would like to see you before some forkbeard monster puts an end to you. Let them know why it was all worth it. Work hard on that one, Gallow. Maybe if they believe you then I might too.'

But Gallow stayed where he was. 'I made an oath, Arda. I said I'd stay, and so I will.'

'And I release you from it for this one thing. I don't want to, but Valaric's too proud to ask if he thought there was someone else. And I know you, Gallow Truesword. You want this.'

Gallow shook his head and held out the red sword in its sheath and then dropped it in the dirt and took Arda in his arms instead. 'I do. But I want this more. If I'm going to die fighting Medrin, I'll die here, on the walls, with you near me. I'm not going to Witches' Reach, Arda. This time I'm staying here with you.'

She held him tight. 'Valaric's going to blame me for this, you know. You tell him it wasn't my fault.'

Gallow buried his face in her hair. 'Valaric's wrong – there *is* someone else. Not that he'll like it when I tell him who it is.'

Later, outside a cell not far from the one where Valaric had held Gallow, Oribas and Valaric stopped. Valaric shook his head. 'I still don't like this, wizard, not at all.'

'I know.' Oribas smiled.

'She's a Vathan.'

'It's me who must trust her, not you.'

'You say that and then you ask me to give the Sword of the Weeping God to her? To a Vathan?' Valaric opened the door. He did it carefully and with several armed Marroc guards around him. The Vathan woman glared, full of fury. She looked at Oribas and cocked her head, and Oribas felt he understood her at once. She was the same as Gallow, the same as Valaric, each of them cut from one cloth and then scattered to fall in three different lands.

'You want something,' said Oribas, and he held out the red sword and watched her face flush with wonder. She reached for it and he stepped away. 'You may have it but you must earn it. Isn't that always the way of these things?' He handed the sword back to Valaric and waved the rest of the Marroc away and sat down with Mirrahj and set to telling her, right from the start, of Witches' Reach and the shadewalkers and the ironskins and the Mother of Monsters that had made them. When he was done, he found he couldn't read her face at all, and she followed him out of the dungeons meek and quiet as a dog, and he had to keep reminding himself that she was more wolf than dog and more tiger than either.

Valaric kept asking how they were going to get past the forkbeards. To Oribas it seemed strange that he was bothered. The castle had been made by Aulians. Of course there was a secret way out and of course he'd found it. The wonder was that he hadn't found more.

28

THE HUNTRESS

No one knew who started the rumour but it spread through the castle like a plague: Sixfingers was dead, that was why the forkbeards had pulled back. Not that it meant they'd leave, but for now the Marroc cheered and drank and sang songs and threw taunts down the mountainside to where the forkbeards were building wooden shields to protect the lower tiers from Marroc stones and arrows. Gallow watched. If Medrin was dead then the Lhosir would make the mother of all pyres for him. They might just burn the whole of Varyxhun. They'd speak him out for days too, one after the other, those who knew him telling of his deeds over and over as he walked the Herenian Marches to the Maker-Devourer's cauldron. And maybe it was all true, and Gallow did see many pyres when he looked down from the castle to the city, but none near big enough for a king. Even so, the Marroc paraded Reddic around the castle walls: the hero who'd put an arrow into the forkbeard king – and maybe he had, and Medrin was just slow to die.

The Marroc had seen Gallow fight too. They'd seen him stand up to the shadewalkers and stand up to the forkbeards at Valaric's side. Foxbeard they called him now, and quietly put aside what he was though he made no effort now to hide the fork growing in his beard. The ones who'd seen him hold the shield wall behind the fourth gate all remembered Andhun now as though they'd never forgotten how he and the red sword had turned Medrin Twelvefingers into Medrin Six.

Oribas found him staring out over the valley as he always did at sunset. Everywhere else it seemed the Marroc were waiting for the Lhosir to give up and go home. But the Lhosir weren't like that, although no one wanted to hear it and even Valaric called Gallow a sour old man who preferred fighting to being with his family.

'I leave for Witches' Reach tonight,' said Oribas quietly. 'The quicker it's done, the sooner the ironskins will trouble you no more.' He looked furtively around as though afraid they might be overheard. 'I wish you would come with me. It's not that I don't trust this Vathan, but ...'

Gallow slipped the belt from his waist, slid the scabbard from the loops that held it there and handed it to Oribas. 'Take it. Let her keep it, Oribas, no matter what happens.'

'Hunting a monster again. It'll be strange not to have you at my side. I've searched the library but there's nothing. Salt will bind it, I think, but to make an end ...' He nodded to the sword. 'The Edge of Sorrows. If anything can.'

Gallow put a finger to his lips. 'Do your best, Oribas. No one will fault you. Now take a moment to be quiet and watch the sun go down.'

Oribas sidled closer. 'Sixfingers isn't dead. I know this.' Gallow turned sharply, but before he could speak Oribas leaned in and whispered in his ear, 'There were always ways in and out of this castle, my friend. Aulian ways. Achista has been to the Lhosir camp. I will tell you where. Decide when it is right for others to know.' He stepped back and shook his head. 'There is still a secret to this place, old friend. Something I haven't found. I feel it. Look for it if you can while I'm gone.'

'You can't wait to go. Why?'

Oribas shrugged. 'Since I came here, I have watched men fight one another. I have led many to shameful deaths and I am made small by what I have done. This creature, though? It gives me an honest purpose once more.'

For a while Gallow said nothing. They stood together and watched the sun set until the last brilliant crescent of orange slipped behind the mountains on the far side of the valley. As that last light died, Oribas nodded and turned to Gallow and clasped his arm. 'And so now I go. Farewell, friend. We each have our monster to face.'

Gallow took his arm and held it fiercely. 'And we'll slay them, wizard, and I'll see you again, if not here then in Middislet, a little past the Crackmarsh in Nadric's forge. Look for me there.' He smiled. 'But if you want your welcome to be a warm one then come filled with stories and not more adventures! Fare well, Aulian.'

'Fare well, Lhosir. I vow I will not die first.'

'Aye and so do I, and that's one of us an oath breaker right here.' Gallow pushed him away and watched him go, then turned back to the darkening sky across the valley. After a little while he left that too to be with the people who mattered most of all.

A quiet fell over the castle after sunset. Men slept or kept watch. The forkbeards were skulking at the foot of the mountain and Addic was limping his way to the kitchens. He went there every night after dusk and struggled his way to the cool caves deep in the mountainside that passed for pantries and cellars. He leaned on a staff that had once been the shaft of his spear but now had a crook on the top from which he hung a lantern. Short of sitting on the battlements dropping rocks on forkbeards, there wasn't much else he could do. So he came every night and counted the sacks of grain and the barrels of onions and beans and the hams to make sure all was as it should be. They had food for weeks and everyone had full bellies but he liked to be sure. And to be useful.

Now he caught the flash of a lantern ahead, quickly hidden, and stopped. That people might take to stealing food was why he came to do his counting; but that he might catch them at it was something he hadn't imagined and now he wished he had – that, and that the shaft of his spear still had a point on the end instead of a lantern and that he could still walk without it.

He took another step. 'Who's there?'

The lantern ahead flared into life again and started bobbing towards him. The air was cool after the stuffy warmth of the evening outside, although night would swiftly bring its chill. 'Addic?'

'Achista?' He stopped as she came into the circle of his light and he saw her. 'What are you doing here?' He smiled. 'You're not stealing food, are you?'

Achista came closer and stopped in front of him. 'How's the leg today?'

'Like it's on fire, just like it was when you asked this morning.'

'Oribas says you should rest it. You should listen to him.'

'Oribas says that to Valaric too. Do you see *him* listening?'

She smiled but he could see that something was wrong. 'Pig-headedness a disease now, is it? Suppose it must be.'

There was a rustle and a scrape from the caves further on and then the glow of another lantern, and slowly two more figures emerged from the shadow – Oribas, who spent half his time in the castle library carved high into the mountainside with its balcony and its hundred long thin doors that let in a glory of light when they were opened. And then the Vathan woman. Last he'd heard she belonged in the dungeons. They both had sacks slung over their shoulders.

'What are you all doing here?'

Oribas frowned at him. 'I told you to rest that leg. Does no one in this castle listen? Do I speak the word badly? Rest? R-e-s-t. Is that not correct?'

The Vathan woman shook her head and tried to push on past but Addic hopped into her way. She glared at him. 'Getting food for our journey, Marroc.'

Ah. He looked at his sister Achista. 'What journey's that?'

Achista took the staff gently out of his hand and passed it to Oribas, then put his arm over her shoulder and led him back to the kitchens. 'Oribas has something to show you.' A spikiness crept into her voice and he knew that whatever it was, he wasn't going to like it. 'There's a passage under the gates that runs beneath the Aulian Way right to the bank of the Isset. A way out. And Sixfingers isn't dead.'

The Vathan woman growled. 'I mean to change that.'

'He keeps a monster in Witches' Reach,' said Oribas quietly. 'The mother of the iron devils. We must kill it.'

Addic almost laughed. 'I see. A wizard and a Vathan. And what, sister, will you do?'

'Someone has to show them the secret ways.'

'The Aulian knows them, or he knows enough.' But he was wasting his breath and he knew it. She was going so that she could be with him, one way or the other. To keep him alive or die by his side, and he had the sudden sense that he was never going to see her again, a horrible sickening feeling in the pit of his stomach worse than the pain in his calf when the iron devil had cut him open. And now that it mattered the most, he couldn't think of a thing to say, because nothing would change anything.

Achista led him down into the cisterns where fresh water from the tarn above the castle drained through a series of tunnels and channels. They hobbled together to the far side where the water lapped at a hole in the wall not much bigger than a man.

'The water makes its way down to the Isset.' Oribas sounded smug. 'It took me a while to work it out, but if you squeeze through the tunnel quickly widens. There are steps. I think it goes down the mountain under the gates but I suppose it hardly matters how it gets there – what matters is where it ends.' He knelt down by the hole and squeezed into it, feet first, dragging his satchels behind him. 'I told Gallow where it is before we left. Since I know you will now tell Valaric too, make sure he posts a guard here. The Lhosir may see us. It's best to be sure, and though I have not yet found them, there may be others.' He vanished into the gloom of the hole. The Vathan woman followed him. She had a sword now, Addic suddenly realised. Someone had given her a sword even though Valaric had forbidden her from carrying one. And then he looked again and saw what sword it was. He backed away and shook his head.

'What are you doing, Achista? What are you doing?'

She took his hand in both of hers. 'We go with Valaric's blessing, brother.'

Words dried up and stuck to his tongue. 'The Vathan. The sword. Does he know?' He stared at her and saw it in her face. Yes, he did. And he hadn't said a word.

Achista turned away. She'd never been able to lie to him. Then she turned back and embraced him. 'Goodbye, brother. And good luck. Modris watch over you.'

'Over you too, little sister.'

She let him go, handed back his staff and his lantern and slipped quietly into the hole without another word. Addic stayed where he was, watching long after she was gone. There were tears in his eyes.

Eventually he turned his back and hobbled up through the castle to the room that Valaric the Wolf had taken for his own.

29

THE WIZARD'S WAY

Valaric stormed around the castle. Gallow watched him hobble in a fury from one battlement to the next, taking it out on anyone who happened to be near and swearing at Gallow now and then. For his own part, Gallow shrugged it away. So the Aulian had given them a way out, so what? It was all the better, wasn't it? When Medrin broke through the last gate, maybe they could slip away.

'A fine gift,' Gallow said, which only made Valaric storm even louder, but by the evening he'd limped down to see the tunnel for himself, cursing and snapping and snarling at his injured leg.

'And what does one do with this gift, Gallow Foxbeard?' he snapped when he'd seen it. 'If I had a new leg I'd be out there in the middle of them in the small hours of the night, wreaking havoc.' His eyes narrowed. '*You* know forkbeards better than any of us.'

There were plenty of Marroc who could have gone instead of Valaric, but with Addic crippled, Achista gone and Angry Jonnic dead, Valaric was in a mood for arguing. Maybe it was his way of getting his own back for Gallow refusing to go to Witches' Reach, and maybe even Arda felt a twinge of guilt for that because when Valaric told her what he wanted, she only closed her eyes and nodded. By the middle of the next night, Gallow was at the bottom of the shaft with the last of Achista's Hundred Heroes behind him, a handful of the Marroc who'd seen him fight at Witches' Reach and a few

Crackmarsh men who'd heard of the Foxbeard of Andhun and believed in him enough to follow him into a fight. There should have been more, and if it had been Valaric with the red sword leading the way then every Marroc in the castle would have come. But it wasn't, and despite what he'd done in front of them all, there weren't so many Marroc ready to fight beside a forkbeard, not here in Varyxhun.

Oribas's tunnel rose higher into the mountain but it was the going down that interested Gallow. They crept through the trickle of icy water, ever lower until the tunnel ended in a hole and the trickle splashed through it into some reservoir below. There were no steps, no ladder, only a gap the height of a standing man and then ice-cold water and a darkness that seemed to eat the light of their candles. Gallow peered and lowered a lamp and looked about and then handed the lamp to a Marroc, closed his eyes and dropped. The cold was shocking. His mail and his weapons dragged him straight down, but when he found his feet and stood on the bottom, the water only reached his chest. He looked back up. The lamplight from the shaft lit up a cavern shaped like a tadpole, the tail rising up out of the water into the heart of the mountain. Where that passage went not even Oribas knew.

He waded forward. It was slow and difficult and he kept losing his footing, and the cold was like a vice gripping him ever tighter. Ahead of him the roof of the cavern dropped to the water, pushing down on him, making him duck. Oribas had said there were Aulian pictograms etched into the stone where the water would lead him out but it was too dark to see them. He ran his fingers over the rock instead, feeling until he found their notches and ridges and then took a deep breath and then another, filling his lungs one last time before he dipped his head into the freezing water. Snowmelt, he remembered, that's what Oribas had said. Water that had made its way down from the tarn above the castle. He could feel himself freezing, his arms and legs already sluggish. He reached up, hands to the stone ceiling above him and walked and fell and floundered and stood up again, pushing himself forward as quickly as he dared. His head broke the surface in a second cavern, utterly pitch black. The floor rose and the water fell away until he was out, shaking himself and his furs, jumping up and down, making his heart pump faster again. Made him wonder how people as small as Achista and Oribas had come through without freezing to death, but maybe Oribas had some potion or powder for that. *Straight ahead*, the Aulian had said. *Straight ahead until you crack your head on the wall and then veer to the right and you'll see some moonlight*. So he walked with one hand reaching ahead of him and when he felt stone he veered to the right, and half a minute later he saw moonlight reflected in the dampness of the walls. He thanked the Maker-Devourer, not that the Maker-Devourer either listened or cared, and turned back to call the rest.

Reddic dropped into the freezing water, the last Marroc to go. He squealed as the cold shocked the air out of his lungs. The Marroc ahead of him turned and glared. 'Quiet, boy.' He followed the man in the darkness through water that reached almost to his neck.

The soldiers held hands, each whispering to the man behind what was coming, pulling each other onward. Reddic ducked his head beneath the water along with the rest of them and prayed to Modris, but when he felt the stone close over his head he still knew he was going to drown; and when his head found the air again and he breathed a deep chestful of ice-cold air, he felt a relief like the moment the sun had risen after his night with Jelira and the ghuldogs. He hurried after the rest, all of them picking up speed now, keen to keep moving, shaking off the water and the cold and eager for the fight. Out of the cave they scrambled up a vicious path that twisted from the bank of the Isset up to the Aulian Way as it wound along the valley beneath Varyxhun castle. He followed the others and they crouched in the shadows of an overhang.

Reddic found he could barely meet the Foxbeard's eye. There he was, hunched over two bodies. Dead forkbeards, and somehow knowing that the Foxbeard had killed two of his own only made him even more terrible and Reddic was suddenly very aware that he'd lain with the Foxbeard's wife in the caves of the Crackmarsh and then spent the night of Shieftane staring at the moon with his daughter, or someone he thought of as his daughter. He hung back. Sarvic, Valaric's right hand now, squatted beside Gallow. Rumour had it they'd once fought together against the Vathen at Lostring Hill and that the forkbeard had saved Sarvic's life. Hard to imagine when you looked at Sarvic now.

Gallow's eyes raked them. 'Medrin and the Fateguard will be in the heart of the camp. Fateguard don't sleep. Keep away from them.'

Sarvic glanced at Reddic and Gallow's eyes followed. 'The Aulian wizard says the iron devils can't cross a line of salt. Any of you bring salt with you? Any of you keep it dry through that sump?' He bared his teeth and drew his sword and pointed it at Reddic. 'On the left, you're with the Foxbeard. You wait out of sight for a hand of the moon and come at the camp from the castle road.' Where the forkbeards' watch was sharpest and they all knew it, but Sarvic left that out. 'On the right, you follow me. We go around the other side. There are Marroc in Sixfingers' army, our own kin. We need their arrows. You see a bow, you take it. A bowstring, you cut it. Kill and fight as much as you like but remember it's the arrows that the Wolf wants from us. Watch the road and remember your path. Every man makes his own way back. We'll not wait past dawn.'

None of the Marroc spoke. Gallow rose and began to lead

his men away. Reddic decided the sword must have been pointing to his right and followed Sarvic instead.

There were men here he knew, Gallow had no doubt of that. Most of Medrin's army would be younger Lhosir, men like the ones he'd seen when he'd sailed with Jyrdas One-Eye to take the Crimson Shield. But there'd be some older men too, men like him who'd fought in the Screambreaker's war and found a taste for it in their blood and never given it up. For almost twelve years he thought he'd been free of that hunger but Mirrahj had taught him he was wrong. He knew better now. He'd never be free of it. He could put it aside – for Arda he could do that much – but be free of it? No.

He took his time. When he reached the edge of the Lhosir camp he kept the Marroc down and out of sight. He watched the waning half-moon creep up through the sky, wondering how long Sarvic would need before he found where Sixfingers' archers kept their arrows. Wondering how far he, Gallow, might get among them before someone realised who he was. If he could get to Medrin himself, and if he did whether that would be enough to make them go away. But that wasn't how it worked among the brothers of the sea, and besides Sixfingers still had his ironskins. They'd spot him long before he could run a spear through Medrin's heart.

The moon crept over the top of his hand. Time enough. With a sigh and a snarl, half-regret and half-hunger, he stepped out of the shadows to where the nearest Lhosir sentry must be. 'Hoy! Filthy *nioingr*!' He couldn't see the man but he was there, and sure enough a furious Lhosir came striding out from a cluster of stones long fallen from the mountaintop.

'What flap-eared piece of—' Gallow rammed into him shield first, battering him back. The force knocked the sentry off balance, and he stumbled and fell. Gallow drove his spear through the Lhosir's neck before he could say another word.

'Gallow Foxbeard,' he hissed, 'that's who.' He stepped over the body and quickly on.

Sarvic dropped to the banks of the Isset and crept through the shadows, hidden from the moon. Reddic followed. They slipped into the fringes of Varyxhun where the river touched up against it. The Isset was flowing fast and high, still rising every day as the late spring warmth reached the deep valley snows. There were no walls here and it was easy enough to creep into the deserted streets. The emptiness put Reddic on edge. He was used to the quiet of the Crackmarsh but he'd been to towns often enough on the back of his father's cart to know they were bustling places, full of life. Varyxhun was dead, abandoned. As they crept deeper in, they began to pass the gibbets where Sixfingers had hung the Marroc who hadn't run. From the castle they hadn't seemed so many, but now Reddic saw them all. A hundred of them and more.

'Sixfingers wants his kin-traitors to remember what they're fighting for,' hissed Sarvic, and Reddic winced at the savagery in his voice. Kin-traitors. That's what the Crack-marsh men called the Marroc who fought for the forkbeards, but the forkbeards had their own word for it. *Nioingrs.*

Sarvic stopped. He waved the other Marroc into the shadows and crouched down and put a finger to his lips. Reddic strained his ears. He heard voices. Marroc voices.

Three Lhosir sat beside their fire at the edge of Varyxhun, picking dirt out of their fingernails and trading battle stories. They'd been fighting the Vathen in Andhun, and not long ago at all by the sounds of it. They heard him coming and were already up and on edge as Gallow strode towards them out of the dark. As he stepped into their circle of firelight and they saw his face, they scrambled to their feet. None of them wore mail.

'I'd be very pleased to hear more.' Blood still dripped from the tip of his spear as his arm whipped back and he threw it. It struck the middle Lhosir in the chest just beneath the breastbone. He flew back and fell, twitching, trying to raise his arm as blood poured from his mouth. Gallow hefted his axe. The other two were quick, he'd give them that, with their shields propped up by their sides and their spears leaned against their shoulders. But not quick enough. He was up close before they could bring their spears to bear and between them before they could overlap their shields; and while he barged one back, he dipped almost to his knees and swung his axe across the earth – low enough to snip the stems of spring flowers and also to snap an ankle or two. A Lhosir screamed. The last one dropped his spear and went for his sword but he was too hesitant. Gallow stood and his axe rose high and came down, over and inside the guard of the other man's shield and into the Lhosir's collarbone. It bit deep. The Lhosir clutched at Gallow. His eyes rolled like a madman. He sputtered and coughed, blood welling up in gouts in time to the last few beats of his heart and then his arms went limp. Gallow pulled his axe out of him and turned on the other. The crippled Lhosir was gasping for breath. Hopping back. He was desperately young, young like Gallow had been once when he'd first crossed the sea.

'Medrin took an arrow through his chest from a crazy Marroc when he was your age. Didn't stop him from being king.' Gallow scratched at his mangled nose, his own reminder of a first year of war. 'You know who I am?'

The Lhosir didn't answer. He had his back to the mountain now, and so to the dozen Marroc creeping up behind him out of the darkness.

'I'm the Foxbeard. I'm here for Sixfingers. Built a new ram yet?'

He caught a flash of a glance away and then perhaps the Lhosir heard a noise: he turned sharply in time to see three Marroc come out of the night to pull him down. They dragged him to the fire and pushed his face into it until he stopped screaming. Good enough a way as any to get some attention, Gallow supposed.

Sarvic waved them forward. They kept low, creeping through the fringes of the Marroc camp. A few Marroc soldiers stood around a fire in the middle, looking off to the commotion on the other side of the town. In a ring around the fire were a dozen hunting shelters, branches lashed together and draped in hides. They'd each have ten or maybe twelve Marroc inside. The arrows would be at the end near the fire in leather quivers. In the Crackmarsh they did the same.

Sarvic nodded. He pointed to three of the Crackmarsh men and then to the guards and drew a finger across his throat. They moved silently forward and then struck all at once, one hand over the mouth, pulling back the chin, the other with a knife to open the throat, the way every Crackmarsh man learned for when they met a forkbeard one day. Some guards, Reddic knew, wore mail across their throats, and this was exactly why, but Sarvic had known without looking that these Marroc wouldn't have such a thing. They were Marroc and so they only got what the forkbeards threw away.

They lowered the dead guards to the ground around the fire and Sarvic beckoned the others forward. He pointed at them and then to the shelters, made a creeping silently gesture and then another throat-cutting motion. And it took a moment before Reddic realised that he really did mean them to creep inside and kill every single Marroc here.

Gallow sent half his Marroc looking for the Lhosir ram. The rest scattered across the town, kicking over fires and kicking in doors, setting roofs alight, murdering forkbeards where they could get away with it. With a bit of luck they might find some place where the Lhosir kept something that mattered – food, boots, arrows, anything they could take or smash or ruin. There were Lhosir in the houses all around him, asleep, half-asleep, in the middle of waking, but few on the streets. A man stumbled out of a house – Gallow darted sideways and split his head open. The more chaos the better. Let them think they were under attack by a thousand. Keep moving, that was the key – plenty of gloom and shadow in a town at night. And noise, and while the Marroc made mayhem, Gallow ran straight and in silence with one thing on his mind: Medrin. And he almost reached the heart of Varyxhun too, the big barn-like hall beside the market square. Almost, and then Lhosir were running towards him to cut him off, and they were armed and carried shields and none of them was afraid to face him, and when they were close enough for Gallow to see their faces, he understood why. He slowed and stopped and braced himself for a fight. 'Hello again, Ironfoot.'

'Foxbeard.' Ironfoot nodded. 'Your warning about the gates of Andhun was timely. Without it my men and I would all be dead. So I thank you for that.' Ironfoot was limping. Survived then, but not without a scratch.

'I heard men talking. Medrin took Andhun and held it then, did he?'

Ironfoot nodded. 'He holds the castle and what passes for their king as a hostage. Frankly, the Vathen could help themselves to the rest any time it took their fancy, but who knows? Maybe they're like the Marroc and like to keep their kings alive.'

Gallow laughed at that. 'And you, Ironfoot? Do you want to keep yours?'

'If you had Sixfingers or old Yurlak or even the Scream-breaker himself up in that castle of yours, Foxbeard, do you think I'd hesitate for even a second before I came at your walls? Would any true Lhosir?' He laughed too and shook his head. 'We're not like them, Foxbeard. Why are our shields not locked together, you and I, side by side?'

'Because you follow Medrin and Medrin is no Lhosir.'

'I disagree. He's a brother of the sea and our king.'

'Yet you wouldn't hesitate for a second if I held him?'

'Not one heartbeat.' He smiled again. 'You don't like him, find him and call him out. The old way.'

'I'm here, Ironfoot. But I don't see him, I see you.'

Ironfoot shrugged again and let out a sigh. 'You picked the wrong night, Foxbeard.'

For a moment they looked at each other, smiling and remembering how they'd fought together once, remembering the men they'd known, the mighty and the small, the noble and the craven. And then slowly a change came over Ironfoot's face and he lifted his shield another inch. His grip tightened on his spear and quietly they set to killing one another.

Reddic slipped into a shelter, easing in, careful as could be. There were quivers of arrows piled just inside. He crawled past to the first Marroc. They were pressed together, sharing their warmth, wrapped in too few furs for a mountain spring night. He slipped out the knife he was supposed to use to cut their throats. Valaric and Sarvic and a few of the others had shown him how to do it back in the Crackmarsh, how to come up behind a man and open his neck the way Sarvic had done to the guards outside. Do it so he'd bleed out in a few heartbeats and die without a sound. But here, to a man wrapped in furs, lying asleep. To a Marroc?

He slipped back outside, pulling the quivers after him. Behind him the closest of the Marroc muttered and turned in his sleep. And he'd barely got out when a shout went up and inside one of the shelters a struggle broke out. He saw the hides bulge at the side and two men roll out. Then a scream went up from another and Sarvic popped his head out of the next and looked sharply around. There was blood on his knife and blood all over the rest of him. He stank of it. He dived back in and pulled out a dozen quivers then thrust them into Reddic's arms. He glanced at Reddic's knife as he pulled away, frowned a little and then shrugged. 'Hard to kill a man in his sleep, even if he's a kin-traitor. I'll not say more. Now go!'

Other Crackmarsh men rolled out of the shelters clutching quivers, and Sarvic sent each one scurrying away. As they ran, Marroc tumbled out after them, clenching their fists and shouting. Sarvic waited long enough to stab a few and then ran too. There seemed to be a lot of them to Reddic, so perhaps it wasn't just him who'd found it hard to kill a man in his sleep.

Ironfoot lunged with his spear at Gallow's face. The man on his right tried to hook away Gallow's shield with his axe but Gallow tipped back a couple of inches at the last moment and the Lhosir missed. For a moment his arm was open. Gallow's spear flicked up and down and sliced an exposed wrist, cutting deep; the Lhosir howled and fell back. One fewer to fight; still, that had been enough for Ironfoot to ram his spear point at Gallow again, creeping it inside the rim of his shield, straight through Gallow's sodden furs and into his mail hard enough to knock the wind out of him. Gallow lifted his shield over Ironfoot's spear and turned his body, catching the spear in his cloak. Ironfoot dropped it and stepped smartly away, pulling an axe from his belt, but Gallow kept turning, snatching up the tangled spear in his shield hand and lashing it at a third Lhosir, making his head ring under his helm, and he would have lunged with his own spear and finished him too if Ironfoot hadn't barged him away. As they staggered apart, Gallow shook the spear free. The three men eyed each other.

'I'll give you a good death,' said Ironfoot.

'I'd speak you out myself, Ironfoot, but I doubt your friends will allow me that luxury.'

'You turned your back on us, Foxbeard.'

Gallow snorted. 'We've all turned our backs. We're not what we thought we were, Ironfoot. I've travelled half the world to learn it, but really we're nothing more than a pack of savages. And whatever nobility we had – if we ever did – it's dying. Men like you and me, there won't be any more of us. Whether Medrin wins or whether I kill him, it makes no difference. Our time has gone. We'll grow old and look at the world and wonder what happened to it, and as we turn feeble, we might wonder whether it would have been better if we'd died in our prime and thought ourselves heroes and seen a little less of what was to come. But by then it'll be too late.'

Thanni Ironfoot shook his head. 'We're Lhosir, Gallow. We are what we are.'

As one, Ironfoot and the other Lhosir charged. Ironfoot went for Gallow's head. Gallow ducked and ran past, shifted his grip on his spear to take it behind the point and stabbed it into the back of the other Lhosir's neck as though driving in a knife. The Lhosir stumbled and fell and a spray of blood spattered across his shield and across Ironfoot's face. For a moment Ironfoot was blinded. Gallow kicked his shield down and rammed his spear into the hollow of Ironfoot's neck. He collapsed without a sound and Gallow stared at what he'd done. A good man. One who remembered the old ways. His shoulders slumped and with a weary sigh he levelled his spear at the Lhosir who'd gathered to watch, some in mail and some not, weapons drawn and wary but not wanting to interfere in another man's fight.

'Speak him out. Speak him out well.'

He turned his back and walked away.

30

THE FIFTH GATE

They travelled through the night and most of the day that followed and then bedded down in an old goatherd's shelter high above the Devil's Caves. Achista and Oribas wrapped themselves tightly together in their furs. The Vathan woman slept alone, haughty and cold. Achista thought they might stay there through the day too, but when she scouted the paths around the Devil's Caves she didn't see signs of any forkbeards and so they pressed on. By the middle of the afternoon they were at the mouth of the cave that led into the Reach and the shaft to the Aulian tomb. This time Oribas lit a lamp, a tiny flame that guided them as far as the water. He handed them each two satchels full of salt. 'One to sit on each hip. Keep them open. As soon as you reach the top, make sure you have a handful of it ready.' He twitched. 'I don't think there will be any Lhosir, not after what I saw last time, but the creature will be close.'

Achista looked at him, eyes big in the lamplight. 'Oribas, why didn't you kill it when you were here before?'

'I didn't know how and I was afraid. Too afraid to think clearly.'

'And you're not afraid now?'

He squeezed her hand. 'You are my courage.'

The Vathan woman rolled her eyes. Oribas smiled and started to climb. He felt slightly stupid leading the way but he did it anyway.

*

Three Marroc never returned to the castle. They just didn't come back, and no one would ever know if the forkbeards had got them or if they quietly ran away. Others came racing to the sump cave with forkbeards running after them. They bolted straight into the water and vanished as the forkbeards watched, bemused. Valaric supposed they'd work it out and they'd surely put a watch over the caves now, but it made him smile to think of them pulling up short at the edge of the water only to watch the Marroc going deeper and deeper until their heads went under and they never came back. It probably didn't happen like that, but that was how Valaric imagined it.

Some of those forkbeards had come back out of the cave only to find more Marroc running straight at them. And Gallow, and that had gone badly for the forkbeards by all accounts. There was a bloodiness to the Foxbeard now, a viciousness, a vengeful anger. All the things Valaric had seen in Gallow before but now unfettered. He wasn't fighting for pride or honour or glory. He was fighting to keep his wife and his children from being ripped apart and hung in bloody shreds for Varyxhun's ravens.

The forkbeards came at the castle again in the morning. Valaric limped down to the battlements over the fifth gate. All the stones he'd been planning to drop on them as they climbed up the mountain were piled up behind it now and it was hard to watch forkbeards march through the third gate and do nothing. They turned the elbow in the road at the end of the third tier and started on the fourth, and there the barrage began, every Marroc soldier in Varyxhun lining the walls above. They didn't have any great boulders here but they did have a lot more arrows now; and the Aulian might not have been with them any more, but that didn't mean they hadn't talked about the best way to keep the forkbeards at bay. For a dozen yards in front of each gate the road was covered in salt to keep the iron devils back.

Not that it would work for long, but it would serve for a while, and that was the point.

The forkbeards forced their way up the fourth tier and through the sundered gates and out the other side. They broke ranks and charged, eager for the fight, as they turned the elbow to the fifth tier. The battlements of Varyxhun castle itself were above them now but no Marroc appeared to pepper them with arrows. Valaric let them come; but as the first forkbeards reached the gate he yelled the order that half his Marroc had been waiting for. Up on the battlements a hundred men leaned out and emptied a hundred burning pots and pans and bowls, and for one glorious moment the whole mountainside was draped in a curtain of fire. It didn't last but it was the most glorious thing Valaric had ever seen. He laughed and whooped and howled as he watched the forkbeards scream and burn. Arrows rained into them after the fire, their own arrows stolen the night before, and this time Valaric let his archers fire at will. As the first flames burned themselves out, he bellowed up at the castle, 'Give them a hand, lads! Put the rest out for them!' Up on the walls the Marroc returned with their pots and cauldrons now filled with boiling water. The forkbeards howled and milled around, trying to guess where the water would come. They crashed into each other, slipped over the edge and fell down the cliff to the tier below in their panic, and then Valaric slashed his sword through the air. The fifth gate swung slowly open. From behind it, Gallow and Sarvic and a hundred and fifty fighting men, the best the Crackmarsh and Varyxhun had to offer, lifted their shields and spears, cried out to Modris and hurled themselves at the forkbeards.

Even from the bottom of the shaft, Oribas could hear a tapping from the top, the ringing of metal on stone. He climbed as slowly as he dared, as quietly as he could, and when he reached the top he clenched his fingers around a fistful of salt. There was light, just a little, from the other side of the broken crypt door. Not the cold white light of the Mother of Monsters but the orange flickering of a candle. The tapping was loud now, a pick hammering at stone. With slow deliberation he climbed onto the edge and inched forward on his hands and knees until he found the line of salt he'd left before. He felt his way along it, filling it out where it seemed thin, and by the time he was done, Achista was crouched beside him and the Vathan woman too. He showed them the salt and whispered, 'Whatever you do, don't break the line.' Then he stepped over, crept to the crypt and peered through the broken stone door.

The Mother of Monsters wasn't there. The tomb was empty except for a pair of Lhosir digging at the tunnel to the crypt itself. One was inside, swearing vigorously. The other sat and watched, muttering sympathy. They had a lantern between them and a weariness too, as though they'd been there for hours. On the floor lay one of the pieces of iron armour that had reminded him so much of the Fateguard. Oribas pointed and shook his head and the Vathan woman let out a silent laugh and slipped through the broken door. She moved like a ghost until she was behind the sitting Lhosir and then reared up with a rock held in both hands and brought it down onto the Lhosir's head in time to the striking of the pick inside the tomb. She caught him with her knees as he slumped and then put down her stone and dragged him out of the way, off into the shadows, all without a sound.

The Lhosir in the tunnel said something. When he didn't get an answer he said it again. The tapping stopped. He started to shuffle out of the tunnel. The Vathan woman waited out of sight, and as soon as his head was clear she brought the other Lhosir's axe down on the back of his neck. They dragged him out of the way. The rest of the tomb was empty. No monster, no ironskins, nothing. Oribas stared

278

at the piece of metal armour on the floor. *The back plate, was it?* He didn't know. He shook his head. He'd thought he understood. The creature – whatever it was – had come back to claim the pieces of its skin that long ago it had been forced to leave behind. But where was it then? Not far away, surely. He whispered in Achista's ear what she must do and then crawled nervously into the tunnel. The other piece of armour was still inside the crypt but all the salt he'd once left there had been meticulously brushed away.

Outside, Achista took the red sword off her back and handed it in its scabbard to the Vathan woman. 'For when it comes.'

The red mist called him. It begged and pleaded with him as he saw his kinsmen climbing over the stones and he knew he couldn't refuse. The Lhosir were battered and scalded, bruised, some of them burned. Men had died screaming all around them and men still were – friends perhaps, or brothers or cousins, fathers and sons – but these were Lhosir, unafraid, furious and ready for a fight, and who better to bring it to them? Gallow ran ahead, leaving Sarvic and his Marroc behind. A part of him knew that all he was doing was drawing it out, slowing the forkbeards down, making it harder for them to form the wall of shields and spears that would sooner or later come marching up the road. Making it easier for Sarvic when the time came. But the deeper truth was that all he wanted was to drive these men out of his home for ever by stabbing them with his spear and hitting them with his axe, and when he closed his eyes all he saw was a heap of corpses burned in the castle yard with his Arda and his children among them. That was the future if Medrin took Varyxhun. Every Marroc from the mountains to Issetbridge, butchered and burned, and he, Gallow, would not let that happen.

And so he screamed at the Lhosir stumbling over the

stones that littered the road; and as they saw him they screamed right back and charged, too maddened to wait and form their wall of shields and face him as a Lhosir army should. The first to reach him was bright red in the face, scalded by boiling water and mad with rage. He roared loud enough to shake the mountain and lifted an axe in both hands. He didn't even have a shield. Gallow hurled his spear with all his strength and drove it right through him, then dashed up and pulled it out before he fell and ran straight on past to the next, kicked the man's shield and stabbed his face. Pulled back, blocked an axe, twisted inside a spear thrust and slashed open the belly of a Lhosir stupid enough to come to a battle with no iron over his skin. His next lunge skittered off mail. Another Lhosir came at him with a spear – Gallow twisted the point down into the ground and stamped on the shaft, snapping it in two.

He moved through them fast, before they could make a circle or lock their shields, sliced the hamstrings of another and ran on up to the the stones and leaped up onto the last boulder right behind the gate. A Lhosir on the other side looked up. Gallow jumped, landed on his face, and stamped on it. A man with an axe hacked at him and Gallow howled, part-rage, part-glee, part-despair, while his spear lashed out with a will of its own. He couldn't help himself. Medrin's Lhosir were swarming through the gates now and he could only take a few of them, but he killed another and another, and now the rage was fading from all of them.

Medrin's men were starting to think like soldiers again. Most got past him as best they could, scrambling through the debris to the open road where they could lock their shields. And then Gallow looked up and saw Valaric, and a moment later an iron portcullis crashed down, crushing three Lhosir into bloody smears and splitting their assault in two. Sarvic and his men came storming down the road with their shields locked and their spears low and hit the trapped

Lhosir like a battering ram while Gallow turned and fell on them from behind. Out on the road on the other side of the portcullis, another sheet of flame fell like a blanket over the Lhosir on the road and finally they turned to run.

Achista emptied one of her satchels of salt into the other. She put the iron back plate into the empty one and then filled it up with salt again. Mirrahj went to the other entrance, another heavy round slab of stone that had been smashed. She stared at the remains and then stepped through and looked at the strange drawings and carvings in the wall and the stone circles that turned like wheels on the other side. She reached out to touch one, then heard voices from above, loud and full of purpose. She ran back to the tomb. 'Forkbeards coming,' she hissed. As she moved to take them from behind as they entered, she drew the red sword for the first time. It felt strange in her hand. Long and yet light. She looked at it, wondering if there was any more to it than what it seemed. Gallow called it cursed, yet the Weeping Giant had carried it and the Weeping God before him and so would it not then carry a charge? An energy? And yes, perhaps a curse if the hands that clasped its hilt weren't Vathan hands? Yet she felt nothing. Oribas's words rang in her ears. *You have to earn it.* In that moment, with the red sword in her hand, she understood: he didn't mean paying a debt to him or to Gallow or to the Marroc who'd imprisoned her. He meant to the sword itself.

Achista ran to the hole where the wizard had gone. 'Oribas! Get out!' Mirrahj didn't hear what the wizard said back. The forkbeards were coming down the steps. Earn the Comforter? How? By killing the Aulian's Mother of Monsters?

'Oribas!'

The first forkbeard ran at Achista. He didn't even see Mirrahj and so she let him go and the next one after him too, and it was the third one she took in one clean slice as he ducked through the broken door and came up the other side without a head. She kicked him in the chest as he crumpled, shoving the body back into the forkbeards behind him. Inside the tomb one of the forkbeards was grappling with Achista. The other turned to face her. She ran at the forkbeard. He raised his shield to fend her off as they always did, ready to run her through at the same time as his shield hit her. And it was kind of him to lift his guard like that because it meant he had nothing to protect his legs, and instead of crashing into him she dropped to the ground and rolled and slid past him, and as she did, Solace smashed both his shins and down he went screaming.

The wizard was pulling himself out of the tunnel. The forkbeard who had Achista smashed her head into the wall and threw her to the floor. He pulled an axe and faced Mirrahj. More forkbeards were coming through the broken door. She faced them, grinning. It was a pity Gallow wasn't here. He'd have liked this. They fought well together and they could have held this space against anyone.

And then her eyes narrowed as the real prize ducked into the tomb, carrying the Crimson Shield before him. Sixfingers himself, king of the Lhosir. She bared her teeth and hissed, 'I came to kill a monster and so I shall!' and hurled herself at him bringing Solace down with an irrevocable force. And he didn't even move except to lift his shield, didn't even try to get out of the way, but as the sword and the shield met, a pain shot through her arm so harsh and sharp that she dropped Solace and doubled up at his feet, whimpering.

Medrin's expression never changed. He looked down at her and shook his head. 'Well now, I was expecting the Foxbeard. *He'd* have known better after the last time.'

'Lhosir! Behold!' She heard the wizard but her eyes were screwed shut at the pain in her arm. A brilliant light filled the room as she opened them. The forkbeards cried out and she looked round. The wizard was there, a hand falling from his eyes. He threw the satchel with the salt and the armour inside at her. 'Take this! Take it to Gallow and our bargain is done!' He barged her aside, crashed into Medrin and knocked the Lhosir king down. A forkbeard grabbed him, half-blind, and threw him aside. Mirrahj dropped her shield, shrugged the satchel over her shoulder and picked up the red sword. She almost stayed to fight, but with only one good arm it was obvious the forkbeards would win, just a question of how many she could take with her.

'Go! Now is not your time to die!'

As soon as she had her back to the wizard, another blinding flash of light filled the tomb and for a moment she could see exactly where she was going. She ran and slid through the line of salt and over the edge and down the rungs in the walls and took them three at a time, and when the forkbeards reached the top of the shaft and started to drop things on her, her sword arm was strong enough again to lift the wizard's satchel like a shield over her head. One last cry from Oribas echoed after her. 'Tell Truesword to melt it down and forge it again with salt. Fire and salt will kill it!'

She didn't stop to see if any of the forkbeards came after her but they didn't, and when she got out of the cave and back onto the mountainside and the bright afternoon sun, she saw why. They were already pouring out of Witches' Reach and down the slopes, arrowing after her.

Valaric waited a while and then raised the portcullis, and the last few forkbeards trapped behind it turned and ran. The battle-crazed Marroc charged after them, Gallow at the front, waving his blood-drenched spear like a madman, hurling curses like slingshots. He ran on past the turn in the road to the tier below and only then had the sense to finally stop. Sarvic screamed at his soldiers to grab any arrows they could find. A few hundred in the end, but that was still a few hundred that could be fired again.

Next time the forkbeards would probably take the gates but for now it was a victory and Valaric meant to make the most of it. For the rest of the morning he and Addic limped and hobbled among the forkbeard dead, laughing and joking with each other about who was more crippled while Sarvic's men stripped the corpses of anything they could use. When they were done with that, they kept on going until the bodies were naked and then took all the clothes back up to the castle and soaked them in pitch to be set alight the next time the forkbeards came. Valaric had the corpses beheaded as Achista had done at Witches' Reach. The heads went on spikes over the fifth gate, the bodies went over the edge of the cliff, tumbling and bouncing to the tier below, arms and legs spinning; and some of them, he saw, hit the road and slid over the next edge as well. It amused Valaric to imagine a few of them bouncing and falling all the way to the bottom.

In the middle of the day the Lhosir came to take the bodies of their fallen. Valaric spread his best archers along the walls to pick off any they could. Even collecting their dead would be a misery for the forkbeards. Everything. For ever. Until they left.

But they didn't leave. A few hours passed, that was all.

From the fifth gate Gallow watched the Lhosir march up the castle road for the second time that day. There must have been a thousand of them, snaking up through the tiers, and they had huge wooden shields with them this time, peaked things like the roof of a house and almost as wide as the road itself. Not many but he could see how they'd huddle under them, hidden from the Marroc arrows and stones and even from the fire, not that Valaric had much of the precious fish oil left. Boiling water and rocks then, the two things they had in abundance, and cloth from the morning's dead, soaked in pitch and set alight. It would stick, and their wooden shields would burn.

The Lhosir turned the elbow of the road into the fourth tier. As the barrage from above began, the shields moved to the front of the column. The rest of the army stayed where it was and the shields came on like a giant armoured cockroach inching towards the gate, maybe enough to hide a hundred men if they were packed tight together.

'Is there a ram under there?' Valaric stood beside him. Gallow looked but there was no way to know. 'If your Aulian wizard was here, he'd have thought of a way to turn that against them.'

And that might have been true, but Oribas was gone. Gallow picked up a stone and waited as the shield-roof came closer. It reached the gate stuck with arrows like a hedgehog but there wasn't a single dead man left in its wake. He put the stone down. Wasted. Any minute now the ladders would come and—

'What are they doing under there?' There were no sounds, no battle cries, no axes striking the gates.

'I've never heard of—'

'The salt!' hissed Valaric. 'They're clearing the salt. They've got another iron devil under there!'

Of course they were. Gallow turned away from the battlements and looked to the rope ladder that ran down from the gatehouse to the road below. If they were clearing the salt then there'd be an ironskin in the vanguard of the Lhosir. He'd face them, and Sarvic and his Crackmarsh men would face them too, and they might die or they might not. 'Open the gates again, Valaric. The fight comes either way. We broke them once this way and we can break them again.'

'Wait.' Valaric put a hand on his shoulder. 'It's not too … Jonnic!'

A burly Marroc had climbed between the merlons. He

had an axe in each hand and he grinned at Valaric with a mad gleam in his eye. 'Tell my sister how I died, Mournful. Tell her I went well.'

'Jonnic!'

The Marroc dropped. He landed on the first of the shield roofs and slid, and then slammed first one axe and then the other into the wood and caught himself, pulled himself up and sat astride the thing. 'Throw me a rope, Mournful!' At first Gallow had no idea what Jonnic meant to do. Valaric threw him the end of a rope and the Marroc tied it around one of his axes. The shield bucked and heaved beneath him but he sat fast, grinning like a madman and beckoning for more, and now Gallow understood and so did the Marroc. They tied axes to lengths of rope and threw them down, and Jonnic struck each axe into the wood as deep as it would go. A forkbeard slipped out from underneath and tried to grab him and a dozen arrows took him down. The back of the shield dropped almost to the ground and then tipped sideways as the forkbeards tried to roll him off, but Jonnic just held on to the axes and moved on to the next and the next until the shield was held fast in a dozen places. He gestured to the men on the gatehouse to lift it up.

Valaric threw another rope. 'Get back here you stupid Marroc!' Fat Jonnic shook his head and jumped down from the shield-roof and vanished beneath it, a knife in his hand. A shout went up from the Marroc as they heaved at the ropes and the shield lurched and shifted and then suddenly tore free of the Lhosir beneath and swung away. The forkbeards were like ants nested under a rock with their shelter pulled aside. They fell under the storm of stones and arrows, but not quickly enough for Jonnic, who fell, flailing in the midst of a handful of stabbing Lhosir as the second shield roof moved forward over him.

'Drop it! Drop it on them!' Valaric was seething, and Gallow half expected him to go over the edge as Jonnic had

286

done. But he didn't, and the Marroc pulling on their ropes let go and the first shield-roof crashed onto the front of the second and brought it down, scattering the Lhosir yet again. Yet amid the scrambling chaos Gallow glimpsed the rusted and broken remains of a Fateguard's armour lying still and empty beside the gate.

'We were too slow,' he whispered.

Further down the road the forkbeards were moving again, the first hundred of them coming forward at a run. They had a ram. Quietly Gallow turned away and climbed down the ladder to the road. When the Lhosir smashed the rusted hinges down and were swarming over the stones then he'd be there to meet them again, with Sarvic and the Marroc of the Crackmarsh, sword for sword with nowhere else to go.

The flash blinded the forkbeards a second time. For a moment Oribas was free. He shouted what must be done to Mirrahj and saw her run. Then he scrambled to Achista and lifted her head, terrified by all the blood on her face, but she moaned when he shook her and so he held her tight and cradled her in his arms and by the time he could think again the Lhosir had hauled him up and pulled them apart. Oribas supposed they meant to kill him right there and then but they didn't, and after a few moments the Lhosir King came away from the shaft and looked at Oribas. A smile pinched his lips. 'I remember you. The Aulian wizard.'

Oribas dipped his head. 'I would bow properly if your men did not hold me so tightly.'

'After we met on the road I did tell them not to kill you if they found you. I said nothing more.' Behind the smile there was strain in the Lhosir king's face. He was in pain. He held up the iron hand he wore in place of the one Gallow had taken. 'What have you done, Aulian?'

'The creature my people entombed here left behind two

287

pieces of itself when it escaped. I have encased them in salt. A common enough preservative.'

King Sixfingers pointed. 'You. Go and see if he lies.'

A Lhosir crawled into the tunnel to the crypt and a few moments later crawled out again. 'There's one piece there. Covered in salt.' He sounded bemused, as though wondering why anyone would do such a thing. Oribas smiled.

The king cocked his head. 'And the other piece, Aulian? Where's the other piece?'

They'd seen Mirrahj go and they were neither stupid nor deaf. Oribas bowed his head. 'The Vathan women took it. If she does as I asked then she will take it to Gallow Foxbeard who will melt it down and forge it again in salt.' He shrugged. 'The Mother of Monsters will be weakened. Perhaps together we can defeat it.' He looked about the tomb. 'I had imagined it would still be here. That is why I came. To kill it. Tell me, King of the Lhosir, do you serve the monster, or does the monster serve you?'

Sixfingers laughed and a twitch of a smile lingered on his lips. 'Come with me, Aulian wizard, and I'll show you something.' He turned away and addressed his men. 'Keep them alive. Strip the woman of her weapons and the Aulian of everything but his clothes but *don't* throw anything away.' He took a step back and then stopped and gave Oribas a queer look. 'I knew you'd come here, Aulian. But I was certain it would be Gallow who brought me the red sword. Then we might have talked some more about what you came here to do. Might even have been the three of us could have reached some accord.'

'The Edge of Sorrows is not yours, King of the Lhosir.'

Sixfingers laughed again. 'A Vathan? A woman? Alone in the valley? Shall we make a wager, Aulian, on how long it is before I have her?'

*

288

The ram smashed down the fifth gate as it had smashed the third and the fourth. Under the shelter of the gatehouse another iron devil spent itself turning the portcullis to rust and the Lhosir poured through the ruins. Gallow met them as they climbed through the debris scattered across the road. Grim-faced Marroc with spears and shields locked together stood either side of him. They'd beaten Medrin's Lhosir once today so they knew it could be done and the knowing fired their blood. When the soldier beside Gallow fell to an axe buried in his helm, another stepped up to take his place, and when he too fell, a spear stabbed through his foot, another came forward. Gallow and Sarvic held the Marroc line together and close to the rubble in the road, so close that the Lhosir had no space to make a wall of their own to face them. For every Marroc that fell, two Lhosir died.

Gallow's legs ached, his shield arm had turned to lead, his shoulders ground like broken glass, yet the arm that held his spear lunged and slashed and stabbed with the same strength it ever had. He remembered how the red sword would sing to him when he held it, softly in his head and only he would hear. It sang of the end it brought to suffering and pain and woe, of the sweet nothingness of oblivion that was its gift. He had a dozen cuts and bruises: a slash on his arm from a Lhosir spear, a throbbing in his shoulder from being hit by the Marroc beside him jerking his shield, a twinge in his ankle where he'd trodden on a stone in the fighting and turned it, but they were holding. Barely, but they were.

And then the Lhosir in front of Gallow pulled suddenly back, and out of the stones strode the iron-skinned men – Fateguard, nine of them. For a moment Gallow thought the Marroc would hold, but then the Fateguard closed on the line and spear thrusts sparked off their iron skins, swords skittered aside, axes dented but didn't slow them and they came as though they didn't care. One grabbed a Marroc from the centre of the line by the arm, pulled him out and rammed a sword though his chin before throwing him over the edge of the road to the tier below.

'Salt!' Gallow dropped his shield and threw salt from the bag at his hip into a Fateguard's face. It reeled, and he rammed the iron point of his spear through the slits of its mask. The metal split and the Fateguard fell. When Gallow looked down, he saw its face disintegrate before his eyes. There was no blood. 'Salt!' They had it – Sarvic and Gallow and dozens of others. Oribas had seen to that.

Two of the Fateguard turned on him. Around him the Marroc fought on but he felt the fear wash through them like a river in flood and then in a moment they were breaking, screaming at the men behind them to run, to flee back to the castle and safety of the sixth and last gate.

'And what then?' Gallow screamed at them. 'What when they rot that one too and smash it down like all the rest?' But the Marroc didn't hear, or couldn't, or chose not to, and now they were all running and five of the Fateguard were marching up the road, battering aside the missiles thrown at them from above. Three others had him pinned, cutting off his retreat, but they paused for a moment instead of killing him. They seemed to eye him with interest.

Suddenly a single screaming Marroc sprinted down the road, hurling fistfuls of salt into the faces of the Fateguard as he passed. He reached Gallow and two of the Fateguard lurched away, caught in clouds of the stuff, but the last stepped up and ran the Marroc through. The Fateguard and the Marroc stood together for a moment, and Gallow saw the Marroc's face and knew he'd seen this man twice before, the drowning Marroc pulled out of the Isset in Andhun three years back, and then in Varyxhun when Angry Jonnic had meant to hang him.

The Fateguard threw the dead Marroc over the edge into the road below. Gallow turned back, stabbing his spear into the salt-blinded face of the ironskin in front of him. He drew out his axe and hacked the hand off the second and then its head, but now the Lhosir had returned. Shields locked together, they swallowed the Fateguard into their ranks as they came up the road at a slow run towards the sixth gate, the last before the castle of Varyxhun itself, and Gallow retreated before them. At the open gates of the castle with the Dragon's Maw at their backs, Sarvic had managed to rally the Marroc at last.

'Salt! For the love of Modris, who carries salt?'

The Lhosir stopped a dozen yards short. The last handful of Fateguard stepped forward again. Before the Marroc behind him could break and run a second time, Gallow stepped forward too. The ironskin in the middle took another step and saluted him. 'Gallow Truesword.' He took off his helm and his mask and crown. The face underneath was as sallow and as pale as Beyard's had been.

'Do I know you?'

'You were meant to be one of us, Truesword. My brother the Screambreaker was meant to bring you to us. Fate gave him that time for that purpose.'

'Your brother? Who are you?' But the Screambreaker *had* had a brother – everyone knew that. It just wasn't possible, for the Moontongue had been drowned at sea almost twenty years past.

'You know my name, Foxbeard. All Lhosir know my name and spit upon the sound of it. I am Farri Moontongue, brother to Corvin Screambreaker, and I am dead.' He levelled his sword at Gallow's heart and came forward, and Gallow backed away because, even before someone had wrapped him in an iron skin, there was no man alive or dead except the Screambreaker himself who could beat Farri Moontongue, the thief of the Crimson Shield. Gallow caught the first blow on his shield but the Moontongue was already lunging again, and Gallow moved barely in time; and then the ironskin had an axe in his other hand, and it came so fast that Gallow hardly even saw it before it smashed into the mail over his ribs and knocked the breath out of him; and Moontongue's sword was already flashing at his face, and Gallow lunged, not caring that he was about to die as long as he might take this abomination with him.

And at that moment, in the tomb beneath Witches' Reach, Achista poured salt over the armour of the Eyes of Time, the first of the Fateguard. On the top of that same tower King Medrin dreamed that his iron hand burst into flames, while somewhere not far from there the Eyes of Time felt a pain that seared through all its creations, and on the road outside the gates to Varyxhun castle the last of the Fateguard staggered and clutched their heads and fell to their knees, and the thief of the Crimson Shield paused in the blow that would have killed Gallow but Gallow's spear did not. He drove it through Farri Moontongue's throat and twisted. There was no blood.

'I did not mean for this, Gallow Truesword,' said the creature that had once been a man, 'when I did what I did.'

Gallow's axe rose and fell, he bellowed and roared, the Marroc swarmed over the other writhing Fateguard with salt and iron and fire until the ironskins were done, and then it was the Marroc who charged, not the Lhosir, and the forkbeards who melted away, too stunned by what they'd seen to stand and fight.

31

THE EYES OF TIME

'I will tell you a story, Aulian, and then perhaps you'll tell one to me.' The king of the Lhosir rode on his new horse and Oribas rode beside him, wrists tied to his saddle. Behind them some five hundred Lhosir fighters were marching up the Aulian Way to Varyxhun. 'I don't know how the Eyes of Time came to our land. Your people brought it here, whatever *it* is. They buried it in salt. It was meant to stay here for ever.' He fixed Oribas with a look that bored into the Aulian. 'I have to imagine they didn't know how to destroy it, otherwise they would have done so, but then how is it that *you* do?'

Oribas met his eye. 'I came here to do what I could, King Medrin of the Lhosir. I had thought the Mother of Monsters had made you its slave. I see now I was wrong. It is the other way around.'

'No, Aulian, you still have that wrong. My mind is my own and always has been, though a fine battle we've had on that score, but the Eyes of Time serve a mortal?' Medrin smiled up at the sky. 'I think not.' He chuckled to himself. 'Aulian, I'll kill you if I have to, I won't pretend otherwise, but I'd prefer you alive. Maybe it lightens your thoughts to know that. You travelled with Gallow a while so I suppose he must have told you about the day he and Beyard and I entered the Temple of Fates?' His six-fingered hand tapped the Crimson Shield. 'All we wanted was to see it, not to steal it, but we were found and taken for thieves. I ran and left

Beyard and Gallow behind. I don't know what happened between them – something very noble, I suppose. Somehow Gallow escaped as well. I didn't know him then, had barely even heard his name before that day, but Beyard was my friend and he was taken by the Fateguard, and I was a coward, too afraid to own up to my part in it. When I begged my father the king to save my friend, he told me I must do it myself. And he was right, and I should have gone to the temple and given myself to them. Both of us should, Gallow too, but neither of us did. No one else knew, of course. To this day no one else does. Beyard took our names with him to his pyre.' He looked across at Oribas from the back of his horse. 'Gallow was only there because his father was a smith. We needed helms that made us look like the Fateguard and someone who could climb the temple walls, and he could give us both.'

For a long time the Lhosir king stared into the distance, into the past. There was shame in his face, Oribas thought, and pain and regret and perhaps a little longing, and it took a while before he shook himself and came back. 'After Beyard was gone I came across the sea to fight with the Screambreaker. I asked him for his help. I thought, after the Fateguard had stolen King Tane's shield from him, he might harbour a grudge, but he only looked at me with scorn and shook his head. I fought beside him anyway, with the passion of a shamed man and in due course I found the punishment I was looking for.' He patted his ribs. 'It was a bad wound. I didn't even see what did it. They say it was a spear, but whatever it was, it punched through my mail and ripped me open. The wound went bad. My flesh started to rot. If I'd been anyone else they would have let me die and burned me and that would have been the end, and if an honest man who knew the truth had spoken me out, they'd have said that I'd abandoned a friend to die and remorse drove me to follow him. The Maker-Devourer doesn't take a man like that for his cauldron, Aulian. Deeds are what matter, not remorse.'

Medrin stopped as another rider drew alongside, and for a while Oribas rode between silent guards while the king did whatever it was that kings did when they rode to war. He let the sights of the valley wash through him. The sky was blue without a cloud in sight and the sun was already warm. Not hot like the desert and it never would be, but almost pleasant – he might even sweat later – and then he wondered whether that helped the Marroc of Varyxhun or the forkbeards or made no difference at all. In the morning the castle was in the shadow of the mountain. The forkbeards would prefer to fight in the mornings then.

His eyes drifted to the river. This far down the valley the Aulian Way ran a little away from the Isset, carved into the lower slopes of the mountains that channelled the water. Between the river and the road lay a steady succession of abandoned Marroc farms, most of them burned. The river ran fast and high; now and then whole trees washed by. The fields were littered with stray boulders, even the trunk of one colossal Varyxhun pine, swept down by the spring floods of years before when the river burst its banks. The Aulians had carefully built their road where the floods wouldn't reach, carving notches into the mountains where they had to, building bridges over the sharp-sided ravines and valleys between. The Aulians had always liked to dig and they'd liked to build too. The streams under the bridges rushed and hissed and foamed. The winter snows were melting, and it was a pity, Oribas thought, that he wasn't going to live to see the valley in summer. It was probably a pretty sight.

It wasn't until the middle of the afternoon that Medrin came back, and when he did he looked annoyed. 'Tell me your name, Aulian.'

'I am Oribas, O King.'

'And that Vathan woman?'

'Mirrahj Bashar.'

The king laughed. 'Bashar is a title, Oribas of Aulia. Thank you.' The more Oribas studied the king, the more he knew he was wrong about something. The king had been vexed by Mirrahj's escape and the loss of the red sword, but no more. 'I wish I'd met you back then, Aulian. So much might have been different. Do you know how to cure flesh rot?'

'You must cut out the rot. All of it.'

Medrin laughed again and shook his head. 'I was the son of a king. No one dared. They took me to Sithhun flat on my back in a cart. The Screambreaker thought it was bad luck to have his prince die in the middle of the army and so he sent me away to die alone instead. Oh, he said he was sending me back to my father but I knew better. Away, that was all that mattered. Flat on my back, and I a proud Lhosir prince.' He snorted. 'In Sithhun there was an Aulian wizard. A man like you.' He turned and looked down at Oribas and smiled. 'He said I couldn't be saved but he did his best anyway. I was close to my end. He made potions – I don't know what they were – and had me drink them. I was delirious. He talked to me as he worked and I told him about Beyard. I don't know why. Because it preyed on me and because I thought I was dying. I remember how he changed when I spoke of the Eyes of Time. His face, his voice, everything about him, as though he was suddenly a different person. We were in Sithhun among the Marroc. The Fateguard had crossed the sea and taken the Crimson Shield and so they *had* been seen, but this Aulian knew them by another name, one I'd never heard.'

Oribas didn't try to hide his curiosity. 'Another name?'

'He spoke it but I was delirious and didn't properly remember it, only that he said it.' Medrin spat. 'The Aulian opened my wound and drained it. I remember the stench. It made me want to retch and I thought it was one of his potions and then I realised it was me. I can't tell you how it feels to smell such a terrible thing and know it's your own putrefaction. I don't remember much after that. As far as I can put it together, the few friends I had left heard my screams and ran into the room. When they saw what the Aulian had done they murdered him on the spot.' He shook his head. 'We are not reasonable people, Oribas. Perhaps you've seen this already. I think what saved me in the end was that they thought that I too was dead. The Aulian had filled my wound with maggots and honey. Do you understand?'

'To eat away the bad flesh.' Oribas looked up. He'd seen no sign of Achista and not knowing what had happened to her was wearing him down. For all he knew she'd been hanged before they even left. 'Mighty king, You told your soldiers I should not be killed. You did this for a reason. For the knowledge I—'

'Are you trying to bargain with me, Aulian? After everything you've done? Perhaps I want you kept for a very special death.'

Oribas bowed his head. 'I do not take you for a wasteful man, King of the Lhosir.' He took a deep breath. 'The Marroc woman from the tomb. She was nothing but a guide. I will give—'

'Don't lie to me!' Medrin bared his teeth. 'You've been in that tomb before and have no need of a guide, and besides which she was with you when we met on the road and you turned back my ironskins with your circle of salt. I know exactly who she is, and you'd failed before we even spoke if you meant to hide what she means to you. You'll give me all your knowledge but only if I let her go, was that it? But I won't, and you'll give it anyway if that's what I want from you. I'll keep her. Cage her and never hurt her but always let you be very sure how thin is the thread of her life. Yes. And you are right, of course: maggots to eat away the bad flesh. My stupid friends couldn't bring themselves to touch me and so the creatures were allowed to do their work. For two days I lay there, pickled in the Aulian's potions and eaten by his creatures but by the end the rot was gone. I didn't die. I suppose I started to recover, though it hardly felt it at the time. It took a very long time before I could even walk without gasping for breath.' He patted his side, just under his left breast. 'It's not a pretty sight. It had spread a long way.

'When I could speak again, I asked after the Aulian who'd cured me. When I had the answer I sent the men who'd killed him to seek out his family, but he had none. Later, when I looked for myself, I learned this Aulian was not such a pleasant fellow after all. He had a fine house in Sithhun. A palace almost, yet none of the Marroc would go near it. They said he was a witch. In time I went to his house myself and there were strange things there – few that I understood – and even now no one goes to that Aulian's palace unless I say they must. I heard he had a woman, a wife perhaps, and I heard that she fled after he died and that the Marroc caught her and tore her to pieces. I don't know if that's true but I never did find her – either in one piece or many. What I remembered, though, was how he'd changed when I spoke of the Fateguard. How he asked questions about them, about where they came from. He even spoke the name of Witches' Reach, although it wasn't until years later that I learned of the fortress that guards the Aulian Way. I spent a long time in Sithhun in that Aulian's palace. The Screambreaker was off fighting his war and I was recovering my strength from a wound that should have killed me, and when I had that strength again, I found I had no desire to fight beside a man who'd sent me away to die alone. So I stayed in Sithhun until I had my answers, and when I thought I understood how to destroy the Eyes of Time, I went home.'

Oribas looked up sharply and found Medrin was looking at him again, smiling faintly. 'That never occurred to you, did it, Aulian? Not once. Admit it. Not that I once wanted the same as you want now.' He smiled wryly at some private memory and nodded. 'One thing for which I thank my father – that he forced me to learn to read a little Aulian as well as our own tongue. The Aulian's books called it the Edge of Sorrows, and so that's what I looked for, Oribas of Aulia, and found nothing because I knew only its Aulian name. Other matters occupied me: the Screambreaker and his war, my father falling ill, the Screambreaker eyeing his throne.' He was laughing out loud now, shaking his head. 'And then after Andhun and the Vathen I found to my amazement that someone had walked this path before me. No less than Farri Moontongue, the Screambreaker's big brother.'

He might have said more, but that was when a shout made them both look up and back to where a Lhosir was pointing up the mountain. When Oribas squinted, he picked out a lone figure leading a horse along a trail hundreds of feet above them. It took a moment to realise that the figure was standing still, looking down at them, and a moment more to realise that the figure had a bow.

King Medrin snorted. 'From all the way up there? He can't possibly hope to hit anything.'

Oribas judged the angles and wasn't so sure. The archer was a long way away but he was a long way up too.

'What's he shooting at? Us?' Medrin had stopped to look. He didn't sound at all concerned.

'I can't see, O King.'

'He's shooting at something in the road ahead but I can't see what. Look.' Medrin pointed. A moment later Oribas saw a puff of dust from the middle of the road some fifty yards ahead of them. 'What *is* he doing?'

'That is Mirrahj,' said Oribas, too quietly for Medrin to hear, 'and she is finding her range.'

32

MOONTONGUE

'Farri Moontongue.' Gallow lay slumped in the castle yard, too tired to even yelp with pain as Arda washed his wounds and bound them. The yard was full of exhausted and battered Marroc, some still bleeding but all savouring the evening quiet. A moment of bliss. A moment to make peace with Modris, a moment to laugh, to remember or perhaps to forget. Some men stared, eyes far away. Others wept.

'People will remember us for what we did today.' Valaric sat beside Gallow, trading bawdy jokes with Sarvic and a few of his Crackmarsh men. 'We turned the forkbeards back. We slew the iron devils, every one of them, and when they come tomorrow the sixth gate will stand closed and that's how it stays. And you're sitting there thinking of some old forkbeard dead the best part of twenty years?'

Gallow said nothing. He'd seen the Moontongue once. He'd been ten summers old and there was no way to tell whether the dead thing he'd killed today had been the same man. The Moontongue he remembered had been a thundercloud filled with storms and lightning but also with laughter.

'All I know is he stole the Crimson Shield from your iron devils and then sank into the sea. Pity I can't say the same for the rest of you.'

'He was the Screambreaker's brother and they were the bitterest rivals. Yurlak favoured the Screambreaker and

Moontongue thought he was better. That's about as much as I know. I only saw him the once before I crossed the sea but that was enough. He wasn't the sort of man you forget.'

'I heard he was tight with Neveric the Black. Neveric would turn on Tane and then the two of them would turn on you forkbeards and Neveric would sit on the throne of Sithhun and the Moontongue would be king across the sea. So Moontongue stole the shield and then Neveric turned on him and they all died and good riddance to the lot of them.' Valaric snorted. 'Neveric was always a bastard. Still, it's easy to tell tales of the dead. If it's all the same to you I'll keep my mind on thinking what tales they'll be telling of us.'

Gallow flinched as Arda poked a graze on his shoulder. 'Doesn't need stitches but I'll be dropping some brandy on that.'

'No, you won't!' said Valaric and Gallow at once.

Arda snorted and did it anyway. 'It's what your wizard would have done.'

The next arrow came straight at Medrin. The first Oribas knew of it was when the Crimson Shield suddenly shifted and the king jerked in his saddle. For a moment Oribas thought Medrin had been hit.

'Maker-Devourer!' When Medrin lowered the shield Oribas saw the arrow. Medrin looked at it. 'That's a Vathan arrow meant to pierce mail.' He laughed. 'No, wizard! This is some trick of yours. I'll not believe your Vathan woman is up there with a bow now, already ahead of us! No.' He pulled the arrow out of the shield and closed on Oribas. 'This arrow isn't real. And the archer on the mountain? Not real either. What are you doing, wizard?' He grabbed Oribas by the shoulder and stabbed him with the arrow's tip. Not deep or hard but enough to draw blood. His face changed: the smile fell away and left a cold hardness beneath. He shook his head. 'No, Aulian. Not your Vathan woman. Just some Marroc.' He kicked his horse to a canter and sped away, a dozen Lhosir at his heels while more began to climb the slope towards the archer. A soldier took the reins of Oribas's horse and led him away too. The last time Oribas looked back he saw several Lhosir still labouring up the slope. The archer hadn't moved. He had no doubt at all that it was Mirrahj.

They slept in the open that night. Oribas dozed now and then, wondering what the Lhosir king had done with Achista. Twice he jerked awake to shouted alarms from the Lhosir sentries but the commotion never came any closer. In the morning they dragged him to his feet and hauled him back to his horse, and then Medrin took him to the edge of the camp to where a gang of surly Lhosir soldiers were dragging a bound Marroc by a rope. The king shouted at them to stop, and it dismayed Oribas how his heart jumped when he realised who the Marroc must be even before he saw her face. She glared at King Sixfingers and spat into the dirt in front of his horse. Medrin laughed.

'See, Aulian, she still has all her arms and legs and most of her blood on the good side of her skin. She has nothing I want, so how long she stays that way lies with you.' He turned to the Lhosir. 'Beat her though, for her disrespect. Aulian, you may stay and watch or ride with me now, as you prefer.' Oribas didn't want to watch but he knew he had to, and so he stayed as the Lhosir punched his Achista to the ground and then kicked her half to death.

'It was the Aulian of Sithhun who set me on the path, and you're an Aulian too. That's really the only reason I haven't made ravens out of both of you.' When the army was ready to march, Oribas found himself led to Medrin's side once more. 'You deserve it for what you did. Burning men like that, their bodies sunk into water where no one will ever speak them out.' He spat. 'You think I want the red sword, don't you? Three years ago I wanted it more than anything.

Not any more.' He shook his head. 'The Vathen came and my father was too old and fat to lead an army. It fell to me to go to Andhun, to be the king of the Lhosir across the sea whether I liked it or not. In Andhun I learned that the sword the Vathen carried to war was the Edge of Sorrows. I learned, at last, its other names.' He chuckled again. 'I wanted that sword, Aulian, and if Gallow had ever stopped to wonder why, if he'd ever asked me, perhaps all of this might have been different, perhaps we might have sailed side by side to the frozen wastes and the Iron Palace amid the Ice Wraiths and put an end to the Eyes of Time, each of us with one hand on the sword together. I just wanted to avenge Beyard and if he'd known, he'd have had a piece of that too, I think.' He laughed bitterly. 'I never even knew the Eyes of Time had made an ironskin of Beyard. I just thought he was dead all those long years ago.'

He unbuckled the Crimson Shield from his arm and held up his iron hand. 'For running away that day in the Temple of Fates, Gallow cut off my hand with that sword in Andhun. I was Medrin Twelvefingers before. Now I'm Sixfingers, Medrin Ironhand. I should have died. Gallow should have killed me, or the wound he gave me should have done it. But for a second time I lived.' He tapped the shield and strapped it back to his arm. 'The Vathen took Andhun and everything east of the Isset. My men took me back home. Yurlak took one look at me, flew into a rage and rushed across the sea to put down the filthy Vathen or Marroc or whoever had had the audacity to damage his son.' Medrin spat again and there was an edge of bitterness to his words. 'Never mind that it had been a Lhosir, never mind that I might die, he crossed the sea and got away from the sight of me as fast as he could. He died within the year and I shed no tears. He'd done what was needed. He'd outlived the Moontongue and the Screambreaker and that was all I was ever going to get from him. And while everyone else was fighting, I spent my time at the Temple of Fates and looking for the Screambreaker's fortune.' His face wrinkled into a suppressed smile. 'All those years of fighting and winning should have made him as rich as a king but he never took much. He did it for ...' Medrin shrugged. 'I really don't know. But by the end of my looking it was the Moontongue I came to understand. They say the Moontongue stole the Crimson Shield as a gift to Neveric the Black of the Marroc, that he meant to betray his brother and his king and that Neveric betrayed him in turn, but Moontongue had a sea more ambition to him than that. When I understood, Aulian, for a moment I was in such awe of him that I forgot to breathe. I had found a Lhosir I could finally truly admire, safe in the knowledge that he was dead. You see, the Moontongue stole the Crimson Shield for himself, not for some Marroc, and he stole it because he believed it could make the Eyes of Time into his servant. He believed he would see the future, know all things before they came to pass, and with that knowledge he would crush Yurlak, grind his brother to dust and lead a conquest the like of which the world hasn't seen since the glorious days of Aulia. He wasn't killed by some renegade Marroc. It was ironskins who sank his ship.'

He sighed. 'I took salt with me, Aulian, and other things, and I took the Crimson Shield. I took the knowledge I found in the house of the wizard of Sithhun and in the secret letters of the Moontongue.' He smiled again, although his smiles never touched his ice-blue eyes. 'Of course, nothing was what I thought. I was more careful than the Moontongue perhaps, but still ignorant.' The king lifted his iron hand. The fingers flexed and Oribas jerked in his saddle.

'How ...?'

'The Eyes of Time made this hand for me. Through it the Fateguard obey me. I learned quickly enough why I was so favoured. I did the same as you – I threw salt. Now when I do that, I burn too.' Medrin slipped the shield back over his arm. 'I keep it hidden. I already have a finger more than most men and there are limits to how much witchery a brave Lhosir warrior will take. I found I couldn't make the Eyes of Time my slave, but with the shield nor could I be easily dismissed. We bargained. In the end, for this hand I gave my blood oath that I would search for two pieces of iron armour, lost for hundreds of years somewhere near the mountain crossing to Aulia. I knew, as I gave it, that I would never find them.'

He reined in his horse abruptly and turned in the saddle to face Oribas. 'And then you came. You and Gallow, whom everyone thought was dead, and the Edge of Sorrows, and I have to wonder what is coincidence and what is fate. That the Fateguard I unwittingly sent to Varyxhun was Beyard? That he had the red sword in his hand and Gallow in his grasp and did nothing? That you found the two pieces of iron? Coincidence or fate, Aulian? I must believe that the Eyes of Time knew, as we struck our bargain, that these things would come to pass.'

Oribas looked away. 'King of the Lhosir, my people do not believe in fate.'

'But mine do.' Medrin rounded on Oribas and now his voice took on a sharpness. 'What did your people entomb out here so very far from their home? What will it become if it's made whole? Answer me that and answer in truth and I'll give you that palace in Sithhun and everything in it. You can live out your days there in service to me. You can have your Marroc woman too, as long as she never leaves the walls of your house. Otherwise I make her into a raven and you will watch every moment of her agony.'

'What will it become?' Oribas shrugged. 'What it already is – a monster.' He looked at the river, at the rushing water still rising. A man who looked for it could see how the water was higher today than it had been yesterday.

*

Night after night Gallow and Valaric stood on the walls and watched the forkbeards at the bottom of the mountain. Sometimes Addic came and stood beside them and sometimes Arda. Sometimes Gallow brought the children, Tathic and Feya and Jelira and even little Pursic. He showed them the Lhosir and told them that these were his people. Then Arda told them stories, Marroc stories of men who were more than men, slow to anger and reluctant to lift their swords yet who fought with a relentless fury when evil came, protecting the folk around them until the bitter end. In Arda's stories they always won but at a terrible cost, so they died in the end.

And then Gallow told his own stories, the ones he'd learned as a child, and his too were of men who were more than men, and sometimes they too protected the weak who looked to them for shelter, but more often they fought against those who claimed to be strong and did it for no better reason than it was there to be done, and sometimes they won and sometimes they died, and often they lost a hand or a foot or an eye and none of it ever for any reason but to see who was the better man. They weren't Marroc stories and they didn't follow the Marroc way, and when Tathic asked which was better, Gallow only shrugged. 'All our stories say one thing. That a man must speak his heart and speak the truth he finds there. That he must defend both with his life if he has to.' He pointed down the mountain. 'I'm here beside you and my people are down there, and soon we'll fight because our hearts follow different songs. But I'll tell you this and they would tell you too: a man who lies, a man who gives his word freely and without thought or meaning, is a man who is worthless. This is what my people mean when they say *nioingr*. A traitor to his kin, but worst of all a traitor to himself. It's not our nature to be kind or merciful. Those are Marroc ways and my brothers of the sea sneer at them, but even so only our beards are forked, never our tongues. That is what it means to be Lhosir.'

In the afternoon, Oribas was with the first riders as they came into Varyxhun and suddenly King Medrin was beside him again. They walked their horses off the Aulian Way and through the town and into streets filled with Lhosir soldiers. Medrin led the way to the edge of the river and stopped there. 'So, Oribas of Aulia. I keep seeing your eyes stray to the water as we talk. Will it flood and wash us away? Do you know the answer or do you simply wonder?'

Oribas let out a deep breath. 'I do not know the answer, O King of the Lhosir. Perhaps the mountains are angered or perhaps they are not.'

Medrin shook his head. 'The river is a river and does what every mountain river does: rises in spring. Yet Varyxhun is not washed away and rebuilt each summer. The river will not save your Marroc friends. So … the Eyes of Time. Do you have an answer for me?'

'Beyard was Gallow's friend and yours. Make your peace with Gallow. Whatever the creature is, he will destroy it. He will help you. I will see to it.'

'Make peace with him?' Sixfingers held up his metal hand, almost shouting in his outrage, 'He took my hand, Aulian, and Beyard is dead now.' He stared across the river and up the valley to the mountains that towered over the distant Aulian Way. 'I'll crush the Vathen if I must but my heart lies across these mountains now. The Lhosir will build Aulia once more.'

'I do not think it can be done.' Oribas shook his head. 'Not by any king, no matter how great he might be.'

'Nothing is done that is not tried. Isn't that an Aulian saying? And should it *not* be tried?' His hand swept up the valley to the castle of Varyxhun. 'Look at what you made, Aulian. Look at what you were!'

'But we were not wise, King of the Lhosir. We dug until we found something we could not contain and should not have found and with a stroke it brought everything to ruin. Nothing is done that is not tried does not mean all that there is *should* be tried. That is a saying of my people too.'

'What did your people bury here, Aulian?'

'I do not know, O King. The libraries of the castle do not say. I do not know why it was brought here and nor do I know what will happen if it is whole again. It is something unique in its danger. Perhaps in this palace of which you speak there is more ...'

Medrin nodded. 'You disappoint me, Oribas of Aulia, but I thank you for your honesty.'

He left Oribas at the side of the river staring at the water, filled with thoughts about the castle that the Aulians had called the Water Castle and the legends which spoke of a dragon who would drown any army who broke the sixth gate. Filled with the knowledge of his ancestors and their craft and their cunning and the certain understanding that he'd missed something. But filled most of all with thoughts of Achista.

Later, the Lhosir led him into the heart of the town. As the evening drew in they took him to what had once been the market, where a dozen carpenters were hard at work building what looked like wooden shelters, each as long as a hanging shed but with no walls. Sixfingers was walking among them and he smiled when he saw Oribas. 'It seems my Fateguard are all gone.' He held up his iron hand and looked at it. 'A precious gift this, once, but now it burns and serves no purpose. Thanks to you, Aulian, and so I won't be so sad to lose it again. I should have known, of course, that every gift would come with a price. I'm sure *you* would have known that.' He looked at the road leading up to Varyxhun castle, at the Lhosir moving about on the lower tiers and then across the market square where a bedraggled band of

Marroc were being herded. He stood and watched as the Marroc were beaten and forced onto the wooden frames and tied there, hand and foot; and when it was done he looked at Oribas. He stayed silent but his eyes asked if Oribas understood, and Oribas bowed his head and nodded, because yes, he understood perfectly. The Lhosir would carry these human shields over their heads when they attacked the gates once more and Achista was among them.

'What do you want?' He could hardly speak.

The Lhosir king nodded slightly. Arms gripped Oribas and forced him down, holding him helpless while others tied him to the wooden frame. 'Oribas of Aulia, you came to Witches' Reach filled with purpose, yet you say you know nothing?' He shook his head. 'The Eyes of Time is here, not far away at all. Do you not feel the presence? The Fateguard are gone, the pieces of iron are found, and so our bargain is done. I fear we have become adversaries once more and so my patience for your knowledge has become frayed. Perhaps a night out here will help your memory.'

A wave of despair shook Oribas. 'I would tell you what I knew if I had the knowledge to share. Why would I not?' Desperation filled every word. Not for him, but for his love. 'The red sword. Salt and fire and salt and ice and last of all iron. There is nothing more to know! That is enough! It is all I have to give!'

But Medrin was shaking his head. 'Tomorrow I'll take the last gate of Varyxhun. I might go alone, if you convince me. Otherwise we all go together.' The king squatted beside him. 'In the morning I'll let you go. You can walk beside me. You can carry the shield for me.' He chuckled. 'If it was the other way round, we both know she'd let you die. But it isn't.' He held out his arm with its iron hand and cut the skin above his wrist with a knife. 'The Eyes of Time. My blood oath, Aulian. Tell me its secrets and I'll keep your woman from harm. Otherwise what use are you to me? What use are either of you? Think on it. You have until the morning.'

He walked away. Oribas watched him go and felt his heart turn to lead, for there were no secrets to share.

33

THE SIXTH GATE

Somewhere far away the sun began to rise. Oribas watched the snow-painted tips of the mountains across the river light up in orange fire and listened to the morning watchmen as they shuffled into the market square, yawning and rubbing their eyes. The Lhosir who'd stood guard through the night slunk away to doze before the morning battle began.

'Guard! Guard! I have something to say to your king!' Because if what Medrin needed was to hear a story about the Eyes of Time then a story he could have. It wasn't an easy thing to lie, not for one like Oribas, but he'd done far worse since he'd crossed the mountains.

The nearest watchman laughed and spat at him. 'If Ironhand wants to hear your begging for mercy, he'll come in his own good time.' He walked away. Oribas looked across the yard for Achista but he hadn't seen where the Lhosir had tied her, and when he called out the Lhosir kicked him until he was quiet. His eyes flickered about the square, searching for inspiration. He could only see two Lhosir now, not the three who'd first come into the square, but then he spied the third again, slipping out of some alley, and one of the Marroc must have said something for the Lhosir suddenly started kicking and snarling like an animal. The second watchman went over to him and the other spun around and smacked him in the face with such violence that even Oribas winced. The two fell to the ground wrestling. The first ran over, and then suddenly the third Lhosir was up again, sword drawn, and the next thing Oribas knew the other two were being murdered right in front of him. It was brutally quick and happened almost without a sound. The Lhosir dragged the two bodies under the wooden shields and ran to Oribas and crouched down beside him, and at last Oribas saw her face.

'I have to kill a monster,' she said in her singsong Vathan voice. 'So I will kill this Lhosir king.' She cut the ropes that held him. Across the square he saw another figure rise and crouch down again.

'Achista?'

Mirrahj helped him to his feet. 'Run and hide. Get away. I want the Lhosir king.'

Yes, he could do that. Or they could get back into the castle the same way they got out. And he found himself thinking of the shaft that ran up under the gates and into the cisterns and on up into the mountain, and finally his eyes flickered up to the castle and to the tarn above it, brimming full of snowmelt. He gripped Mirrahj's hand. 'No!' Across the square Achista was freeing the other Marroc. Oribas pulled Mirrahj after him. 'I know how he means to break through the last gate.' He stared at the rushing waters of the Isset, full and ready to burst its banks. 'I have to go back. I know why they call it the water castle. I know its secret. I know how to stop him. He will lead his army himself this time, I know it. You can be there, waiting for him.'

Mirrahj seemed to think on this for a moment and then nodded and handed him his precious satchel. 'Then you might want this.'

Once again the Lhosir climbed the mountain road and once again Gallow watched them. They came with a banner in their midst this time, the banner Reddic and Jonnic had seen before. Valaric looked at him. 'Are there any iron devils left, or was that all of them?'

As far as Gallow knew no one had ever counted the Fateguard or known how many they were. Not many, that was sure. He shook his head. 'Someone had better tell Reddic that Sixfingers is coming back for seconds.'

The Lhosir wound steadily closer and Valaric left to stand over the sixth gate. The Lhosir had the big wooden screens they carried over their heads again and Gallow wondered how many more Fat Jonnics there were among the Marroc. Not many.

Sarvic quietly came and stood beside him. 'Sixfingers must think he's going to win. He wouldn't be here otherwise. So there's more iron devils after all. Must be.'

'Maybe Valaric will shout the right words into the Dragon's Maw and draw out the beast to eat them all.'

They both laughed at that. Sarvic shook his head. 'Never thought I'd see you again, forkbeard, after Lostring Hill. You saved my life from the Vathen. A Marroc saved by a forkbeard. I hated you for that. When they were going to hang you here, I paid you back.' He drew off his gauntlet and pulled the knife from his belt and cut his arm. 'Yours today, forkbeard, and freely given. I'm proud to stand with you.'

Gallow did the same. They clasped arms, their blood mingling. 'You're not the man I remember, Sarvic. If all Marroc were like you and Valaric, the Screambreaker would have turned back at the sea.'

Sarvic laughed. 'I wish that were true.'

'Watch over my Arda and my sons. If Sixfingers breaches the gates and takes the castle then he won't be kind. Don't let him take them.'

'If I still bleed I'll defend them with my life.'

'Just let Reddic get them out, Sarvic. He knows the way. You should get out too. It doesn't have to be the end here.'

'For most of us it does, Foxbeard. For most of us it does.'

The Lhosir came on up the road through the smashed

lower gates. They marched along the fourth tier and Valaric loosed a single volley of precious arrows to remind Medrin's men that they weren't safe, not ever. After that the Marroc watched as the Lhosir marched under their sea of shields and their wooden roofs and turned the corner to the last tier, to the broken fifth gate and then, at the road's end, the sixth. All the oil was gone and also most of the stones piled up behind the gates to hold them shut and brace them against the inevitable ram. Shouts started up, taunts and insults raining down, but even as the Lhosir came up to the sixth gate, the Marroc held back their last precious arrows. Then a shout went up from Valaric on the gates and all along the battlements the Marroc rose. Stones crashed on the forkbeards' wooden roofs, knocking them askew. Arrows flew through the gaps. Boiling water rained over them, though it was hard to see whether it ever scalded Lhosir skin. Men snapped off the icicles that had formed overnight and threw them like spears. Gallow smiled as he saw that. Oribas would have done the same.

'No ram,' said Sarvic beside him, and Gallow saw it was true. The Lhosir had come up the mountain road with their shields but nothing else. So Sarvic was right. They had more ironskins after all. He looked at the sacks of salt lined up along the battlements and slit one open.

'Give me a hand with this?'

Sarvic nodded. The first Lhosir were at the sixth gate now, arrows thudding into their shields, and Valaric had his own sacks of salt and all manner of other things to throw down on them. Medrin and his banner were moving up under their own wooden roof. It looked different, but it took a moment for Gallow to realise why.

There were people tied to it.

As the sun crept down the mountains across the Isset, Mirrahj swore softly under her breath in her own tongue.

When Achista and Oribas were finally done freeing the rest, she grabbed them both and hauled them away into the darkest shadows she could find.

'Look!' Two forkbeards stumbled bleary-eyed out of a house across the street. 'They're waking.'

'They mean to attack again this morning. King Sixfingers told me this.'

The alley where they hid ran between a jumble of yards to a wide street by the river, the obvious place to go. If they reached a boat, the current would take them and the forkbeards would never catch up on foot, but they'd need to be quick. The other freed Marroc were trying to slip away. One of them, at least, would be seen. The hue and cry would go up at any moment and forkbeards would come swarming from everywhere.

Mirrahj fingered the sword hilt at her belt. Maybe Sixfingers would come to see for himself – now there was a thought. But Oribas wanted to go back to the castle, so Mirrahj pulled him and Achista into a yard instead, and then through the back door of a house. A place to hide.

Three forkbeards looked up at them as they burst in. They were sitting in a circle on the floor. The one staring right at her froze mid-yawn. The nearest had his back to her. She kicked that one in the head, jumped on his back, drove the red sword through the one who was still yawning and then swung a backhand slash that cut open the face of the third. The one she'd kicked had time to let out an angry grunt and turn and look up and go all wide-eyed before she drove Solace through his heart. Two spears leaned against the wall. Achista snatched one. Oribas went for the other door but Mirrahj pulled him back. 'We wait here.'

Achista laughed. 'Shall we fight the whole of Sixfingers' horde?'

As a shout went up outside, the first of the fleeing Marroc seen, Mirrahj gripped Achista. 'They expect us to run!

315

Perhaps they won't look so close. And yes, little Marroc, if we have to then we fight every forkbeard in this valley. Isn't that what you came here for?'

Oribas pulled a fur off the floor. He wrapped himself in it and lay down.

'What are you doing?'

'What if there were six forkbeards here, not three, and all had been killed? Who would know any better? Who ever thinks to look closely at the dead?'

More shouts and then one right outside: 'Marroc! Marroc!' Another shout: 'Ironhand wants them alive!'

The Aulian shifted so that his eyes were on the door but the dead forkbeards hid his face. 'Lie in the back in the darkest shadows with your weapons close and ready. Sixfingers plans to take the castle today. He has a way through the last gate and he won't wait. They won't look for long, I promise you. The castle is his prize today, not us.'

And he was right. Mirrahj settled uneasily into the far corner of the room and slumped against the wall, the red sword close to hand. When a pair of forkbeards burst in on them, she stayed very still as they stopped with the sunlight streaming behind them and squinted into the gloom and shook their heads. They left the door open and so now and then she saw others hurry past, back and forth for a while with noise and commotion all about, and then the noise faded and no forkbeards came past any more, and when the three of them finally emerged, hours after dawn, the army was all gone, marching up to the castle and Varyxhun was almost empty. Mirrahj led them from house to house, shadow to shadow, until she reached the edge of the river, and there Oribas stopped her. He looked up to the column of forkbeards steadily climbing the mountain road. 'Find a rope.' He looked her up and down and then poked her in the hip. 'And a stout piece of wood that stands this high off the ground. And be quick.'

Sarvic drew back his bow and took aim. 'Don't say a word, forkbeard. Not a word.' His voice was harsh and hoarse. He let the first arrow fly and it struck one of the Marroc in the chest. Sarvic drew another. Medrin was climbing the last tier now, about to pass through the fifth gate and in range of the boiling water and the stones, yet nothing was hitting his human shield. At least there was no hearing the screams over the shouts of the Lhosir and the Marroc on the walls.

Sarvic shot another arrow. It struck a second Marroc in the throat. A good clean kill. Gallow squinted, trying to see if Achista or Mirrahj or Oribas was a part of Medrin's shield. Under the rags and the dirt and the crusted blood it was hard to be sure.

Sarvic fired again. As Medrin's banner passed beneath he killed the last of the screaming Marroc, threw down his bow and ran along the battlements, howling at the top of his lungs, 'There! Down there! Sixfingers! Never mind the rest of them, he's the one! Kill him! Kill the forkbeard king. Look at him! *Look!*' He picked up a stone as big as his head and staggered under its weight, hefted it up to a merlon over Medrin's banner and tipped it over. It bounced off the wall and smashed into a corner of the shield. For a moment the back end wavered and sank. 'Kill him! Use everything!'

The Marroc went wild. Arrows flew at every opening, no matter how small. Men ran up and down the battlements with stones and pots of boiling water, slopping it, burning their hands and scalding their feet but they didn't care. A torrent came over the wall down onto Medrin's roof and banner. Another great stone hit square in the middle and snapped the beam that held the shield together. Smaller stones pinged off the sides and it was riddled with arrows. As Gallow watched, the roof began to break apart. The Marroc cheered but now Gallow wasn't looking at Medrin's banner, he was looking everywhere else. There was too little Lhosir in Medrin to stand beneath his own banner come what may, and yet just enough for him to be here somewhere. And he was looking for the Fateguard too because there had to be one. He could see small rams carried under the following roofs. Nothing big enough for the gates of the castle as they were, but rust their hinges to dust and ...

Another whoop and a cheer went up from the Marroc on the sixth gate and a cloud of grey showered down. The roof at the front of the Lhosir army tipped sideways and lay on its edge, about to topple over the cliff onto the tier below. Lhosir soldiers hastily lifted their shields and cowered. Medrin's roof was almost at the front of them now, bent in the middle and sagging but still carried onward. Sacks and sacks came over the gatehouse, each of them ripped before they went. The air was suddenly thick with salt but still Medrin's banner came on. Then with a great shout from the gate, a stone block the size of a man toppled from the wall. Gallow watched it plunge into the front of what was left of Medrin's roof, shattering it. The spear flying his banner snapped and exploded into shards. The roof disintegrated, the Lhosir crushed beneath it trapped screaming while others scurried for shelter, pressing themselves against the walls. Everywhere the Marroc cheered and hooted. 'For King Tane!' 'Go back to your sheep, forkbeards!'

Gallow peered frantically among the forkbeards who'd come up behind Medrin's banner, looking for the one Fateguard who had to be among them to rust the last gate. Looking and not seeing, and then he caught a glimpse: Medrin. A flash of him almost at the front, with his helm and the Crimson Shield in his hand, and then he was gone again, hidden among the press of men.

'He's not dead!' He pulled Sarvic to the edge of the wall and pointed. 'He's not dead, Sarvic. He's there.'

They looked, both of them, but all they saw now were Lhosir shields, and then three Lhosir ran for the gates and behind them the rest began to move again. 'There!' In the middle of the three. Medrin.

Sarvic let fly. His arrow hit the Crimson Shield. He tried again but it was as though each time Medrin saw the arrow coming and lifted his shield to catch it even though he never once looked up. He reached the gate, crouched down and raised a hand to touch it, the iron hand that the Eyes of Time had given him, and the shields of the Lhosir closed around him. Almost at once a cry went up from the men in the castle yard. 'The gates! It's happening!'

'Stop him!'

But how? The Marroc had thrown all their stones and the Lhosir had Medrin wrapped in shields to catch their arrows and the ground was already white with salt and their oil had gone. Gallow bowed his head. He gripped Sarvic's shoulder. 'Stay here, friend, with your bow and the best archers you have. When the gates fall they may drop their guard in their rush to kill us. Use your arrows well and then come. I'll hold a place in the line for you.' His lip curled. 'I promise there will be plenty of them left.'

He left the battlements and walked with a steady stride down into the yard, to where the Marroc soldiers waited with their shields and their spears for the gate to fall. When they did, the Lhosir would be there, and Medrin would be at the front and Gallow would call him out, and Medrin would have no choice, in front of all his men, but to accept.

Oribas and Mirrahj and Achista ran along the banks of the Isset. The forkbeards were up on the road, marching on the last gate, and the rain of stones and arrows from the Marroc had already started. Oribas could hear the shouts wafting from the mountain on the breeze. He bounded down the path with Achista behind him. Mirrahj followed, carrying their rope and the piece of wood. He ran into the cave and the winding tunnel, and if there were any forkbeards watching then he never saw them. He reached the water and ducked under the surface and felt his way through to the inner cave.

It was dark, utterly dark, and so it took a long time and a great deal of cursing before they found the hole in the roof of the cave and poked their stick through and stuck it fast. Mirrahj shinned up the rope and then Achista, then Oribas last of all, hauled up by the others. They started to climb the shaft.

'Where's Sarvic?' A runner from the gates looked up at him. Sarvic looked back.

'Here.'

The runner gave him an arrow. 'Valaric says this is for you.' The runner darted away again. Sarvic looked at the arrow and then peered more closely at the tip.

The arrowhead had Medrin's name scratched into it.

34

THE CRIMSON SHIELD

'I understand it!' In the blackness Oribas scrambled up the shaft, feeling his way one hand at a time. Achista and Mirrahj climbed behind him. 'The Dragon's Maw behind the bars. The gates that no one can enter!'

'That cave has a dragon?' Mirrahj snorted with derision.

'Yes! A *water* dragon.'

'I don't understand.' Achista kept grabbing at his feet. He was slower than either of them.

'The stories! When the Aulians built the castle, they dug into the mountain and awoke the dragon, and the dragon in its anger flooded the valley and the river rose to the walls of the castle itself and wiped everything away. And the dragon will come again to devour whoever breaks the sixth gate!'

'There are no such things as dragons.' Mirrahj spoke with a flat certainty.

'No, but—'

'My people killed them.'

Oribas cackled to himself. 'No no, there's no dragon hiding here that no one has seen for two hundred years, that is true. But what if the water was real? What if there really was a flood?'

It was Achista's turn now: 'The Isset rises every spring, but up to the castle walls? That's not possible!'

'But what if it was not the river!' Oribas was shaking with excitement. 'What if it was ...'

'The lake!'

'Yes. The tarn above the castle.' He felt the change in them after that, both of them, as the possibility coursed through their thoughts. Aulians had built the castle. Aulians liked to dig. They'd burrowed into the mountain and they'd dug their tunnels, tunnels like this one. But somehow they'd hit the underside of the lake or some flooded cave beneath it and the waters had rushed out of the Dragon's Maw and through the sixth gate and down the mountainside and washed away everything in their path. The whole lake, emptied into the Isset in one single torrent. And because they were Aulians, they went back into their tunnel after the waters had subsided and they built a wall. And slowly the lake had filled again. He could see it all as though he'd been there.

The sixth gate shuddered under the blows of the ram and with each one the rusted iron flaked and cracked. Gallow stood tense and ready. When the gates finally broke and fell they might tumble onto the Lhosir. In that moment of confusion the Marroc would fall on them, charging out of Varyxhun castle before Medrin's warriors could form their wall of shields.

The pounding stopped. The gates still stood, a haze of dust clouded behind them. At Gallow's back lay the cave, with its bars too thick to break and too close for a man to enter. He'd have given a lot to put some Marroc archers inside that cave and never mind the dragon of stories. He stood with his spear poised and waited. On the battlements above, the Marroc fell quiet. The gates creaked and groaned and one seemed to sag a little. A tension seized them – even the Lhosir fell silent now. The gates groaned again and then one of them began to fall, twisting under its own weight. The bars that held them closed caught it for a moment, but then the rusted iron that held the bars wrenched and tore and split. Corroded metal shattered in bangs and puffs of

322

dust and retorts that Gallow felt through his feet and then the first gate hit the ground. The second was already falling, and outside on the road he saw that the Lhosir had moved back and had already formed their wall of shields and spears. One man alone stood in front of them. Medrin raised the Crimson Shield high and Gallow could see that the arm that held it ended in a ragged stump – the shield was not held but was strapped to his arm. Medrin looked right at him. 'See this, Foxbeard?' he cried. 'You did this.' He gestured at the castle, a sweep of his arm that took in Marroc and Lhosir alike. 'You did all of this.'

An arrow flew at him. Medrin caught it on the shield. Then he lifted his spear and lowered his head and started to run, and behind him the other Lhosir ran too and a great howl went up from them. The Marroc on the battlements screamed and threw their remaining stones and Gallow roared a battle cry of his own, and all around him the Marroc of the Crackmarsh lowered their spears and braced their shields to receive Medrin's charge.

Warm distant light poured into the shaft like liquid honey. Mirrahj knew at once where they were – the cisterns of Varyxhun. The Aulian was a slow climber and the ascent felt as if it had taken the whole morning though she knew it must be far less. The light drew closer. The shaft reached the cisterns and went on past, rising steadily into the mountain. Oribas kept on climbing. Mirrahj stopped. 'Aulian, where are you going?'

'To the water dragon, Vathan.'

Mirrahj shook her head. 'There's no dragon, Aulian. Only stories and their ghosts.'

'Wait and see.'

'I have a creature of my own to kill. One that's real.' She turned and pulled herself through the hole where the cisterns drained. Medrin Sixfingers was near. The sword knew it.

They took the Lhosir charge and met it, staggering a half-pace back under the crashing impact. The Lhosir pressed with a frenzied strength and the Marroc fought back with the wild abandon of men with nowhere left to run. Gallow looked for Medrin in the press of shields but the crush of bodies was too thick. He lunged with his spear and sliced open a man's arm and then stabbed him in the face. He barged with his shield and reversed his spear and stabbed the next Lhosir in the foot. But the Marroc, for all their heart, never fought together as a wall of men like this. When Gallow tore a shield aside, no spear thrust came from behind to finish the man he fought, yet when the Lhosir did the same, that thrust came fast and deadly. The Marroc to Gallow's right had his shield hooked by a Lhosir axe and pulled down and instantly a spear slashed his neck. The Marroc on the other side lifted his shield to hold off a barrage of blows and a spear plunged into his knee. He lurched, screaming, and another took him in the throat. Slowly the Marroc line fell back.

A shout went up from the sixth gate and another rain of missiles fell on the Lhosir from Valaric's Marroc, stones and arrows and boiling water and the last sacks of salt. The Lhosir fought with mad desperation to press away from the gate and for a moment the Marroc found a new heart. Gallow lost his spear, bitten in two by a Lhosir hatchet. He drew his own axe and rained blow after blow on the enemy before him, battering them back, beating them to death beneath their mail and shields. Another Marroc fell beside him. For a moment he felt something give, the whole line falter. He stumbled, forced by the press of the Lhosir to step back, and for a moment he felt the Marroc about to turn and rout – but then a cry went up: 'The Wolf! The Wolf!' And though Gallow couldn't see, he knew that Valaric, crippled or not, had come down from the gates to pick up his sword, and at the sound of his name the Marroc found their courage again. They held with bitter resolve while the Lhosir pressed like a storm. And now, at last, Gallow saw Medrin, sword raised high, driving it into the Marroc ahead of him, blow after blow after blow.

'Medrin! *Nioingr!*'

Over the noise of screams and howls Medrin turned and saw him, and then each pressed towards the other, pushing and shoving friend and foe alike aside until they were close enough for their swords to touch.

Oribas barely noticed Mirrahj go. He climbed on because he was an Aulian and he knew how an Aulian thought, and what an Aulian thought was that any good thing served more than one purpose. The tunnel from the cisterns was a way for men to escape, and that was one thing, but why then tunnel up as well as down? The anticipation gave wings to his thoughts. It was a way for water to escape without flooding the castle and so it must be that the water that might make that flood would lie at its top. And when he reached that top he stopped and tried to see, but there was no light at all, not the tiniest bit of it. With a reluctant huff he reached into his satchel and fumbled for his lamp. Nothing was where it was supposed to be – Medrin had clearly gone through his powders while they'd been riding – but eventually he found it and lit it and held it high so that he and Achista could see what they'd found, and it was enough to make Achista sigh with wonder in his ear. A rift ran up and down the inside of the mountain before them, too deep for his light to penetrate, wrinkled twists of tunnels and chasms vanishing in all directions. From where he stood, steps carved hundreds of years ago climbed the wall of the cave. From somewhere ahead he heard the hiss of water. The air was damp.

Achista rested a hand on his shoulder. 'Is it here?'

'I think so.' He started to climb the steps, creeping on his hands and feet.

'Oribas, if it is, I have to go. Valaric needs to know.'

He turned awkwardly and held her briefly. In the darkness he grinned. 'Tell him his dragon waits for him.' He watched her go and then returned to the steps. They wound around the edge of the cave wall, carved into it, narrow and old and slippery, and then spiralled up into an inverted funnel. The sound of hissing water grew stronger. Now and then he felt a waft of spray on his face. The steps took him to a ledge where the stone above closed into a narrow shaft clearly carved by men. Its walls were flat and slick and as he stepped closer, dripping water spattered his face, so much that he had to shield his lamp. Down beneath his feet was nothing but a dark void. He looked up. Above, at the limit of his light, the shaft was blocked shut. Stone blocks pressed against one another so tight that no knife blade would slip between them, and yet from the cracks ran a steady trickle of water, drips in some places but in others tight hissing jets of it as though squeezed through the very stone itself by an irresistible pressure from above.

He giggled. So there it was. The Aulians had tunnelled into the mountain and struck the bed of the lake that lay above the castle. And after the flood they'd sealed the hole the way only Aulians understood, with an arrangement of stones that would only grow stronger as more and more weight piled onto it. And as with the gatehouse he'd described to Valaric back when the Lhosir had first come, somewhere would be a single stone that held it together. A single stone that, if it was pulled away, would cause the entire structure to collapse.

His eyes gleamed. There would be a chain. And there was, hanging right down in front of him, and that was when he remembered the other part of the story he'd told to Valaric.

The fighting stopped around them. Gallow and Medrin faced each other amid a ring of men, half Marroc, half Lhosir. In the middle of the fiercest battle they would ever see men set on killing each other stepped away to make space and lowered their blades.

Medrin cocked his head and lifted the Crimson Shield. 'Marroc! Look at me! You call upon your god Modris to protect you, yet here is his shield. *His* shield! I am your king and I am your protector, and yet you've turned your back on me and so Modris spurns your names.' He looked at Gallow and bared his teeth. 'And you, Foxbeard! You were supposed to be here waiting for me with the Sword of the Weeping God! With Solace, the Comforter, the Peace-bringer, the Edge of Sorrows. Our clash would have been of titans, a myth made flesh. But no, you sent the sword away with some Vathan. Was that to spite me?' He cut an arc with his sword, pointing at the Marroc around Gallow. 'I came to Varyxhun not for some strange blade, nor for some faithless *nioingr*. I came to crush these men to bloody dust so that all Marroc might understand that we are now one. One kingdom, one crown, one people.' He smiled. 'You! Look at you, Gallow Foxbeard! A Lhosir living among the Marroc, and you fight me, and yet that is what I offer: Lhosir and Marroc together, side by side. Why not?'

'We'll not be ruled by a forkbeard!' shouted Valaric, and the Marroc cheered.

Medrin threw back his head and roared with laughter. 'You'll be ruled by a king! What difference does it make whether he's born on this side of the sea or that? He might as well be an Aulian for all the difference it makes. A king is a king is a king, and kings do what kings do and whether their beards are forked or straight or they have none at all, it makes not a whit of difference. *I* am your king, no more and no less, and you are traitors, every one of you, and so you will die.'

Gallow let out a deep sigh. 'Thank you, brother of the sea.' He drew his sword. 'Thank you for letting this be clear.

Because you're right: it's not about your beard, it's simply that as kings go, you're a bad one.'

He lunged, and the Crimson Shield swung down and caught his blow.

For a long long time Oribas stared at the chain. It was right in front of him, a massive thing of iron links each the size of his fist. He could reach out and touch it. It hung straight down from the clot of stones above his head and ran into the darkness of the void below. When he looked down, he could just about see a piece of stone the size of a man dangling from its end.

He wondered what to do. Such a massive chain and such a weight hanging from it and such a weight pushing down from above, what difference could one man possibly make? But then he peered more closely and saw that not all links in the chain were alike. At the level of his eye was a single link of a different colour, and Oribas understood. This was not iron but a milky glassy stone, stained by years of rust from the links above but definitely different, and he knew this stone, a kind of glass sometimes found in rough round nuggets in the fields of old Aulia itself, stronger than iron yet brittle. One good sharp blow would shatter it. And when he rubbed away at the stains to be sure, he found it marked with pictograms that left no room for doubt. Air and earth, water and the dragon. The chain would snap and the weight would fall. Earth would become air and water would become the dragon. It wasn't about pulling the chain but about snapping it.

He looked up. He couldn't see how it worked but maybe that didn't matter. A counterweight mechanism perhaps. The intent was clear enough.

His first problem was having no hammer to shatter the brittle link, but that wasn't much of a problem at all because there were loose stones right at his feet. His second problem was a bit harder. How not to die when a ton of stone and a lakeful of water crashed down on his head. And he was still pondering that one and realising that it probably didn't have an answer when he heard Achista's desperate cry echo through the caves. 'Oribas! The sixth gate is shattered! The forkbeards come! If you've found your dragon then let it out! Let it out!'

Gallow charged into Medrin like an angry boar, crashing into him, shield on shield. Medrin was smaller, weaker, sure to buckle and fall, and yet it was Gallow who reeled away as though he'd run headlong into a wall of stone. He charged again and Medrin simply stood unmoved as though he barely noticed. Breathing heavily, Gallow faced him more warily. 'What sorcery is this, Sixfingers? Has the witch you keep put a spell on you and made you into iron?'

Medrin's eyes never left him. 'I carry the shield of a god, Foxbeard. What did you expect?'

Gallow shook his head. 'It's just a shield.'

'So it is.' Medrin came at him then, slow and sure, his sword swinging in a steady barrage of blows. Gallow took them on his shield and struck back, yet Medrin caught Gallow's sword on the Crimson Shield each time with ease. 'Shall we see who tires first?' He snorted. 'A dull fight this is for our men to see. How about this? If I beat you, all your Marroc will throw down their arms and I'll let one in every four go free, chosen by chance. One in four, Gallow. Better odds than I offer with my army. And if you beat me, then what shall we say? One in three? *If* they throw down their arms, that is.' He cackled with glee. 'I'll make it sweeter. If you beat me, one in three may live, most chosen by chance but you may choose a dozen of them. Got any friends here, Foxbeard? Or family?' Then he looked at his six-fingered hand and at his stump behind his shield. 'No. We shall say six, not twelve.'

Gallow spat at Medrin's feet. 'I will cut you down, prince of cowards, and the men behind you too while the rest of your army turn to their heels!'

'No, Gallow Foxbeard.' Medrin smiled back at him. 'That's not how it will be and you very well know it.' And he jumped forward and barged into Gallow with the Crimson Shield and it was like the kick of a horse, a battering that would have shaken even old Jyrdas One-Eye in his prime. Gallow reeled and before he could do more than stay on his feet, Medrin hit him again, another hammer blow, and another, and with each blow Gallow staggered back and the Marroc behind him withdrew to make space, and Medrin and the Lhosir advanced beyond the gates and the Dragon's Maw and into the castle yard, until on the fifth blow Gallow stumbled and there was no time to recover, and when the shield of Modris struck him again, he fell exhausted and beaten. King Medrin Sixfingers pointed his sword at Gallow's face. He wasn't even breathing hard.

'Do you not see? Do you not understand? *Just* a shield? It's the shield of a god, Foxbeard. A *god!*'

'Oribas! *Oribas!*' For a moment he froze, too terrified and torn, but then he heard the sound of feet on stone and knew she was climbing the steps.

'Achista! Wait!' If he let her come she'd die beside him.

'Oribas! The forkbeards are in the yard!'

'I have the dragon. I've found it! Go! Turn back and I will release it!'

He closed his eyes and picked up a stone, and when he opened them again there were tears on his cheek. Not for himself but for her, for the years, for the hours, for the minutes they wouldn't have. It was a cruel trap these long-dead Aulians had made.

'Oribas!'

'Do not be angry, my love,' and roundly and loudly he

cursed every god he knew as he drew back his rock to smash the brittle link and snap the chain in two.

Gallow felt as if he'd been trampled by a herd of wild horses. He tried to get to his feet but it was so hard and then Medrin kicked him back down. The Lhosir king walked towards the Marroc soldiers, lifting his shield high so they all could see it. He shouted at them, 'The shield of your god! Modris!' Wherever he approached they quailed and backed further away.

As he lay on the stone, Gallow felt the mountain quiver beneath him. A whisper of a rumble breathed from the Dragon's Maw, too quiet to be heard over the noise of Medrin roaring at the soldiers around him. 'Lay down your swords and your shields and sink to your knees and bow your heads, Marroc. One in four will live, that was my promise. Or fight and you can all die. Here I stand! Who will face—'

'More than happy to kill you, Sixfingers.' Valaric limped out from amid the Marroc, swinging a sword in his hand. Gallow pulled himself to his hands and knees. 'Shame my spear missed you in Andhun but I'll be happy to—'

Medrin moved like quicksilver. He barged Valaric, shield on shield, and Gallow saw Valaric's face as he reeled back, the shock and surprise as if Medrin was not one man but ten. The Wolf crashed into the Marroc behind him and slowly picked himself up. Medrin turned his back. Valaric took a deep breath and picked up his sword and this time, Gallow knew, Medrin would kill him. Valaric probably knew it too, but that wasn't going to stop him.

'I'll fight you, King Sixfingers.'

Mirrahj. She pushed her way through the Marroc. She carried no shield, but in one hand was an axe and in the other the long rust-red blade of the Edge of Sorrows. Medrin opened his arms to welcome her. 'Good for you,

Vathan. About time someone with a proper sword came to this fight.'

The glass-stone link in the chain exploded. Shards like knives stung his face. Something hit him in the eye – a bright burning pain. The upper part of the chain flicked like a whip, lashing with all its pent-up energy into the stone above Oribas's head. The bottom of it plunged into the dark. He heard the crash as the stone at its end hit the floor of the cave somewhere below. Then something else came hurtling down the shaft. Another stone on the end of another chain. It jerked to a halt right in front of him and he understood. The counterweight. Somewhere above, the force of its arrest would jerk something free. He closed his eyes, waiting to die under the deluge of stone and water, but none came.

'Oribas!'

He opened one eye, the one that would still open. His face had blood on it.

'*Oribas!*'

He was alive. The dragon had failed and now he didn't know what to do. 'It didn't work.' He swore. Then he swore louder. 'It didn't work. Stupid …' How old was it? Stuck? Rust? He didn't know. Didn't know what to do.

'Oribas, the gate is breached! The forkbeards come! Do it!'

He nodded, not that Achista could see him. 'Then we have to leave. The way we came. There is no dragon after all. It did not work. I am sorry, my love, but it is dead from age.'

'No!'

He squeezed his fists as though he could somehow squeeze an idea out from between his fingers. Only a fool gave up at the first attempt. Maybe there was another … He froze. Cocked his head to listen.

'Oribas! What are you—'

'Be quiet!'

The hiss of the water pushing out from between the stones had changed. Very slightly, but it wasn't the same sound it had been when Oribas had come. He looked at the chain and the stone dangling in front of him. Water ran down it now, trickling off in a steady stream. It hadn't done that before. And it had come down after the first stone had hit the cave floor. The mechanism was higher up the shaft than he'd thought.

As if to answer him, a rumble shivered down the shaft – stones falling somewhere above. Awe ran cold across his skin.

'Run, Achista. Just run!'

The hole the Aulians had filled and left behind them wasn't big, easily large enough for a man to climb through but little more. Yet the pressure of water from the lake above was as though every Lhosir assaulting the walls of Varyxhun was hammering in that one place. And in that elaborate working of stones upon stones, as Oribas released the chain, something high above had shifted, and it was enough.

The rumbling grew louder. The shaft shook suddenly, right above his head. The stones that blocked it trembled. He could hardly see, and all he had was his tiny lamp in all this darkness and one eye still burned and wouldn't open and he had no idea how long he had. A few seconds perhaps. Or perhaps for ever. But either way he ran, scampering down the stairs, dancing from step to step with the crazy grace of desperation and dreadful fear and unexpected hope. A sharp crack sounded behind him. He felt it through the walls of the cave and heard a sudden spray of water, and then another crack and a terrible crashing roar as the weight of the lake at last crushed its way into the cavern. The Aulian stones plummeted past him and smashed into a thousand fragments and behind them came such a torrent of water that for a moment the whole mountain shook and almost threw him off its walls. A shock of air rushed and tugged at his limbs. He felt the mountain quake and heard its drawn-out rumble, and then he was at the top of the passage down to the cisterns and Achista was there and her arms were around him, dragging him in, hauling him to somewhere safe, and he clasped her hand and hugged her tight and kissed her while the great roar of water thrummed in his ears and the air filled with soaking spray.

'The dragon,' he whispered in her ear. 'It seems it was only sleeping after all.'

Up on the battlements Sarvic felt the mountain quiver too. He looked at his last arrow, the one Valaric had given him. The one with Medrin's name scratched into its iron head. With exaggerated care he rested it against his bowstring and drew it back and took aim. The back of Sixfingers' neck, that would do. But then a shout came from the gates, and then another and then more, and he heard Lhosir cries full of fearful warning and he couldn't help but turn to look. Water rushed from the Dragon's Maw and, even as he watched, the river became a torrent, so hard and fast with such force that all the forkbeards in the gate were swept back onto the road, and the ones on the road shouted out as the water tore over them, rising around their ankles and sucking at their feet.

Medrin waited. The Vathan woman danced around him, twirling her sword and her axe. She raised the Edge of Sorrows as if to swing it at his head and he lifted the Crimson Shield and smiled. From the corner of his eye he saw Gallow stumble to his feet and open his mouth to shout a warning. Three years ago in Andhun Gallow had struck the shield of Modris with the Sword of the Weeping God and learned a hard lesson. But this Marroc had learned it too, in the tomb under Witches' Reach. The red sword slid through the air past the Crimson Shield, turning away at the last moment as the Vathan woman struck at him with her axe instead, then drove the point of the sword low, too fast for the shield to follow but still not quick enough. Medrin saw and jumped away.

A rumble came from behind him, from the gates. He heard his Lhosir cry out. The Vathan swung again, backhanded, axe and sword at once, striking for the head and for the knees, and he saw what it was she was trying to do – to strike two blows at once so that the shield couldn't possibly deflect both.

He smiled a last smile. Too ambitious by far. Her axe struck the Crimson Shield and stuck fast, torn out of her hand. Medrin caught the red sword on his own blade, which shattered, leaving him holding a jagged stump of iron. He threw it away as they stepped apart, breathing hard. The Vathan woman looked past him, up to the castle walls, but Medrin only shook his head. 'Do you think I'm so easy to fool?' And then it seemed to Medrin that the Vathan closed her eyes and something came over her. She took the red sword in both hands, lifted it high and brought it down straight at his head, and it was the easiest thing in the world to lift the Crimson Shield.

Sarvic watched in awe. A flood like the Isset in all its rage was sweeping down the road now, washing the forkbeards away. They dropped their weapons and clung to the cliffs, climbed the walls, scrambled for any high ground they could find, for any handhold they could reach, but for every forkbeard who found safety Sarvic saw another plucked from his feet and tossed by the waters over the cliffs.

He shook himself. Laughed and then turned away because glorious as it was, he had other business. He looked back to the yard and Sixfingers and lifted his bow again. Sixfingers and the Vathan woman had stepped apart. She'd broken his sword but she'd lost her axe. He raised his bow and saw her look up, right at him, and it seemed that a glimmer of understanding passed between them. Then she looked away and lifted the red sword to split the Lhosir king in two. Sarvic took aim and his fingers released the bowstring.

Gallow watched as Solace struck the Crimson Shield. Mirrahj screamed in agony and dropped the blade. Medrin screamed too. He lurched bizarrely and half spun, eyes wild, the shield slicing down behind him at nothing at all while Mirrahj staggered away, clutching her arm to her side, doubled up in pain. Gallow was the first to move. He sprinted the few yards between them and snatched up the red sword. He turned on Medrin, ready to make an end of it, but the king was already dead. He tipped over and fell face first in front of Gallow, lying still, and it took an age for Gallow to see the arrow sticking out from the back of Medrin's neck.

35

KING OF THE VALLEY

Valaric stood on the sixth gate and looked at what was left of the valley below. The five tiers of the road from the castle to the Aulian Way. The five gates below him, all gaping holes scoured clear by the flood. And down in the valley the forkbeards' camp washed away and half of Varyxhun with it. All vanished in a lake of mud and rubble.

The Lhosir weren't all dead, not by any means, but the ones who hadn't been washed away had still gone. Maybe they were at Witches' Reach by now, licking their wounds, choosing their new king. More still were crossing the Aulian Bridge from Tarkhun. Maybe in a few days they'd be back again. Or maybe they'd had enough and they'd keep on walking, all the way to the sea and beyond, back to their homes.

He'd sent Medrin's body down on a mule. Chased it off after the last forkbeards along the Aulian Way for the forkbeards to do whatever forkbeards did. He hadn't liked doing it – what he'd wanted was to take Sixfingers' head and hang him by his feet from the gates but Gallow wouldn't let him, and his leg was giving him grief again, and in the end it had just been easier to let the crazy forkbeard have his way.

When he looked away from the valley and back into the castle, he saw that Gallow was coming to bother him again. He was with the Vathan woman and one of his Crackmarsh men, the one who thought he'd killed Medrin for a day or so. They seemed to take it in turns to make sure he had no peace. If it wasn't Gallow then it was the Aulian, or the worst of them all, Arda.

'Well? What now?'

'I came to say goodbye.'

'I need a smith.'

Gallow clapped him on the shoulder which made him stagger, and that made his leg hurt. 'Goodbye, Valaric. Come see me if you need your horse shod or a new blade for your scythe.'

Valaric winced and growled, 'So that's it? You just go now. After all this, you just go?'

'I'm going home, Valaric.'

'Well I do need a smith, but I shan't be sad to see the back of your wife so I suppose it evens out.'

'I'm taking Reddic too. Forge could do with another hand.'

'Yeah.' Valaric smirked. Reddic and Arda's firstborn. Half the Marroc in the castle knew by now. 'Anything else you want? Maybe to cut off my arms and legs too, before you go?'

Gallow held out the red sword in its scabbard.

'Taking that, are you?'

Gallow shook his head. 'In Andhun you told me it was cursed. You were right.' He cocked his head at Valaric and then handed the sword to the Vathan woman. 'This goes back where it belongs. Do we agree?'

For a moment Valaric remembered how it had felt to hold the Comforter. How strong and powerful he'd seemed. He bowed his head. 'Go on then, Vathan. Take it.' He tapped the Crimson Shield, which now hung from his arm. 'Don't bring it back, mind. You know what happens if you do. So just go home.'

Later he watched them go, picking their way down the castle road on their mules, Gallow and Arda and their children, Nadric and Reddic and the Vathen. Off to the Devil's Caves and the Crackmarsh and then their separate ways, and he wondered quietly if they'd all get home and find there what they wanted. He supposed he'd never know. And he was still wondering when Sarvic came and stood beside him and did that lurking thing again, shuffling closer and closer, except this time he managed to spit it out before Valaric hit him. 'I think you'd better come,' he said. 'Your soldiers have made something for you.'

'What's that, then? A list of demands?'

'No.'

'Gates? Is it new gates? Because we could really do with some new gates.'

'Just come and see. And don't mind me if I can't stop laughing if you ask me to start calling you Your Majesty.' He sniggered.

There was one other person to see before he left, and Gallow went to see him alone. He clasped arms with Oribas long and hard and it seemed that his hands didn't want to let go. Then Oribas closed his eyes and took a deep breath, and it felt to Gallow as though the Aulian was letting go of everything between them. Or at least perhaps loosening it a little. 'I have climbed to the lake, Gallow. Under the water my people built something. Something that was meant to stay hidden. I wonder now if it was no accident that they drained it. I have not told any other. Should I leave it be, Gallow, or should I see what lies beneath?'

Gallow smiled and shook his head. 'You know very well to leave it be, old friend.'

'I will seal the hole as my ancestors did before me. The snows are melting. It will be hidden again before long.' He bowed and then picked up a heavy satchel filled with salt and handed it to Gallow. A corner of iron poked out. 'I have one thing for you to take, Gallow.' He laughed and shook his head. 'I would shower you with gifts if I had any to give, but instead I have only this burden.'

'My hunting days are done, Oribas. I gave the sword to Mirrahj.'

But Oribas pressed the satchel into his hands anyway. 'Just this one thing, Gallow. Take it with you. Take it to your fire. Melt the iron down and forge it again with salt. Then throw it away, far from where you live. Or send it back, or drown it in the Isset, or lose it in the Crackmarsh, or hurl it into the sea. Whatever you like – just be rid of it.'

Gallow took a deep breath and then took the satchel. 'Make it work, Oribas. Make it work.' And he didn't know whether he meant Valaric's kingdom, which he was about to find he had, or holding off the Lhosir if they came again, or simply being married to a wilful Marroc woman – and the Maker-Devourer himself knew how hard *that* could be.

'I will do my best, old friend. I will do my best.'

EPILOGUE

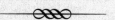

The Vathen rode slowly through the ruins of the village. There was little left. Burned-out huts, not much else. They stopped at the edge, at what had once been a forge. One of them dismounted and poked through the rubble. Whatever had been done here, it had been a while ago.

'The forkbeards call themselves men of fate.' She said it without much feeling one way or the other, as if noting that the clouds had turned a little darker and perhaps more rain was on the way.

'This is a Marroc village,' said one of the others, with a voice that was keen to push on.

'Yes,' said the first. 'But a forkbeard lived here once. They called him Gallow. Gallow the Foxbeard.'

ACKNOWLEDGEMENTS

If you've read this far, I'm kind of hoping you've read *The Crimson Shield* and *Cold Redemption*, because otherwise you probably had a real *who on earth is he* moment somewhere in the battle for the fifth gate. If you have, then I'm sorry for repeating myself. I'll be brief. Thanks go to Simon Spanton, who commissioned this and to Marcus Gipps, who edited it, and to all the people who put together the wonderful covers these books have had. They go to the copy-editors and proofreaders and booksellers and the marketeers and everyone who makes books possible. They go to you, for reading this.

And thanks, still, to all the crazy people who think the best way to spend a week in February is to strut though York in mail carrying an axe.

As always, if you liked this story, please tell others who might like it too. And if you did like it, there are other stories out there that you might like too, ones that had a touch in shaping these stories or ones that I read afterwards and wished I'd read before, including:

Legend by David Gemmell (Varyxhun castle has six gates after the six walls of Dros Delnoch);

Wolfsangel by M. D. Lachlan (I can still smell the blood and the iron); and

The Ten Thousand by Paul Kearney (The fight scenes – ouch!).